The First Volume Of

The
Shadow Histories

The Empty Land
A Murti Schofield

Grateful acknowledgement to the following Authors & Publishers for granting permission to use their material in this book.
Extracts from Three Quadrants Of Mind © TK Edwins
Courtesy of (Two) Tangents Publishing
Passage from God Weaving And Dream Paths © Suskind Gromsen
Courtesy of Abandonit Publishing
Quotes from Gone Is The Sky © BA Wyeth
Courtesy of Inheritance Press
Lyrics from Hobo Holocaust © Rue Brawler
Courtesy of Hot Tonic Records & ArtDisk Publishing
Quotes from Commentaries On Lao Tzu & The Effective Hand In Combat
© Beowulf Clark
Courtesy of Sidetrack Publications and Bo-Bulletins
Selections from Lethal Lullabies And Cautionary Tales © Jean Frecé
Courtesy of Herald's Banner Publications
Passages from Waelbeorc's Stand © Brough Savage
Courtesy of Hexagram Song Press
Selections from Cullie Brown articles and works © Cullie Brown
Courtesy of Arkadashim Print House & egl.albionlore.co.uk
Extracts from Gifts To Come, Mortal Fields Of Time & other works by Thomas Carlan Morledge
©Thomas Carlan Morledge courtesy of Reuel Title Imprints & egl.codesign.co.uk

All Shadow Histories material © A Murti Schofield 2006
Sigil cover artwork by Kev Crossley
Sigil design & background artwork — A Murti Schofield

British Library Cataloguing In Publication Data
A Record of this Publication is available from the British Library

ISBN 978-1-84685-549-8

First Published 2007 by
Exposure Publishing, an imprint of Diggory Press
Three Rivers, Minions, Liskeard, Cornwall, PL14 5LE, UK
www.diggorypress.com

DEDICATION

For the truest angel - endearing innocence.
Codie Tia.
Always on my mind and in my heart.

And to Dilys. In admiration of the extraordinariness
of an ordinary life lived well.

WITH THANKS TO:

Jerry Oldreive, Royd Tolkien, Kev Crossley, Dave Gibbons, Bro Chris, Emma Schofield, Bev Bright, Mary Loveday, Amber Houlders, Berni, Liam, Holly, Adham, Priya, Claire, Wayne Rawlinson, Bhagawan SR, Scott, Bee, Dave Taylor, Em, Tessa, Bernard Platt, Kurtis, Beryl Heather, Paul Houlders, Fehmi and my English teacher at St Gregory's Ardwick Green 1965-66 - Mr Fitzpatrick, for nurturing a love of words and TS Eliot in particular.

And especial thanks to dad, Edwin Schofield 1918-1995, who showed me true magic and simplicity of spirit around the Lake District camp fires of the 1950's. It takes a long time to become young again.

CONTENTS

Continued...

PREFACE

SIDETIME
A SNOWFIELD NEAR SKAERKABORG.

IT is cold, bitterly cold but the girl is too terrified to let this bother her. She knows she must keep moving pushing through the heavy snow if she is to stay ahead of her pursuers. They can't be far behind her now. She can hear their cries, a thin wailing sound in the wind and she pictures their hideous shapes scuttling after her like clockwork scarecrows. The Vil-kind! If they touch her again she knows she will lose her mind. It would be better to throw herself off a cliff than be dragged back into those nightmarish caves. She'll do it, she knows she will! Nothing will get her back into that suffocating cell.

The filthy white smock is no protection against the wind as she struggles to keep her feet moving. Its edges are torn and soaked from trailing in the crust of snow that comes half way up her shins. The buckles at the back have torn loose where she ripped herself away from the metal cot and only a few shreds of cording keep the grimy canvas on her shoulders. Loose strands whip and crack across her frozen skin. The heavy iron boots lashed to her feet drag her down at every step. If only she could work the thick straps free she would move faster but there's been no time, no time to think, no time to breathe, no time to plan, just frantic flight from her tormentors, every step a silent scream of pain and fear. And they are coming for her. She can hear them. But she won't go back — she won't - not ever!

Her eyes are stinging with cold, blinded by the whirling snow and she can barely see more than a few metres ahead in the darkness. Twice already she has tumbled down slopes and crashed into the trunks of trees. She knows her reserves of strength are waning. Numbing cold makes the crude sutures on her back and arms throb with pain. A dried trickle of blood remains where she pulled the tubing out of her wrists. There is no pain in her hands now; numb, all numb.

A sudden shriek from behind pierces the night almost freezing her limbs in panic. Her head whips around. Where can she hide? There is no cover. She is in the open, surrounded by a circle of silhouetted trees. For a moment the wind drops, as if in anticipation of some terrible event. She must get rid of the iron boots! In a panic of clawing fingers she tears at the heavy straps around her ankles, sobbing as they refuse to budge. It's no use. They're frozen in place. She can't...oh she can't...it's no use. She sinks helpless into the ice her breath leaking from blue lips in a thin stream of vapour. The inevitable is upon her. It is the end. She can go no further. Her head sinks to her chest and her frantic mind slowly clears as if flushed by a warming draught of spring air. If she can just find a drop to throw herself from...she feels oddly calm, dreamlike, unreal. Is it the cold? Is she already dying of the cold? Everything has slowed down. Her breath trickles away like strands of cobweb.

Then a new sound, a voice. Soothing, gentle. A voice speaking words she doesn't understand. And hands, smooth strong hands reaching down to loosen the bootstraps. The boots fall away. The hands lift her slowly to her feet and she steps out of the cruel iron weights and onto the snow. She notices, calmly, that her feet are black and trailing tatters of bloodied skin. She starts to look up at her helper but at that moment hideous wails shatter the dreamlike calm and everything snaps into high speed. The line of trees has spewed out a pack of nightmare figures charging across the snow. The Vil-kind have found her! Every movement of their twisted joints is grotesque as if jerked on strings but their speed is terrible. The girl feels herself propelled, almost thrown, towards the darkness on the opposite side of the clearing. She stumbles half running half falling into the gloom ahead totally confused by what is happening. Her feet feel light without the iron.

She has taken scarcely a dozen steps when her elongated shadow leaps out in front of her thrown by a brilliant flash from behind. The broken keening of the Vil-kind stops abruptly. The light dies as quickly as it appeared. She turns and sees a tableau of hellish forms crouched, standing or squat, held at bay by a lone figure which faces them poised like a dancer, balanced and serene but somehow...deadly.

2

Then as if at a silent signal the scarecrow shapes launch themselves at the figure stabbing and hacking with mindless ferocity. The noise of shrieking becomes deafening and the girl is held mesmerised by the intensity of hatred that beats at her in waves. The figures blur in a melee of flailing limbs and two Vil-kind crash to the ground one inert the other choking its life into the snow. Without a pause the rest throw themselves at the figure who weaves like a storm tossed leaf evading and whirling, dealing out ballettic violence in total silence. The carnage is hypnotic, terrifying. The girl finds it impossible to tear her eyes away.

With a start she hears the voice inside her head again, assuring and calm. The words are unknown but the sense is clear, 'Go! Flee. Be quick! Leave now.' She sees with horror that one of the Vil-kind has broken free of the rest and is leaping over the snow towards her in an uneven loping run. Already it has halved the distance between them. Already she can see the horrible tangle of rags and shreds that is its face. With stupefying clarity she sees the clawed hands, the barbed hooks of filthy iron lashed to its arms and wrists with wire and sinew. The jagged mouth is open in a scream of rage...
...and the nightmare shape erupts in gouts of flame as a needle thin lance of light rips through its chest from behind. The light is so intense that the entire clearing is illuminated as if by lightening. The Vil-kind spasms in mid air, lifted by the force of the impact, and then crashes into the snow. It skids face down, steam spurting from its back, snow hissing furiously. Fierce blue flames lick along the grotesque corpse. The girl is blinded for a moment by the contrast of the returning darkness.

And again the voice urges her, 'Run! Flee! Only a little time.' And she does, not looking back this time although she can hear the furious struggle continue in the darkness behind her. It is not just her body that is numb now. Her mind and emotions are like silt. Her entire being is about to shut down in protest at the excess of everything she has undergone...so that when she comes to the sudden drop she hardly hesitates in her stumbling flight but plunges over the edge in a surrender to gravity and air that takes her down into welcoming oblivion. Whether it is the fall or the ice crusted river that closes her suffering she has no idea. She knows only that the fear has finally stopped. And the silence and dark welcome her in.

One
VILLAGE IN BLOOM

CODY could see Clayton Bar church eight hundred feet below with nothing but space between her and the spire. Cold air was rushing into her lungs and she gasped in exhilarated delight as the microlite lurched and fell into a stomach churning drop before righting itself and soaring on. The pilot, whose name was Corbin, yelled over his shoulder asking if she was OK. His head was only two feet from hers but the words got shredded by the wind and the deafening drone of the engine.

'Yes. Wonderful,' she yelled back. A cheery thumbs up told her *message received.*

There had been turbulence during the whole ride out over the Cheshire Plains. The unexpected lurches and sudden moments of weightlessness were one of the best parts of flying for Cody. She loved it! This was her third flight this year and hopefully there'd be time for many more before the season was over.

Below them the details of her village were crystal clear. She could make out every roof tile, every item of washing on the lines, every sunlit ripple on the canal. A flock of starlings scattered in alarm when the microlite's shadow swept over the oaks at the west end of her school grounds making her laugh out loud. The pilot yelled to hang on and the tiny craft turned in a long graceful arc that took them east towards their landing strip. The flat field was next to the meadow where the weekly Albion fayre was spread out in a riot of striped awnings and tents. As they swept over the crowds people tipped back their heads and waved. She couldn't make out where mum and dad were. When she took off they had been stood by the old oak at the top end of the field but they weren't there now. They'd probably be at the landing strip when she touched down.

She couldn't wait to tell them about the things she'd seen from the air. Beeston Castle pale and heat hazed in the distance, a tiny horse and plough working in fields a dozen shades of tan and yellow, little farmyard buildings and windmills looking like toys from so far up and the large circular patch of inert Bloom tar out beyond Tarvin glinting black in the brilliant sunlight. She knew for a fact that it was over a hundred yards across but it seemed less sinister from this height. They'd also taken a turn over the outskirts of Chester peering down at the river winding through the semi deserted city. She'd waved at people on the boats and those driving carts across the bridge near the castle. All the tiny figures trundling along the streets had looked like models in a toy town.

After one more pass over Clayton Bar they began their descent towards the landing field. A row of bright red and yellow striped windsocks stood on poles at each end of the field showing the wind's direction and strength and the pilot began to ease down towards the strip of battered grass that was their runway for today. It was at this moment that Cody became aware of a disturbance in the people below, a sort of ripple moving across the tightly packed crowds in the meadow. Although it was impossible to hear anything above the engine's roar it was clear that some disturbing news was passing from person to person. She could sense the sudden spikes of anxiety like a charge of electricity peaking and building. People's faces were turning towards the gate at the top of the field. She saw several stricken expressions before the microlite dropped behind the high trees and flashed towards the ground for a bone rattling finish in the ankle high grass.

By the time the microlite had come to a halt Cody already had her helmet off and was climbing out of the tiny bucket seat. She couldn't see her parents anywhere.

'Thanks Corbin. That was great,' she yelled hurriedly. 'I must go. Something's wrong. I...I have to go. See you next time.'

The young pilot cut the engine and the mad hornet roar died away.

'Don't worry,' he yelled at her retreating back. 'See you around. Watch out for ground now!' He couldn't help grinning as he unbuckled his own helmet and shook his hair loose. Cody was already over the brow of the incline and still running. Always in a rush these kids. Couldn't wait to get up in the air, then once down they couldn't wait to tell their friends everything they'd seen. He watched as another microlite made a wide turn into the wind ready to begin its descent. Business was good today. His next customer was waiting over by the oak tree. Corbin waved and walked over with a big welcoming smile. The teenager was stood with an awkward grin fixed to his face like a mask. Nervous. Not one of Corbin's regulars.

'Good afternoon young sir and welcome to the sleekest, trimmest lite craft in the airs above Cheshire on this beautiful day. Have you flown before?' The youth's sickly expression widened but no words came out. Corbin put his arms around the youth's shoulders and reassured him, 'Don't worry. We'll only be flying at fifteen hundred feet. Hardly even off the ground.' He barely had chance to jump aside as the youth bent double and emptied his lunch onto the ground.

*   *   *

Cody reached the top end of the meadow and could feel the peaks of anxiety coming at her from like waves from the crowds gathered amongst the multicoloured stalls. There was a general movement towards the gates at the far side of the meadow and she found herself being pushed that way too. Then she began to distinguish what was being shouted and felt in her own spine the same chill that had swept across the meadow like a winter breeze.

'Bloom! There's been a Bloom outbreak near Beeston Castle! A big one!'

This was the thing all communities lived in dread of hearing. Every passing day every adult and child knew that deadly Bloom spores might drift back into their lives and change them forever. Apart from the catastrophic consequences of the world wide outbreak back in 1991 there had only been eight small outbreaks in the region in the last three years. Fortunately they had been caught in the early stages when still manageable and had been dealt with by the ever alert fire crews based around the county. A large outbreak was something else entirely. The implications were too terrifying to think about, the consequences could be devastating.

As she pushed through the crowd pressed against the stonewall at the gateway to the meadow Cody could sense that at least some part of the excitement rushing through the crowd was the expectation of seeing Clayton Bar's own fire carts go into action. She managed to lean over the top of the wall to catch her breath and was relieved to see her mother approaching.

'Oh Cody, there you are. I'm sorry we weren't there when you got down from your flight.'

'That's alright Mum. Where's Dad?'

'We heard the Bloom alert being broadcast over the short wave and he had to get to the station.' Cody's heart jumped in her chest.

'You mean Dad's on the fire cart? He's on call today?'

'Yes dear, I'm afraid he is. They're...' a huge cheer went up as a magnificent Green Goddess fire engine roared out of the station and braked while a couple of men in fire outfits loaded some Napetroleum canisters onto the back. Cody's mum gripped her hand as they watched. The old reconditioned engine was an inspiring sight with its brilliant emerald paint and flashing red light. Some of the younger watchers cheered again but Cody's stomach dropped as she caught sight of her dad sitting grimly in the side cabin of the engine. He was too busy pulling on his uniform to notice her.

'There's Dad,' she said weakly. They both waved futilely as the klaxon blared and the massive engine took off down the road headed for Beeston mound seven miles away.

'Look sweetheart I just have to go and check with Mr Short about where they're going. Are you OK here for a moment?'

'Of course Mum. I'll be fine.' She watched her mother weaving through the crowds towards the fire station further down the road. Cody was being brave. The truth was she felt she was drowning. Being surrounded by so many distraught adults like this intensified her own natural anxieties and made her feel she was slipping beneath a whirlpool of emotion bigger than she could cope with. There was nothing she could actually do, she knew that, and the anguish coiled inside made her fists clench and unclench until they ached. She had to find space to breathe, to talk out some of the storm raging in her chest.

'It's at Newton,' gasped a voice beside her, a small boy with a mop of sandy gold hair. 'That's only five and a half miles away.' The excitement in his voice was obvious.

'Oh, how do you know?' she asked distractedly, watching as one of the red fuel tankers roared out of the station and shot after the Goddess its klaxon blaring. Her head was beginning to throb slightly. She squeezed her eyes to ease the tension.

'I was at the back of the station when the alarm came in.' The boy spoke breathlessly, unable to take his eyes off the speeding vehicles.

7

Clearly this rated as much more exciting than anything the fayre had to offer this week end. The terrible anxieties of the adults around them, the panicky looks on their faces, the emotions of dread moving through the crowd like a tide, all this was lost on him. Too young to notice. But it was affecting Cody. Her left temple was pulsing now with a dull pain.

'I heard the location being called to the driver,' he yelled above the hubbub. 'It's a big one this time. Two hundred feet across. Right next to Newton village itself.'

Shocked, Cody glanced through watering eyes at the excited youngster. An outbreak that big! How could it have gone undetected for so long?

'But that's terrible' she whispered. 'Can it be dealt with in time?'

A second red tanker was already roaring down the lane of poplars by the old hall chasing the Goddess which was now out of sight. Half a dozen figures ran after it waving and calling encouragement, mostly excitable boys.

'Oh there's bound to be fire carts from other areas. At least eight I'd guess. They'll do it just right. Wish I could be there.' Cody looked at him thoughtfully. He was what...six, seven? A ragamuffin with a boys' adventure comic sticking out of his pocket for goodness' sake. It wouldn't be considered cool to be seen talking to someone so young, she knew, but he intrigued her. And anyway she wasn't generally swayed by the opinions of others her own age. Such stubborn independence guaranteed her treatment as an outsider of course but it wasn't just that. There were other things about Cody that made her peers vaguely uneasy in her presence. Unfortunately they were things she wasn't prepared to change. So...

'Are you always hanging around such odd places?' she asked as casually as she could. The tension at the back of her eyes was making her wince. 'You were caught on the roof of the church last week weren't you?' The boy shrugged noncommittally. He was a pleasant faced lad. She recalled having seen him in the playground many times running around like a mad thing, arms waving, being an aeroplane or something. It must be fun to be able to still do things like that. He turned and looked directly at her with thickly lashed eyes. 'Want a chewing gum?' Caught off guard by his directness Cody laughed.

'No thanks...erm...'

'Miles. Miles Oldfield. But you know that.'

'Yes. Yes, of course I do.'

'You spoke to me last week by the canal basin. Showed me how to skim stones right across to the other side.'

'Course I did. Sorry. I'm a bit forgetful at times.'

'I know. You're famous for it. But I don't mind. Are you alright?' He stared intently as she rubbed her temples.

'I'm fine thanks. Must be the sun. Too strong for me today.'

'Oh! OK. I have to go now,' and he was gone, just like that, ducking between the chattering crowd at the gate. Cody turned back to the fading sound of the klaxons. The gap where the road vanished between the poplars was hazed in blue shadow giving the impression of having swallowed the speeding carts…blue, lethal blue, the colour of deadly, active Bloom…the waves of adult anxiety coming at her from all sides became a roar…then faded rapidly to silence making her almost stagger at the sudden contrast. A vivid picture of her father formed in her mind; she could see his face in astonishing detail. He was frowning, concentrating as he struggled with his uniform in the confined space of the cabin. She sensed the closeness of others in the same space, heard their voices, could smell plastic and leather and perspiration, could feel the swerving motion of the Goddess as it roared down the narrow lanes. The sensations and colours came at her in a great unstoppable flood and everything around her was blanked out by an overwhelming spasm of fear for his safety.

A dozen colliding thoughts flashed through her mind, things she's been told or had read about Bloom, such as fire being the only way to clear areas that had been infected by the deadly growth. She knew that such work was terrifyingly dangerous. How many times had dad explained how difficult it was to control the combustible materials used by the fire trucks. The fire hoses weren't too accurate and of course fire itself was indiscriminate. Accidents happened. If the outbreak was in a field or a forest or on open hillside it wasn't too bad but if it was near to someone's home the risks were greater. People got hurt. There'd been a situation like that last year at a farm. A fireman volunteer had been badly scorched when caught in the firestream from another truck. Luckily the Bloom itself had been caught early enough to stop the patch of blue growth expanding beyond fifteen to twenty feet across. Only an outbuilding and a pigsty had been infected. The pigs had already perished by the time the fire trucks arrived – fortunately the farmer and her children had been taken to safety.

At school it was drilled into everyone how they must always be alert for telltale signs of the Bloom and report any sightings immediately. They had been shown endless films of how the lethal blue mould would start as a tiny blotch no bigger than a 1p coin and gradually expand to smother everything it touched in a writhing fur like growth. If left unchecked it would go on expanding indefinitely like an immense circular stain. Anything caught inside a Bloom circle, living or inorganic, would be broken down and absorbed by the creeping blue infection. Sometimes, for reasons no one yet understood, the Bloom would simply stop growing and turn into a black tarry goo. The same thick residue was all that was left when Bloom was incinerated by two or three dousings of Napetroleum.

There were massive tar spots all over the country, all over the world, on which nothing had grown in the twelve years since the first outbreaks. Either way the original forms of anything caught within the Bloom died or were lost. Vegetation, machinery, people, stone, animals, soil, all went the same way. There was no known cure and only fire could eliminate it. That was why life in every community placed so much stress on the need for constant alertness. Bloom outbreaks could occur anywhere at any time.

And today it had occurred five and a half miles away and her dad was rushing into danger to save people's lives! Again she felt the drowning sensation as the tide of anxiety around her threatened to overwhelm her. She began to slip...

'Hello dear. I'm back. Are you alright?' Her mother's voice broke through the crashing silence and she let her arm be taken and steered down the road.

'I'm fine Mum, really. Oh, I just remembered, what about the concert tonight in Chester Cathedral? We've got tickets and everything!' Her mother laughed as they walked,

'I don't really think we need bother too much about that do we. Dad'll have other things on his mind after this call out. He'll be exhausted and smelling of gasoline and whatever else goes into that stuff they use.'

'I suppose so. It just seems such a shame. I know he was so looking forward to hearing the Tallis choir. We all were.'

'Well, some things take priority. But there'll be other times.' They walked in silence for a while following the path across the recently mowed acres at the back of the school playing fields.

'Look, I think you should go on ahead and wait at Granma Bees' till dad gets back. I need to go and use the Post Office phone to cancel those tickets...and a few other things. Is that OK?'

'Course it is. Will we be having tea there?'

'I should think so. See what Granma Bees says.' Cody could tell her mum was distracted and didn't want to add to her worries. She kept up her brave face.

'Alright mum. I'll see you later then. How long will you be?'

'I don't know dear. But not long.' She bent down and gave her a peck on the cheek. 'I'll bring some preserves along. I got some at the stalls today. Apple.' She looked steadily into her daughter's eyes for a moment and then the distracted look returned. She hugged Cody warmly and strode off towards the village centre waving over her shoulder. 'See you soon dearest.'

'Don't forget the preserves mum.' Cody was reassured to hear her mum's laugh drift back on the breeze.

Cody continued on the path that eventually cut around the old pond and plucked at the waist high grass on either side as she walked. There was birdsong overhead and in the distance she could hear the drone of a microlite coming in to land beyond the row of beeches. It was a beautiful day. Life went on despite the shadow from the past passing over their lives. She knew she ought to relax, stop worrying so much and let the adults look after things she had no control over anyway. It would be good to see Granma Bees, she would help. She wasn't really family, everyone in the village called her Granma Bees, but the old lady had kind of adopted the Conmar family when they arrived in the village three years ago and Cody always felt welcome at the rambling old cottage with its outhouses and barns and animals. Bee, as she called her when they were alone, was a really great cook. She...poch!...

...something hit the back of her head and bounced into the tall grass. Cody whirled round.

'Hey there!' A stocky figure about Cody's age in worn jeans, T-shirt and sleeveless jacket jumped out from behind a tree grinning.

'Bron! How are you! Have you heard all the excitement today?'

'Have I ever. Bloom outbreak wasn't it?'

'A big one too from what was being said.' Cody paused and looked at her feet. 'Dad's on the fire truck. He's on duty today. I'd forgotten.' Bron put her arm around Cody's shoulder and they strolled up

11

to the stile set in the hawthorn hedge. It was built between two huge upright blocks of sandstone set deep into the ground. The slabs were sloped at an angle pointing out across the fields and there were dozens of them around the boundaries of the village. For some reason they always put Cody in mind of sentinels guarding the neighbourhood.

'I shouldn't worry about your dad. He'll be OK. Bloom is a part of life now, you know that. And they know how to handle it, the adults. It can be stopped and killed.'

'I know. But it's not just me. Everyone's really anxious. I can feel it. The fayre won't get going again till much later this evening.' Cody climbed over the stile startling something in the grass that scuttled away.

'Well, the evening bonfire should cheer things up. A good sing song and some roast spuds. That's how community works best.'

'I suppose so. I'm off to Bee's.'

'Thought so. I'll walk you there. Where's your mum?'

'She'll be along later. Got some calls to make in the village.'

'OK.' Bron dug into a pocket and pulled out a small package. 'I've got some chewing gum.'

'What! Where did you get that?'

'Want some?'

'Sure. They're all out in at the village shop. Everyone's run out except the hoarders at school. Jesmina and her cronies had some of course but her dad works at the base. They can get all kinds of stuff there.'

'Is she still being a pain?'

Cody snorted, 'Always. I don't think she knows any other way to be. You should hear what some of the other girls call her behind her back.'

'I could add a few names of my own. C'mon. We can cut past the pond.'

'Don't forget to share out that gum.'

'Who said anything about sharing.'

'You are too! Hand it over Bron.'

'OK but I think you'll find your piece is a lot smaller than mine.'

'It'd better not be!'

'Time has many currents and levels, many aspects above and below the present moment we perceive with our limited senses. Sidetime is an interweaving of parallel events and realities which are hidden or revealed at moments of intersection. Such intersections are often glimpsed in our dreams.'
Extract from Gifts To Come by Thomas Carlan Morledge.

Two
NEWS OF THE DAY

CODY and Bron finally arrived at the back gate of the orchard where Granma Bees kept her bee hives. They waved goodbye. Cody felt a lot better for having spent time with Bron. She always did. They had skimmed stones across the pond seeing who could get the most skips and they had talked. And talked. And talked. Bron was a good listener, not the kind who is obviously waiting for you to finish so she can trot out what she has been rehearsing in her head.

As she walked across the well cropped grass towards the cottage Cody put the gum she'd been chewing back into it's wrapper and slipped it into her waist pouch for later. Two goats on long tethers looked up at the newcomer, their neck bells clanking. Clouds of black and yellow insects swirled drowsily amongst the trees. Occasionally one bullet like individual would zoom past on some mysterious errand but most of the hive were quiet. They were a docile breed imported from the continent after the catastrophic Bloom and Ice Year of '91 killed off most strains native to Britain. In all the years she had kept them in her back orchard Granma Bees boasted that not a single person had been harmed except for a few who had no right to be there. Some youths had once decided to rearrange the hives as a prank and been seen off when the normally docile swarms showed how fiercely protective they could be towards intruders.

She reached the back door which was always unlatched and popped her head inside,

'Hello Bee. Anyone home? Are you there?'

'Yes dear,' Bee's voice called back from somewhere within the cottage. 'I'm busy. Change your shoes and come through. Be with you in a minute.'

'Is there any news about dad yet?'

'What was that dear?'

'There was a Bloom alert, you must have heard, and dad had to go off on the firetruck and…' Bee leaned round the kitchen door smiling, arms full of jars and hands wrapped in a towel. Cody continued, 'I'm worried about dad. They said it was the biggest outbreak in years. Do you think he'll be safe – is there any news yet?'

'Mrs Bentley came across earlier and said the firing was going well. Your mum rang her and said to tell you not to worry. She'll be along in time for supper. Tell you what, you come in and sit down and we can talk properly over a drink,' and her head disappeared. 'Then you can give me a hand with supper. Ben will be back in a while.' Ben was her husband, Mr Ben Onnercott, which of course made Bee Mrs Onnercott, though Cody had never heard anyone call her that, not in three years.

She slipped off her outdoor shoes and picked a pair of soft leather slip-ons from the rack behind the door. The small porch smelt of baking bread and what was probably a cherry cake. She entered the kitchen and slipped onto a stool by the table where a cold glass of apple juice had been set for her. For a while she watched Bee tidying things in the sink humming to herself. A knotted scarf held a great mane of dark hair trailing down her back. She was dusted with flour and her wide figure was wrapped in a floral apron whose pattern was echoed in various plates and carvings on wooden panels around the kitchen. Occasionally a bee would drift in through the open window and buzz around Bee's head or explore the kitchen before flitting out again. For the first time Cody noticed how Bee's humming and the drone of the insects matched. It was a relaxing, almost hypnotic sound that reached right inside her chest.

She finished her drink and began to help out by stirring bowls of delicious smelling ingredients and setting the table. They chatted easily as they worked. It was a familiar routine engaging enough to take her mind off her nagging worries. Bee wanted to know all about Cody's ride on the microlite and then asked who had been at the fayre this week. She was particularly interested in any storytellers who might have turned up. Cody was well known for hanging around the tellers' tents. She had a passion for old legends and mythic tales and had been lucky to hear some of the most gifted storytellers in the country during the last three years. They all passed through Clayton Bar sooner or later. Many people her own age felt that the story tellers were old fashioned. They were only interested in dress trends, the current music scene or the growing use of netsites that you could look at using computers. Granted there were only a few computers in or around Clayton Bar, most of them at school, but it was a growing trend especially with boys for reasons that Cody couldn't begin to understand.

'Was Old Tom Morledge there today?'

'The one who calls himself The Dream Collector!' laughed Cody. 'Yes he was.'

'That's interesting. I thought he was on the continent. Well he's obviously back again. Glad to hear it. Did he do any of your favourites?'

'Yes he did the Ice Year saga, you know with mad subterranean scientists unleashing the Great Bloom on mankind and the world getting saved by the twin angels Ceulwas and Occitan...'

'They weren't angels dear.'

'I know that Bee but that's one of the twists he gives it. There were variations in all the stories he told. I think he's one of the best I've heard.'

'He has a very inventive mind does Old Tom Morledge. He's worth paying attention to.'

Bee went on to ask details about any new stalls or newcomers that Cody might have noticed. Cody was just describing a new fortune teller's tent with green and black awning that she'd seen some girls from school going into when Ben arrived.

'Madeline, why didn't you say we'd been invaded. Keep the ruffian busy with biscuits or something and I'll go fetch my shot gun!'

'Hello Mr Ben,' Cody giggled despite herself. Mr Ben was a small wiry man, quite old by her reckoning, with a shiny bald head like a coconut. He claimed to have been a tumbler and entertainer in his youth. There was certainly something of the mischief she'd seen in clowns and conjurors in the way he acted around her. Bee's part in this family routine was to appear unamused by any of Mr Ben's antics.

'You giddy rumpus! Get yourself cleaned up. We're ready to eat in two minutes. And don't trail sawdust across my kitchen or you'll eat in the fireplace with the other old sticks.'

There was a rush of hand washing and final preparations for supper and Cody became aware of how late it was getting. She was becoming fretful about her parents again. Bee assured her that either they would either turn up soon or send a message via Mrs Bentley.

'But perhaps I should go and find her Bee.'

'No, I don't think so. It'll be getting dark soon and she said you were to wait here. We don't want everyone wandering about in the dark missing each other and having to send out searchers for the searchers now do we.'

'And what were you up to at the fayre today my young adventuress?' asked Mr Ben busy stacking wood by the Aga at the end of the kitchen. 'Big crowds I heard, and some new faces? You were telling Bee there was a new reader, in a green tent...?' Cody was distracted and missed the quick look that passed between the two adults.

'Green tent...oh, yes...yes it was all in green, dark green and black. She was dressed in the same colours and she looked really good in them. Green gloves too even though it was so hot. And she didn't have any signs or chairs outside, or a table or anything so I don't what her name was. You just had to wait your turn in the sun.'

'Were you on your own?'

'Mum and dad were buying some preserves at the fruit stall.'

'Did you go in then, for a reading?'

'No. Two fifth formers from school were there waiting for their friend and they tried to get me to go in. But then the reader came out with the fifth former and stood kind of staring at the crowds, and she saw me and gave me a look. It was odd.'

'Oh, what do you mean odd?' asked Bee as she lifted a pan off the hotplate.

'I don't know. Hard to say. I couldn't even see her eyes properly because she was wearing these dark green glasses, rectangular with no frames. But I could sense she was staring at me. I pretended to see someone I knew and ran behind a tent. It didn't mean anything. She probably wasn't even looking at me really. Just my imagination. But there was something about her'

The ticking of the hallway clock filled the kitchen for a moment. A solitary bee buzzed around Bee's head. Mr Ben had paused with a handful of kindling in mid air.

'Did she see you again after that?' he prompted quietly.

'No, it was my turn for the microlite and I went to join mum and dad.'

Bee lifted the heavy iron pan onto the table and spoke briskly,

'Well I'm sure she meant nothing by it. Some visitors come from a long way away to visit our Cheshire fayres and their style and manner differ from ours. Here we are. Food's ready. And if I'm not mistaken that could well be your mum coming up the path right now.'

Hurried footsteps could be heard outside on the gravel path and there was a loud knocking on the front door. Someone was gasping, half sobbing as if from running...or in great distress,

'Cody! Cody where are you? Mrs Onnercott! Are you there?' It was her mum's voice! She turned to Bee whose face had a hard expression she'd never seen before. Bee nodded to Mr Ben who moved rapidly towards the front door hallway. As if moved by a counter weight Bee slid behind Cody's chair and rested her hands on the girl's shoulders. Cody's chest felt constricted with sudden panic at the sound of pain in her mother's voice. She tried to rise but Bee pressed her back into her seat.

'Easy my love. Easy. Ben can let you mother in.'

'Mum! Mum, what's wrong?' but somehow she already knew, even before she saw her mother's face or heard her speak - she knew. Her mother came rushing into the kitchen radiating panic, heartache and terrible terrible loss. She ran stooping to wrap her arms around her daughter still sat at the table.

'Oh sweetheart, there's been an awful accident.' She could hardly get the words out between sobs. 'It's dad!'

Cody never heard the rest because the world came crashing in, great suffocating shadows piling in on her from all sides. It was a relief in a way but the word *dead* pursued her eerily as she tumbled down the twisting airless tunnel that finally squeezed her flat.

BLOOM: the planet wide algae bloom of 1991 aka 'The Event'. A blue self replicating nanofungus that nearly destroyed all life on Earth in three weeks of February 1991, aka the World Eater. Characterised by a sickly sweet odour. Intermittent outbreaks still occur today.
Entry from News Archive Services egl.bloomhistory.co.uk by Jem Barnstable.

History Of Bloom:

Reliable data on the origins of the Bloom outbreak of 1991 is scarce. What is known is that in February of that year reports of a blue algae like growth started appearing on news programmes world wide. Expanding blue circles were destroying everything they came into contact with. The circles could be metres or tens of kilometres across. All vegetation, buildings, land and animal and human life was being digested, absorbed and rendered beyond recognition. Nothing survived.

Rumours and theories were rife; the Bloomcircles were said to exhibit characteristics of nano technology run amok. Another theory blamed biological weaponry; another claimed it was the result of genetic modification on plants or animals or both. But no one knew the truth.

Within 26 hours of the first large outbreaks the astonishing rate of expansion was computed. Bloom was present on every land mass and in every climate. Bloom circles observed in polar regions grew more slowly than elsewhere. Extreme heat, such as around volcanic vents, destroyed it altogether. Extreme cold slowed its growth and seemed to render it inert. Nothing else had any effect on the rate of devastation. The areas affected grew exponentially doubling in leaps and bounds. It was predicted that the entire planetary surface would succumb within 28 days! Unless a solution was found extremely quickly the world was effectively lost. Panic ensued and world order collapsed.

Only the occurrence of Fimbulwinter, a freak fourteen month arctic year, saved Earth from total devastation. Zero temperatures killed Bloom more slowly but as completely as burning.
[See references on The Ice Year aka The Ice Event, the Arctic World Shroud.]

Three
WREATH DAYS

THE days up to the funeral passed in a blur for Cody. Her mother rallied and tried to be a comfort but it was obvious she was very badly shaken herself. Granma Bees and Mr Ben were there for them in an unobtrusive way. Other members of the community showed their support with offers of help at the Conmar house and everyone dropped by with cards, flowers and good wishes. Despite people's good intentions however Cody would have preferred to be alone with her mother. At least together they could find some comfort in simple domestic routine and each other's company. But that was an unlikely option in such a small community where no one's business was truly their own. Teddy Conmar had been well liked in the village and everyone seemed to take the loss personally. He was the first Clayton Bar casualty in years and nobody could understand how it had happened. The procedures for tackling Bloom were tried and tested, based on years of experience and hard learned lessons. Those were well trained, well equipped men out there – so what could have gone wrong? Details of the incident were sketchy and fire crew members who'd been at the Newton outbreak refused to talk, traumatised by what they'd seen. For this reason nobody probed too much into the details. But they did gossip and something did seem to be odd about the Newton outbreak.

Word was that Teddy Conmar had tried to rescue someone trapped by the Bloom, a young boy possibly, no one really knew the truth of it. The youth, possibly a vagrant or a runaway, had got trapped beneath a derelict farm building that was being steadily engulfed by the Bloom. Somehow they both became cut off and other members of the fire team hadn't been able to get them clear in time. No knew who the boy was or where he came from but that wasn't uncommon in a time when many people travelled around the country looking for work or trying to track down long lost family members. And why did Teddy Conmar get trapped at all? He was an intelligent well trained operator who would never take any unnecessary chances. Had he been careless, unlucky or what? The lack of details was frustrating for people hungry for news of anything Bloom related. It certainly didn't stop some very fanciful versions of the fatalities at Newton from circulating although people were careful not to voice them around Cody or her mother.

The service a week later was held in the commemorative grove on the edge of the village. It was well attended. Many people remarked how dignified Cody looked with her mid length blonde hair tied back with a black ribbon and her black dress and top. She suddenly appeared a great deal older than her twelve years carrying herself with dignity and poise. Mother and daughter held hands the whole time during the readings, Mrs Conmar shaking with sobs throughout and Cody squeezing her hand to reassure her.

The distress of those around her, especially her mother, was hard to bear. Apart from Granma Bees and Mr Ben the faces around the clearing were mostly a blur with two major exceptions – Bron was stood half hidden in the shadow of some nearby trees. Her bright green eyes were focussed intently on her friend, radiating strength. Miles Oldfield was there too, six years old diminutive Miles, whose name Cody usually had trouble remembering. He was stood close to her left hand side. His eyes too were focused on her face with a seriousness that might, in other circumstances, have seemed comic but which today made her feel infused by warmth. Cody acknowledged them both with a small smile then returned her attentions to her mother and what was being said about her father by the readers. When the small plaque was placed on the low brick wall next to a photograph of her father's smiling face she almost felt her control slip. With Bloom deaths of course there was no body. Not a single fragment of any victim remained after being ingested by the insidious creeping growth, added to which, once a Bloom circle had been scorched inert with Napetroleum it reduced to the familiar thick black tar and nothing could be retrieved. At least in the case of cremation you would have the ashes of a deceased loved one to place or scatter as you wished; with Bloom demise there were no tangible reminders. Grievers were left with a plaque and memories, nothing more.

The entire fourteen-man contingent of the local voluntary fire crew turned out in full dress uniform, in fact men from all the Cheshire fire units were there. There was even a representative from the Chester City Fire Service with a tribute and a wreath and another from the Cheshire Police College out at Upton. An intriguing detail that started more rumours circulating was the presence of a man from the National Census Department based in Chester, a Mr Peter Loren. Census Officers had an ambiguous role at the best of times in recovering Britain. It was rumoured they had powers exceeding even those of the police force. They were known to be part of the Mainland Protectorate Headquarters based in London who were directly responsible for national security. Why would he be here at a local ceremony? Was there after all some truth in the rumours of something 'weird' having occurred at Newton? No one knew what to make of it all but the truth about Teddy Conmar's death might never become public knowledge and people would just have to accept that.

After the funeral it was hard for Cody to adjust. She felt suffocated by faces she knew and many she did not. Her particular sensitivity to others' feelings meant she had to handle not only her own grief but her mother's and that of everyone she came into contact with, many of whom were trying to be sympathetic. Her waking hours became dreamlike and her dreaming hours took her into strange landscapes where grotesque shapes chased her and her family through dripping blue caverns that howled and closed in on them. She began to retreat into herself and her memory lapses, which had been troublesome since the accident three years before, now became worse. All her school work suffered and she was absent from class several times in a couple of weeks. Her teachers made allowances of course but not everyone was so considerate.

Jesmina Feydon was a troublemaker in Cody's year, a troubled girl who delighted in exploiting the vulnerabilities of those around her. She was a bully. She was also a coward, as all bullies are. Her taunts were sly, done in a way that could be denied if any teacher drew attention to it. She was totally insensitive to anyone's needs but her own and she had never liked Cody who even as a newcomer to the village had stood up for herself. The two girls had had several face to face run-ins and each time Cody had proved more than a match for the tall scrawny misfit. With her cronies, a sad pair of similarly disturbed unfortunates, Jesmina did her best to make Cody's life as miserable as possible. Mr Conmar's death seemed the perfect time to get some good hits in. But in the immediate period after the funeral neither Jesmina nor anyone else ever knew where Cody was.

Cody had taken to spending a great deal of time with Bron running wild in the fields or walking the country lanes together. Some of this was during school time but Mrs Tansley the headmistress told staff not to make a fuss because it wouldn't go on for too long. Some reaction was understandable with what she had been through recently and so long as someone kept an eye on her she would find her feet again. The staff were concerned but in secret many of them admired Cody's capacity to handle her own problems in her own way, which they felt sure was what she was doing.

For Cody the pressure to get away from the village became almost unbearable. One hot sunny day a week after the funeral she decided to enquire if anyone in the village needed any small items couriered into Chester. The response was good. Five business letters and a couple of small parcels needed delivering. She and Bron grabbed their bikes, stuffed the packages into their panniers and set off along the towpath. It didn't take long to make the deliveries round the town (it was a pretty small city and everyone Cody knew referred to it as 'the town') which gave them the rest of the day to wander about Martin's Gate market. This rag taggle gathering was located around the canal basin where the river Dee, the railway and the canal system converged close to the ancient city walls. It was the city's one commercial hot spot, ideal for picking up bargains or large consignments of goods. Everything exchanged hands here, legal or otherwise, and Cody found it invigorating. She loved it. OK, so the stalls weren't as decorative as the gaudy awnings used at the Albion fayres but there was an edge, a rawness that the country affairs lacked. And the sheer range of goods being bought, sold and haggled over was breathtaking. And there were always plenty of people from out of town, travellers and traders dressed in the most outrageous and fascinating styles.

Bron pointed out a few microlite pilots, 'Liters' as they liked to be called, cruising the market stalls, distinctive in their thick padded jackets, leather helmets hanging from battered backpacks and wind burnt faces. Liters were a common sight at any market in the county. They bartered much of what they needed to keep their aircraft in the air and were a constant source of salvage lifted from isolated areas encircled by tar Bloom that no one else could reach. Ruined Manchester, for example, was surrounded on all sides by a five mile wide tar belt and had provided rich pickings for teams of lite salvagers for years. Liters loved haggling over the rare items they lifted from within the tar zones. Their lifeblood was flying, salvage and barter, oh and giving occasional week end rides at Albion fayres to earn a little cash and goodwill from rural communities. On the surface it was a romantically exciting life and Cody loved being around them.

They treated themselves to a couple of small honey toasted biscuits and Bron was just making a point about how much better this was than being stuck in a stuffy school room when they spotted someone they knew. It was Corbin, the pilot who had taken her up on the Barter 'n' Ride flight at Clayton Bar a couple of weeks back. She was just about to go over and say hello when she noticed who he was talking to. It was Enwyn Carter, the sixteen year old daughter of the post mistress in the village. Enwyn wore her hair in a pull-back pony tail and in black jeans, T-shirt, short sleeveless leather jacket and biker ankle boots looked more beautiful and self confident than anyone had any right to be. She and Corbin radiated an air of maturity that Cody found somehow daunting. They were laughing quietly at some shared joke. Cody was suddenly flustered. What was Enwyn doing here? She was always popping up in unexpected places like a bad penny. It was almost as if she was following her around. She ducked behind a stall and began to scuttle away, followed by an amused Bron.

'Why are we doing this Cody?'

'Oh, I dunno. I don't want them…her to see me.'

'Why?'

'She makes me feel uneasy. She's so…so…'

'Attractive?'

'No. Well yes, I suppose so. But it's not that. She's always…there! Wherever I turn round she's hanging about somewhere.'

'She's got more reason to be in Chester than we have. Doesn't she attend classes here or something?'

'Who cares. I don't want her hanging around me all the time. She's like a shadow.'

'Pretty good looking shadow if you ask me.'

'I didn't. Are you going to shut up now! Can we kindly go now please?'

Bron giggled again.

They pushed their bikes up steep stone steps that led to the top of the ancient city walls, which surrounded the entire centre of Chester. Their route would lead them around the edge of the magnificent cathedral grounds. Bron, in an attempt to distract her friend, suggested they should creep up into the spires and throw bits of moss at anyone below, something they had done on a number of occasions before and always thoroughly enjoyed.

They could use a path that led through the cathedral buildings without being spotted. Once inside they would have to creep along tiny twisting passageways and up a narrow set of steps that led off from a miniature arched doorway set in an obscure corner of the transept. The tiny oak door was always kept locked but that never presented a problem to Bron who had a knack for getting into places she wasn't meant to be.

'OK,' said Cody. 'Race you.'

As they peddled around the walls Cody had to admit to herself that she knew exactly why Enwyn upset her so much. It was because, secretly, Enwyn was very much how Cody herself wanted to be; tall and mature and confident. If they could somehow be friends that would be great but the age gap was too massive. And whenever Enwyn looked at her there was something hard in her eyes, something judgemental, as if she thought Cody was just an annoying kid! She laughed at herself. How silly, getting continually tied up in knots about such non issues. Who cared what Enwyn Carter thought about anything!

As it turned out they couldn't get into the cathedral because there were workmen everywhere being bossed around by clergy overseeing repairs. Not too disappointed they sat on the city walls eating their apples and cheese and gazed out over the rooftops level with the walls. They were by a tall stone structure called King Charles' Tower. From this vantage point it was possible to see right across the Cheshire planes, past the imposing mound of Beeston Castle which stood like a misty blue pyramid high above the flatness of the rolling farmlands. The sun was hot and they wore neck scarves wrapped around their heads like a couple of pirates. The roof tiles of the abandoned houses shimmered in the heat.

Cody and Bron had explored many of the derelict buildings below. They had once found a small cache of pre-decimal pennies under some floorboards. Each coin was about an inch across and made from heavy copper. At first Cody thought they'd uncovered a real treasure trove but Mrs Carter, the post mistress, who also happened to be a collector, had checked them out and there was nothing terribly valuable. So Cody had got to keep them all. She carried one with her all the time, like a good luck charm.

Everything useful in abandoned Chester had long since been cleared by salvage teams or vagrants. Like most of the rest of the Isles, much of Chester remained unoccupied because, as her father had explained, there simply wasn't the demand for living space in built-up areas. The entire population of Britain was still only a fraction of pre-Event totals. People preferred living in the countryside because new outbreaks of Bloom could be spotted more quickly and dealt with in the open. For many who had survived the hardships of the Ice Year, towns and cities felt claustrophobic. The ruins were thought to be inhabited by the spectres of past terrors – or perhaps it was simply bad memories.

Cody didn't have much patience with talk of ghosts and mysterious happenings, which she regarded as childish. Too many children in her class got all worked up about 'things' they heard in stories. Someone, who knew someone, who knew someone else had once seen 'something' wandering about preying on unwary victims. It was so silly. Even so, Cody was definitely aware that some kind of 'presence' could be felt in parts of the deserted town.

'Have you ever seen anything in the ruins Bron. You know, like...?'

'Like what?' prompted the sturdy youngster, chewing on a tough piece of cheese.

'I dunno. Like, y'know, ghosts. Or voices. Have you ever heard voices?'

'Have you?' asked Bron quietly, gazing casually out at the shimmering landscape.

'Well, no, not as such...not really.' Cody glanced sideways to gauge her friend's reaction. 'One particular time,' she continued hesitantly, 'Last winter it was, when the snow was still thick, I was standing near the old amphitheatre waiting for dad to come out of St John the Baptist church after a concert. I was looking down into the arena and without warning I suddenly felt as if there were people all around me talking, in a whisper. Not at me, they were just there talking. Amongst themselves. For a moment I felt as if I could push through the air and step into that place where they were. It would be so easy.'

'And did you?'

'No. Of course not. How could I. You do say the oddest things sometimes Bron.'

'In some places the membrane dividing the past from the present is thinner. It is more porous, like a piece of sacking, so that thoughts and dreams can leak across the time streams.'

Cody peered at her companion, a little taken aback,

'Bron! That doesn't sound like you.'

'Hardly surprising really. They're not my own words.'

'Oh?'

'There's a netsite by someone named Cullie Brown that goes on about "*old places of power in the ancient and present landscapes.*" There's also articles on myths of the Ice Year, Dream Lore, stuff like that. You'd find it really interesting'

'Where on earth do you get access to a computer?'

'The library.'

'But there's always such a waiting list to get on those terminals.'

'Not if you go late enough. When there's no one about. Say after closing time.'

Cody laughed in surprise, delighted and outraged at the same time,

'You mean when it's locked! But that's…that's…'

'It's very quiet, yes. C'mon we'd better be getting back. People will want to know that their deliveries have arrived safely.'

'Oh, I suppose so. And school'll be finished soon.' Cody really wanted to ask Bron about that quote and what she had been doing in the library when it was closed, but they began stuffing their water bottles into their panniers and scooting their bikes along the top of the city walls. At one of the narrowest parts, where there was a drop of fifteen feet on the side without rails, Bron threw her leg over the saddle and accelerated away at a dangerous wobble. Cody was caught by surprise and yelled in protest but didn't catch up till they reached the massive bell tower by the cathedral. Racing side by side along the deserted wall they disturbed a flock of rooks that took off in an explosion of black wings and angry cawing. The girls whooped with glee sending echoes bouncing off the high walls.

They chattered all the way along the canal towpath heading back towards Clayton Bar, but they did not mention voices or myths or Dream Lore, whatever that was. When they reached the outskirts of the village

Cody's back tyre got a puncture and they had to wheel the bikes for the last quarter mile as neither of them had brought a repair kit. Even that didn't spoil it being a great day out, a welcome contrast to the suffocating closeness of Clayton Bar. They delivered the courier receipts in no time and were soon waving goodbye and heading their separate ways home for tea.

*   *   *

Cody burst into the house exhausted but smiling. Her mum was pleased to see her in such an uplifted mood. After hearing where she'd been all day Mrs Conmar explained tolerantly how in future she wanted to know where Cody would be, even if she was bunking off, but she didn't labour the point. It was on everyone's mind in the village that young Adam Bowman, a boy in the year below Cody's, was still missing after disappearing a week ago and no one had a clue where he might be. The anxiety level of every parent in Clayton Bar was racked up, especially after the Newton outbreak, but Mrs Conmar knew it would be wrong to try and rein her daughter in too much at a time like this. Recent events meant they'd both been under a great deal of pressure, particularly for a twelve year old. Anything that lifted her spirits was obviously to be encouraged and the day in Chester had clearly done that.

After tea Mrs Conmar watched through the kitchen window as Cody repaired the puncture in the back yard. Blonde hair fell across her daughter's face as she struggled to disentangle the inner tube from the tightly fitting tyre. What a picture she made, so lovely, so capable, so ... vulnerable. Observing her daughter this way Mary Conmar was suddenly ambushed by an emotionally confusing upsurge of panic and love for the young miracle her life was dedicated to protecting. Teddy was gone. She'd have to get used to that. For a moment the responsibility of keeping at bay all that would be pitted against this young life in the years ahead seemed monumental. She wasn't alone of course, there were many allies and friends, but the burden of it weighed her down. So much at stake! At the same time she knew the task to be one she would embrace whatever the cost to herself.

Bathed in the evening sun that slanted into the back yard Cody, hands black with oil, glanced up to see her mother watching from the window. She gave a little wave and a smile before continuing to wrestle the inner tube off the metal rim of the wheel. She whistled quietly to herself unaware how her head was haloed by golden hair fired by sunlight.

*   *   *

Three hours earlier that same afternoon, eight miles from Chester, nine year old Martin Burnside burst into a farmyard on the edge of Delamere Forest and fell wild eyed and incoherent into the arms of one of the farm hands. Everyone rushed out to see what the yelling was about expecting to have a Bloom sighting on their hands. Ben Cartwright, the farm owner, knew the procedure for that, who to alert and so on. But it wasn't Bloom. This was something different. Unfortunately the lad was dry retching and unable to speak so no one could make head or tail of what had distressed him so much. After he'd been calmed down they were wondering whether to take the lad into Chester for proper care. Mrs Cartwright was talking gently to him when he blurted out something that made them decide to call the local police. Something about abandoned lorries at the derelict outhouses – with things inside them.

'No, not animals...things! Things!' That was all the boy could manage.

'That's it,' said Ben, 'I'm calling the police. Betty look after the lad.'

Two police officers accompanied Ben Cartwright to the spot young Martin had described and found the lorries easily enough. One of the constables ran back to the farmhouse to put a call in immediately to the Central Constabulary at Chester. He was told they should cordon off the area until someone in authority came to take charge. Neither of the constables would comment on what had been found to anyone at the farm and even Ben, normally quite talkative, was oddly reluctant to say what they'd seen. No, it definitely wasn't Bloom, but he couldn't say what, not right now. Later he confided to his wife that everything around the vehicles and outhouses had been scorched and a sickening smell from inside the lorries clung to the clearing. Even his clothes reeked of it, he complained. She could detect nothing unusual on his clothes and said so. But he protested the strength of it kept making him nauseous. Beyond that, an official cautioning from the two officers had convinced him to remain quiet. No one on the farm pushed for more details, reluctantly.

Everyone was used to inexplicable events as a part of their lives these days. It was all part of the Bloom legacy but it had never involved officially enforced silence before. As things normally went the authorities were keen for signs of anything strange to be reported and broadcast as widely as possible throughout the county. An informed county, the often repeated phrase went, was a vigilant county. But not on this occasion. Clearly something more than usually disturbing was going on.

About nine o clock that evening one of the farm hands passed the old outhouses, 'Just taking a small diversion on me way back from the top field, like, 'cos it was raining'. He was astonished to see the police no-entry tape still in place but the lorries gone.

FIMBULWINTER: a fourteen month global arctic winter (March 1991 to April 1992) cause unknown. This freak global event killed off the original outbreak of Bloom algae and over half of the world's population — exact figures unknown. Aka The Ice Year, The Ice Event, The Bloom Killer, The Arctic World Shroud, Zero Winter.
[For relevant articles see: egl.fimbulwinterfacts.co.uk
egl.mythsoftheiceyear.co.uk
egl.govtrecoveryprogram.co.uk] Cullie Brown.

Four

DARK MANOEUVRES

'Mortal man must be shielded from an excess of reality.'
T.K. Edwins.

THREE miles away a motor bike and sidecar roared through the darkened streets of Chester, headlights flashing on puddles and glistening brickwork as the BSA 500 gunned towards the river at the bottom of Lower Bridge Street. The roar of the engine boomed louder as the driver shot under the city walls then dropped to a throaty growl as the vehicle swung away from the bridge and right along the banking towards Chester Castle. The ancient stronghold loomed in silhouette against night clouds dwarfing everything around its base. Fifty yards on from the bridge a sharp right turn swept up towards a gateway set in the castle wall and the motorbike took the corner at speed, skidding violently on the wet cobbles. With a screech of brakes the BSA juddered to a halt mere inches from a metal barrier. The driver leapt from the saddle, threw the barrier open then remounted. He wore goggles, leather helmet, gloves and a hooded cape belted at the waist. His face glistened from recent showers and his jaw was set into a grim expression. He revved the engine, accelerated away between massive stone buttresses with inches to spare and skidded into a courtyard where he killed the engine. Leaping off the machine he stormed through a low doorway.

The figure pounded along narrow tunnels oblivious to the darkness or crumbling sandstone walls. At various intervals light switches dangled from tangles of electric cable, but he ignored these moving through the musty gloom with the assurance of complete familiarity. In some sections a faint glimmer came from low wattage bulbs set into alcoves but most of the twisting passageways remained sunk in shadow.

Echoes of his progress pursued him along the passages, cape rasping against the rough walls, boots thudding on flagstone.

Finally he threw open a heavy wooden door and mounted a rickety stairway. He was now in an open space lit only by the flicker of monitor screens in a distant corner. This had once been the castle chapel but the original forty foot high space had been divided into two levels by a crudely timbered floor. Any impression of solemnity or grandeur had long since been dispelled. The dry air muffled all sound. On every side, beyond the reach of the feeble light, were shelves where mouldering boxes sagged against each other or spilled onto the floor like dusty waves. No one knew or cared that these decades old records existed and no one would ever come to retrieve them. They were testimony of a redundant past. The general neglect contrasted sharply with the clutter of hi tech equipment in the far corner.

Census Officer Peter Loren pulled off his leather helmet and gloves as he strode across the creaking floor to his swivel chair and threw himself into it with a sigh.

'Let's see what those bloody fools have been up to,' he growled. Fingers tapped ferociously at the keyboard and he peered hawk like at the data that scrolled before him. He snorted and reached for the phone. A short pause.

'Hello sergeant. Loren here from the Census Office. Yes it is late. What's happened to the two abandoned lorries at Delamere? I was just up there and they've been moved!' What he heard next did not please him but he controlled his temper by consciously lowering his voice.

'I understand...I understand, but who gave the authority to have them moved? I informed your superior I was interested in the incident and needed to take a look myself. Yes, I understand they can be better guarded at the barracks but I needed to see them where they were first discovered. Alright, look. Ring ahead to security at the camp and inform them I'll be along in twenty minutes, thirty at most. I don't want to be kept hanging about at the gate. Thank you. Most obliged.'

He took care not to slam the phone down and leaned back letting out a long controlled breath. 'What can they have been thinking!' he murmured. He raked fingers through damp hair and stared up towards the chapel ceiling somewhere in the gloom overhead. Then in a blur of motion he was at the keyboard attacking the keys with grim determination, reading at ferocious speed as data scrolled up the screen.

He tapped several curt messages, mailed them and leaned across to a low metal locker from which he hauled a heavily padded camera lens case. Slinging this over his shoulder he grabbed his helmet and goggles and pounded down the rickety stairway back the way he had come. Bursting into the courtyard he adjusted his gloves and head gear, gunned the BSA's engine, glanced impassively at the cloud laden sky from which a steady rain was gathering strength, and slipped his goggles down before roaring off. The metal barrier was still open.

He had to skirt the small Tar-Zone that cut off the most direct route through Broughton but twelve minutes later he arrived at the gates of Saighton barracks to the southeast of Chester and was admitted by armed guards after a brief formal challenge.

A non commissioned officer on duty instructed Loren where to park his bike by the gates and waited whilst the dripping wet Census Officer grabbed his camera case from the sidecar and zipped the heavy lens case to it. A Land Rover drew up driven by a private and with Loren and the officer on board took a direct route to a compound four hundred yards inside the camp. They stopped at a large unlit structure that Loren recognised as a vehicle maintenance bay. The officer hauled back the sliding doors and they both stepped inside,

'Both lorries are in here...Mr Loren. Is there anything else I can help you with?' The officer seemed wary of the Census Officer despite his clearance to enter the base. He kept glancing at the camera bag slung over Loren's shoulder.

'No thank you corporal. Do we have lights in here?' The corporal leaned his head out into the rain,

'Do we have lights private Feydon?'

'Yes sir! Flood lights connected to a generator sir. Should I...'

'That's OK private,' Loren interrupted. 'I can work it out. Thank you. Any chance of a hot drink?' The private glanced sideways at the officer and got a nod.

'I'll ring through...sir. Coffee OK?' The slight hesitation before 'sir' showed the man's uncertainty about Loren's status.

'Definitely. And anywhere to hang my wet things?' Water was streaming from Loren's cape onto the stained concrete floor.

'Nail by the door, to your right there...sir.'

'Thanks.' He strode into the echoing space watched by the corporal from the door. Loren noted the officer's reluctance to enter the building. Fine. That would mean no interference. The cold air smelt of engine oil and rain soaked soil…and something else hard to pin down. Weak light came from a single bulb by the entrance. He could just make out two lorries parked at the far end of the otherwise empty bay. Sets of floodlights on stands had been arranged around the rear of the nearest but were switched off. He approached the vehicles. Winking lights from two security cameras high up on the wall showed that there was at least a basic security system in operation. Someone somewhere was keeping an eye on these lorries – or should be. So far this situation had been handled atrociously. What would London have to say about such a shambles? He grinned and gave an ambiguous finger gesture to the cameras.

Stepping up to the rear of the lorry he flicked the light switch on the squat control box cabled to the floodlights and heard a dynamo start up somewhere in the darkness. The interior of the filthy scorched vehicle flooded with light and there, stacked three high and lashed with thick roping against the truck sides, were about fifteen shapes in grimy black plastic. The wrappings reminded Loren of body bags. He'd seen enough of those whilst flying recon and salvage missions in the late 90's during the government's national recovery programme. A frayed length of the rope used to lash the bags to the lorry lay on the grimy floor. Footprints had been scuffed into meaninglessness. There was an evasive dankness on the air…decay? Nothing too unusual for a place like this where fuel and oil got spilled regularly and the neglected structure itself bred mildew but…there was something…

He removed his gloves, unslung the camera and took half a dozen photos from different angles. Then he clambered onto the tailgate and prised open a tear that had already been made in one of the heavy black wrappings. Inside was something shiny and also black. Very black. He took more pictures swapping lenses twice from a selection kept in the heavily padded side pouch. At one point he hopped off the tailgate to turn the floodlights off and took close up shots with a lens that looked like a bundle of transparent pencil stubs lashed together. With the floodlights once again filling the claustrophobic space he squatted low staring at the scene, his eyes gliding slowly over every detail. There were exactly fifteen bags. There were tears in at least two other bags that he could see.

Whatever the shapes inside the wrappings might be they were coated in a tacky substance similar to inert Bloom-tar. Its surface shimmered with little spectrum patterns like oil as he moved his head from side to side. It was impossible to tell what lay beneath the thick coating. Prising a thick wooden splinter from the lorry's floor he pressed it into the tough surface. It seemed to break through an outer skin and when he pulled it away a glutinous gummy strand trailed from the wood like molasses. In seconds the goo had spread, coating the splinter to within centimetres of his fingertips. He dropped the mess back onto the tar where it sank from sight, absorbed into the surface before he had time to straighten up. The fact that the tar didn't stick to the plastic of the outer bags was intriguing. If this was Bloom-tar he'd never seen it in a situation like this before. He stared at the shapes piled around him, an uneasy suspicion gathering strength at the back of his mind.

Footsteps crunched across the concrete from the bay door.

'Coffee's here...sir.'

'Great. Thanks. I'll come over,' but the footsteps continued to approach. Loren pulled out his survival knife, locked the longest blade and made a determined stab into the tar. He twisted sharply opening a soft edged gash about three inches deep. Before the muck oozed back to seal the opening a marshy smell whiffed out of the incision and made him cover his face. Advanced decomposition, a smell he knew well. His subconscious whisperings had been correct. The shapes could be bodies – this one almost certainly was. But bodies of what? And how many were in the second lorry? An avalanche of questions cascaded into his mind.

'Your coffee...sir.' The private stood silhouetted against the glare of the lights beyond the truck. Loren hadn't tried to conceal what he was doing. He held the knife blade downwards so that the tar wouldn't spread up to the handle.

'Thanks. Do you happen to know the officers who brought these lorries in?'

'No idea. Local constabulary was all I heard. They left once the lorries were signed over...sir.'

'Anyone have any idea what these things might be, at all?' Loren gestured vaguely at the sinister shapes behind him. There was a moment's pause and Loren felt the man's tension roll over him.

'No sir. Is that all...sir?'

'Sure. Thanks for the coffee.' The guard's stroll back to the doorway was a study in controlled nonchalance spoiled only by the furtive backward glance as he reached the doorway. He might not know what was in the black wrappings but he obviously had an active imagination – not always an advantage for a soldier.

When Loren attempted to scrape his blade clean against the truck's side he had to give up. Nothing was going to shift the viscous muck completely. He put his coffee down and with a quick slash cut a length of the plastic wrap from the already opened bag and folded the knife in that before sealbagging it and zipping it into an ankle pocket. He jumped down and moved to the second lorry. With a slim pencil torch taken from a shoulder pocket he counted another fifteen bags. Exactly. There was nothing more he could do right now. He had no proper facilities. It was time to report in.

Back at the guard's hut the corporal agreed, after hesitating just enough to register his disapproval, that Loren could make a landline call from there. Loren dialled a fastlink connection to a number in London. He recognised the voice at the other end, female, Amuna, nice voice but a tough lady who took no prisoners. He was curtly instructed to email a report from the secure line in his office asap and include all digital data including images from the location. He replaced the handset, thanked the corporal and guards and five minutes later was roaring back to the Castle Chapel mulling over the implications of his trip.

The rain had stopped and the easier driving conditions allowed him to review bullet points of the situation as he negotiated deserted streets with no lighting. This was definitely one for the anomaly file even though there was little enough hard information to chew over. He'd have to see what London wanted done. Proper examination of what was in the lorries would need specialist equipment and that would take time to arrange. Shouldn't be a problem though.

*   *   *

Peter Loren was the officially appointed Census Officer for all of Cheshire. His job was to monitor and chart population movements between his jurisdiction and adjoining counties and keep the National Census Office in London up to date. Officers of lesser status were sited at hundreds of locations throughout the British Isles working closely with local police, military and civil administration receiving regular reports from traffic and control agencies countrywide. The exact boundaries of his job were ambiguous enough to allow him certain liberties when dealing with local authorities none of whom understood the true extent of his duties and powers. He never hesitated to exploit this uncertainty wherever possible. It saved him a lot of time. The visit to Saighton barracks was a good example.

The truth was Loren's duties as a Census Officer were a front for a variety of undercover activities carried out on behalf of an officially appointed government department, the Mainland Protectorate, which happened to run a number of covert divisions responsible for national security. No one outside the Protectorate knew quite what its operatives were capable of, legally or otherwise. And no one in the regular forces wanted to challenge someone who might, just might, be one of the Protectorate's specialists. All of which suited Loren perfectly. There were 'situations' other than the movement of the population at large that needed constant monitoring; situations that sometimes required him to operate outside of strictly legal guidelines.

Peter Loren's covert function was to record and take action on anomalies. In a recovering world only twelve years on from the most devastating natural anomaly of all time, the appearance of Bloom and the catastrophic winter of '91-'92 that effectively killed it off, there was never any shortage of unusual sightings, disappearances or superstitious panics amongst the population. Most of them, such as the occasional reappearance of Bloom, could be dealt with by standard response bodies such as the fire services, armed forces or local constabulary. The list of recorded enigmas on file beggared belief. Every family in every community had their own repertoire of mysteries. Half the population thrived on the reinvention of myths and believed in the significance of dream interpretation. The unknowable was woven into the fabric of twenty first century life.

But anomalies, true anomalies – well, that was something else entirely. Anomalies were classified as anything considered serious enough to have implications for national security. And that interested the Protectorate very much indeed. Special measures were in place to identify and deal with anomalies and Loren was part of those special measures.

Since his placement in Cheshire eighteen months ago he had investigated an increasing number of high priority anomalies and the dark nature of his findings had begun to gnaw away at his beliefs in the safety of the recovering world. Basically, twelve years on from the Bloom outbreak, most people accepted the more radical changes to everyday life in Britain. Families and communities prospered by accommodating to those changes. And it was a common belief, actively encouraged by the powers entrusted to safeguard the population's welfare, that higher forces were in place guaranteeing everyone's safety. Wise guardians and benign government were a bulwark against the return of a darkness that had changed life forever, and taken it from many. It would not happen again!

Unfortunately Peter Loren knew this not to be the case. Knew it for a fact. And that worried him deeply. His own dreams had grown disturbed of late. He had begun to leave things out of his officially submitted reports. Too many bizarre occurrences fed a growing suspicion that something obscure was at work in the world, something furtive but growing increasingly careless about masking its presence. The signs were there, indicators, things he had been trained to look for. He could track them, record and report them but he lacked any accurate way of interpreting what on earth they meant. As an operative out in the field he lacked the status that would grant him access to the bigger picture; his face was pushed up too hard against the gritty details. And he was finding it increasingly difficult to blindly trust the procedures meant to deal with the kinds of things he uncovered. London didn't always listen to what he had to say. And he could not shake the suspicion that he was occasionally being sabotaged. For example, who had ordered the lorries driven to Saighton barracks? Not the local constabulary. So who? No one in London was saying. His immediate superior, Amuna, had been her usual enigmatic self when he spoke to her from the barracks, no help at all. For someone with such a foxy voice she had a habit or treating him like a total non ranker, which was frustrating as well as worrying. What in blue hell was going on?

Now, driving through the rain he prioritised his moves. First process the photo images he'd gathered. Start a basic breakdown of the goo on his survival blade. Then check in with London, hopefully Amuna wouldn't still be on duty. He'd have to arrange for proper equipment at the barracks to carry out extensive analysis on the bag contents. That tar like substance was worrying. Then check out the farmhouse at Delamere again. It was going to be a stimulating night.

He wondered what kind of restaurants Amuna liked eating in.

'*All is pattern, everything is code. We have been evolving since before life threw up something recognisably man-like and we must recognise that the nature of humanity is not fixed. Nor is our physical form. Being a pattern of energies and flesh, thoughts and dreams, we are also part of a vast motif that includes landscape, megalithic forces and mystery. We are a miracle amidst wonders. And we can become both greater and stranger than our present familiar configuration.*'

From a lecture on Mystery And Evolution given by Thomas Carlan Morledge at the Recovery Institute of Britain. [For full text see egl.mysteryandevolution.co.uk]

Five
POULTICES AND VENOM

'Defend all your weaknesses, failings and mistakes and you will surely get to keep them.'
David C Beltane.

THE boys came screaming and yelling into the front orchard as Granma Bees was tending her goats to the rear of the cottage. They were spinning in all directions swatting the air around their heads although nothing was near them - but something had been! The state of their arms and legs proved that. They were covered in stings. Granma Bees ran over to calm them down and ushered them into her kitchen to administer one of her miracle remedies, a suspect looking brown goo concocted from honey gel and herbs.

'Now, you sit on the old sofa there, and you little one, let's have you on this big chair here in the light where I can see you properly.' The boys did as they were told and sat squirming with the discomfort of their wounds. Granma Bees fetched a flat wooden box big as a coffee table and as deep as a tennis ball, raised the lid and began to take things from the many compartments inside.

'I don't know what the pair of you looked like dancing around out there,' she smiled as she smeared thick brown grease from a jar onto gauze squares. She applied each poultice gently to the boys' stings and then covered them with cotton pads taped into place. At least they'd calmed down a little now. It wasn't uncommon for sting victims to suffer from mild shock and Bee needed to assess how bad a state they were in; it was clear from their moans that they were in considerable pain. The older boy tried to sniff at the pad as it was applied to his arm. His face wrinkled in disgust but changed to a reluctant smile as he realised the smell was in fact quite pleasant.

'You'll have to keep still now dear. This looks quite bad.' The smaller of the two was near to tears but whether from pain or general distress at the whole experience it was hard to tell. In contrast the bigger youth was putting a brave face on whilst still obviously overawed by being in Bees' cottage, a place that had a name in the village as a witch's cottage. Bee's reputation as healer and general oddbod with a flair for the magical had been carefully cultivated to keep the younger element from prying where they weren't wanted. She studied the boys as they fidgeted and moaned. They were what … ten years old?

'What were you two doing in my orchard anyway?' she asked casually as she worked.

'We weren't in your orchard Mrs Bees, honestly! We weren't even near your hedge were we Doug?' Doug glared at his companion for using his name so carelessly but spoke directly to the large woman stood over him,

'No, we were on the lane at the end of the road.'

'They just came at us.'

'Just came at you?' puffed Bee unbelieving.

'We weren't bothering them or anything, were we Doug.'

'No, we weren't Mrs Bees.' Doug was making a good show of standing up for himself and his friend. 'We just got chased by this huge swarm of bees.'

'Stinging bees,' added the smaller boy, unnecessarily, his chest wracked with sobs. Bee could see he was having trouble breathing. So was Doug, though he fought to control it with more success.

'My bees don't attack anyone minding their own business and certainly not on the road outside so you'd better get your stories right if you expect anyone to believe you.' Granma Bees was used to being firm with rascals who tried for her apples but she had to avoid upsetting these two too much if she was going to be able to help them properly. They had been lucky, there were no marks on their faces but as she examined the patches of blue-black swelling on their arms and legs her own sense of calm was beginning to tilt a little. These markings didn't look good. She placed a hand on the older boy's forehead. Ice cold, but his face was red and sweaty. Both youngsters were the same. Could they be having identical allergic reactions to the bee venom? Unlikely, and yet…! Granma Bees had dealt with allergic reactions before and had a preparation to hand if that were the case, but she had never seen anything quite like the mottled blotches that were spreading out from angry red centres where the stings had penetrated the skin. Both boys' breathing was laboured and their hands were trembling. She may need to get help with this situation.

'Hush now,' she added quietly. 'It's hard to apply these patches if you keep squirming. Press them down firmly if you want the stinging to go away.' Two pairs or eyes stared at her beseeching her words to be true.

There was a sudden clatter at the back door and everyone turned to see Cody pushing backwards into the kitchen carrying a large tray wrapped in a tablecloth. When she saw the strange scene her mouth dropped in disbelief.

'Bee, there are dead bees on the path all down the lane! What's been going on in here?' she placed the tray on the wash surface by the sink.

'Dead? That'll be due to these two bad 'uns here is my guess. They've been tramping around in my orchard and upsetting my workers.' This started another round of protests from the invalids,

'We weren't Mrs Bees, truthfully!'

'We weren't. It's like we said we were at the top of the lane when this swarm came at us ...'

'... couldn't see where we were or anything...'

'... didn't even know we was outside your place, honest.' The boys' expressions were wretched. Their eyes were brimming. Granma Bees pitched her voice low to keep them calm,

'Now, now, no need to get all agitated boys. I'm not intending to tackle you about it yet, except to get this swelling down a bit. Hold that onto your arm young 'un. It's coming off ...could you help out dear?' Bee turned to Cody and handed her the box of linen squares and a screw top jar containing the thick brown paste.

'Of course Bee.' Cody took the items and began to smear ointment onto the squares without being told. She spoke to the big lad on the sofa as she knelt to apply tacky cotton strips to the smaller of the two sat on the high back chair.

'You're Doug Feyden aren't you? Jesmina's brother?' The lad stiffened warily. He wasn't as awed by the twelve year old as he was by the large framed woman with the lion's mantle of thick dark hair.

'So! What of it?' He had to speak between gasps. It was difficult for him to breath.

'Nothing. Just wondered if she was around when this happened.'

'Nope. Been acting kind of weird this last week, she ... why do you want to know about Jesmina?'

'Oh, no reason.' Cody glanced back at the smaller casualty whose eyes were closed showing dark blue eyelids. She shook his arm gently, 'And what's your name?' Silence. The lad's breathing had a rasp to it but he managed to flicker his eyes open and stare back into Cody's. She could feel the waves of distress and desperation that kept him paralysed in the high wooden chair. The poor thing was really terrified. She tried to apply a gauze to the back of his knee but felt his body go rigid with panic under her hand. It wasn't her touch that caused the reaction however; his bulging eyes were fixed on a solitary bee that had drifted into the kitchen and was circling Bee's head as she cut more strips of gauze with a large pair of scissors. A low moan came from Doug on the sofa. The sheer terror radiating from both of the boys was like a scalding pulse of fire in Cody's head. She forced it aside and addressed Bee in a low voice,

'Bee, they're scared.' She indicated the two terrified figures with a nod. Bee's stout face looked puzzled for a moment then lit up as realisation dawned. She rose and gently shooed the tiny worker insect out through the open window. Cody turned her attention back to her patient. He relaxed slightly.

'Come on Vas,' she encouraged, her voice pitched low the way Bee had been doing. 'I know your name really. It's Vas Brown isn't it.' The boy unglued his gaze from the window for a moment and nodded uncertainly. She smiled at him, 'We're going to help you.'

'Can you make the pain stop?' His voice was a whisper and his eyes darted between her face and the window.

'I'm sure we can.' She began to roll back his sleeves to expose the stings and saw how the dark bruised patches were now linked with threads of angry red tracery like tiny streams joining up to make a river. Something deep within Cody made her heart go still for a moment as time... seemed... to... slow. She'd seen this before ... somewhere. But where? Sounds receded. Warmth was flooding out from her chest down her arms and into the space between her hands where it bobbed like a glowing ball of energy. She placed her palms onto the boy's icy flesh and for a moment her eyes closed. It was like touching a cold skin of silk stretched taut over a stream with fish kicking beneath the surface flicking at her fingers. She could feel herself sinking into the depths, surrendering

43

to the pull of the currents... chasing the fishtails darting amongst swirling shadows. She followed the flickering forms down, away from the light, deeper into the muffling darkness...

'Cody, are you alright! What are you doing?' Bee's voice was like a light being switched on inside a darkened room. With a shiver Cody slid back into herself, back into the kitchen and opened her eyes. Vas seemed to be asleep, his breathing low and even.

Bee... I'm here!' Cody had to push her voice out as if it had somehow become locked in her chest. It emerged deeper than usual. She looked at the stout figure still wearing her outdoor apron used for cleaning out the goat trough and was taken aback to realise she was staring back with an expression of barely concealed amazement, perhaps even a touch of fear.

'What were you doing just then?' Bee whispered looking flustered.

'I... I don't know Bee. Something's wrong here. Terribly wrong. But I don't know what it is.' Bee appeared to rouse herself with an effort and indicated a high shelf above the window.

'Yes, I know dear. Very wrong. But everything in its time. Fetch me that green wood box on the top shelf would you, quick now.' Cody rose and pulled a chair over so that she could reach. As she stretched up a low groan made her turn.

'Bee! Look out!' Vas was sliding slowly off his chair as if his bones had turned to water. The heavy woman made a lunge and only just managed to prevent his head from smacking onto the hard tiled floor. She cradled him in her arms suddenly alarmed that the boy was so deeply unconscious. Doug was likewise slumped on the sofa, a puppet with its strings cut

'They've slipped into a coma,' Bee gasped. 'Anaphylactic shock! Quick, bring me the box! I have a serum in there to counter it.'

Cody jumped from the chair and placed the wooden box on the floor next to the inert form in Bee's arms.

'No, it's OK Bee. Really.' She rested a hand on the woman's shoulder. Her voice was still low, husky as if strained by shouting. Bee was about to say something but stopped, registering what Cody was saying. 'They've passed below the level of pain and the danger's held - for the moment. These aren't bee stings. I don't know what they are but we must draw the toxins out. If the venom connects across the whole skin surface they'll stay unconscious and be lost. There'll be no recovery after that.'

Bee was fighting a rising sense of urgency to take care of the boys as well as combating the shock of what she was seeing in Cody. She felt anaesthetised by the girl's voice and manner. Jumping to her feet she bustled around the kitchen opening drawers and gathering jars and pots. 'I have an unguent that can draw the toxin,' she spoke over her shoulder, strain evident in her voice. 'We must be quick. We need all the bandaging in the house. There are some old sheets in the landing cupboard upstairs.'

'I'll get them Bee. You make them comfortable.' Cody rushed to the top of the house whilst Bee busied herself opening various containers and placing them where they could easily be reached. As she placed each of the unconscious boys in comfortable positions her mind was in a turmoil at what she had seen the twelve year old doing. Surely the child wasn't ready for this yet. Her voice had held such authority. Her manner was different. The changes couldn't be happening already – could they? This was wrong. She needed to tell the child's mother, and the others!

When Cody returned they both worked frantically covering the inflamed parts of the boys' skins with a variety of ointments and poultices wrapping them with gauze and strips of linen. Between each layer of bandage they wove sprigs of strong smelling herbs taken from the large medicine box. All the while Bee was trying to shake herself free from the numbness slowing her brain. She must concentrate on what had to be done to save the boys, but her thoughts wouldn't hold still. Besides her Cody worked without pause, her hands flying over the boys, winding linen strips, placing pungent leaves over the infected areas and securing the wrappings. She was totally engrossed in her task. The air felt thick from the aromatic herbs they were using. Bee imagined she could feel heat radiating from the youngster as they worked.

By the time they were finished the two ten year olds pretty much resembled a couple of miniaturised mummies with only their faces peeping out of the swaddling. The final step was to trickle a few drops of tincture down the slack throats. Cody cradled their heads whilst Bee carefully administered the colourless liquid.

'There. Done.' Bee sat back on her heels avoiding looking directly at Cody as she checked pulses in the limp wrists. 'We can keep them here to make sure they're stable but we should call for an ambulance as soon as possible. They seem through the worst.'

'They're safe Bee. They're young and strong. So long as they're not disturbed their bodies will throw off the effects of the venom without any more help. Don't worry. I should go and tell their mothers,' but Cody made no move to leave. The two women regarded each other in silence, one mature, the other no longer as young as she appeared. Bee felt sure there was an older mind regarding her from behind the eyes of the twelve year old. She deliberately slowed her breathing and pushed back her hair playing for time wondering what to do. Cody sniffed delicately at the herbal traces clinging to her fingers – then she lifted her head and looked around the kitchen as if realising where she was.

'Bee what's happening? ' The husky tone in her voice had receded and when Bee peered hard into her eyes the old presence behind them had gone too – if it had ever really been there.

'I don't know dear. I thought you might know. What were you doing when you had your hands on young Vas? Do you recall?'

'I have no idea. I... I can't remember what I did... I mean what happened when I did... whatever I did. You were scared weren't you, I know that!'

'No dear, I wasn't scared. I was... oh alright, I was scared, a little. Those poor boys could have died here in my kitchen.'

'That's not what I mean. You were scared of me for a moment weren't you?'

'You... were different Cody. I haven't seen that side of you before so I'm not sure what I can say to you, but your manner changed. You seemed older. That's all. And what you did was remarkable. Young Vas was slipping away, they both were, and you spotted it in time for us to save them. I've no idea how you knew what was happening, but I'm glad you did.'

'Oh Bee, it was so strange. It was like when I get these memory losses. Usually it's just forgetting simple things but this time... it was like I was remembering – or something!' Cody was twisting a braid of hair distractedly as she spoke. Bee leant forwards and stroked her face.

'You have the potential to be a great healer young one, I've always told you that. So has your mother, and your father, rest him. But what you did with Vas was unusual. I've shown you a lot but you're not supposed to be able to do things like that yet.' Bee nodded indicating the boys. 'Not yet. It's too early, I mean you're too young.'

As she listened Cody felt a baffling sense of exhilaration and vertigo as if she was about to topple from a great height. Something was trying to claim her, tugging at her attention, trying to open a door in her mind. The impossible familiarity of it left her feeling agitated. She sat down heavily on the floor her back against the sofa.

'Bee, what do you mean I'm not ready yet?' Her eyes were threatening to fill with tears and she didn't want that to happen. 'What's going on with me? What aren't you telling me? It's to do with the accident three years ago isn't it?'

'Ah my precious, who can say. The doctors said you had amnesia afterwards and that it would reoccur from time to time. Truth is I don't think anyone really knows. The only thing I can say for sure is what I've told you before, you have a powerful gift for healing and I wouldn't have you fretting about that. It may not be a gift you want but it is a gift none the less. It's in you and you're learning how to use it. In time you'll no doubt have its full use, but not yet. You will though. As I know my name you will. Give it time.'

'I don't like being like this Bee. I can sense what's in other people but sometimes I don't have a sense of myself, as if I'm not really here but watching myself from somewhere else. Other girls at school aren't like this. Why am I different?'

Bee moved over to sit besides the forlorn girl on the floor and put her large arms around her shoulders.

'In time you may be glad that you are different Cody. You'll be able to do great things one day I promise, things that'll surprise you. And me too!'

'Do you get images in your head Bee? Can you tell when someone is hurting like I can? And I'm always forgetting things. Do you know I have to write down lists in case I forget to do things. Old people have to do that. Lists! Next thing you know I'll find myself standing at the top of the stairs wondering what I went up there for. What's wrong with me?'

'Wrong? Who said there's anything wrong! You're a bit forgetful and you pick up on people's feelings more strongly than most, that's all. I've told you before, it's a gift. There's nothing wrong.'

'But no one else I know has this. I don't fit in.'

'So, you're growing up differently. You're learning to be yourself. It's something we all have to do. And it's never easy. You're doing well. You really are.'

Cody's hands were twisting and knotting inside each other. Gently Bee reached across and put a hand on the girl's arm. The twisting stopped and Cody sighed. They sat in companionable silence for a moment listening to the sound of breathing from the bandaged figures on the floor and the quiet buzz of a half dozen bees that came nosing into the cottage. The insects collected in tiny orbits around Bee's head.

Talking things over with Bee always helped. Very often nothing was solved, no great conclusions were reached, but simply having someone listen whilst you struggle to put your worries into words was a comfort. It was the same talking to Bron. Her viewpoint was, 'Wrap your worries in words and share 'em out like sandwiches.'

Bee suddenly noticed the cloud of insects around her head. She came to with a start.

'Oh my, we'd better shift ourselves. You'll have to go and use Mrs Bentley's phone across the way and call for an ambulance. I'll keep an eye on our sleeping princes here. And give a shout for Ben would you. He should be about somewhere.'

Cody got up and moved towards the door. The insects around Bee's head buzzed more insistently.

'My bees!' The big woman jumped as if stung. 'Cody, you said they were lying dead outside?'

'Some were, yes, in the lane.'

'Were there many?'

'I'm afraid so. They were scattered all over the ground.'

Bee looked stricken,

'I'll need to have a look when we have the boys taken care of. Now you'd better be off. These lads need better help than I can give them on the floor of my old kitchen.'

'Alright Bee.' Cody started to move for the back door again.

'Just a moment young 'un. Come here.' The great lion of a woman folded her arms around the confused girl in a massive embrace. 'Everything will be alright, you'll see. Now get along with you. And don't forget to call Ben. He can fetch your mother, or Mrs Bentley can put word round the village for her.'

'OK. I'll be quick.'

Bee watched from the front door as Cody ran down the path and out along the lane. The woman heaved a sigh as if shouldering some invisible weight. Although her face was a mask her mind was flitting about like a dragonfly. There was a lot to discuss when Cody's mother arrived. Plans would have to be made and people contacted. Things were coming to a head faster than anticipated.

'In time,' she sighed to herself. 'Everything in its time. I do hope so.'

*   *   *

It was fortunate that the boys still weren't conscious when the first layers of bandages came off rank and stinking with the toxins drawn from their recovering bodies. Cody's mother turned up in time to help Bee, Cody and Ben Onnercott dispose of the pus saturated linen and apply fresh dressings. The swellings were much reduced; the boys' colour was better too, less bruised looking. By the time the lads regained their senses they were cheerful enough to start a chorus of feeble complaints about their injuries which evoked a dutiful amount of sympathy from the paramedics who arrived around five o clock. The idea was to take the boys to St Werburgh's hospital on the east side of Chester where there were facilities to care for what sounded like an anaphylactic reaction to bee venom. Both lads' parents appeared just as the ambulance was drawing away. Young Doug's mother was strident and abrasive, as most of the Feydon family seemed to be, accusing Granma Bees of keeping dangerous insects that should be destroyed. The Feydon family were an unruly selfish bunch, what Cody's father called a collective case of NRDA - normal rules don't apply. They behaved as they liked and took little account of the effects their often selfish and untidy habits had on the community. Young Doug was the only half decent member of the whole Feydon tribe. No one was in a mood to take much notice of Mrs Feydon's ramblings and to ease the situation the paramedics, who knew Granma Bees well, invited both sets of parents to ride along in the ambulance. And so that problem sorted itself out.

Six

BETWEEN THE LINES

'There are no dead ends. There is always a way out, even if it is the way you came in.'
From Amber Child, A Tale of Mythic Codes and Abnormalities, by Lapis Kent.

BY evening the Onnercott's cottage had returned to its customary quiet. It was decided that Cody and her mother should sleep over for the night. Cody would have her usual room tucked under the eaves with a view out onto the back orchard. After a very late supper Cody said good night and the adults remained downstairs talking in low voices.

Once upstairs Cody couldn't get to sleep immediately and was leaning out of her window enjoying the night scents coming off the fields and looking up at the Moon. She was missing her dad. It was worse some times than others. She was also feeling exhausted after the excitement of the afternoon and having difficulty making any kind of sense of her part in the events in Bee's kitchen. Her hands still tingled from the energy she had felt flowing out of her chest. She was about to close the window when there came a low whistle from some trees at the edge of the lane. A figure was standing in the shadows.

'Bron! Is that you? What are you doing out?' Cody hissed.

'Watching all the coming and going. You OK?'

'I'm fine. Tell you all about it tomorrow.'

'You want me to come up?'

'Better not. I'm jiggered and they could have a fit downstairs. I'm supposed to be asleep. Tomorrow'd be best.'

'OK. Get some sleep then. You can call me up if you want. I'll be around.'

'Thanks Bron. Sorry I'm so tired out.'

'Not a problem. See you tomorrow.'

Cody yawned massively and waved as she watched Bron's silhouette stroll slowly down the lane. Barely visible in the darkness was another figure coming the opposite way towards the cottage. As it passed into a patch of moonlight Cody was puzzled to recognise Enwyn Carter. What was she doing here at this time of night? She saw Bron slip unnoticed into the shadows as she passed. To Cody's surprise Enwyn turned in at the gate and walked up to the back door. What on earth did she want? Probably delivering some message from the boys' parents or something. 'Oh, who cares. It's nothing to do with me. Enwyn can come and go as she pleases.' Another huge yawn. Barely able to keep her eyes open she tumbled onto her bed and was soon drifting amongst brightly coloured streams filled with glittering fishtails.

           *   *   *

Around midnight an unusual group was gathered downstairs. There were important matters to be discussed. Madeline Onnercott, Ben Onnercott and Mary Conmar were sat around the kitchen table their faces lit from below by a number of lanterns placed at ground level around the walls. Their shadows danced high on the wood panelled walls. Enwyn Carter was stood with her back to the door arms crossed in a pose that would be easy to mistake as languid. And yet, for one so still she radiated the subdued intensity you might see in a lion stalking something it was about to kill. On the table rested a rough thrown pottery bowl half filled with water. There were a variety of stone shards and seeds balanced around the thick rim. Madeline spoke,

'Is everything secure outside Enwyn?' The teenager closed her eyes as if concentrating on an inner voice and replied in a hushed tone,

'The Behelian shield has us covered. No one knows we're here.'

'Good. Then we'll start. Mary, what's going on in the village?'

Mrs Conmar appeared ill at ease and was struggling to summon a measure of calm. She suddenly blurted out almost involuntarily,

'What happened with Cody today Madeline? What happened with those two boys?'

'In a moment Mary. Tell us how things stand in the village first. And remember to direct your voice over the bowl.'

' I'm sorry, yes.' Mary leaned forward slightly over the table.

'What about sightings around the village - strangers?' asked Ben Onnercott as she was about to resume. Mary paused, glancing at her open palms before replying punctiliously,

'Every newcomer is being carefully watched whether here on Fayre business at week ends or during the weekdays.'

'What about that woman Cody spoke of, the new reader at the fayre. You say her interest in Cody struck an unusual note. Has she been seen again?'

'Only around the Peckforton Hills and twice on the Wales border. Nothing closer than that.'

Madeline glanced over at Enwyn stood by the door and the teenager nodded. Madeline turned back to Mary,

'Do we have her name?'

'Not yet.'

'It would be useful to know. Go on.'

'Rumours and all reported night sightings have been followed up but nothing has proved out of the ordinary. Anxiety is still high around the village after the Newton outbreak and you'd expect people to be gossiping. In the absence of hard facts they will invent their own. No more Bloom circles have appeared anywhere in the county.'

'What about the missing boy? He's been absent since the week end of the Newton Bloom.'

'Adam Bowman, yes, nothing has been heard I'm afraid. I doubt it will now. He's untraceable, or gone.'

'I agree, it's been too long,' agreed Ben Onnercott in a restrained voice. The lines of his face were thrown into extreme relief by the low lighting. There was nothing of the clown in his manner now. 'We should concentrate on what we have before us and can control.'

'But what about today! We didn't control that,' insisted Mary. 'What was it that attacked those boys Madeline? They could have died!'

'My assessment is that it was very possibly a spore swarm.' A long silence hung thick in the dim room after this statement. Mary Conmar's face wasn't the only one to pale. 'A directed spore swarm,' Madeline added soberly. 'The first I've seen in five years or more.'

'Directed! Do you really think so,' Ben whispered aghast.

'It seems the likeliest explanation,' continued Madeline. 'Whatever it was that attacked the boys it was killed by my bee sentries, at a cost. Every insect involved died, which was why I had no warning of what was going on. The only thing capable of that which I'm aware of is a spore swarm.'

'The boys are still convinced it was a bee swarm that attacked them. We can leave that story uncorrected,' said Ben.

'They are young. The only things that hold their attention for more than ten minutes are computers and anything with an engine that roars,' said Madeline with the briefest flicker of a smile.

'Was it directed at Cody do you think?' asked Mary her voice rising. She was becoming increasingly thrown by the unfolding situation and when another voice joined the exchange she stiffened upright in her chair. Her eyes flew to the bowl at the centre of the table from where the voice, a man's, rich and resonant, caused minute ripples on the surface of the water.

'*Calm yourself Mary. The measures in place around Clayton Bar are strong and certainly sufficient for now. Our charge is safe.*' the voice said. Everyone's eyes were focused on the bowl. '*However, we must treat the Newton outbreak and the sinister circumstances of Teddy Conmar's death as significant indicators. Also the boy's continuing disappearance, and now this swarm event today. There is evidence that something is gathering and our defences must be reviewed and strengthened. Madeline, Do you think Cody is becoming aware? Has her shield been breached do you think?*'

'She recognised that the boys' stings weren't caused by bees! And she spotted that the smaller boy was slipping into a lethal coma, the second boy too. It happened spontaneously I'm certain, but how much her mind will retain of what she did I have no idea. Her voice and manner shifted but were restored soon after. She has been her 'usual' self since. I think her shield is still in place.'

'*Then we still have time. I think this is a good moment for Cody's godfather to visit Clayton Bar and spend some time with her. There are things she needs to hear. And preparations to make in case of a possible relocation.*'

'That would be an excellent idea,' agreed Ben. 'I'd feel easier in my mind if she was moved. There are other sites so much easier to protect than this one.'

'*There are, though not as many now as we could wish.*'

'True but the very insignificance of our location has been one of our strongest advantages thus far in remaining hidden,' said Madeline. 'Though I have to admit my worries too would be assuaged by a relocation.'

'Is there word of Thomas Morledge's whereabouts?'

'The Dream Collector is in the provinces somewhere. We've heard nothing for several weeks,' stated Mary eying the bowl as if watching something she didn't quite approve of.

'He should be contacted.'

'I'll attend to that,' said Enwyn calmly from the doorway.

'Good, then that is a beginning. Your handling of the situation with those boys today was well done Madeline.'

'Thank you Kanulf.'

'The fact that our charge's primary personality resurfaced, even briefly, is an alarming development demanding our most intelligent vigilance. Why did the child's personality shield slip on this occasion? It is imperative we understand.'

No one seemed willing to speak at this point until Enwyn approached from near the door and bent over the table to address the bowl,

'It seems likely that, being confronted by the prospect of the boys dying, her innate gifts were spontaneously called up. This caused a partial and temporary awakening.'

'Go on.'

'With the threat to the boys' lives reduced her 'primary' returned to somnolence.'

'Thank you. Is that Enwyn?'

'Yes.'

'That was the gist of my own deliberations too. We must never forget there are those who would welcome our charge's premature awakening, with all the inherent dangers that that implies for her - and for all of us of course. She will be extremely vulnerable for a considerable period to come. We must determine where this spore swarm originated and whether it was in fact directed or a random occurrence. Abominations do leak into the world from the shadows from time to time. Was this leakage or strategy? I will confer higher on this with our allies.'

'Are they... ?'

'Yes, they are close. They must be informed. As to the rest, keep vigilant. Even though the signs indicating possible interest in our little Cheshire haven are few they are still signs. It would be foolish to ignore them. In encouragement however I would remind you that at times of greatest peril even one alert mind can be enough to save the day. Now review the measures in place for me and let us be creative in improving them. We are all aware of the enormity of what is at stake here, are we not.'

A subdued but sincere chorus of assent came from all in the room.

*   *   *

Upstairs Cody Conmar dreamt on, running through landscapes she was certain she had known once. By her side ran someone whose name radiated light – *Lucian*. The word reverberated through her dream like a call from the past. Safe within the protective folds of sleep she remained oblivious of the forces being woven around her destiny by minds intent on her protection. Mercifully she was also unaware of those seeking her for other purposes, less benign purposes.

In the kitchen the council went on late into the night deciding many things and wishing for a great many others.

'Who knows how much sooner or more widespread the global network would have been if the originators of the Electronic Global Linkup (EGL) had not perished during the 1991-92 Bloom Event and subsequent Ice Year. In the mid 1990's the EGL was built at the re-established University of Oxford by Professors Bernard Timmersly and Nate Limberton using programming data developed before the Event. They believed that much of the pre-existing hardware of the internet, the data banks, wiring and actual computers, could be salvaged. And so, world wide electronic communication in the recovering twenty first century was re-established and taken to a new level. It is now possible for any school or library in the land to have access to text and still images and, with the right equipment, moving images and sound too.'

Extract from The Increasing Use Of The Electronic Global Linkup by Cate Waverly at the University of Bangor 2002. Taken from egl.computersandthenet.co.uk

Don't Look Under The Bed
by Jean Frecé.

Isky Frisky Dora
Climbing up the stairs.
Isky Frisky Dora, Covered all in hairs.
Creeping through the darkness
In the dead of night
Biting all the children's toes
Giving them a fright.

Isky Frisky Dora
Black as darkest pitch
Isky Frisky Dora, Evil spidery witch
Eyes like shattered marbles
Teeth like jagged shears
Giving children nightmare screams
Feeding on their fears.

(Taken from Lethal Lullabies & Cautionary Tales.)

Seven

SOMETHING NEW, SOMETHING BLUE

PETER Loren's BSA skidded into the sun baked courtyard of Chester castle, the roar of its 500cc engine amplified into a deafening boom by the four high walls and narrow confines. The edge of the sidecar narrowly skimmed the edge of a tarpaulin covered bulk in one corner. Every time he parked in the courtyard the sight of this heap affected Loren terribly. It was the shell and engine of a microlite he'd been hoping to renovate ever since coming to Chester eighteen months ago. There hadn't been a spare hour to work on it and the only time he'd spent airborne was when ordered onto a services flight down to London for important personal updates with his superiors. He hated having someone else at the controls of any plane he was in. The period he'd spent flying light aircraft during the government salvage and recovery programmes of the late 90's had been some of the best times of his life. And what was he now – a desk jockey! Well, not quite. He could scorch around on the BSA, which was great fun but it wasn't flying.

He glanced morosely at the tarpaulin covered shape. There was never any time for anything these days. Actually, had there ever been...? He hadn't even been able to get to his Kendo martial arts class at Upton for weeks. And when not filing long detailed reports he was zooming around Cheshire checking out possible anomalies or interviewing witnesses. Eighteen months on and he still hadn't stripped the microlite engine! That baby had a range of two hundred and fifty miles on one tankful; that's four hours in the air at 60 miles an hour, and at 60 in a buggy like that you felt you were breaking the sound barrier. Nothing like it. But not in the state it was in under that sheet. Dammit!

He'd been fending off offers to buy it from every Liter in the county after word got out he had the hulk a pre-Event Pegasus Q stashed in his back yard. But it just wasn't in his heart to let it go. Not till he's flown it himself. He pulled off his gauntlets and hung them across the handlebars of the BSA before running his hands over the tarp, patting the chassis beneath with sad affection. One day. One day this century perhaps. Ah well! Time to report in.

He stomped all the way to the Chapel and swept into the gloom of his personal domain flinging leather helmet and goggles onto a black padded armchair he'd liberated from the derelict town hall a week ago. He kept his flying jacket on expecting to be back on the BSA again within half an hour. It could be chilly in the chapel.

He'd just returned from checking out a possible anomaly case involving a 'sighting' that had seemed to merit investigation. He'd interviewed two highly disturbed itinerants at St Werburgh's hospital, both suffering from shock and claiming to have seen a ghostly screaming child when they were sheltering from the rain in a derelict mansion. He'd get very little useful information from them in the state they were in. He had recce'd the mansion where the event had occurred, taking extensive photographic evidence as well as a range of other readings. Now it was time to process the data and zip it to London by fastlink. He'd only just entered the files to be sorted on his computer when a screen prompt popped up reminding him to check on the tar goo analysis he'd requested weeks ago. The stubborn black coating was still on the blade of his survival knife from that lorries case. It wouldn't come off completely and he missed that knife. Replacements were hard to come by. The tests he'd run with the fairly comprehensive equipment installed here in the castle, two floors below, hadn't got very far. The substance seemed identical to Bloom tar, which he knew was impossible – or should be. So he'd sent a sample to London for further testing expecting a rumpus of excitement within the day. There'd been nothing! Not a peep. Luckily, as a backup, and as part of his increasing habit of working outside of standard procedures, he'd also sent a sample to a colleague up in Lancaster. It wasn't strictly speaking forbidden to do so; all Census Officers were valued for their initiative, but this felt like sedition on his part – good!

Census Officer Cas Winters was one of the sharpest and most irreverent minds he'd met in the Census Officer training programme years ago. She could throw a roundhouse punch that'd floor a bear, outrun an avalanche and was almost as gifted a flier as himself...almost. She was also someone he trusted completely – well let's say enough anyway. They'd shared some tough spots together.

Cas had access to lab facilities in Lancaster University he'd kill for and she owed him a favour; he owed her too but he reckoned he was ahead at present. When he accessed her linkup site using a secure password there was a coded note waiting for him:

'Wren sample results need f2f. On field mission Serious^{2}6. Contact on return. SxM.'

Wren was his nickname; f2f meant face to face i.e. a personal meeting in secret. Serious^2 6 meant the situation was urgent. SxM meant Satan ex Machina, Satan in the Machine, which implied there was something highly sinister working within the system. SxM was pretty extreme. If Cas was being this cautious some serious stuff was going down! Loren scratched excitedly at the tattoo on his left palm, an unconscious habit Cas had pointed out to him on several occasions and which he kept meaning to put a stop to. He'd give anything to know where she was but he knew she'd check in via a linkup. He tapped a message into his own secure site: 'Loki name day & location. Apex blocking. Approaching Serious^2 too.'

Loki was her nickname, after the Norse trickster god; Apex was London; 'Serious^2 too' meant things were becoming urgent and he needed to see her asap.

The moment he finished typing a landline phone rang. It was Amuna – oh no! He sighed inwardly. Was she never off duty?

'Why don't we have your latest reports yet Loren?' came the cool tones he adored and dreaded at the same time. He'd never actually seen Amuna in person or on screen but he had an image of her features firmly in his mind. In the early days she'd been pretty.

'Processing as we speak.'

'Good. And the report on the unidentified remains and L.O. at Nantwich you said would be completed yesterday?'

Damn! That was the other case he'd been working on when he got news of the manifestation & fatality at Frodsham. An L.O. was a levitating object, supposedly. Someone had been exploring an ancient rotunda on a small island in the middle of a lake and come across a massive slab of granite hovering inexplicably where the building had partially collapsed. 'No visible means of support' the report had said. Yeah, sure. He'd broken all land speed records getting to the salt mining town of Nantwich, run a routine check and concluded there was nothing to merit the excitement. The slab lay crushed under the debris of the now flattened rotunda. He figured someone's imagination had been working overtime.

'That report'll be with you tomorrow Amuna, interviews and all. Guaranteed. There's no rush. It wasn't an L.O. I took all standard readings. No show.'

Sssssssssssss...

Silence hissed down the line at him. He considered being stubborn and waiting for her to speak first but his nerve gave way,

'Surely this manifestation & fatality at Frodsham takes precedence. I mean...'

'Not your decision Loren. We need data, images and both reports from you asap. Is there a problem?'

Loren made a last effort to salvage the initiative,

'But what about the bodies in those lorries some weeks back?'

'What bodies Loren?'

'The ones found at Delamere Forest, covered in Bloom tar or something like. I have good reason to believe the thirty bags crammed into the backs of two badly burnt lorries may have contained bodies... of some sort... '

Sssssssssssss...

This time he was determined not to speak first. He tapped a pen against his teeth and checked his desk to see if he had any chewing gum left. It was getting harder to come by these days.

Sssssssssssss... he'd wait, he'd wait, he'd – oh what the hell!

'Hello, London?'

'Put that observation in a separate report Loren. And get onto the very real body you have in the Frodsham manifestation.'

'I have. That's what's being processed right now. Can't you give me a verbal on the lorries situation? Why were they moved from the farm at Delamere and then from Saighton barracks with no notification? I was going to process that case.'

'Follow procedure Loren. Send us the contemporary images & data you collected. Report as you've been trained. If you need to be informed about any other cases you will be contacted. That is all. Anything else pressing?'

'Did anyone read my reports on the scorched earth around the Delamere lorries? Or the embryos embedded in fourteen inch thick glass slabs beneath the abbey walls at Northwich? Or the phosphorescent shapes swimming about in the flooded basement at Alderley Edge that attacked the landlord? Or the nascent rebus maze on the cathedral floor right here in Chester?'

'Are any of those pressing Loren?'

'No.'

'Out.'

Click - the line went dead.

Loren sat stunned. What was going on here? Why was he constantly submitted to this kind of condescension. Was it an officially sanctioned procedure to keep agents in the field on their toes? If so it stank. It was insulting both personally and professionally and it was dangerous. He suspected Amuna of deliberately misdirecting him on a few notable occasions which had left him insufficiently briefed in circumstances that might have had nasty consequences. Mistakes could be lethal in the dark corners he had to poke his face into, like that woman with lungs rupturing from crystalline growths on the Welsh border. That'd been a close call! He'd swear it felt like he'd been sabotaged at the time; in fact he did swear. It felt good.

He was learning to dread the sound of Amuna's voice however silky-smoke smooth it was. Perhaps it would help to imagine her as an ugly person or a pre-Event computer generated voice – they'd had those once.

The console bleeped interrupting his reverie. The data was ready to send. He fastlinked it with an insulting icon attachment. Alright, it was petty but he was in the mood for petty after the day he'd had. The neglected pre-Event Pegasus Q wasting away in the courtyard nagged at him. They could have his written reports when he'd done them. Let 'em wait.

Then a couple of onscreen message flashes caught his attention. One was notification that his superior, Edwin Kanulf, would be paying a visit from central office in London. Apart from heading the agency branch of the Central Census Office Kanulf was a highly placed figure in the government think tank for recovering Britain, a major panjandrum in the Mainland Protectorate and a big cheese in who knew what other heavy brigade. 'What the hell does he want?' puzzled Loren staring glumly at the screen. 'Has someone actually been paying attention to my reports at last? Hm!'

The second onscreen message was a follow up on the report he'd submitted on the big Bloom outbreak a few weeks earlier. His report had been approved (oh, good) but he'd tagged the file asking to be included on any updates. This was it. He noticed that the file listed as: 'Bloom outbreak – Newton #27-CH-233' was now recorded as the most serious to occur near an inhabited area in three years over the entire country. He had personally checked the tar circle's 55 metres diameter, (that was about 180 feet!). The outbreak had been effectively dealt with except there'd been a casualty, an exemplary fire team member from Clayton Bar. That was unforgivable. Such a large Bloom should never have gone undetected for so long. Someone had slipped up. Badly. And a life lost unnecessarily. Inexcusable! He'd attended the funeral in his official capacity, always a good way to get local colour and detail on any case that concerned him.

Whilst in Clayton Bar he'd followed up a rumour that some disturbing details of the unfortunate death were circulating around the village. Supposedly, eyewitnesses on the fire force had seen a shape leaping out at the fire team member from within the Bloom circle itself and somehow dragging the poor man down. That was impossible Loren knew. Nothing survived long enough inside an active Bloom circle to be capable of jumping anywhere. The creeping blue mould started ingesting everything it made contact with instantly. The longest you'd last under the blue goop was seconds - at most! Following a series of discrete interviews with the still traumatised firemen in question he had strongly suggested to the investigating constabulary that this version of events be shut down immediately. The public didn't need to be distressed by inflammatory spook sightings. Place a legally enforced ban on witnesses repeating what they thought they had seen and circulate an official version saying that a brave rescue attempt involving an unnamed itinerant and a fireman had gone wrong resulting in two fatalities. Loren got the distinct impression that the witnesses were actually glad of an excuse not to talk about what they had seen – or thought they'd seen.

Loren had driven over to Newton to check out the site for himself but of course there was nothing to see except the massive patch of glistening black tar. There would be no evidence to collect. There never was after a Bloom outbreak. He remembered kneeling at the edge of the tar zone and thinking 'Stagger me! Look at the size of this thing! How did nobody spot this before it spread so far?' Once the standard readings had been taken he had walked the circumference of the outbreak. Nothing inside the patch moved. Nothing protruded above the glistening undulating surface. The goo gave off an unpleasant smell from the highly combustible chemicals used to incinerate it. That was all. And somewhere in this muck were the dispersed molecules that had once been Teddy Conmar.

Going over the scene again in his mind something about Clayton Bar nudged at the fringes of his memory. He leaned back in his chair, tipping at a dangerous angle with both feet on the desk and stared at the chapel shadows far above his head. What tiny alarm bells was that name ringing? Then he had it! Eight months back he'd casually looked into a case of vandalism at the central library records department. It was only a small incident, no one hurt, nothing major. Someone had broken into the map reference room and smashed the place up a bit. The files clerk had complained that some items had been stolen. What had prompted Loren to make a cursory check was that no one could work out how the vandals had got in or out.

It was only by chance he noticed that one set of maps had been tampered with. It was quite cleverly done and only a highly trained eye like his would have noticed the signs. The area surrounding Clayton Bar and the village itself had been changed subtly. Having no original to compare it to he had no idea what the changes might be but he knew he was right. He made a mental note to get back to it and dig further some time but never had; too many urgent things competing for his attention. But now he remembered the incident it returned to nag at him. Why on earth would someone want to alter a set of maps? It was often the smaller details that gave the lie to some bigger deception; tip of the iceberg cliché and all that. And now that he was on this thread a few other links to Clayton Bar came to light. There had been a disappearance some weeks back, around the time of the Newton Bloom as he recalled, a young lad called Adam something. Yes, here it was listed in another report, Adam Bowman, 11 yrs old. Reported missing at the Albion week end fayre.

As separate incidents they were serious enough. As an accumulation of incidents they alerted his instincts. Maybe it was time to take a closer look at Clayton Bar. Poke about, see what might come to light. He'd shuffle a few priorities in the next couple of days and get out there, perhaps talk to the deceased fireman's family, see if they could shed any light on the more puzzling aspects of fireman Conmar's demise.

Extract from Suskind Gromsen's God Weaving And Dream Paths.

'Fathoming dreams is like walking a maze; it involves deeply hidden pathways leading towards unknown goals. Both hardships and incredulities will oppose your progress but having penetrated to the centre of the mystery you will encounter forces that impose contour and context on all our lives, at both conscious and unconscious levels. A skilled dream walker, an adept, can use Dream Lore to impel those primal forces and direct them. Our dream landscape can be shaped. Supposing for a moment that an individual's dream experiences can be tilted and coloured by an exterior force it follows that influence may be exerted on thought, hope, behaviour and memory in our waking world too. This means that any child, adult or community can be protected or subjugated by anyone who knows the way to the centre of the dream labyrinth. There is a fascinating section of the enigmatic Peaks Engravings, uncovered during the Resettlement Programmes of 1994 in a long abandoned mining complex. It translates as: 'The Meldae seek to mould all tangible worlds from the labyrinth's centre.' I believe this passage refers to the use of Dream Lore in some unspecified past.'

[N.B. approximate meaning of Meldae would appear to be shape changers or chameleon beings.]

Eight

ANOTHER NOTE

'We are all hiding, wanting to be found. Our terror is that there is no one searching.'
From *A Many Divided Strength* by Fidious Leath.

CODY sensed the little group before she heard their shouts. It was like having a small shock in her chest or something sour bursting at the back of her throat. Oh no! Not again. They were at it again! Bloody Jesmina and her crew. Alerted, she turned to follow the direction of the disturbance. As she did so, snatches of jeering came from somewhere beyond the Almshouses that backed onto the canal. Accompanying this was a burst of animal delight, a mindless urge to hurt that Cody knew only too well. There was a distinct note of cruelty that was characteristic of Jesmina, that and an unpleasant twist of glee from some others with her. As she walked towards the jeers Cody detected another note, something unusual, something that drew her to whatever was going on by the canal.

The path skirted a high brick wall to the rear of the National Waterways warehouses where several barges were busy unloading, men with thick arms and rough voices shouting to each other as bales and crates were hoisted between land and deck. Cody walked past whitewashed cottages on the near side and emerged on the towpath next to the Walker's Arms. From a hundred yards away she could see what she already knew. There at the water's edge was a small, agitated crowd of about half a dozen figures in school uniform. And they had someone trapped against the canal's edge. It was the new boy, Josse ... something. His stick thin figure with a mane of uncontrollable spiked hair stood at the centre of the agitated group. Even at this distance there was something unusual about the scene. For anyone who could read the signs the new boy's stance spoke of someone both confident and capable of handling himself. Whilst those around jeered, hardly able to keep still with the ugly excitement of mindless violence he was calm, casual even. His arms were relaxed at his sides and he simply watched those who taunted him. The contrast pricked at Cody's senses. The boy's emotions were a pool of readied calmness, disdain even. Unusual. Cody hung back a moment for a better reading of the situation fingering the small silver locket around her neck that her mother had given her recently.

The motley group was a predictable mix of easily led non-entities. Most notable were Jazzer Dean (dough faced, small, B.O.) and Kendal Brown (skinny, bow legged, too much make up) stabbing the air and mouthing some taunt or other at their would be victim but they were clearly annoyed to be getting so little response. Jesmina Feydon, the dark centre of the bunch, stood at a safe distance behind the others from where she could make a quick get away if things went wrong. Typical. Cody made her move. She approached from the rear without being noticed and stood behind the gawky gang leader. Her quiet words were projected at just the right pitch,

'You can stop this. Now!'

The result was very satisfying. There were little shrieks and several gasps as heads whipped round to see who had caught them in the open, in the act. Their emotions ricocheted between dismay, fear, resentment, panic and from Jesmina a blast of fierce outrage.

'Push off Conmar. What do you want?'

'Nothing. But Mrs Tansley wants you. She said you should be in detention, right now. She's looking for you. You'd better get back. Hadn't you.'

Cody had no idea whether Jesmina should be in detention or not but it was a safe bet. At the very least the bluff would push some of the girl's buttons. As the bully's face twisted into a variation of the ugly snarl she habitually wore Cody followed up with,

'How's little Doug doing? He feeling better now?'

Jesmina didn't respond to this reference to her brother. The moment had changed but it was still threatening. The others were waiting to see what would happen. Some were hoping Jesmina would precipitate some action. Others just wanted to be away from there. Erratic currents of emotion sparked like invisible fireworks amongst the little mob. Things were coming to a head. Cody glanced at Josse to see how he was taking this. His face was aglow with amusement. There was a bad graze on one knee, blood trickling down onto his untidy sock. Unusually, no pain registered in the wiry lad's inner calmness. In fact, he seemed to be enjoying the situation. He was radiant. Cody turned her attention back to the raggle taggle lynch mob staring at each of them one by one. It took a few heartbeats to register that two of the stocky lads in dishevelled clothes had nose bleeds. They were sullen rather than dangerous. Then other details connected. Three of the girls' uniforms were doused in milk. A couple of school satchels dangled out of reach from the branches of a nearby oak. A jacket was floating in the canal. A torn comic lay trampled on the ground. None of these were Josse's. He still had his. Realisation dawned. The calm, wild haired, wiry boy on the canal's edge was far from being an unresisting victim. He had been dishing it out, generously! Cody stepped up closer to Jazzer and Kendal who both stared down at their feet. She snorted quietly,

'Been giving you a bad time has he?' Angry, furtive glances darted between the group.

'What do you mean Conmar?'

'Well, he's got you outnumbered hasn't he. Need any help sorting him out?'

Now it was Josse's turn to snort. He smiled at Cody and winked. He still hadn't spoken a word. His hand was in his jacket pocket grasping something. Cody edged past the two shamefaced hangers on and stepped closer to Josse. By this time Jesmina's face was puce and she was scratching angrily at a livid red rash around her neck and chest. It had angry crimson threads spreading out from blotches of bruising as big as fingerprints.

'Look at you two! A couple of freakos together. I bet...'

A new voice boomed at them from the bridge fifty feet away. Enwyn Carter, beautiful in the sunlight, was walking along the towpath towards them. Every graceful move and economic gesture radiated confidence and maturity.

'What're you kids up to? Is that you Jesmina Feyden? Shuffle along there's a good delinquent.'

'Get a grave artsy girl!'

'Do you know you speak in exclamation marks Jesmina.'

'Wh...what? What are you on about you...you hippy!' By now Enwyn was only a few yards away. She stopped and folded her arms looking at the gathering like a disapproving school teacher.

'There see. You did it again. You have no emotional spectrum, no down switch Jesmina. Everything you say is in exclamation marks. You're a cartoon.'

'I have no idea what the hell you're on about. And I don't care. Come on...!'

...she stopped in astonishment as a half eaten apple core bounced wetly off the side of her face. Her expression was a mask of congealed incomprehension.

Quick as a humming bird Josse seized Cody's sleeve and barged between his two nearest attackers letting out a high pitched ululating wail that had them scattering in panic. Jazzer Dean spun dangerously close to the water's edge and before anyone had time to react they had brushed past Enwyn and were running clear and heading for the bridge. Cody was mightily impressed both by Josse's aim and his sense of timing. They began to giggle uncontrollably as they ran. By the time they were on the far side of the canal there was a distinct skip to their steps. No one had followed them. Some workmen at the quay had stopped working briefly to watch what all the commotion was about but quickly resumed when they saw it was just kids messing about.

'Just a minute,' gasped Josse. His voice had a slight accent. 'I have to return something.' He trotted along the bank to a point opposite the furious gathering on the far side. 'Hey, gargoyle,' he shouted across the water. 'This is yours.' He held up an expensive looking fountain pen and waved it for everyone to see. Before anyone could react he flung it in a low arc towards the other bank. 'Catch. If you can.'

Jesmina jerked forward with an expression of dismay but she was nowhere near fast enough to catch the glittering prize. Whether by accident or malice Josse had thrown the fountain pen to land just short of the bank. In a mad scrabble the desperate ringleader skidded to the water's edge, made a wild swipe as the pen struck the stone edgings of the canal and spun like a tiny windmill. Then is disappeared with a plop. Jesmina barely managed to recover her balance but fell heavily on the rough sandstone. It must have hurt. She shrieked words that had no sense in them. Her pain registered with Cody like a face slap before she was able to push it aside.

'Oops! Sorry,' yelled Josse, clearly delighted. 'Now we both have nothing to write with. Never mind.' He let out his ululating cry again and added in a voice that only Cody could hear, 'She threw my pen in the canal before you showed up.'

Cody looked at him, confused and delighted by this wild child. Josse gave Cody a knowing look brimming with mischief then grabbed her hand and they both ran off doubled over in hysterics.

Later they sat eating ice cream scoops in front of the village store. Cody stared sidelong at her new found ally with wary pleasure. The newcomer had only been in Clayton Bar for a week but was clearly someone you went up against at your peril. The semi punk hairstyle was a warning to the unwary, as well as a fashion statement. Josse spoke with his mouth full,

'Who was that? And I don't mean the gargoyle.' Cody found his touch of accent very attractive.

'Oh that was Enwyn Carter. Her mum is the post mistress.'

'She's very…impressive.'

'Do you think so. I find her a bit overbearing. She does a Tai Chi class near Chester and thinks she's really cool.'

'She is. I like her dress sense. Got a lot of presence.'

'Hm.' Cody didn't really want to be discussing Enwyn Carter. It always made her feel inadequate. She was sick of turning round and seeing her there like a pet dog or something. So annoying!

'She makes me feel uneasy that's all. She's alright I suppose,' Cody added attempting to be generous.

'Should we move then?' asked Josse.

'Why should we move? I'm just enjoying this mint and vanilla scoop.'

'Coz she's coming this way.'

Cody was dismayed to see Enwyn approaching with the unhurried graceful swing that always made the lads turn and stare. A couple of them on bicycles did just that narrowly missing a couple of pedestrians trying to cross the road. Cody was even more put out when Enwyn stopped by their table and sat down only a couple of feet away. She was acting as if she hadn't seen them. But Josse wasn't having any of that.

'Hi,' he said brightly. 'My name's Josse.'

'Yes it is. You're new in Clayton Bar aren't you,' replied Enwyn glancing over her shoulder.

'Been here all of a week. It's a quiet place isn't it.'

'It used to be. You can handle yourself young 'un.'

Josse didn't reply but fixed Enwyn with a stare so neutral it could have meant anything. Enwyn returned his look calmly.

'So what started all the hoohar back there?' Enwyn intoned casually.

'Oh nothing serious,' said Josse. 'Just some bunch of kids. Their ring leader needs a couple of lessons in politeness, that's all. Not too bright I think.'

'You and your dad are newly arrived from the continent aren't you. Get into a lot of fights there did you?' smiled Enwyn thinly.

'What?'

'Fights? You?'

'Only when the odds are in my favour. How about you? Trained in martial arts I hear.'

Enwyn chose not to reply but regarded the spirited boy with the penetrating look Cody always found so unnerving. Josse broke the eye lock pretending to concentrate on his ice cream. 'Are you going to ask to see my passport then?'

'Not necessary,' Enwyn got in quickly. 'There's not much use for passports in the village. We are interested in how people behave though. Very interested.'

'...I'd...' Josse was showing the first signs of losing his composure despite himself, '...I'm going to finish my ice cream.'

Cody felt annoyed to be left hanging around on the edges of this sparring match but was mesmerised by what was unfolding. If was like watching some awful slow motion accident. And it was taking the edge off her sense of triumph over Jesmina.

'I'm interested, for example,' continued Enwyn still staring at Josse, 'Why was Jesmina picking on you particularly? Doesn't she like you?'

'I don't really know. Or care, about her or you come to that,' replied Josse staring hard at the table top and then out at the people passing by in the street. 'But she's rather hard to ignore sometimes. Like you.'

'Jesmina is a troubled soul,' replied Enwyn. 'Ask Cody. She knows all about Jesmina, don't you Cody.'

'Why are you being so unpleasant Enwyn?' Cody asked exasperated. She was about to suggest to Josse that they move on when Enwyn slid gracefully to her feet and strode away.

'Don't eat too much of that stuff. Bad for the complexion. Give you a rash,' was her parting shot as she sauntered up the street and disappeared round the next corner. Cody was quietly stunned by such a show of rudeness.

'I told you she was overbearing but that was a high tide mark even for her.'

Josse continued eating his ice cream as if nothing had happened. He came over calm and dark like a deep pool. Cody was puzzled by the unusual lack of disturbance in his emotional currents. Even when he had been outwardly riled by Enwyn's offensiveness there had been no change in his inner stillness. This was one remarkable individual. She stared at him impressed until she noticed the dried blood on his socks.

'We should get that looked at, your knee. That's a bad scratch.'

Josse carried on eating his scoop unimpressed,

'Oh it's OK. I've had worse. That's a nice necklace.'

Cody realised she was playing with the locket again.

'It's a locket actually. Silver. Mum gave it to me.'

'New?'

'Yes, how did you guess? Well not really new. Mum said it was my grandmother's. Look, it's got a tiny photo on the inside.' She flicked the catch and leaned over to show Josse the miniature black and white portrait of a smiling child.

'Who is it? It looks like you.'

'Mum said it was my grandmother. I never knew her though. This is the only picture there is of her. Go on, you can hold it if you want.'

'Naw, that's OK.'

'It's pre-Event, I mean obviously it is. So is this,' she reached into her pocket and pulled out a large brown coin.

'What's that? Some kind of medal?'

'No, it's a coin. A pre-decimal penny. Imagine your pocket full of these things. They'd weigh a ton. It's one of a set I found in Chester with … with a friend. Feel the weight of it.' She dropped it into Josse's hand and leaped as the boy flung the coin onto the table as if he'd been stung.

'Yeeow!'

'Are you alright?'

'Yes! Yes, I'm fine. It was so cold that's all.'

'But it's warm. It's copper, see, and it's been in my pocket all day.'

'Copper, ah, well, I'm allergic to copper. It's a condition I inherited – on my mother's side. It's just a skin sensitivity. Nothing to worry about.'

All through this Cody was surprised to feel a fierce peak of fear emanating from the boy, fear verging on panic. It was more reaction than there'd been during the whole nasty exchange with Enwyn or when cornered by Jesmina and her little mob. And it was only an old coin. Josse fidgeted and unconsciously edged his chair away a fraction. Cody retrieved the old penny and glanced at it before carefully replacing it in her pocket. She found herself chattering to cover the awkwardness.

'I don't know what you think of Clayton Bar. It's quiet but I like it. My family came here three years ago after a serious car accident.'

Josse seemed relieved to have something to distract him.

'Oh, right. Was anyone hurt?'

'Someone died. The driver of the car apparently but I don't know who they were. And I got amnesia. Can't remember a thing before I came to the village.'

'That must be weird.' Josse sat upright in his chair and half heartedly dusted his creased jeans. Cody noticed how bony and scarred his fingers were.

'Yes, it is a bit, I suppose. What about you?'

'Me! Oh my dad works at the Institute of Commerce and Waterways, the big building on the edge of the village, by the canal.'

'I know it.'

'Course you do. You've lived here for ages,' laughed Josse embarrassed at himself for the first time since they'd met.

'So is he a lecturer or something?'

'No. Janitor and grounds man. We live above the stables at the back. We've got a caravan too. All our stuff is still in it at the moment.'

'So where were you before? You've got such a nice accent you know.' Josse didn't react to the compliment.

'In France. My family got stuck there during the Ice Year and afterwards it was years before there were any ferries in operation. So we lived there awhile. We came this way twelve months ago trying to track down some relatives in the Midlands but the trail went cold and we ended up here in deepest Cheshire.'

'Is your dad French then?'

'Look, I don't want to talk about all this.'

72

'I'm sorry. I wasn't prying.'

'No, it's OK. I just want to forget about the past. Most people do I think. Dad does. You're lucky, you've got amnesia.'

'I suppose that's one way of looking at it,' laughed Cody. She found it hard to understand the point of people trying to forget because there were so many gaps in her own life she would love to fill. But she did understand that for many, the past was a terrifying place. The Ice Year and the years that followed were times of terrible suffering and loss. No one had been left untouched by it and she would guess that Josse's story was one of the hard ones. It was lucky he had ended up here in Clayton Bar where things were so safe and predictable season after season - or as safe as one could be anywhere in the world. On an instinct she leaned across and put a hand on the boy's thin shoulders. There seemed hardly any flesh over the bones. He jumped, taken by surprise.

'I'd better be going,' he said abruptly. 'Dad'll be wondering where I am.' He got up to go.

'Yes, of course. See you around, or at school'

'Yep. I may pop by for you, if that's OK. You live in the white house don't you, the one set back from the road up that little drive; Brimrose or something. Up near the Little Heath.'

'That's right. How did you know?'

'Just noticed as I passed once. Well then, bye for now.'

'Just a minute,' said Cody quickly. 'We haven't even told each other our names. I know you're Josse.'

'And you're Cody Conmar. I'm Josse Ailet. So there we are. See you around.'

'Bye,' said Cody spooning the last of her ice cream out of the pot. She watched the wiry figure of Josse Ailet trotting down the road and wondered what his story was; those scars on his hands had a tale to tell for sure. How had he had spent the years in France and what must his family be like, or was it just him and his father? He was so wonderfully intense and even if his emotional blankness was puzzling it was refreshing to be around him. Things were going to be different at school this term she could tell.

Cody wondered what Bron would think of him.

'There is a new war coming, one that will not be fought in the sight of men. There are minds at work in men's lives whose wish is to rule, to harvest the forces of Hell and nourish tyranny. The only hope for humankind lies in the gifts concealed in your sleeping flesh by earlier generations. You will be redeemed by evolution, a force that never rests and will not be denied.'

Address given on the eve of a great battle by an Aelim ally to human forces, from the mythic sagas of Ceulwas and Occitan compiled by Cullie Brown.

SIDETIME
A DISMANTLING.

A young girl stands in bright sunlight at the centre of a three sided courtyard. She is facing an ancient barn with shuttered windows and a sagging door. The girl's slim figure throws an inky shadow at her feet. She is motionless. There is no sound in the baking heat, no wind, no crickets, no birdsong. Everything is hushed. Expectant. Waiting. With a slight turn of the head she glances towards a small figure sat cross legged in the shadows furthest from the barn. A boy, no more than six years old. His eyes are closed. His breathing is quiet and his hands are held palms up in his lap. The girl turns back to face the barn. Her arms hang relaxed by her side, palms open towards the sagging door. Stones can be heard ticking in the fierce heat.

Suddenly from the rear of the building comes a shriek and the sound of smashing timbers. The girl closes her eyes but does not move. The sounds increase, growing closer from within the depths of the barn. Neither the girl nor the boy show any sign of having heard.

With a terrifying abruptness a monstrosity erupts from the darkness of the barn's doorway smashing the door to splinters and staggering to a halt blinded by the sunlight. About the size of an adult ape it is twitching uncontrollably. Blisters are forming on its pallid skin as it stands blinking in the bright light. The girl's eyes open to reveal an icy blueness that is shocking in so young a face. Neither tremor nor sound shows what she might be feeling. She stares intensely at the quivering thing before her, her palms still facing forward. The monstrosity's body is erupting in pale, fleshy tendrils that thrash and swell and burst open scattering drops of pink flecked fluid onto the dusty courtyard. It screams then lurches towards the unprotected girl. Its savage-edged mouth drools venom. It staggers, collapses in the dust, lashing out with grotesque limbs, trying to reach her.

But the thing is dying in the sunlight. Even as its frenzy increases and its screams become more liquid it covers half the distance to the girl. The tears in its flesh are spurting more quickly now, its body is collapsing, rupturing, withering. Orange dust from the ground coats the thrashing limbs. The thing has crawled to within twelve feet of the abnormally calm girl but it will not get any closer. The fierce sun is roasting it, baking it, killing it where it lies. With a blood-strangled cough the thing stops, quivers, sags in on itself. Blackened blisters pop open. Soon even their oily trickle stops. The thing is shrinking, collapsing at an impossible rate leaving only a dried out husk like a giant toad killed on the highway, an obscene leather thing withering in the sun, angles of bone protruding through the skin. Time slows. Silence and heat settle over the scene.

The girl turns with simple grace and walks over to where the boy has fallen onto his side as if asleep. She sits besides him and lifts his head onto her lap where he continues to breathe quietly. She strokes his hair. "That's it. You did well little one. Rest now. All done. All done."

The small figure stirs, his face serene. Gently she strokes his hair.

Without a sound a third figure steps from around the open end of the courtyard and gestures to them. The boy opens his eyes, and looks round smiling. He and the girl rise together, walk hand in hand towards the figure where light shimmers in the heat. They all leave in silence. Only the husk of tattered brown leather is left in the courtyard. It is already devolving, turning to dust and shreds, scattering before hot gusts of wind. Soon there will be only dust. And silence. And the burning light.

Nine
NIGHT SOUNDS

IT took seven or eight weeks for things to settle down in the village after the tragic Bloom outbreak at Newton. People had their lives to be getting on with and the unwelcome reminder of how precarious life was under the constant threat of new outbreaks slowly faded into the background of everyday life. One difference was that everyone, all ages and all walks of life, became even more watchful than before in looking for Bloom sign. But in general things returned to established routines consisting mainly of work and, for those fortunate enough to be young, of learning about the big wide post-Event world of the twenty first century.

Cody spent quite a lot of time with Josse or with Bron, although never at the same time. Bron was Cody's longest standing companion and friend and it upset her that she was so wary of the newcomer, whom she never referred to by name but always as 'The French boy.' Bron made it clear that in her opinion there was a lot to be said for being wary of anyone you didn't know particularly well. Cody challenged this but didn't push Bron too hard about her suspicious attitude. She respected her friend's views the way she respected her preference for avoiding other children. Much of Bron's time was spent alone in the fields around Clayton Bar wandering the borders of the village and generally running wild. That was the way Bron was and surely part of true friendship was accepting people as they were. It was just a pity that Bron seemed to be more than usually absent these days. She said she had a lot to do and left it at that. Cody took her at her word.

Mum wasn't' finding it easy without dad. She was constantly on edge and her face had developed a kind of haunted look. She gave little jumps if Cody spoke to her suddenly, which was amusing the first few times but then became worrying. She obviously missed Teddy. It was heart wrenching to see. Cody missed him too, his strong reassuring presence about the house, his jokes, his whistling and singing in the workshop behind the house. Occasionally Cody would go and stand in the now silent shed amidst the sawdust and unfinished chairs and cabinets her father would never finish. She loved the smell of resin and cut wood that filled the well lit workshop. This had been his space. It was easy to remember his features there. In the light beams from the glass panels set into the sloping roof she could still see him dressed in overalls, his strong hands smothered in wood shavings. His tools were still out on the workbench where he had left them a lifetime ago.

At Granma Bees' suggestion Cody took to spending more time at the cottage. This suited Mum who said she was glad to have Cody somewhere 'safe', whatever that meant. The cottage had always felt very much like home and as Cody kept a change of clothes and a few personal things there anyway it was a good arrangement. Bee was a wonderful cook and Ben was a constant source of jokes and distraction. Nothing ever seemed to cloud the little man's good humour.

And so life continued. There were good times at school; Cody began to get back into her schoolwork and was on the winning team for a netball tournament. There were a couple of outings she enjoyed, one to a book and barter fair held in the grounds of Chester Cathedral. Another was to a mab-music festival staged at a natural amphitheatre in the hills behind Frodsham ten miles from Clayton Bar. Mab was definitely the in thing to be listening to this year. The two day event was a change from the traditional Albion fayre music with appearances by current bands such as Stone Souls, Ice Foundry, Kreuel Hearts, Legions of Glass and the Goth revival band Hell Pearl headed by Rue Brawler the lead singer that everyone was talking about that summer. Hell Pearl were a local band which had toured country wide and had a strong following amongst the edgier, more rebellious youth element especially the Liters who were there in strength camped out in the fields around the site.

Cody was accompanied by uncle Ben who said he wanted to look at a new batch of the tough little Shire Ponies bred for use on farms throughout the county. The stud farm was close to the festival field and Ben was particularly interested in two sturdy Belmin mares imported from the continent – and of course he also liked the 'young music' as he called it. They had hitched a ride from a group going to Frodsham on two large horse drawn carts owned by one of the Clayton Bar canal merchants. It saved walking, although some of the younger kids were over excited and had to be made to walk a fair distance to siphon off some of their high spirits. Josse was put on the cart behind Cody's by his dad, a thin agile looking man with a mad shock of white hair like an older version of his son's punk spikes. It didn't take long for the two of them to get together and they spent the journey chattering about the relative merits of the bands on the bill.

They arrived mid afternoon and by evening the crowd had swollen to well over two hundred, a big gathering by post-Event standards. There was a constant rotation of acts varying from OK to good but the big event was the first night's appearance of Rue Brawler billed for about nine o clock.

Around eight thirty, fires and lanterns were coming on around the amphitheatre piercing the gloom like earth bound stars. Cody was queuing at a soup tent whilst Josse kept their places on the grass bank that served for seating. Uncle Ben was finishing off his business with the pony dealer at a drinks tent nearby. He waved to her and continued his haggling with the rugged faced farmer. Cody was reading through the menu pinned up on the side of the tent trying to decide what to choose from the wonderful selection there. As she did so thoughts of Bron kept popping into her head. This had been happening a lot recently and she would dearly have liked to catch sight of her friend amongst the crowds. She was missing her these last weeks and wanted to talk so many things over with her but the strong minded girl was stubbornly independent and continued to remained absent whilst Josse was around. It troubled Cody to think she had upset her somehow but you could never tell with Bron.

Cody was only a few places from the front of the queue when something alerted her to a disturbance some distance away behind a thick hawthorn hedge. The footpath to Frodsham ran just the other side of the hedge cutting through some tangled woodland before weaving its way down to the town below. Something with an unpleasantly familiar savour was going on in the darkness beyond that hedge. There were plenty of people nearby, youths dressed as Goths, Liters, couples, family groups, but no one else was paying any attention to what had alerted Cody. This was because no one had picked up on the creepy emanations that were as clear to her as if someone had been shouting for help. She left her place in the queue and slipped through the gloaming towards the source. Jesmina! Of course, it had to be Jesmina again. She hadn't come along with everybody else on the carts but she wouldn't miss a gathering like this. No doubt she'd be up to something typically mindless and brutal, but there was an odd variation to the troublesome girl's emotional currents that was hard to identify. They were confused even for Jesmina.

When Cody had gone about a hundred yards from the nearest lamp light she could hear voices. Only one of them was recognisable. It was Miles Oldfield, the young lad from the village and he was protesting feebly at something. The other voice seemed adult, which was strange because the only other person in sight was Jesmina. It was unusual for her to be on her own with no zombie posse in tow. She had Miles pinned up against a tree and was hissing at him menacingly in an almost animal way that was rather grotesque. The light was poor under the dense foliage and Cody was picking up more from the emotions flaring around the couple than by what her eyes could distinguish but it was clear that little Miles was trapped and very scared. She called out to them as she approached,

'Leave him alone Jesmina. He's half your size.'

The girl swung round furious and hissed like a snake at Cody's approach but said nothing. For a moment Cody would swear her eyes were glowing. Miles didn't move. He was petrified.

'Miles, c'mon. You're OK. Come over here.' The lad still didn't move. Jesmina was crouched over him in the dark her back bowed and arms hung claw like at her sides but still didn't speak. Her breathing was hoarse and rasping as if she'd been running. Cody walked slowly over to the boy and took his hand all the while keeping her stare fixed on the silhouette of the school bully. They began to make their way towards the lights and the scarecrow figure stepped haltingly behind them as if uncertain whether to follow. Cody never dropped her eyes for a moment, walking with face turned over her shoulder. As Jesmina's thin figure emerged from under the deeper shadow of the copse Cody could see her properly for the first time. She was not a pretty sight. Her hair was matted and tangled, she staggered stiffly as if covered in extensive bruising but worst of all was her face. It was twisted into a gargoyle exaggeration of her usual grimace with eyes afire with malice. Her shirt was open at the neck and it was hard to see in the starlight but her throat and one side of her head appeared to be covered in welts and blotches that writhed in the pale light. She opened her mouth in a grotesque leer.

'You won't get away,' the horribly gasping voice hissed like steam. 'You are…'

'Leave them alone! Go!' said a strong female voice from far back in the shadows. A tall figure was coming towards them at a measured pace. Jesmina halted and began to twitch her head from left to right in peculiar jerky movements like a badly projected film. Her expression dropped its leer, became blank. In the darkness Cody could see her eyes making rapid flickers back and forth in all directions. Her breathing became shallow and rapid like a dog's. Then her eyes glazed and slid slowly to her feet. She shuddered and turned to shuffle away down the path towards the town. The figure coming towards them was somehow familiar – then Cody had it. It was the woman from the Albion fayre, the reader from the black and green tent. She wore a long dress reaching to the ground and what might have been a cape. Astoundingly in the deepening darkness she still wore her dark glasses and Cody also noted the long wristed gloves she remembered from the fayre. The rectangular glass over the woman's eyes reflected the starlight like mirrors.

'Ah, thank you,' said Cody. 'I think we'd have been alright though.' The figure raised a hand in a gesture that could have meant you're welcome, but said nothing. 'But you never can tell with Jesmina,' Cody added lamely. 'We'd better be getting back. Thanks again.'

She gripped Miles' hand firmly and they walked towards the amphitheatre and the lights just as the next number struck up from one of the bands. A cheer went up from the crowd. It was Hell Pearl coming on early. When Cody turned back the mysterious woman was stood in the same spot watching, her eyes lit up like miniature television screens.

Back at the food tents Uncle Ben was seriously put out that she had disappeared repeating what everyone seemed to be saying to her these days that she should never wander off without saying where she was going. Miles' big sister, who was supposed to be looking after him and who had been growing frantic, threw her arms around him in a confusion of relief and annoyance that he had gone in the first place. The six year old couldn't properly explain what he'd been doing away from the tents on the wooded path except to say he'd thought he'd heard someone calling his name. He remembered being scared and was glad when Cody came to hold his hand. The explanation satisfied no one but what could you do with a six year old. The important thing was he was safe now, and feeling better. He kept smiling at Cody with his long lashed eyes.

Word had spread and soon a group from Clayton Bar had gathered wanting to know what had happened. Josse came running up asking why Cody had left her place in the soup queue and what would they do for food. His expression was sombre as Cody explained and he made no further comment but peered around angrily as if wanting to attack someone.

A couple of adults ran off towards the path where Cody indicated she'd found Miles followed closely by Josse who ignored Cody's calls to come back. It was decided to make an immediate return to the village despite loud protests from all the younger member of the party. It didn't matter how many bands there were still to perform, Uncle Ben stated firmly, they were leaving - now! The memory of young Adam Bowman's disappearance was fresh on every adult's mind and the irritated group was herded together efficiently by a ring of grown ups and, Cody was miffed to notice, a few older teenagers including Enwyn Carter.

The two adults returned followed a few moments later by Josse, his face set grim in lines of frustration. The adults said they could find nothing in the dark, to which Josse nodded his agreement, though no one paid him any attention except for Cody. Ben organised buying enough food from one of the stalls for those who had missed their evening meal and as the sounds of Rue Brawler's throaty roar and Hell Pearl's rocking guitar backbeat hit the night the Clayton Bar contingent set off.

Sounds of the concert faded slowly behind them as they walked grumpily downhill to the paddock where their carts had been left. The two huge dray horses were being rapidly harnessed and within ten minutes the return journey to Clayton Bar had started. Cody hadn't realised there were so many people from the village at the concert. There must have been nearly fifteen adults as well as the same number of youngsters. They made quite a caravan with groups of grown ups walking ahead and behind the two carts chatting together and obviously totally unbothered by having missed the rest of the mab-music on the programme.

Uncle Ben was clearly desperate to question Cody about what she'd seen on the edge of the woods. Jesmina's peculiar behaviour interested him but he was especially keen to learn of the tall woman from the fayre. Unfortunately any more lengthy exchanges had to wait until they reached home. Josse was sat next to Cody and Ben whispered it wasn't appropriate to be discussing such things in the crowded carts with so many youngsters within earshot. Cody felt a small warmth as he said this. She liked being distinguished from the kids as a more responsible adult – well almost. She had still wandered off without telling anyone but Ben didn't comment on her actions any further and said they'd talk later. Bee and her mother would need to hear all about this. It wasn't said in any threatening way, just as a statement of fact. Cody nodded her head seriously. He smiled and began to do a few conjuring tricks to try and distract the younger ones. It was a relief to see him smiling again after what had happened. Cody had never seen him so serious before tonight.

As the plodding carts cleared the borders of Frodsham and took the back road via Manley, Mouldsworth and Tarvin, lanterns were lit on poles set into front and rear brackets on the carts. Some of the youngsters were making comments about missing the main act of the night and pointedly looking at Miles murmuring that kids wandering off like babies were nothing more than a nuisance. It wasn't meant viciously, merely an expression of deeply felt disappointment but they were loud enough for everyone to hear. In the swinging light from the lanterns Cody could see Miles' unhappy face at the top end of the cart near the driver. A partly eaten sandwich was poised half way to his mouth as he peeped apprehensively at those talking about him. Then his eyes met Cody's and he smiled, just as he had at her dad's funeral. She gave him an encouraging 'come here' signal and he clambered over legs and backpacks to her side. He snuggled next to her on the side away from Josse.

'Can I sit with you?' he asked simply shuffling into the heap of blankets and cushions everyone had brought. Cody looked over at his big sister but she was too busy chatting to one of the teenager boys walking beside the cart to notice.

'Course you can. Are you feeling OK now?'

'Uhuh,' he murmured, but as far as she could tell he was already fast asleep sandwich forgotten on the blanket beside him. Cody and Josse grinned at each other over his head. The sounds of the concert were still faintly audible in the darkness behind them. It was obviously a great shame to miss Rue Brawler but that didn't hold her attention for too long as they rattled along the night time road. Rather it was the state that Jesmina had been in that filled her thoughts. What on earth had she been up to terrifying young Miles in that way? Being a misfit and pain in the neck was one thing but the disruptive youngster was seriously disturbed. For one thing that rash on her face and chest had looked awful. She badly needed help. And her parents should be challenged about her behaviour by someone they'd listen to; she couldn't be allowed to carry on like this.

The timely appearance of the woman with the dark glasses and gloves was puzzling too. What had she been doing there? Not a Hell Pearl fan surely.

Like a light turned on in a dark room a vivid image of Bron's face suddenly leapt into her mind. Instantly alert Cody sat up and peered anxiously around hoping to spot her friend. For an instant she glimpsed what might have been the old familiar face with some adults on the edge of the lantern light thrown by the leading cart. But it was just shadows. No Bron. Cody's heart sank a little.

Uneasily her thoughts shifted back to young Miles murmuring quietly at her side. Poor kid. Fancy being dragged along by a sister who so clearly had other things on her mind. It was no way to treat someone of his age. Shivers ran up her spine at the thought of what might have happened to him, though thankfully no specific details came to mind. Uncle Ben was right of course, it would all need serious discussion when they got back. Someone in the village was going to have to do something about such thoughtlessness and irresponsibility.

There was no sign of Jesmina or any of her tribe on the journey home. And the image of Bron's face stayed with Cody all the way back to Clayton Bar.

Extract from article on Aelim in Human History by Cullie Brown taken from egl.aelimlegends.

'*In the astonishing array of myths and legends that sprang into existence after the Ice Year of 1991-92 a recurrent theme was that of the Aelim. This race of ethereal beings featured as the benign force in a titanic struggle that had been going on for the fate of humankind since before recorded history. The prize was humanity itself. Their opponents, the Chameleons, were the exact shadow aspect of their hated enemies. One force sought to protect and the other to enslave. Both were capable of terrible ferocity and, unlike the idealised version of angels in established mythologies of every country world wide, the Aelim were fallible; they made mistakes, committed crimes, betrayed their principles or sometimes went mad, for all of which they had to pay fearsome penalties. They also performed acts of unbelievable self sacrifice and bravery to protect humanity whom they loved for their courage and vulnerability.*'

'Aelim were a complicated race existing primarily at an etheric level of vibration. As luminic beings they were bound from meddling directly in the fates of their earth-bound charges by the code of Karishmaha or "directed non-interference". They could voluntarily manifest physical bodies for themselves in order to work more intimately with those they protected but in so doing would be limited by the laws of the physical world. And so, in the popular tales, we find Aelim involved in rescuing foundlings, masterminding perilous intrigues, tracking down Chameleon monstrosities, accompanying heroes on epic quests and fighting never ending battles above the ice fields, planes, mountains and deserts of the physical planet.'

'Any Aelim who transgressed against the Karishmaha code could be exiled in fleshly form, or made Excidiat, until they had atoned, usually by completing a course of redemptive tasks. Time spent on the human physical level was considered by some Aelim an essential part of earning the right to their higher state. However it wasn't uncommon for Aelim to forget who they were and become irredeemably lost on the physical level. The sagas are full of tales of the 'Perdu', heavenly exiles or Excidiats, lost after decades or even centuries of wandering.'*

*See poem by Bronco Mason 'We who are lost, wanting to be found.'
egl.linesofsight.co.uk

Ten
SIGNS AND FROST

TWO nights later Cody was roused from a frighteningly realistic dream where a battle of some kind was raging high above vast fields of ice. Indescribable shapes clashed in mid air as a disembodied voice called to her from within a cavernous hole in the earth...*find...please...lost, perdu...help me...so cold!* She cried out his name...*Lucian...I am coming.*

The village bells were ringing. It was 3am, the time of night when people are most deeply asleep. Her head was muzzy and for a moment she felt confused, the sounds in her dream mixing with voices from somewhere a few houses away. The voices were crying what sounded like '*Doom*', no it had to be Bloom. Bloom! Instantly alert she threw open her curtains as her mother rushed into the room whispering fiercely,

'Cody, get dressed. We have to get to Bee's now. Quickly.'

Cody was staring out at the night time skyline of trees and rooftops and was horrified to see lights flickering on the edge of trees over by the church. Something was on fire. So it wasn't Bloom. It was a fire! Behind her in the room mum was grabbing a bag already packed and repeating, 'Cody, we must go. Now!'

'Mum, there's a fire over by the church somewhere. I think it's the Old Hall.'

Just then an alarm bell began to ring from the centre of Clayton Bar. The fire station bell. That was the Bloom alert this time. So there really was an outbreak! Cody snatched up her own shoulder bag and hurried after her mother.

*   *   *

As they left the house, tugging the fronts of their coats together and shouldering a matching set of satchels, another set of bells began to toll. The deep sonorous tones filled the night. Then a siren. And more shouts. Towers of sparks shot up into the night sky dancing like fire flies. Another fire had leapt into life on the eastern edge of the village opposite the church. The streets were filled with the silhouettes of people running, flitting shadows, voices calling to one another and a rising sense of raw panic which Cody hadn't felt since the day of the Newton outbreak. What was going on? Amidst the clamour of frightened voices one word kept repeating – Bloom!

It was bedlam and everyone was running in all directions at once. Mrs Conmar grabbed her daughter's arm and drew her away from the main road down a narrow passageway that ran behind a row of houses with high back walls enclosing gardens or yards. A dirt footpath ran alongside the walls overhung by a high thorn hedge on one side. They began to make their way along the pitch black tunnel. Cody shivered finding it surprisingly cold for a summer night, even at this hour. She glanced back as they bustled through the darkness. There was a cloudless sky directly overhead between the branches of the hawthorn and she could see the edges of chimneys picked out by the light from fires on the far side of the houses. The sounds of screaming and confusion made her feel she was caught up in another of her disturbing dreams; there'd been an increasingly number of those lately.

'Mum, where are we going?'

'To Bee's dear. Keep moving.'

The dirt footpath snaked its way through the dark heading steadily north towards the Onnercotts' cottage a four minute walk away.

'Why aren't we going to see if we can help out or something? We should at least find out what's going on.'

'Keep your voice low. No, we have to get away. We have to reach Bee's. Hurry, we must hurry.'

A fire van roared past a gap between the houses, it's flashing lights briefly illuminating their faces. Cody caught an unpleasant sickly sweet smell drifting on the air.

'Mum, can you smell that?'

'No dear. Keep moving.'

'Mum, everyone's dashing about in the dark. Someone could get hurt. Shouldn't we at least stay in one place.'

'She'll be expecting us and we'll be safe there. We have to reach the cottage.'

After that the only reply her mum would give, apart from muttering distractedly to herself as they pushed on through the dark was 'Hurry. Hurry!'

Although it was only a four minute walk to Bee's it took ten in the dark by the route they were following and it seemed a lot longer with the terrifying noises coming from the village behind them. It sounded as if more fires had broken out and the shouting and yells were amplified by the night. And the air was getting colder too. Bitterly cold, far colder than you'd think possible. Their breath was puffing out in white clouds that hung, faintly luminescent in the dark as they ran. By the time they arrived at the thick hedge surrounding the Onnercott's orchard Cody could feel her cheeks hurting from the intensity of it. Their footsteps were making an odd crunching sound as if they were walking on egg shells. Cody glanced down at the brittle surface beneath their feet sparkling with reflected starlight. There was frost on the grass!

They pushed open the back gate glinting with ice crystals and started to make their way across the whitened lawn. The sound of their feet was loud in the still air. The cottage was in complete darkness, which was unusual if Bee was expecting them. Cody's eyes wandered down to their feet again and she gasped reaching out to grasp her mother's arm.

'Mum. Look!'

The entire surface of the orchard was covered with a carpet of dead bees – hundreds of dead bees, frozen white and glittering in the faint starlight. They had been walking on dead bees! Her mother's eyes were white with horror in the darkness.

'Oh no! This can't be right! Bee wouldn't let this happen.'

They were both rooted to the spot, unmoving and unable to think. Not for the first time Cody felt that she hadn't woken up at all and must still be in her bed at home. Her head was pulsing and there was a deep irregular rhythm to her heartbeat. Heat was growing in her chest, flooding slowly into her lower trunk and limbs.

'Mum, what's happening? What are we doing here? And where's Bee and uncle Ben?'

'I don't know dear. I really don't. I wish I did.' She gripped Cody's hand hard. 'We'll have to take a look inside. Stay close now.' Her mother was making a huge effort to master her fear and Cody was relieved to hear that her voice had become steadier. They stepped cautiously over the crackling carpet of tiny frozen corpses. It was useless to try and avoid them. They covered every inch of ground. To one side of the path lay a couple of frosted humps on the grass that could have been the Onnercotts' goats lying on their sides beneath a dusting of white.

They reached the cottage door, which was ajar. A drift of dead, frozen insects lay against the side wall. Cody thought the sound of their breathing was deafening in the still air. Their breath hung around their heads like mist. Mrs Conmar called into the darkness,

'Madeline? Are you there? Ben? Anyone?' There was no reply. Cautiously they stepped onto the porch and crept into the kitchen. Inside everything was covered in hoar frost, thick and crusted like crushed glass. There was broken pottery on the table and floor. Mrs Conmar became transfixed when she saw this.

'Oh no...no please!'

'Mum, what is it? Is there no one here?'

'I don't know. We have to find out. Let's keep our voices down. This way.' Cody could feel her hands pulsing gently now, waves of warmth filling her palms, ebbing into her fingers. She could still feel the chill on her face but the cold didn't affect her at all.

Far away, from a distance of miles it seemed, as if the cold was muffling everything inside the cottage, they could still hear the sounds of bells and shouting from the village. Their feet crushed ice crystals as they stepped out into the main hallway – and then another sound, a groan. From nearby. From the front parlour. They trod gingerly into the wood panelled room and stood in the darkness trying to make out where the noise was coming from. Barely noticeable light came through the leaded windows allowing them to see the slumped shape in the corner when it let out another low groan. Granma Bees was collapsed half upright against the far corner almost hidden by the grandfather clock. Her face was turned to the wall and her entire body was thick with a coat of granulated ice. She was feebly trying to move.

They ran to her with sharp intakes of breath and her head swivelled jerkily at the sound of their feet. Where her face had been pressed against the wall was free of ice but her mouth hung open, her entire face pulled to one side like a stroke victim. They tried to lift her but she gasped in pain,

'No don't. Move me. Limbs solid. Frozen. Move me. And I'll. Die.' She had to pause for breathe between each utterance and her voice was thin and croaked. Cody took a lantern and matches from the nearby fireplace dragging her sleeve down over her fingers to handle the icy cold metal. She removed her shoulder bag and lit the lamp placing it on the floor next to the frozen figure. Bee was too far gone even to shiver.

'Bee, what can we do for you?' asked mother bending and putting her face close to the suffering woman eyes. Bee's breath was shallow producing hardly any mist in the icy room. Her eyes kept rolling back into her head but she made a great effort to rally her strength.

'Mary. Must get. Cody. Away from. Here. Find Enwyn. Or one. Of the. Others. And get. Away.' An alarming spittle of red foam was coating her lips but she carried on. 'Must head. For Haven.' Mother nodded her head grimly unable to tear herself from the spot.

Cody could feel the heat from her chest building up, rising, threatening to spill out uncontrollably. Her distress at seeing Bee like this was unbearable, beyond words.

'We can't leave you like this Bee. You need to get warm. Let me put my arms round you.'

'No!' The bark sprayed more blood flecked spittle over Bee's chin. 'Mary! No time. I. Don't count. Get. The child. Away. Now! Being attacked!'

Mrs Conmar jerked as if she'd been slapped and pulled herself to her feet grabbing hold of Cody's arm - but she stopped taken by surprise. The heat radiating from Cody's body was flowing into her hand as if from a furnace. She stared at her daughter numbly and saw how the light from the lantern seemed to gather around the kneeling girl and form a tight ball of radiance around her chest. Even in the darkened room the pale golden ball was barely more than a glimmer in the air but as it extended outwards like a gently questing tendril it pulsed with the rhythm of a heartbeat. Each beat added to its length and it grew, reaching towards the stricken woman on the floor until Cody leaned in to wrap her arms around Bee and the pale tendril was hidden between their two bodies.

Cody could feel the tremendous outpouring of energy from her chest flowing into her friend's cold frame, wrapping and penetrating the frozen limbs and trunk, easing the unnatural solidity of the muscles, restoring pulse and rhythm to the faint heartbeat, warming and healing. It was as if the energy was a third hand reaching from her heart to touch in ways no physical limb ever could. She could almost feel fingers on the imaginary hand flexing as the energy coursed into Bee. Soft moans came from the large woman's shuddering body as she shifted in the girl's arms. Her damaged face was stretching, trying to speak again,

'Wait. Stop. I know. What you're. Doing. No time.'

'Be still now,' soothed Cody. 'We've no intention of leaving you here like this.'

'No. Listen. Really. Isn't time.' Cody stroked the invisible hand of energy across Bee's face, warming and softening the lines of pain there. She wiped the blood from around the mouth, felt the eyelids cease their flickering as she touched them gently like a wisp of down. Bee's breathing became deeper, her exhalations misting in the air like drifts of steam. Her eyes opened and held Cody's own steadily.

'Cody. Listen to me. Really listen. You must go. Now. There are things, coming, from the dark, for you. You must flee and hide, where your mother tells you. Do you hear me? You must get to Wrayhaven.'

'But Bee, I don't know where that is.'

'Your mother knows! Leave me here now. You must get away. You must find Veriman. The shadows are coming for you!'

'We are all that is left of a race who were once beings of light.'
Translated fragment from the Peaks Engravings.

Eleven
LIGHT AND FLIGHT

'May your dreams protect you, and bless these fields of men.'
A Sufinam warrior's invocation.

CODY could hardly comprehend what was being said to her and she didn't want to believe any of it. Bee's breathing was making a bubbling sound in her chest. She needed protection and Cody's strongest impulse was to scream no to all this talk of running away. Sensing the rebellion in the youngster the old woman turned her head appealingly towards Mary who was still staring at the two of them in shock.

'Wrayhaven Mary. You must get her to Wrayhaven. And Veriman.'

'I...yes. Yes of course. Come Cody.' Again Mary put her hand on her daughter's arm tugging gently to separate her from the slumped figure.

'No Bee. I'm not leaving you like this. You can't make me.'

Bee held her gaze and a great peace settled on her face. She was taking in the girl's features, drinking them in hungrily, almost desperately.

'You must my dear. I am only here, to help you, to protect you, young one. You are our hope, and I am of no use to you like this. You are what is important. And you must go.'

Cody could sense that Bee's body was warming itself slowly, drawing on a small reserve of strength. It wouldn't do to rush the process. She allowed the column of energy from her torso to withdraw, felt it reabsorbing, retreating, snaking back into her chest. She flexed the fingers of the phantom hand as it settled inside her.

'Bee, I won't.'

'You will because I tell you. And because I say to you *Sercetes Eloin Hauna Ceulimas Bimhir!*'

A small window opened in Cody's mind, a shaft of clarity in a fog of forgetfulness. An illuminating flash of recognition shone out from somewhere deep within herself, but recognition of what she had no idea. It awoke a sensation of being at home in herself that was oddly disturbing. She could almost hear music, notes heard so softly that they might not have existed at all, but it was just the fading echo of the words Bee had uttered.

'Old Tongue. Caebimhir. You're speaking Old Tongue.'

'Do you know what I have said to you?' Bee whispered fiercely her eyes bright.

'No, but I...yes! No. What is it? It's so familiar.'

'Then that is enough. For now. That is all there is time for. You must leave. I want you to leave my dear.' There were tears in Bee's eyes but her face was joyous.

'Can't we help you Madeline?' said Mary, voice full of pain.

'No! I am hurt but not yet lost. I may even survive now that the worst of the cold has been taken from these old bones,' and indeed Cody realised that the frost covering had dropped from Bee's upper body. She realised several other things too, all in a rush and one of them was that what Bee had said was true. They had to leave! Something terrible was about to happen.

'Who is Veriman, Bee?' Cody almost sobbed. 'Can he guide us to where we have to go?'

'Your mother knows. Go! Head north...'

There was suddenly the most awful keening wail from outside the house. It dug into the nerves behind Cody's eyes and stabbed at her ear drums. Mary ran to the window and rubbed frost from a small pane to peer out. She gave a weak cry,

'Oh no! There's something on the lawn Madeline!'

Bee stirred herself with a great effort.

'Something Mary? *Something?*'

Cody joined her at the window and rubbed a second pane clear with her coat cuff. All she could see was a tall pillar of shadow on the white lawn at the centre of a large circular patch of darkness.

'What is that thing mum?'

From behind them came Bee's voice tense with fervour,

'What is it Mary? Speak!''

'It's a Shadow Hein Madeline. A predator! We can't go out that way.'

The hideous penetrating sound wailed on, its pitch rising to a point almost beyond hearing producing a numbing effect on the brain and nerves. Bee was struggling desperately to rise, her feeble efforts heroic but ineffective with limbs still incapable of holding her upright. She yelled at Mary with surprising force,

'Check the back, quickly.' Mary ran from the room. Cody tried to help Bee to her feet as they heard her mother's frantic footsteps rushing from room to room. She returned as Cody was trying to prop Bee against the side of a large padded armchair that creaked beneath her weight. Her palsied attempts to move more than the muscles in her face were distressing to witness. Mary ran to the window again gasping,

'Both sides and back Madeline. More Shadow Hein. We're surrounded.'

'How close?'

'Almost at the front door now…oh great saviour, there's Ben!'

Cody made sure Bee was safely propped against the armchair and ran to the window. Outside Ben had appeared from between the ranks of whitened apple trees and was moving hesitantly towards the hideous shape of darkness towering above the frosted lawn. He was yelling at the top of his voice and furiously swinging what looked like a set of thin chains around himself as he approached - but whatever it was he was doing it appeared to be having no effect.

Cody ran to the front door yelling,

'He needs help ! We must let him in.'

Her mother made a lunge to grab her but missed and staggered after her. Collapsed on the armchair Bee also shouted,

'No, he's not trying to get in. He's trying to save you. Don't…' but her words were lost in the ear shredding wail of the terrifying figure on the lawn.

Cody burst out of the front door and stood transfixed by a scene lifted directly from nightmare. A gaunt figure, eight to ten feet high, towered above uncle Ben its form flowing top to toe in a featureless fall of saturated darkness untouched by light. From where its head should be, slow ripples of black on black oozed downwards like melting wax, pooling at ground level in slow waves that radiated outwards in all directions before seeping into the ground. Near the top was a gaping hole, a maw of shadow, frozen open in a perpetual wailing shriek. Nothing else gave any clue that the thing might be alive, if in fact it was.

For the most awful moment Cody stood frozen in shock, drawn into the horror of something her senses were incapable of interpreting. What broke the spell was Uncle Ben screaming at her to get back in the house. He was racing to put himself between her and the abomination but as he passed the nightmare shape it surged forward and the edge of its inky circular stain swept over his leg. He shrieked, dropping the chains onto the lawn and staggered a few steps pushing Cody bodily towards the porch. She missed, crashed into the side pillar and fell against the wall. Over Ben's shoulder she glimpsed two thin slits of yellow open above the mouth of the shadow-being and was almost blasted by an overwhelming wave of mind numbing hatred. The ferocity of the urge-to-destroy carried in that blast threatened to drown her even as she tried to rise pushing with both hands against the rough wall. The keening wail rose to an even higher pitch. Uncle Ben screamed again and tried to rise but was being pulled backwards towards the monstrosity until his entire lower body was engulfed. His face contorted in pain and he began to collapse slowly into the shape, shouting to Cody as he did,

'Get back. Get back! Ruuuuuuun!'

He was clawing at the ground as the shadow swept over him. His limbs thrashed and twisted as the creature's keening note rose and fell as if in triumph. Within seconds he had been totally absorbed into the writhing blackness. And the Shadow Hein came on. It was only yards from where Cody lay.

At that moment her mother burst out of the cottage doorway screaming incoherently and flung herself full bodied at the black horror. She seemed to collide with something solid at the centre of the shimmering mass causing it to crash over backwards even as it enveloped the kicking, flailing woman. Briefly there was a heap of tangled shapes thrashing about on the frozen ground, a short-lived testimony to Mary Conmar's heroic self sacrifice but then, with sepulchral slowness, the dark form of crawling nightmare began to flow upwards restoring its original height. The shapeless maw opened again and resumed its hideous nerve shredding wail at the same time as the Shadow Hein began to slide forwards. Cody felt paralysed and helpless, her limbs numbed by fear and the terrible cold. She knew she should run but the horror of what she had just witnessed sapped her strength. The thing's eye slits were open again pouring malice, torment and despair into her soul. She knew she would never leave this spot.

The needle thin thread of light that pierced the monstrosity's head was so intense that Cody was blinded for several seconds. Behind the veil of blindness she could still sense the ferocity of the attack and heard the creature's keening soar to a shriek and die abruptly as if cut by a knife. As sight returned Cody could make out the haggard figure of Bee clinging to the wooden porch pillar, something silver flashing in her hands as she swept the piecing needle of light repeatedly across the now silent shape. The Shadow Hein had collapsed in on itself writhing like a harpooned jellyfish, hissing and steaming until all that was left on the scorched lawn was a tangle of broken angular shapes that could have been limbs or tentacles or claws. The stench was appalling.

The light died.

For a moment Cody was unable to move. Then she rushed on shaking legs to Bee's side and took her in her arms. The old woman looked dreadful, skin ashen and sagging, blood seeping from between her teeth, limbs twitching. All the muscles on one side of her face were pulled down and grotesque. She was barely breathing. Cody tried to lift her.

'Stop.' Bee's voice was little more than a whisper but clear as if being spoken directly into Cody's mind. 'Make for. Your father's Grove. Teddy's Grove. Hide there. You must. Go now. No time. Run child. Take these.' Bee's twitching hands were trying to pass what they were holding but the fingers had to be prised gently apart. On her dried old palms were two rings, both silver. One large, one small. Both were hot. Was this what Bee had used to create that spear of light that had finished the Shadow Hein? In a way wiser than she knew herself to be Cody understood with complete clarity that this was the case. There was something of great power here. Tears were pouring down her cheeks. But the old woman was struggling to grasp something around her neck on a chain. Cody reached around to undo the clasp. It was a glass phial the size of a small battery, capped both ends in silver and containing white crystals of . . . what . . . salt? It looked like salt. Clumsily Bee pressed all three items into Cody's hands. It felt wrong to be taking things from the stricken woman when she should be helping her get away.

'Oh Bee. What's going on? Why is this happening?'

'Hush. Take these. To Veriman. Go. Other Shadow Hein. Are coming.' Cody began to protest feebly but Bee's next words stopped her.

96

They were delivered in a weak voice but one clear and fresh as spring water, 'Thank you precious one,' she said, 'for the gift of who you are. It has been nought but privilege.' Her head sagged for a moment and then, clear as if spoken directly into her mind came, '*Kelerim Aogath Ceulimas Mohinr. The Grove. Get to the Grove.*'

With astonishing strength Bee pushed the resisting girl away. Despite herself Cody found she was running, sprinting as fast as her legs could carry her. She ran, ran as if impelled by the words her fallen friend had uttered, words she didn't understand but knew in her heart, faster and swifter, more fleet of foot than she had ever felt before in her life, light as the wind, strong as the earth, pounding and leaping over the frosted grass, past the shattered front gate and swift as thought into the lane. Here she paused and looked back. Two more of the hideous shadow shapes were stalking around the sides of the cottage, their keening note rising and falling in a hypnotic wail. But they were slow, too slow for her she knew, though she didn't know how she knew. The broken tumble of darkness that was her mother and Ben lay smothered by the obscenity that had absorbed them, a stark shape black against the frosted grass. Beyond that Bee lay inert in the doorway, a pathetic mound barely visible in the darkness. Cody's grief and rage rose like a hot rush of lava filling her chest threatening to explode her ribcage and she became aware of the weight of the two silver rings and the phial in her palms. There was a way she could use them, there was – but it eluded her! She knew and yet didn't know. And this wasn't the time to be hesitating. There was chaos and pain everywhere in the night. From the village there still came the sounds of alarms and cries. Fire and columns of sparks shot up into the sky. It was like a scene from hell. Again Bee's words sounded shapelessly in her mind and she knew she had to get to the Grove to find whatever or whoever was waiting for her there. Veriman, she had to find Veriman, whoever that was. She ran, hot tears scalding her eyes and the hand at the centre of her chest flexing and bunching into a fist as if wanting to grip and shake something angrily.

Clutching the three items of silver she fled to the Grove.

'*This has all happened before. And it will all happen again.*'
JM Barrie.

97

Twelve

PAIN AND VOID

'The only thing new in this world is the history you don't yet know.'
Harry Trueman.

PETER Loren was roused from his camp cot in the chapel by the shrill ringing of the phone a floor below. He staggered down the rickety wooden steps muttering things about unearthly hours and vengeance not even pausing to switch on the desk light before picking up the handset. Before he could speak a voice barked,

'Loren get yourself to Clayton Bar immediately.'

'Who is this,' Loren snapped back, realising it was a mistake even as the words left his mouth. The red priority light flashed discretely on the top of the dash box.

'This is Kanulf at the Protectorate – your boss - and I'm calling you at three thirty in the morning. What does that tell you son?'

'It's an emergency sir.'

'Good man.'

'Yes sir.'

'You're going in at the deep end Loren and I need you up to speed if you're to be any use to me, so listen up. You're to come prepared and as quickly as possible. You'll meet me there.'

'How prepared sir?'

'Come heavy.'

'Sir?'

'How long will it take you?'

'I can be there in ten minutes sir. Whereabouts will you be?'

'It's a small place Loren. Follow the noise.'

'I...'

Click!

Loren stared at the phone in his hand for all of two seconds before throwing himself up the stairs three at a time to grab his clothes. He went for a set of padded ankle boots and a thick belt lined with loops and karabiner clips. 'Come heavy' wasn't much of a guide for what to expect so he grabbed a selection of attachments and pouches from his locker and distributed them around his 'working' outfit. Much of his equipment was personalised, a sort of all purpose armoury and field kit. With the variety of tight spots he'd encountered during his time in Cheshire he was confident he could anticipate most likely scenarios – mind you he'd not had a call out like this before. As he gathered his gear the adrenaline rush kicked in. This was it! For Big Cheese Kanulf himself to initiate the call out, things must already have gone over the precipice. Perhaps at last he was going to get some answers to his many questions; questions about the build up of anomalies over the last ten months. Old Indestructible wouldn't show up in this part of the world in person for anything less than Armageddon.

On the next floor he grabbed his cape, helmet and gauntlets and rushed through the darkened tunnels, finally bursting into the night air of the courtyard. He glanced up at the starlit heavens before drawing the tarpaulin from the BSA 500. Clear sky and a full moon. Visibility would be good. Should be no trouble finding Old Sour Whiskers once he reached the village. He grinned as the 500cc engine gunned into life first time and took the narrow turns between the stone buttresses of the courtyard at breakneck speed. The streets of Chester were deserted and Loren's soul sang with the elation of speed and mounting excitement as he negotiated the neglected roads.

*   *   *

Cody slowed down as she drew away from the cottage and began to skirt around the edge of the village keeping to the cover provided by the hedges bordering the fields. The rage she had felt at not knowing how to use the silver rings had subsided and she was back to feeling like a confused and frightened twelve year old again. She needed the protection of parents and friends. She had zipped the silver phial and rings into the inside pocket of her shoulder bag and clasped it to her chest as if for protection.

To reach the Grove where her father's commemorative plaque was she'd need to make her way along the eastern edge of Clayton Bar. The last thing she wanted was to run into anyone she knew and have to start giving explanations. Fires were still raging everywhere, in fact there seemed to be even more outbreaks from what she could tell. People were still frantically running to and fro. Her newly awakened instincts told her to steer clear of everyone until she found Veriman. After that she'd see about perhaps helping out in the village.

Once or twice she thought she heard something following her along the narrow dirt path, a cautious scuttling in the tall dried grass that could have been anything - well almost anything. It was unlikely the Shadow Hein would follow her this way; they were too slow. Perhaps she should be warning people about the monstrosities at the cottage? No, stay focused on following Bee's last instructions. Push on as she'd been told to. People would see the filthy creatures easily enough in time to avoid them if they should head towards the centre of the village.

Firemen and villagers could be seen occasionally through the foliage and voices were calling out names - she thought she heard her own at one point but she ignored that. What was hard to ignore were the waves of panic battering at her from all directions. Her efforts to screen out the assault were like trying to suppress massive static on a radio set broadcasting simultaneous channels at full volume. Perhaps everything was made worse by the night time - or perhaps she was suffering delayed effects of shock after the stunning loss of her mother, Ben and Bee. Being unable to take in the horror of their deaths she had somehow pushed the torment beyond reach to be dealt with at some later moment, but it kept pushing back unwanted, turning her stomach to ice. She was glad to be wearing her warm coat with the hood which she pulled up to hide her blond hair. Everything she did and thought was becoming more difficult. Blanking out the emotional chaos beaming at her from all sides was taking more effort than usual. She had to concentrate hard on putting one foot in front of the other just to walk and her head was throbbing as it often did when under this kind of assault.

The Grove was situated outside the village perimeter close to where a footpath led over a stile set between two of the large stone slabs found all around the village boundaries. The field had been recently ploughed and the parallel lines of shadow gave the ground a surreal appearance drawing the eyes hypnotically towards the far end of the meadows. A soft warm breeze drifted across her cheeks but she still shivered from the cold in her veins.

She wasn't sure whether it was a trick of her eyes but either there were fire flies flitting between the stone slabs or some kind of static was sparking from one to the other. It wasn't especially noticeable; she just happened to be looking in that direction when a rustling in the bushes made her spin round. It was then that a shadow detached itself from the gloom and approached across the broken ground. Cody froze.

'Bron? Is that you?'

It was too small to be a Shadow Hein. Whatever the thing was it moved awkwardly shambling rather than walking. Once clear of the deeper shadows Cody could make it out. It wasn't Bron. It was Jesmina looking even worse than ever, if that was possible. And this time there was no doubt about it, her eyes were glowing, a dull ruby light making the rest of her face retreat even further into shadow.

'Hhhhhhhh – Cody Conmar – hhhhhhhhhrrrr! I knew I'd find you.' The scarecrow figure straightened itself and limped forward with an awkward twisting motion to the hips.

'Jesmina, you have to get back home, right now. There are dangerous things around tonight. I don't mean the fires or the Bloom.'

'Hhhhhhhhrrr – you have no idea – hhhhhhhhhrrrrr – you sssstupid pathetic sack of flesh.' The bedraggled girl changed direction to intersect Cody's route as she tried to avoid her and head for the Grove.

'No Jesmina, you don't understand. You're in danger. Get back home!'

Jesmina lurched at Cody with a surprising burst of speed, her arms raised aiming for Cody's face.

'Get away from me!' The cry from Cody was involuntary. She leapt to one side and ran for the Grove, vaulted over the low wooden fence and aimed a backward swipe with her arm to fend the clutching clawing girl away. Jesmina crashed into the fencing as if unaware it was there and began to scrabble over it like a mindless animal blinded by rage. Cody backed away clutching the back of her hand which was covered in something wet from the backward blow. As she did so her foot skidded over a marble slab set into the ground and she realised they were inside the Grove.

The newly awakened levels of Cody's mind told her that something terrible had taken root in this latest version of Jesmina. She was literally not herself. Cody's panic level rose a notch. In an instant there came the now familiar sensation of heat building up in her chest flooding down her torso and into her arms. It was a torrent of heat so intense she wondered her skin didn't blister.

Then in a rush Jesmina was over the fence and coming fast. Cody could smell the fetid breath, hear the indrawn rasps of air as the grotesque figure approached to within a couple of feet. Jesmina's eyes burned crimson like hot blood. Without realising what she was doing Cody urged the concentrated column of heat outward from her chest and aimed it at the deranged figure hitting it directly in the face. There was a muffled grunt of outrage and pain and the figure crashed to the ground. For the first time Cody noticed that Jesmina's clothes were hanging in tatters and in the moonlight she could see the skin of the girl's body writhing like a mass of worms. Jesmina lurched to her feet and came at Cody again spitting and raking the air, all pretence of humanity gone as whatever mindless force controlled the girl took over completely.

A great calm settled over Cody's mind as she regarded the pitiable horror that had once been the school bully. Silence descended around her and everything moved - into - slow – motion. Cody knew exactly what must be done. She stood poised, hands at her sides with the palms facing forward and as the rabid figure came within reach Cody snapped her invisible arm out at full stretch and grasped the spitting snarling thing by the throat. Jesmina shuddered to a halt unable to move, mouth working soundlessly, limbs convulsing. Fast as thought Cody reached into the upper part of the unfortunate girl's chest with her ghost limb, grabbed at the squirming thing embedded there and tugged. With a wet ripping sound something tore out of Jesmina's body and there, suspended in the air between the two girls, was a knot of translucent stalks and tentacles that thrashed in fury. The obscenity writhed powerless even as Jesmina collapsed to the ground scattering a spray of dark droplets down her front. Cody squeezed harder on the hideous thing and opened the furnace in her chest to direct a burst of such intense heat at the squirming mess that it crisped and roasted within seconds before disintegrating onto the ground in a fall of greasy ash.

Silence hung over the scene like a shroud…then the night sounds of yelling and chaos from the village crashed inwards like a tidal wave. Jesmina lay gasping in pain but Cody could see that her skin was no longer writhing like a snake pit. Where she might have expected a gaping hole there was only skin, dark and badly bruised but intact. Cody's invisible hand withdrew, coiled itself into her chest again clenching and unclenching its fingers and gradually becoming still. She knelt down to check on the suffering girl.

'No, don't touch her,' said a voice from further back within the Grove. 'Her skin may well be poisonous to anyone except herself. I will check her. Stand back.'

Out of the shadows emerged the woman Cody had last seen at Frodsham, the mysterious reader in green and black. The woman's dark glasses reflected the moonlight, even though, as Cody noted almost without realising it, the Moon was behind the woman. Cody jumped to her feet every nerve on the alert, ready to fight or run.

'You did well young one. Are you hurt?' The woman knelt and drew something from a shoulder bag with her gloved hands. In a swift, practiced motion she wound a few lengths of beaded cord around her fingers and thumbs creating a cat's cradle or web. She cupped her hands around the girl's face without touching it sliding both palms down to her chest and along arms and legs. A few seconds ticked by.

'She is fine. The toxins in her skin have been negated.' The woman returned the cords to her bag and regarded Cody without expression. 'Whatever you did to her my young one you have already saved her. All she needs now is rest and the proper care.'

'I...what are you doing here?'

'Why Cody Conmar, waiting for you.'

Thirteen
LEARNING CURVE

CODY could see the silhouette of the woman rising to her feet as gracefully as a ballet dancer. She was fighting the urge to run and the two of them stood tense and wary only a couple of yards apart.

'Waiting for me?' Cody spoke guardedly. 'How did you know I'd be coming here?'

'It was only a guess, but a good one, as we see.'

Cody considered this for a moment. There was no way she could know if she was being told the truth or not, which was a little unusual. But really it didn't matter. She had to be getting away from here...somehow.

'I have to go.' She began to walk towards the yew hedge and low fence surrounding the Grove. 'I've got to be somewhere else.'

'Cody Conmar you must come with me tonight. I know you have many questions, as I do myself, but despite all the horrors you have been through I must somehow convince you to trust me. This will not be easy but it must be done. How may I get you to trust me Cody?'

Cody was exhausted from everything that had happened in the last hour and her thoughts were beginning to feel heavy and sluggish. Her limbs were trembling with the effort of not racing away over the fields. She desperately wanted someone to make it all go away; she needed to rest; she needed help. Yet how could she trust a complete stranger? An insistent inner voice was whispering, *trust nothing, trust no one.* Her natural instincts were all jumbled up.

'Are you Veriman?'

'No, but I know where he is. We can reach him together.'

'You - know where he is?'

'Yes. He waits at Wrayhaven, where you will be safe.' The woman's voice was low and gentle, soothing.

'Wrayhaven...are we...going to Wrayhaven then?' That sounded good.

'You know the name. That is excellent. Yes, Wrayhaven. We will make our way there but we must proceed in great secrecy. There are forces who will stop at nothing to harm us. We must become invisible. Do you know how to become invisible Cody Conmar?'

Some tense inner part of Cody had relaxed at the mention of Wrayhaven. At the same time she was listening to two voices debating backwards and forwards inside her head, one urging her to trust no one and the other gently insisting - *it's alright – safe - safe.* Whether it was her bone aching weariness or the soothing effect of the woman's words making her limbs relax Cody couldn't decide. On the ground between them Jesmina groaned.

'I can't trust you,' said Cody cautiously as if rolling the shape of the words around her tongue to see how they felt. 'How do you know my name?'

'There is very little I don't know about you. I am one of your guardians Cody. My name is Bella Dixon.'

Cody felt an odd sensation of release in her muscles at these words. The soothing voice continued,

'We must travel together for a while until I can deliver you into safe hands again. I know how suspicious you must be after all you have been through. You have seen many confusing things, you are right to be suspicious. The truth is Cody Conmar I have been watching over you for some time. You have been in great danger and tonight that danger is at its worst.' The tall woman peered from side to side as she spoke, her glasses flashing with reflected light. By now Jesmina had ceased even the shuddering sighs she had been making and lay still.

'I was supposed to come here to the Grove.' Cody said, her voice sounding faint even to herself.

'And you did but the Grove is no longer safe. There are ... presences on all sides. We have to leave the village – now! I have said I need you to trust me and so I show you this,' Bella held out her palm to reveal a silver and glass phial on a chain exactly like the one Bee had given her only a short time before. 'Do you recognise this? Are you aware of what it is for?'

'I don't know what it's for but I have seen one like it. Bee had one she...she showed me once.' Even with exhaustion dulling her thoughts and voices arguing in her head Cody held back, resisting the impulse to spill everything that had happened at Bee's cottage. For a moment she almost clutched at her shoulder bag but managed to restrain herself.

'Good. Only guardians posses these. If you have seen one before you surely know what they are for.'

'No I don't and what are Guardians?'

'Good heavens girl!' Bella asked in anguish, 'Have they told you nothing in all these years? Please be patient with me.' She took a deep breath. 'Time is not on our side and I regret we cannot afford the luxury of finesse. It is vital that we get away from this place and you must trust me.'

'But why should I trust you,' said Cody half convinced that the woman was right.

'Because I am your only remaining hope and I say to you *Shirapenith ko beminhir tallis*. You have not been well protected so far Cody. The Shadow Hein got terribly close. *Tash haluman meordir binden*. Do you understand what I have said to you?'

'No. I don't think so. What did you say?'

'The words do not matter, only the sense.'

'Old Tongue. You spoke Old Tongue like Bee did.' Cody's head was filled with fuzzy warmth like an afternoon of summer mists where pastel colours soften the treeline and...she felt suddenly sick. Her chest was pulsing!

'Old Tongue, yes, Caebimhir. *Tash fimutenin bohir nohlae*.' Bella suddenly whirled in the direction of the village. Someone was crashing through the bushes towards them. Jesmina began groaning and trying to rise, dry retching like a cat trying to bring up a fur ball. In the pale light Josse burst through the foliage and skidded to a halt staring wild eyed at the group. Bella spoke first,

'Josse, Cody is safe.' But the boy ignored her. His eyes were on Cody.

'Cody! Where've you been? I've looked everywhere for you. Are you alright?'

'I'm fine.'

Jesmina groaned again. Josse stared.

'Who's that? It is Jesmina Feydon? Holy scuz, what happened to her?'

Cody stared down at the darkly stained figure in the grass. The girl looked wretchedly vulnerable yet the urge to protect her, make sure

106

she was alright, hammered insistently in Cody's heart. However the bully had behaved in the past she must be taken care of. No one should have had to live with that thing inside her. What could it possibly have been?

'It is Jesmina, Josse. She got attacked by something. But she'll survive.' Cody turned to the woman looming over the collapsed figure. 'What are we going to do to help her? She needs our help.' Turning to Josse she pleaded with her friend, 'Josse, she needs our help.'

'Not our help unfortunately,' Bella replied curtly. 'But you are right. She must be left where the rescuers can find her, not out here on the edge of the fields.'

'Why can't we take her with us?'

'Because she would slow us down. She will be safer here. She is not the one *they* want. Josse can you get her to a place where she can be found?'

'Of course Bella.' The lad knelt besides the groaning girl and Bella stepped forward to restrain him.

'Wait. Let me check one more time.' Again she performed the little ritual with the beaded threads and nodded her head as if satisfied. 'The toxin is completely absent. Good. You must tell me how you did that young Cody. Most impressive. Your friend is fine.' Cody was about to say that Jesmina had never been any kind of friend but kept silent. Bella continued, 'All she needs now is rest and the simplest of care. She will recover - in time. Josse!'

The lad bent and dragged the limp figure to her feet hooking one of her arms over his shoulder. He gasped,

'Oh the smell! Yeurch! What's wrong with her? And she's soaking wet!'

'She has been under a great torment. Be gentle with her. You know a safe place?'

'The Oak Gate should do fine. Someone'll soon spot her there.'

'Take care not to be seen. Return quickly.'

Cody made a move as if to help but Bella barred her way. Her voice was gentle but insistent,

'No Cody. Josse can manage. Truly.'

Cody watched as her friend dragged the drooling mumbling girl into the darkness.

'It is not safe for you so near the village. Or here for that matter. Come stand by this tree until Josse returns.' They moved deeper into the shadows beneath the massive outspread arms of an ancient oak giant. Cody's thoughts were moving at the speed of treacle down a wall. She was still battling to keep the distress from the village at bay but the effort tired her. If only her temples would stop pounding and her eyes filling with water.

'How come you know Josse so well?' she asked in a whisper.

'Josse has been a great help to me in keeping an eye on you. He could be there when I could not. He is very fond of you you know.'

'I...I didn't know.' There was a buzzing in her ears, or around her ears. It was approaching rapidly from the branches above them.

'As soon as Josse returns we must move. If we are to reach Wrayhaven safely we must go before...'

Abruptly a great buzzing cloud of darkness had surrounded them and Cody knew they were being attacked by a spore swarm as the two boys at Bee's cottage had been. It was like being hit by a dust storm and she could feel the gritty particles attaching to her hair and skin. There was a sensation of hot needles on her arms and face but before she could do more than slap ineffectively a few times they were gone.

Clear of the massive oak Bella stood with her feet planted wide apart surrounded by the buzzing cloud. She was stirring the air with great sweeping movements of her upper body and arms and as she transferred her weight to the right the swarm darted in that direction twisting and stretching, coalescing and thinning like a startled shoal of fish. As she shifted to the left the cloud followed. Bella's arms gyrated in mesmeric circles over her head, behind her back, up and down and the dark cloud followed – it was a dance, balletic and soaring with the woman's figure the calm still point at the centre. The noise from the swarm was rising in pitch as if furious at being controlled in this way.

Bella was gliding backwards out of the Grove, her skirts and cloak flowing like majestic wings over the low fence without breaking stride, back, back across the dark lines of the ploughed field until she stood only a few yards from the stone slabs of the stile. Suddenly she flung her arms forward in a dramatic gesture aimed directly at the stones and the churning cloud darted between the slabs - and was vaporised by a crackling wall of energy! Everything leapt into stark relief for a fraction of a second before being instantly swallowed again by shadows. The spore swarm had gone.

'And that,' said the stern faced woman breathing hard, 'is that.'

She strode across the furrows towards the Grove and leapt the fence.

'You see. Danger, Cody Conmar! Every minute we remain you are vulnerable.' She jutted her face to within an arm's length of the astonished girl and whispered fiercely, 'We must go – now!'

'What happened? How did you...?'

'Sentinel stones. Part of the defences built around Clayton Bar for your protection. I will gladly tell you more as we travel. Come!' Bella stood with her arm extended in a gesture of invitation.

'Alright. What about Josse...'

At that precise moment Josse appeared abruptly from the direction of the village.

'What the heck was that noise?' he gasped.

'Never mind that. How's Jesmina?' asked Cody.

'Oh, she'll be fine,' he panted. 'Someone's bound to see her there soon. I made sure she was comfortable. There's loads of people running about.'

'Were you seen?'

'No but I saw some troops arriving in trucks from the barracks. Are you alright Cody?'

Cody was unable to do more than nod her head. She rubbed at the half dozen stings received from the spore cloud.

'Fine,' said Bella briskly. 'Then it is time. Let us go.'

'Me too?' asked Josse uncertainly.

'Of course. There is nothing for you here now. There is nothing for any of us.'

'But my dad. He...'

'There is nothing here for you now – not if you would live.' Josse's face showed little of his reaction but he was clearly stunned.

Bella turned and strode away without even looking back to check they were following. Cody felt drawn along in her wake and surprised herself by keeping pace even though she was almost asleep on her feet with exhaustion. It felt such a relief to have someone else take charge. She had no idea how they were going to find Veriman or reach Wrayhaven but she did know that leaving here was good; she knew that.

Josse trotted by her side darting concerned glances at her and at the murky shadows on all sides. Clearly any personal objections he may have had to leaving the village were now reduced to silence. The trio headed into the darkness of the Cheshire countryside leaving Clayton Bar burning like a scene from a medieval painting.

Microlite salvagers.

'Following the Bloom Event and Ice Year of '91-'92 many areas of the recovering world were cut off by Tar Zones, inaccessible except by air. Unless a region contained vital resources needed for rebuilding the lives of the surviving population it was left untouched. In the case of cities, where all kinds of valuable assets were plentiful, the government organised the Isles' Recovery & Resettlement Programme and airlifted most essential materials within the first five years. By the late 1990's there had evolved a culture of government sanctioned salvagers all acting as freelancers. Most notable were the Microlite Salvagers or Scavengers as they preferred to be called. They were also known as Wingers, Sky Gypsies, Liters, Skyguys and Windies.'

'It was a highly dangerous and competitive lifestyle that appealed to the independent spirited, the daring and the displaced but mostly to the rebellious young. Fatalities occurred but the spirited chancers would be the first to say it went with the territory. Crashing a tiny winged craft in a Tar Zone was not a pleasant end and once trapped in the clinging goo a salvager was beyond rescue. They would become hopelessly mired and eventually succumb to exhaustion and suffocation. But life as a Microliter meant freedom, even if it could cost dearly. Despite the gruelling and often mundane reality popular songs and stories romanticised their escapades. They got to soar above it all, chase dreams amongst the clouds, work where and when they wanted. They were the modern day equivalent of pre-Event biker gangs. Their lives were governed by unspoken codes and they gave themselves colourful names such as Baphomet's Tears, the Wind Knives, Zuzu's Petals and One Hand Tied.'

Taken from News Archive Services egl.abandonedcities.co.uk
See also egl.mythsoftheskygypsies.co.uk
Article by Cullie Brown

Fourteen
THE DEEP END

LOREN was surprised to pass several ambulances on his way to Clayton Bar all heading away from the village. His first real intimation of exactly how serious the situation might be was when he saw carts loaded with evacuees and a steady trickle of people on foot. It was still the middle of the night and the silent silhouettes lining the road brought back memories of his years in the Recovery & Resettlement Programme when he had helped ferry members of the surviving population around the country in an attempt to establish new post-Event communities. That had been a hard time for everyone wondering if life had a future worth the effort of rebuilding.

Approaching the village outskirts he could hear alarms going off all over the place including the Bloom siren; not a good sign. Fields were burning to the north and several blazes raged inside the village itself, stark against the night sky. Total mayhem! No wonder Kanulf was taking charge. But why had he thought it so important that Loren needed to be there? That soon became clear.

The road split from the main A41 to Whitchurch and turned into Clayton Bar over a narrow stone bridge that spanned the canal, a natural barrier to the southwest of the village. A troop carrier was parked on the near side of the canal cordoning off the approach.

A few late stragglers were passing over the bridge through the check point and joining the exodus - no one was going in. To one side an ambulance team tended to the few who needed immediate attention, light burns or scratches mostly, the more serious injuries would already have been transported to St Werburgh's. A half dozen troops stood by a set of flood lights aimed over the canal and into the village beyond. Loren braked his BSA noisily causing a sergeant talking into a field phone to turn round. The remaining guards continued to watch the opposite bank.

111

Loren noticed that two of the troops were hefting flame throwers. Unusual. He approached the officer and flipped his credentials.

'Started the party without me I see,' he quipped. The sergeant responded with a locked jawed calmness that betrayed how tense he was. He checked the ID. Loren noticed the unnatural stillness in the other soldiers, weapons gripped too tight, grim expressions. They were really racked up. Loren could see the whites of one young soldier's eyes when he glance behind to see what was going on.

'Going in Mr Loren…sir?'

'I'm looking for Edwin Kanulf, up from London. Any idea where he might be sergeant?'

'No…sir. We're just on perimeter. There's all kindsa brass running around in there,' the sergeant gave a flick of his head towards the village. 'Specialists. The heavy brigade. All kinds. Other stuff too.'

'OK. I'll find my way. Has Bloom been confirmed?'

'Seems so sir. But the fire boys are there in strength. Got it covered I reckon.'

'Thank you sergeant.' Loren returned to his vehicle and revved the engine. The officer called out to him as he drove past,

'Take care sir. Bloom isn't all that's going on over there. There's some heavy items on the loose tonight.' It was hard to hear over the BSA's engine and the sirens still wailing in the background but Loren waved an acknowledgement as he took the steep backed bridge. It was narrow, the sidecar just scraping between the rough stone walls and he had to go slow. Once clear he was about to accelerate up the road when something caught his eye by the water's edge. It was only a flick on the periphery of his vision, a quick tell-tale caught by the flood lights, but it caused him to steer onto the bank and dismount to take a closer look. He left the engine running, he'd only be a minute.

The burned remains of something the size of a dog lay in a wide patch of scorched grass about thirty feet from the bridge and there were a series of glistening trails leading into, or out of, the canal, slime trails such as might be left by snails the size of footballs. He'd seen something similar some months back when investigating an anomaly east of the Peckforton Hills. It hadn't been good news then and it didn't bode well now. He registered that the sergeant was shouting something at him…it was then that the stench hit him. He spun round.

Something grotesque and scaly was hauling itself out of the canal thrashing the water into a spume of spray as its claws dug into the stone edging. It was huge, about seven or eight feet long. In the fraction of time that his mind registered the creature a cascade of details logged themselves on his senses: the rows of tiny serrated teeth in a vicious slash of mouth, the oily scales on its foot-thick sinuous body muscled like a boa constrictor, the total absence of eyes, the clawed nails digging at the stone. A fetid reek of marsh and decay came at him like a wall. Its speed was terrifying. In less than an eye blink it was arcing through the air in a leap that would take him squarely in the chest!

Loren's reactions went into overdrive. He flung himself headlong to one side putting the body of the bike and sidecar between himself and the monstrosity. The thing landed, whirled and leapt again crashing heavily on top of the BSA buckling it and slithering over the damaged vehicle to get at its intended victim. Jaws sprayed a blast of stinking droplets in his face as its teeth closed on his gauntleted arm. Loren had ripped a bulky reinforced camera case from his belt and jammed the razor rows open wide enough to tear his arm free. With his spare hand he grabbed a stun grip from a side holster and discharge 50,000 volts directly into its open mouth. The thing spasmed and rolled off giving him time to reach the long handled survival knife in his boot. With a swift downward slash he hacked at the body. The blade glanced off the tough scales but connected with the root of its forward leg and cut deep into the muscle and bone. Spitting and spraying slime the monstrosity fell clear as it bucked and kicked from the stunner's charge. By this time the sergeant and two soldiers had joined Loren and let rip with their automatics. The beast was struggling to get back on its feet, the damaged leg hung uselessly as its other limbs clawed frantically into the soft earth. The impact of the rounds smacking into the thickly coiling trunk made it shudder. Wounds were ripping outwards in its side like tiny doors popping open. Its thrashing increased until suddenly ... it froze, slumped heavily onto one side and lay still. Loren jumped to his feet wiping the muck from his face and goggles. He was breathing hard.

'Thanks guys.' He stepped over to the carcass and landed a hefty kick in its side yelling, 'Look at my bloody bike!' then had to leap clear as the tail whipped round missing his thigh by inches. The thing was covered in razor sharp scales. One of the squaddies put another burst of fire into the thing's head.

'OK, OK it's dead,' said Loren taken aback. Overall the thing was about the size of an adult crocodile. It had seemed much much bigger when scrabbling to reach his face. 'That was just nerve reaction. But thanks again anyway.'

'That's OK sir. Stand back please.' The sergeant waved at one of the squaddies with a flame thrower to come forward.

'Wait! What are you doing? You can't torch it. It'll be needed for forensics.'

'Sorry sir. Orders. Everything that comes out of the village that's not human gets incinerated. Orders sir.' The sergeant was not going to back down. 'Things like this been leaping out at us all night.'

'What?'

'Damned boojums are everywhere.'

'As big as this?'

'Bigger, smaller – all kinds.'

For the first time Loren took in the fact that the critter had six legs...what th'...? His bike was unrideable after the pounding it had taken. Its handlebar column had been twisted into a pretzel and who knew what else was damaged. Dammit!

'OK but watch the bike eh. I like the paintwork as it is.'

'Won't burn your bike sir. Safe as houses. Go easy now.'

'I sure will.'

Loren pawed ineffectively at the muck all down his front. Bloody shambles! Not a great way to make his entrance. It was time for some answers. It was time for Kanulf.

*   *   *

He walked into the village rubbing his arm where the thing had chomped on his gauntlets, noticing how the thick leather had been pierced in a couple of places. Behind him the flame thrower roared, throwing his shadow down the middle of the road ahead and lighting up the surrounding trees.

At the centre of the village a couple more troop carriers were parked up on the green in front of the church. Loren could see uniformed fire fighters busy around the rear of a fire engine further down the road. All street lighting was out. Smoke drifted on the air thick, acrid, oily and harsh on the throat. Loren broke out the last half of a stick off gum he'd been saving, halved it, and wadded a piece into his mouth. Stood by the open back of a squat command vehicle lit by the glow from a flickering console was a small group of uniformed or combat clad figures. They were listening intently to message squawks on a field radio. At the centre of the group was a tall white bearded figure with an eye patch wearing a nondescript ankle length black coat. Edwin Kanulf, the old warhorse himself. As Loren got within earshot the old man's gravely voice barked,

'And get someone to stop them ringing that damned bell. We know there's an emergency.'

Rapid orders and responses were being snapped back and forth between Kanulf and others gathered at the vehicle. Loren watched for a moment as reports came in over the com set or were brought by heavily armed runners kitted out in black. There was a sudden outbreak of gunfire in the background as he stepped forward to announce his arrival. Closer to the group he could distinguish what some of the more quietly spoken people were contributing to the exchanges, particularly a child-sized androgynous figure who until this moment had remained hidden at the centre of the assembly. The tiny figure was dressed in shapeless white denim overalls covered in pockets. Now that he was closer he could see that it was she who was conveying Kanulf's orders over the field mike. The voice definitely made the tiny form a she. She spoke rapidly without seeming to take a breath whilst Kanulf consulted intensely with the black suited field agents. But the most arresting detail about the slight figure in white was not that she was a hunchback, which she clearly was, but that the parts of her face and head not hidden behind a large pair of blackout goggles were crisscrossed with strips of surgical tape like a badly botched plastic surgery job.

Out in the darkness the church bells died away as the sirens faltered leaving just the sound of shouts and burning to fill the night.

Loren's eyes were drawn to the hump on the female's back. There was something not right about the thickly padded shape perched dead centre of her upper shoulders. To his eye the mound with its double stitched edgings and contoured piping appeared somehow armoured like the incongruous bulk of an astronaut's suit.

'Loren you made it,' roared Kanulf catching sight of him. 'You look like you've had a little action of your own. Stay downwind though.' Loren was only too aware that he was still sporting much of the nauseating slime spat at him by the thing at the canal. He rubbed his clothes self consciously and decided to disregarded the looks he was getting. Kanulf made room for him by the command vehicle and indicated the figure in white.

'This is Shree, my personal assistant. She doesn't venture into the field as often as she used but we need her here tonight. By the devil we need her.' Kanulf made no attempt to introduce the uniformed figures stood around the vehicle.

'Pleased to meet you Shree.' Loren nodded acknowledgement.

'Loren.' She nodded back.

He hesitated, staring at the incongruous figure with a bemused expression. Something niggled him about her voice.

'We haven't met have we?'

'No.'

'But I know your voice from somewhere.'

'Of course you know her Loren,' Kanulf interrupted impatiently, 'She's your damn supervisor in London. You speak to her on a regular basis. Get a grip man.'

'Amuna ! You're Amuna!'

'Amuna Shree Jensen. Hell of a place for a first meeting eh Loren,' she responded. Loren was so taken aback that his mental faculties took a holiday for several seconds. He made a few snatches at rallying his composure but missed each time. Amuna's mouth cracked a thin smile at his discomfort but her eyes were invisible behind the opaque material of the goggles so it was impossible to see how far her smile went.

'Not what you expected Loren?'

'Forgive me. There's a lot to take in at the moment.' A dull explosion rang out from somewhere near the canal warehouses just as a striking young woman appeared from the opposite direction. She was accompanied by several black clad soldiers. Loren noted the non-regulation uniforms bristling with specialist gear, night vision goggles and innocuous looking weaponry whose simple lines spoke eloquently of their deadly effectiveness. Special Ops obviously. What the hell were they doing here?

The woman herself wore jeans, mid-calf boots and a hooded jacket topped by full Kevlar bodice and carried nothing more than a three foot section of broom handle painted matt black; at least that's what it looked like. Loren knew instinctively it was something altogether more lethal though he had no idea what. She stared hard at Loren until Kanulf assured her,

'He's cleared. Your report please.'

Without hesitation the young woman launched into a stream of details speaking directly to Kanulf and never taking her eyes from his face.

'Villagers all clear and accounted for. Thirteen fatalities,' there were a few intakes of breath from those gathered round. 'Eleven serious injuries, multiple minor casualties. Some unspecified species have been put down after attacking inhabitants. Probably infection crazed; details to arrive. Private Feydon is with his daughter on the way to St Werburgh's — we have someone ready to get her story. The initial fire outbreaks were all synchronised at key positions. All suppressed now. No details on who started them. Seven small Bloom spots, spontaneous and synchronised, all torched or contained. Kleiper says they're not typical in nature, something anomalous. It's got him worried and he wants to speak to you.'

'Not typical? What the damnation does that mean?' Kanulf spoke rapidly to two of the uniformed aides, 'I need this assessing. Get Kleiper and alert two cleanup teams.' He walked some distance away from the vehicle followed by Amuna, Loren and the young woman in Kevlar. They stood in a scrum and Kanulf gave the woman a hard significant look. Loren felt they were all waiting for something.

'OK,' said Kanulf, as if he'd taken a decision. His voice was pitched low. 'Full report now.'

'We have two guardians missing, eleven fatalities, five woundings and two mind wipes. All were specifically targeted including the Onnercotts and Mary Conmar.'

'What were we up against here?'

'Apart from the multiple fire and Bloom alerts, there was an ice lock on the Onnercotts' cottage, spore swarms and Shadow Hein. We may also have had Gaunts or venom slugs with Marsh Kraken on the borders, that's what you ran into at the canal Loren.'

Almost none of this made any sense to Loren but he knew when to remain quiet. His field of speciality was anomalies and he was neck deep in them right now. There was nothing he could contribute so…he nodded.

The details were bewildering but he was impressed by the way the report had been delivered. There was nothing showy about the young woman; she moved and spoke with a grace and economy that implied enormous power and her small coterie of Special Ops lap dogs increased the aura of command she wore so lightly. He noted they had not followed when Kanulf took the little group to one side.

Kanulf was clearly annoyed,

'And our charge? The reason we are all here?' he asked forcefully.

'No sign. She's gone. No trace. This entire show was clearly a massive misdirection. We've been decoyed.'

'How did we miss it?' rasped Kanulf. 'The build up must have been considerable.'

'There are Behelian layers on everything Kanulf. We've run into something new. I want you to take a look at what we've been up against. We came across it in the ruins of the Old Hall. It's this direction.' Enwyn turned to lead the way. 'You really need to see this Kanulf.'

'Watch the storm coming. Your system's in shock.
The Earth's weeping shadows. It's time to take stock.
Hear the sky thunder. There's blood on the track.
The sentinel's waking. It's time to fight back.'
From Hobo Holocaust, words by Rue Brawler.

Fifteen
N.R.D.A.

LOREN kept close to Amuna, who walked with a pronounced limp, leaning heavily on an aluminium stick. She didn't even come up to his shoulder and gave off a faint smell of something medical – with an underlying hint of...honeysuckle? The heavily armed squad fanned out silently on either side. Other dark garbed shapes flitted between the buildings, sinister and impersonal in goggles and blacked out faces.

As the group made its way through the smoke shrouded streets the tiny hunchback suddenly gripped Loren's wrist. Her silk-like voice was pitched for his hearing only.

'There's a lot to take in I know, Loren. Just try to keep up for now.'

'Behelian?' he hissed plaintively. 'What's...?'

'A form of invisibility or amnesia field. Time for questions later Loren. Pay attention to what Enwyn is saying.'

Enwyn was addressing Kanulf,

'...as far as we can tell. It generates a suppression field allowing Chameleon-kind to move undetected. I calculate there must be six more ringing the village. There are teams rooting them out now. Whoever did this established a wyrd zone over the entire region and unleashed everything at once. It was sudden and overwhelming.'

'I'll give you that. Bloody effective,' agreed Kanulf grudgingly. 'But it also contravenes the damned Pact. There's going to be Hell-geld to pay after this. The Chams can't transgress and expect no retribution. I'll see the scales balanced!'

Amuna spoke up from her position a few paces behind,

'We need to update the allies Kanulf and initiate redress.' She was limping badly but no one else appeared to be making any allowances for her so Loren didn't comment but it did make him uneasy. He blurted pretty much the first thing that came into his head,

'Amuna, can I call you Amuna or do you prefer Shree?'

'As you like Loren.'

'OK, what are the guys in black doing here and who's the impressive young woman? I've seen her before, at a funeral I attended here in Clayton Bar.'

'Ah, our resident Amazon. Her name is Enwyn Carter, a key person in what should have been this village's impregnable defences. She is taking it all very personally.' Amuna was breathing hard but didn't slow down. 'It has all gone badly awry. Fortunate that Kanulf was already in this part of the country really. He was able to mobilise the troops at Saighton barracks and the Black Set.'

'Black Set?'

'Specialist forces. All the intense young men hovering around Enwyn.'

'Intense is right. Haven't seen gear like they're toting on any course I've been trained on though.'

'Oh the gear caught your eye did it. And I thought it was our young Amazon. Quite something isn't she. By the way, she's a lot older than she looks.'

'I'm beginning to feel that way myself. This stuff on me – doesn't smell too bad does it?'

'Positively stomach churning. But you're around some pretty tough characters. Don't fret it.'

'Hm.' Loren worked his jaw muscles thoughtfully. 'Want some gum?'

'No thanks.'

'Thought not.'

A smoke streaked man in blue overalls approached the group wiping his face on a navy bandanna. He scuttled alongside Kanulf for a moment jabbering and leapt back anxiously as the shock-haired patriarch stopped in his tracks and barked,

'What's this nonsense Kleiper? You saying this Bloom isn't Bloom?'

'It looks like Bloom sir but it isn't.'

'Not Bloom? Looks like! Be clear!'

'It doesn't appear to be true Bloom. It shares major characteristics but it doesn't check out. My guess is it could be a mimic organism. It's probably harmless. I'll need further tests but...'

'Well let's not get too up tight about accuracy or anything,' roared Kanulf. 'I mean its not as if anyone's life relies on you being right is it. Don't give me your damned guesses Kleiper. Give me an unequivocal report or you can go and handle a fire hose yourself and see how your theories stand up to 18,000 degrees Kelvin. The fire teams are to torch everything. Everything!'

'But I need samples,' the man whined.

'No you don't! We take no chances on voracious self replicating nanofunguses that no one can control and you have no had hard evidence on. It burns!'

Kanulf pushed past the dumb struck man and indicated for Enwyn to lead on.

They were coming to a building that only a few hours before had been the Old Hall, a magnificent three storey structure with elegant gables and mullioned leaded windows. There had been habitations on the site since 1606. There was now a half burnt shell. Two of the black clad operatives stood guard outside and Enwyn guided the party through the soot streaked wreckage down some steps and into the basement. Picked out by the hard beams from their torches was a wall that had been broken open exposing a cavity from which spilled a heap of rubble. Two more Black Set operatives stood guard in opposite corners. Draped over the rubble half in half out of the cavity was a shape glinting in the stabs of light. It was wrapped in black plastic sheeting torn in several places. Loren's heart gave a skip. Surely not! It was impossible to make out quite what lay amongst the soot and filth but the contours were disturbingly familiar. An image of lorries parked in a cold army barracks vehicle bay leapt to mind. There was a pervasive smell of corruption in the confined space.

Kanulf stood over the plastic wrapped form and when he spoke even his voice was more hushed than usual.

'So this is what created the suppression field allowing the intrusions to go unnoticed?' he asked.

'This and six others, yes,' answered Enwyn her voice taut.

'And that is definitely Tar coating the thing?'

'As near as we can tell. Tests on the earlier cases aren't conclusive yet.'

'The Delamere incident, hm, yes, interesting. We need to know how that is done.'

Back in the darkness Loren moved closer to Amuna. Both his palm tattoos were itching for some reason and he scratched the insides of his closed fists with his fingernails as he pitched his voice low for her ears only,

'What is that thing Amuna?' he asked.

'Something new for us. We think possibly a Slumehig, a type of anaerobic unlife that can lie undetected for years if required and then be triggered to project...'

'...a Behelian suppression field – yes I got that.'

Amuna looked at him possibly with respect, possibly not. The goggles made it hard to tell. She had kept her voice low too. It was a small concession and Loren was grateful.

'Also known as an amnesia field or mind shroud,' she added. 'I keep saying be patient Loren. Stick it out. You will get your answers - at the right time. You always were hasty.' Her amazingly mellifluous voice was having the same hypnotic effect on him as when he made his regular reports to London, and it made no difference that her appearance did not match up with any of the images he had fantasized for her. The realization made him feel confused – though in a good way...possibly!

Kanulf boomed on giving orders,

'Crate this one. I want it back at the centre. Incinerate all the rest when they are found. No evidence – got that! No evidence, not a scrap. None of this must get out. Official line is Bloom outbreak and any sightings are the result of hallucination, smoke inhalation, bumps on the head, whatever twist you want to give it. Clear?'

'Yessir.' Enwyn didn't quite salute but the effect was the same. Kanulf waved a hand in Loren's direction.

'Loren, over here.' Loren manoeuvred his way to the man's side accompanied by Amuna who knelt down for a closer look at the plastic wrapped body-Slumehig-whatever. Kanulf did not drop his voice.

'Loren, you're here because it's time to advance your involvement in a side of Protectorate activities which your gifts indicate you to be suited to. You've got to hit the ground running.'

'Already breaking the sound barrier sir.'

A brief expression of distaste flashed across Kanulf's face. He stared at Loren before looking away and continuing,

'Good. Now, question is how much do we put you in the picture? Personally I'm for chucking you in, see how far you get under your own steam.'

Amuna spoke over her shoulder as she knelt by the Tar shape. She had lifted her goggles to get a better look at it.

'Don't pay any attention to him Loren. He's out to rag you. Your reports have been impressing the chrome off him for some time now. You wouldn't be here if you hadn't made an impact.'

'Well all I'm good for at the moment is asking questions because no one is volunteering much information.'

'That's right. It's tough out on the edge,' gritted the old man. 'But there's nothing like having the ground open up and spew a slab of hell right on your shiny new shoes to get a person motivated. So, go back to the field lab at Saighton barracks. See what you can make of this…thing. You've run into them before.' He began to pick his way out of the stink filled basement. 'Give me your report asap.'

Amuna spoke from her position on the floor,

'Is that really the best use of his time Kanulf?' The old man stopped and turned.

'What do you mean Shree?'

Amuna faced round into the room. Loren saw that her eyes were total green on green, no whites, like emeralds. She was looking at him as she spoke to Kanulf,

'He's a field man, not one of your lab lubbers like Kleiper. Send him after the girl.' She was trying to get to her feet. This time Loren helped her; he bent over to take an arm, his face only a foot from the oily shimmering surface of the Tar mass. Kanulf was obviously thinking over Amuna's suggestion,

'But we don't even know where she…'

A single blood red eye opened in the tar not twelve inches from Loren's face. He vaulted backwards across the narrow space dragging Amuna with him. She gasped in pain and collapsed against a wall.

'It's alive! The damn thing is alive!' he yelled brandishing his stun grip in one hand. No one else in the room had moved a muscle. Kanulf ran to help Amuna fussing her quietly as she struggled to her feet.

'It's OK,' said Enwyn unperturbed. 'It doesn't pose any kind of threat. It's alive…' she hesitated. 'That may be the wrong term. Let's say it's active, but immobile. And definitely inoperative.'

123

Kanulf was handing Amuna her stick and trying hard not to glare resentfully at Loren. Loren picked up Amuna's dropped torch and shone it at where the eye had appeared but it had sunk back beneath the slick of goo. His spine felt like ice.

Amuna's outfit was generously smeared with filth but she appeared not to notice as she adjusted her goggles.

'You've got to use him properly Kanulf,' she continued as if nothing had happened. 'Analysis isn't his bag. We all know that.' She moved across to Loren.

'You don't smell so bad. But let's get out into the open air. It'll do us all good.' She leaned on his arm and noticed him wince as she gripped tight. 'Are you hurt?' In answer Loren rolled back his sleeve to reveal a row of tiny inflamed indentations where the Marsh Kraken had taken a chomp. 'We should get that looked at. Could turn nasty.'

'Aw, it's alright.'

'No, it's not. C'mon,' she said heartily, amused by Loren's obvious discomfort. 'Help me up the stairs.'

Kanulf caught up with them outside. The old man flashed him a look that could have meant any number of things, all of them disapproving but he took Loren by the shoulders and led him to one side as two Black Set operatives rushed past with a sling bag on poles and disappeared into the ruined building.

'Amuna is right,' he rasped. 'She usually is. You need to be brought fully into the picture. Everything about this situation is N.R.D.A.'

'Sir?'

'Normal Rules Don't Apply, Loren. You are leaving the world you know behind. Say goodbye to whatever universe you thought you inhabited.'

'What are we talking about sir?'

Amuna took a medi kit from one of the many pockets in her outfit and proceeded to tend to Loren's arm as they spoke. She worked quickly and without fuss and Loren felt it would be ungracious to refuse such attention. Truthfully he was grateful for it, the bites were beginning to be a problem.

'Kanulf, call me Kanulf. Everyone else does and I'll have to get used to it sooner or later Loren.'

The zippered up sling bag was now being hauled out to a low truck with no markings and bundled into the back. A Black Set operative banged on the roof and the vehicle roared away.

Amuna had finished with the arm and Kanulf indicated that Loren should follow him. They strode off towards the eastern edge of the village walking in silence for several minutes. The night air smelt of crushed pine needles mixed with the odd whiff of smoke. People could be heard running purposefully through the darkness in all directions. There were occasional radio squawks from nearby. At the edge of the fields Kanulf stopped.

'It'll be dawn soon. Dawn is good for us Loren. Light is our friend. Are you chewing?'

'Yessir – Kanulf.'

'Gum?'

Loren nodded.

'Got any spare?'

'Just this.' Loren held out a small rectangle of folded silver paper in a grimy palm. Kanulf didn't break eye contact as he reached down, unwrapped the thin pink wad and popped it into his mouth.

'Filthy habit Loren. Hard to come by these days.'

'You're welcome sir.'

A pause. Both men stared at the first lavender streaks of light that heralded the approaching dawn. Flakes of soot were falling like some perverse version of snow.

'All this,' a big sweep of the arm taking in the whole horizon and the village behind them, 'All this Loren, is about one person, one profoundly special and important person. We were charged to protect her and now she's missing. We have to find out where she is.'

'And where do we think she might be sir?'

'We have no bloody idea! She, Loren, is possibly the most important individual you will ever get to meet, if you ever do get to meet her. She – and get this clear – she is the reason we are here. You, me, Amuna, out in the field for the first time in a five year, Enwyn, the Black Set, the Guardians, everyone. She is important.'

'Got it sir...Kanulf.'

'Census Officer Loren I'm going to turn your world inside out. I'm going to tell you what's behind all that you have seen here today, what's behind the anomalies you've been tracking for me for the last eighteen months and I'm going to answer the questions that have kept you awake at nights. You will thank me and you will hate me. But you will stay sane because I need you that way. I am going to give you the chance to repay our enemies in kind for the way they have treated this piece of rural England.'

'Who is she Kanulf?' Loren said this a bit more brusquely than he'd intended.

'Ah, now, that is a question. Who is she? And what is she? Well, there is no short or easy answer you would believe immediately. So we must take this a step at a time. Are you sure your arm's OK?'

'Oh yes sir.' And it was; the irritation had stopped.

Loren's senses had alerted him to a couple of shapes approaching cautiously from under the blackness of the nearby trees. They wore bulky night vision goggles pushed up on their heads. Kanulf spoke quietly into the shadows,

'Ah Enwyn. Join us.' She and her bodyguard had arrived as silently as moths.

'One of the missing Guardians has been found,' she said.

'Oh!' Kanulf looked stricken. 'Was it…?'

Enwyn shook her head. 'No sir. Margaret Tansley, the headmistress. Evacuation of the village is complete and all routes out of the village locked down. Cody Conmar is nowhere in Clayton Bar.'

'That is no more than we would have expected. Do we have any indication yet which routes she might have been taken?'

'No vehicles were spotted leaving during the attack. She could be on foot.'

'So where? North? South? And how? The railway line! There's a request stop to the south by Rowton!'

'We checked whether any trains had gone through recently. One had, headed for Shrewsbury and the south. We have intercepts onto it.'

'Good. What about north? Is the northern line within reach of the village?'

'Yes, at Vicars Cross Embankment. That's a request stop there too. But nothing went through tonight.'

'Check again. Unscheduled runs sometimes get added. We have to cover every eventuality. And pray to the skies we're not too late.'

Enwyn gestured to one of the Black Set bodyguards who began to murmur into his face mike.

'It'll be dawn soon,' said Kanulf sounding a little subdued. 'I don't like that we've been out manoeuvred at every stage of this exchange.' He rallied like a man shaking himself from a dream and snapped, 'Evacuation complete? Perimeters tight?'

'Yes.'

'Incinerate the village. Nothing gets out.'

'Incinerate the village!' The horror in Enwyn's voice echoed Loren's own profound shock. What was the old man thinking?

'But Kanulf, you can't!' Enwyn protested. 'It wasn't Bloom, Kleiper said so.'

'Are you sure of that Enwyn? Sure enough to take a chance on it being some slightly less lethal variation engineered so we don't know how to deal with it; something that can lie dormant like the Slumehig? I'm not. And I have to be sure.'

Out across the fields faint light was rising over the line of Peckforton Hills to the east making an impressive pyramid silhouette of Beeston Castle mound. It lit up Enwyn's stricken face. She was cowed.

'Is this really necessary Kanulf?'

Kanulf's cold gaze was answer enough. He was not taking this decision lightly. She looked away, accepting and distraught. Loren's heart went out to her.

'It's too far gone Enwyn,' Kanulf continued. 'I'm sorry. It really is. Clayton Bar haven is lost. Infection is everywhere. It's not just the Bloom or possible un-Bloom, it's the goddam boojums coming out of every corner and crotch. This place has been seeded! Look how they hid these new abominations right beneath us. A suppression field of their own. Who would have thought it! We found them but what else is lying in wait here? We ... I cannot take that chance. We've absolutely no idea what is going to hatch and rip this place apart if we don't cleanse the field right back to zero.'

Enwyn was made of stern stuff. She didn't plead or argue. It clearly broke her heart but she gave the order to the Black Set operative with a steady voice,

'Initiate field zero.'

The operative relayed the order into his face mike without hesitation.

'We have fifteen minutes to get clear before it starts Kanulf,' Enwyn said neutrally.

Loren realised he had braced himself. Whatever was said or done here he would not unravel. He would let it wash over him maintaining an ice clear focus on all that happened. He would make no judgement. He would let it all pour in, information, details, impressions. Assimilation and understanding would come later. He unconsciously stroked the tattoos on his palms. He watched Kanulf's face like a hawk. The old man became brusque again, his voice commanding.

'Loren, we'll continue our briefing at the barracks. Let's get moving. But first you must excuse me. I've got an old friend I must attend to.' He stalked off.

Loren swung in besides Enwyn as she followed the straight backed figure.

'What did that mean? An old friend?'

'He was a long time acquaintance of one of the Guardians,' she said without looking at him. 'One of the dead ones. They used to be married.'

They walked the rest of the distance in silence.

*   *   *

When dawn did break over the furiously burning Cheshire village of Clayton Bar Cody Conmar and Bella Dixon were already thirty miles away racing through the golden dawn on a train headed towards a future that would affect both the known and the unseen world.

'In order to maximise the limited resources available to a crippled post-Event country, the Recovery and Resettlement Programmes Act of 1994 made many radical decisions. For example it was decreed that control of all fuel would be centralised and subject to rationing. Even after the northern oil fields were reopened fuel was scarce. Privately owned vehicles were strictly limited and public transport systems given priority. Most people's daily work kept them close to where they lived but there were still plenty of personal and commercial reasons to travel, so the official thinking was that any transport systems operating locally or nationally had to provide the most service for the most people at most available times. In keeping with this policy every train route in the British Isles now had a designated number of request stops. Anyone could flag down any train at any time unless there was an officially valid reason for the train being unable to stop. Nominal sums were charged to transport travellers to their desired destination. In many cases the comfort level provided for passengers was crude but for the most part the system worked. Even though the system was inevitably abused by a small proportion of the population it was deemed a success overall.'

Entry from News Archive Services egl.postEventresources.co.uk by Jem Barnstable.

Sixteen
SLOW REVEAL

BY the time Cody, Bella and Josse, had reached the embankment at Vicars Cross a mile north of Clayton Bar, Cody's shock and grief had left her feeling disconnected from reality. Her mother was dead. Her father was dead. Ben was dead. Bee was probably dead too by now; how could she have possibly survived the other Shadow Hein? Cody wasn't really aware of the eastbound goods train grinding slowly to a halt or them clambering aboard. They settled into the fairly cramped rear portion of a carriage stacked with wooden crates and mailbags. Bella dropped some coins into a passenger honesty box bolted to the wall. Next to this was a large red push bell used to alert the driver when someone wanted to get off at the next stop. The honesty box would be emptied later by the driver, or a conductor if the carriage got linked up to a regular passenger service.

Bella made Cody as comfortable as possible on some pull down seats and attended to the stings she had got from the spore cloud by applying an unpleasant smelling ointment.

The train was bound for Manchester but they swapped trains at Warrington and an hour later were approaching Preston. There weren't many people travelling so early in the morning but at least this next train had a proper passenger carriage and they had the compartment to themselves. Cody was still quiet but beginning to take more of an interest in the things around her. Josse was keeping a concerned eye on her but not trying to engage her in conversation. He sat fidgeting and staring out of the window or finding excuses to escape into the corridor outside where he explored up and down the length of the train. At one point he nudged Cody as she stared at the passing landscape through the misted window,

'Cody, would you like something to eat?'

He was perched on the seat opposite scratching at his chest and holding out an apple. The white criss cross scars on his fingers were very noticeable this close. Cody shook her head, no thanks, and turned to watch Bella in the seat nearest the compartment door. The large woman was tearing a tough looking loaf into hand sized chunks. She was still wearing her dark green gloves, which made the process messier than it needed to be, in Cody's opinion, not that she cared much about anything at the moment. Crumbs from the brittle crust were scattering everywhere. Bella's hand movements were clumsy and Cody suspected they might be giving her pain.

'I don't think I'm very hungry,' she said.

'You will be,' Bella said, not looking up. 'Eat something. It will help you keep your strength.' She held out a piece of the torn bread. Cody accepted it and chewed unenthusiastically.

'I need to ask you what happened back at the village.' Bella had unslung her shoulder bag onto the seat and was now taking a number of items from a second bag strapped around her waist. 'We are not out of the woods yet and any information you have might prove helpful before we reach Wrayhaven. We may run into problems on the way. We'll have to change at Preston and again at Carnforth. We will be vulnerable then before we reach the Lake District.' As she spoke Bella was pouring something hot from a small stainless steel flask into a cup.

'Is that where we're going, the Lake District? The line stops at Windermere, I know that, so I guess that's our destination. Is it?' Josse asked brightly.

Bella ignored him and handed the drink to Cody with a smile.

'It is a tonic. It will do you good,' she urged encouragingly.

Cody took it. It smelt herbally with a hint of some sharp fruit and possibly honey. She took a couple of sips then a large swallow. It warmed her immediately.

'You need a draught of something healing to firm the mind,' Bella nodded looking pleased. 'You have been through a great deal tonight,'

'I'll say,' added Josse biting into a chunk of the bread and picking up a square of hard looking cheese. 'There was fire everywhere in the village and I heard people shouting they'd sighted Bloom too.'

'They're all dead,' Cody said lethargically.

'Who?' asked Josse, mouth full.

'Probably everyone. Mum. Ben. Bee. People in the village. Dad too, even though that was ages ago. Aren't you worried about your father Josse?'

'Not really. He can take good care of himself. He always has. We ran into all kinds of scary situations in France. Got surrounded by a Bloom barrier once and ...'

'I'm sorry about what happened to your family Cody,' interrupted Bella, 'Really I am. What did you see at the cottage?'

Cody stared glumly at the toes of her boots. The very last thing she wanted to do at the moment was answer questions about the turmoil churning up her emotions and reliving the horrors of the previous hours. She glanced up to say something and saw a familiar face passing the corridor window behind Bella. There weren't many people on the train but she would swear it had been Bron! In took only a second and her friend has passed out of sight.

'I have to use the loo Bella. Do you know which way they are?'

'Not really. There's usually one each end of the carriage. Do you need me to come with you?'

'Whatever for,' Cody almost laughed. What an extraordinary thing to say! And even more oddly Bella looked put out for a moment, angry even.

'No, I can find it myself.'

She was almost certain a look passed between Josse and Bella as Cody got up to leave but her eyes may have been playing tricks – there was a slight shimmer of colour on the edge of objects, as if she was looking at them through a distorting piece of glass. She closed the compartment door behind her and walked in the direction Bron had taken.

Her friend was waiting around the next bend of the corridor.

'Bron! Oh Bron, it is you! What are you doing here? How did you know where I was?'

'I followed you,' said Bron as if it was the most natural thing in the world.

'Why don't you come and join us in the compartment? We're the only ones in there.' She reached for Bron's arm but the girl pulled away.

'I don't think so Cody. I may be more use to you if I stay in the background.' This was typical of Bron's fierce independence, her dislike of being thrust into company, or of having to mix or be in any way sociable, so Cody didn't press the matter. But she was desperate to know more about the attack on the village.

'Bron, what happened back at the village? I don't really know and I'm getting asked questions.'

'Cody listen. I haven't much time and I can't be seen with you right now. You mustn't tell anyone I'm here.'

'But Bron...'

'No! Listen. I was supposed to protect you and I failed you. I wasn't there.'

'How could you be. We...'

'Cody listen to me! You are still in great danger.'

'I know that. But I have to find someone Bron, somewhere in the Lake District. We could get there together, you and me. We could. We could get off the train at the next stop and we could make our own way. We've run off to places before. Why not now?'

'Because I don't know what to do, and the danger is too great. Cody, I was supposed to protect you, to at least keep a close watch on you and I failed.'

'No you didn't. I'm OK, see. Here I am. And so are you.'

'That's not what I mean. I...I am a coward. I am an exile and a coward and I must stay hidden because...'

There was a sudden clash of doors being thrown open from the next carriage. Cody stepped back to peer round the bend in the corridor.

'It's OK, it's only Josse,' she said turning back to Bron but there was no one there. Josse came round the corner and beamed,

'Oh hi! Did you find the loos? They're usually a bit primitive on these things.'

'Josse! What do you want?'

He looked at her, startled for a moment.

'Bella told me to go and find the conductor to pay our fare. He hasn't shown up yet and she doesn't want him barging into our compartment bothering us, Bella said. She's got a little primus cooker going in there. She's a weird one isn't she. Are you alright?'

'Yes. Yes, I'm fine.'

'You look a bit white you know. Perhaps you should eat something like Bella said. That cheese is a bit strong though.' His cheeky grin was infectious even if Cody didn't feel much like smiling herself. She flicked a quick glance up the rattling corridor as a couple of people came out of a compartment and ran into the conductor going from passenger to passenger. He was asking for fares. No sign of Bron.

'Look, there's the conductor. You go and pay him,' she said, as brightly as she could muster. 'I'll meet you back at our compartment. Perhaps I do need something to eat.' Her eyes were still playing tricks and when she tried to smile at him the best she could manage was a crooked twist of the mouth. He looked at her nonplussed as she pushed past him bracing herself against the sides of the carriage.

'OK Code. See you back there.' He watched her go until she turned the corner.

What had happened there? She couldn't have imagined Bron, could she? Surely not. If only her head didn't feel like cotton wool. Her thoughts were so sluggish, so…heavy somehow. It was like wading knee deep through a cloying dream. There was an awful coppery taste in her mouth. She reached the door of their compartment and paused for one last glance up and down the corridor. Still no sign of Bron. She went in, staggering slightly against the doorframe, and sat down heavily.

Do It Properly
by Jean Frecé.

Oncely, twicely	Please don't ramble	Don't confuse me
Say it very nicely	Complicate or scramble	Baffle or bemuse me
Make it witty	Phrase it tautly	Think alertly
Make it pithy	Snug and shortly	Syntax curtly.
Put it quite precisely.	All without preamble.	Why do you accuse me?

(From Lethal Lullabies & Cautionary Tales.)

Seventeen
TRUTH AS TOLD

INSIDE their compartment Bella had indeed got a small pocket-primus stove going on the fold down table and was adding ingredients to an already bubbling pot of what smelled like soup. She greeted Cody as she poured water from an army issue canteen and returned the container to a hidden pocket in her voluminous coat.

'Ah, there you are. Did Josse find you?' She didn't really seem interested in the reply because Cody never answered and Bella remained focused on her little pan. It really did smell appetising. Cody took a seat.

'I am sorry to press you dear but there are things I need to know. Do you feel alright about that?' Bella spoke as she stirred the pan.

Cody didn't really want to answer more questions. She was feeling terribly groggy but found herself saying,

'Oh, I suppose so.'

'You were going to tell me about what happened at the cottage.'

'Was I. Oh yes. We found Bee badly hurt, Mum and I did. The cottage had been attacked Bee said. Everything was all frosted up. The bees were dead. Horrible black things had surrounded the place – Shadow Hein, mum called them.'

'You saw Shadow Hein?' said Bella taken aback.

'Yes. At least three of them. They killed mum and Ben. Bee too probably.' The tears were welling up in her eyes but she fought to hold them back.

'You are very lucky to be alive if you were close enough to see Shadow Hein. Thank goodness you were able to get away. How did you manage it?'

Once again some deeply buried instinct curbed Cody's natural inclination to tell the full truth and she simply said,

'It was all very confusing. I remember running very fast. That was after Bee said something to me. In the same kind of words you used. Back at the Grove. Old Tongue it was in.'

'But you must remember more details surely. As I have said any information may be of great help...'

The door slid open and Josse stepped in waving three tickets. He was scratching absent mindedly at his arms and chest.

'Josse,' said Cody, relieved to distract attention from herself. 'You got our tickets.' She felt ashamed at this lame attempt and started again. 'You're scratching. Did you get stung by the spore cloud too?'

'No, well perhaps a little. Your stings are settling down a bit.'

Cody put her fingertips to the little red marks on her face and arms and they had stopped itching. The redness had gone too. Bella's ointments must be as good as Bee's.

'Why don't you lie down Josse,' Bella said making a little open handed gesture of invitation at Josse as he sat down on the opposite seat. He looked puzzled for a moment, then his eyes began to flicker and his face slid into a dull expression.

'You look exhausted,' said Bella soothingly.

'I'm ... yes I think I am actually,' he said. ' Didn't get much sleep last night.' He slid his legs up onto the seat in a fluid motion and snuggled into a curled up position facing the wall, all done with his eyes shut.

Bella moved to sit beside him and began stroking Josse's head absentmindedly as she turned to Cody. The rhythm of his breathing indicated he was in a deep sleep. At this moment Cody envied him. Her own eyes felt as if there were angels sitting on them – a phrase her mother used often. The rocking motion of the train was soporific, hard to resist. She'd have given anything to let this day come to some kind of end, although the chances were her dreams would be equally bizarre.

'How do you know it was Old Tongue that I used?' Bella asked watching Cody's face with a quiet intensity.

'I dunno. It sounded like the way Bee spoke. I think. She said I was to get to the Grove. Find someone called Veriman. After that we were supposed to get - to Wrayhaven.'

'Which is exactly what we shall do. It is in Cumbria in the Lake District, not far from Windermere, as our clever little companion here suggested.' She continued stroking Josse's head with her gloved hand. 'With changes of train it will probably take us several hours but we shall get there. And then you will be safe. We shall all be safe. You, me and dear Josse here.'

Even with her thoughts moving like treacle Cody couldn't shake off the feeling that there was something not quite right about Bella Dixon. Some quiet inner voice of caution kept whispering warnings. Trusting someone she didn't know properly was unwise. But when it came down to it what choice did she have? Almost everyone she knew was dead. The woman knew more about what was going on than Cody did certainly. She knew about Veriman and Wrayhaven. And she had a silver phial like Bee had and spoke Old Tongue. Perhaps her oddness was something to be wary of, or perhaps it wasn't really all that significant. It was hard to concentrate. Her mouth had that coppery metallic tang that made her head swim. She wanted to rest but Bella's voice kept on.

'Cody, there are a great many things I think you should know and I want to answer whatever questions you may have. I have been sent to protect you and bring you to safety at Wrayhaven. In the Lakes there will be time to teach you about who you are and the special abilities you possess.'

Cody knew this was stuff she should be paying attention to but her concentration kept slipping. The rocking train calmed her like a lullaby.

'What do you mean Bella, special abilities?'

'You are a unique and gifted individual Cody Conmar. Unfortunately your *gifts* are mostly asleep within you. If you are to have a chance to survive against the kinds of things encountered tonight back in your village you need to have those abilities awakened. You must be able to defend yourself, the way you did when your school mate attacked you at the Grove. Do you recall what you did there?'

'No, not really.'

'No matter, but being able to unleash your gifts as and when you need to is the only way you will be able to fulfil your destiny.'

'What destiny Bella?'

'You are an Eloin. That is not a name you will have come across in your myths and tales at the fayres. An Eloin is a unique kind of human being in a number of ways. For example you are far older than you remember. Even your true name is different from the one you bear now. You are unable to recall anything of your earlier life, is this not so?'

Cody acknowledged this was true. She had always been dissatisfied with the explanation of the mysterious 'accident' of three years ago to explain why she could recall nothing before her arrival in Clayton Bar. Bella's continued softly,

'There are many dangers around you Cody and you will need all of your lost memories and forgotten abilities to survive them. You have been kept unconscious of your true nature for too long now. You must awaken. And so you must tell me anything you can remember of what happened back at the cottage. Do you understand?'

The most Cody could manage was to murmur, 'Yes.'

'Good. Now, were you given anything at the cottage?'

As if in a dream Cody felt her hands gliding to the shoulder satchel beside her and unbuckling the straps. She dipped inside and unzipped the inner pocket. When she withdrew her hand the two silver rings were nestled in her palm. The tiny crystal phial remained in the zip up pocket alongside the old copper penny she always carried for luck. She held out the rings to show Bella. The woman's body had become very still. Something about this felt wrong but Cody had no idea why. It was as if both of them were engaged in some quiet interior struggle of their own. Bella still hadn't moved a muscle.

'That is good Cody. You were given these at the cottage, yes?'

'Yes.' her own voice sounded far away.

'By whom.'

'Bee. Bee gave them to me.' Why was she saying these things? She must be more careful, more guarded.

'Do you know how they are used?'

'No. I feel I should, but it keeps slipping away from me, like fishtails.'

'Pardon? Please explain.'

'Fishtails. It's like chasing a shoal of fishtails always getting away from you, brushing your fingertips but always out of reach.' Bella stared at Cody completely bewildered.

'So you have no idea how to use them...for anything?'

'I have seen them used. I think they are what defeated the Shadow Hein. But I have no idea how they are used. I know they must be kept safe until we reach Wrayhaven.' Cody's voice sounded flat in her own ears as if she were in a dream. Her hand closed protectively around the two silver circles and her arms crossed guardedly against her chest.

'Do you think they are safe with you until we reach Wrayhaven?'

'Yes.'

'You are right. They are in your keeping for now. We have many barriers to cross yet and who knows, the use of them may come to you.'

'Will there be more things like we saw back at the village Bella?' The large woman seemed taken aback by this question, or maybe by the fact that Cody had asked a question at all, but she rallied quickly,

'There may well be Cody Conmar, or worse. The dark forces lined up against us have many creatures and powers at their call. Who knows what we may be accosted by. But I have hope that you will begin to remember. I must help you to unpick the shroud that has been placed around your mind. Your enforced slumber must end. If you had known how to use these rings perhaps you could have saved your mother and the others. Such a waste!' Bella's was agitated as she said this. It occurred to Cody how little she would like to be on the wrong end of this woman's fury.

Cody kept wishing she could sleep. Her eyelids felt like leather and her limbs trembled with exhaustion. But Bella talked on and on. Words that promised explanations poured out of her but turned abruptly sideways and left Cody with no sense of what had been said. Why was she so exhausted? Her muscles ached.

As she peered hopelessly at Bella there was a flick of movement past the corridor window. It was Bron walking with her eyes focused intently on Cody's face. A brief intense moment of exchange, almost a spark of understanding, passed between them, and then she was gone!

Something profound had just happened.

Cody was no longer feeling so sleepy. Her mind exploded with pin pricks of light. A charge of expectation was building up in her mind as if readying itself for some coming announcement that would throw open doors and change her life. She listened to Bella with a rapidly beating heart. It was as if a spell had been broken. The large woman continued unaware of the change in her young audience,

'What was done was done for your own protection and many opinions agree it was the right way for you to be protected. But things have changed.' *They certainly had.* 'Events back at the village prove this. It is time to begin your proper awakening so that your abilities can emerge. I believe this is your only hope, though I freely admit not everyone agrees with this view.'

'But who wishes me harm?' asked Cody making sure to keep her voice flat.

'That is a complicated answer. Possibly everyone, in their own ways, is a danger to you, even those who kept you hidden at Clayton Bar.

They made sure you remained unconscious of your true nature, kept you helpless, reliant on them. Possibly they were afraid of what you might become. Now we are being pursued because of this mistake.

'There are forces at war in the shadows of the world, battling for the fate of humanity, Cody. There are forces of light, Aelim, and those bent on malice who would use you for their own ends, Chameleons. However, despite whatever protestations these so called forces of light would throw up in their defence, their motives are not always entirely free from self interest.'

Cody listened intently, all her senses buzzing with heightened attention. She said nothing. This was a time for listening. There were windows about to open in her mind again, she could feel it. Her old sensitivity to the emotional charges surrounding her was returning – triggered by that contact with Bron.

'There is so much to tell you and none of it simple, so let me be as plain as I may. Aelim regard themselves as saviours. Chameleons are undeniably darker with sinister motives and are widely condemned as such. But there are individuals who fall into grey areas and may be for either force. It is almost impossible for anyone to be entirely sure. Both sides are seeking to control you.'

'I know the legends and tales about Aelim and Chameleons Bella. Are you saying they are true?'

'Not exactly as told by your tale spinners; but in essence, yes. The tales are true.'

'What side are you on?' asked Cody forgetting to maintain the monotone in her voice. She knew that direct questioning could provoke unguarded emotional reactions and she was keen to see what she could pick up in Bella's response.

Bella sighed and looked out at the early light of the day rushing past beyond the carriage windows before replying. She was making the cat's cradle web of threads in her hands that Cody had seen her use with Jesmina back at the Grove.

'There is a third party in the struggle; a human element dedicated to fighting the darkness and balancing the excesses of those claiming the light. These people too do not appear in your myths and tales, not by name anyway. I am of that third party called Sufinam. We are of humanity. It is we who are the balancing point of destiny. We, you and I, Eloin and Sufinam, and the many like us, are the ones with most at stake in this conflict. It is our fate that the Shadow Wars are fought over. Let me show you something.'

Bella tugged gingerly at her gloves to reveal maggoty white, almost skeletal fingers covered in a tracery of scars. Cody stared in fascinated horror at the tips of each finger. It was these that were most shocking. There were no nails – in fact the ends of fingers and thumbs were like nothing Cody had ever seen before. Horny tips of brittle husk extended from above the first knuckle of each digit. The flaking crust was cracked showing red splits that covered the skin. The condition that was obviously very painful. Cody felt sick.

'The Chameleons did this to me. This is the kind of thing they do. They tore away the ends of my fingers and experimented on me leaving me unable to touch anything with love or sensitivity or sensation ever again. I escaped and have fought them ever since in word and deed, in ice fields, on mountains, within abandoned cities, across sun baked plains and rain swept marshes, through cave systems and amongst jungles.' Bella removed her glasses to reveal eyes encrusted with a network of scars that pitted the eye sockets. The orbs themselves glittered wetly like grey marbles, no iris, no pupil, just an oily grey. Cody could have wept to see the pain gouged into the flesh there. And perhaps more significantly she sensed this time that what Bella said was true. The pain of her emotions harmonised completely with her words.

Bella continued,

'I am committed to the defeat of those that did this to me and if possible to their total destruction. I am also ashamed to say that often it is hatred that drives me on. Revenge I suppose for what they subjected me and many others to. Part of my personal battle is to see you kept free of their clutches. I intend to that you will be allowed to understand the proper nature and deployment of your gifts. Many people will benefit from your full awakening. I hope to be by your side when that happens.'

Cody was impressed by the intensity that glowed in Bella's face, and by the conviction in her voice. No wonder the woman was disturbing to be around. Look what she had gone through. She was deserving of compassion not wariness...and yet...!

Bella replaced her glasses with the awkward horn encrusted fingers and slowly tugged her gloves back on.

'So you are not alone in this fight Bella? What about those in the village who protected me. What about my parents? What about...Bron?'

Once again Bella hesitated before answering, busying herself with the food she was heating on the little stove. She crumbled some dried ingredients into the pot.

'Before I tell you what you must hear next you must know that everyone in the village had the highest motives in protecting you. They were brave people, Sufinam like myself many of them. This group of Guardians were your dedicated custodians against those who would harm you, and those of your kind. The people you knew as your parents ... were not your parents. Your true parents perished a long time ago. Mary and Teddy Conmar were given you into their care three years ago after an accident in which those close to you perished. They were brave and selfless Guardians and they paid for their dedication to you. No one expected the attack to be so overwhelming or swift. It took everyone by surprise.'

'I was being protected by other people in the village?'

'Oh yes. Many were involved. There were defences everywhere. It should have been impregnable.'

'Defences, such as the sentinel stones?' gasped Cody in a sudden moment of insight.

'Indeed, as I said to you at the Grove. All this was because you were thought too vulnerable to fend for yourself. But, as I have said already, you have been kept unaware for too long. Your Guardians meant well but were misguided. They died and you must be exposed to the steps that will fully restore your original self so that you will not. You must face reality, relearn who you are - and no more imaginary friends.'

'Imaginary friends? What do you mean?'

'This Bron, this friend of yours who no one else sees or knows anything about. You fondly imagine her to be real don't you. But I tell you this, *Caer macuni chetha nul,* Bron is not real. This is a sign of how fractured your mind has become by having divisions erected in your consciousness. You have a past you cannot recall and only a short life that you can. You have been existing in a waking sleep and Bron is merely part of some fragmented dream. It was always a danger of keeping you so. I know it is not easy to believe but your friend Bron-is-not-real!'

'No. No, that can't be!' Cody's head fell into her hands. She was shaking.

'I am afraid so.'

Everything in Cody rebelled at this idea because although there was some distorted thread of truth in what she was hearing she sensed it wasn't the whole truth. It was like seeing something familiar in the ripples of a badly made mirror. Perhaps she was just too exhausted to deal with this right now. The stuffy atmosphere of the closed carriage was affecting her. Bella's words resonated with truth, or part truth at least. But was she right? Was Bron, dear Bron, merely a manifestation of her deluded mind?

She stared at the landscape rushing past the carriage window as if hoping to find some point of reference there. Josse's gentle breathing showed him to be still deeply asleep. Perhaps, in some dream of his own, he too was meeting and talking to people who were not real.

Cody could no longer find her own thought currents through the storm raging inside her head. She felt she could make sense of it if only she had time to herself. She felt so tired. Bella handed her some hot food and left her alone whilst Josse was shaken awake for his share of the small meal. Thankfully they ate in silence.

It was a huge relief when signs for Preston Station began to appear at the windows. Bella told them to gather the few things they had brought with them and be ready to change trains. She herself was stuffing things into her massive pockets.

'Stay close to me,' she insisted staring pointedly at Josse. 'We have no idea what we will meet. There may be nothing, but be alert.'

'Yeah,' laughed Josse. 'This country needs more lerts.' He sniggered. Cody did too, more from embarrassment than because it was funny. Bella ignored the levity and bustled them down the corridor as the train pulled into the massive vaulted shadows of Preston station.

Eighteen
CHILL STRIKE

THE Victorian edifice of Preston station had been continuously added to throughout the twentieth century. It's daunting mixture of stone, iron, brickwork and less substantial materials lacked all cohesion, and was poorly lit. Prefabricated cabins housed the current ticket office, kiosks and freight departments squatting incongruously along the platforms. Once brightly coloured they now blended into the general gloom that prevailed beneath the soot blackened glass panels of the roof high overhead. The entire upper regions of this imposing edifice were invisible amongst a jungle of filthy black girders and cabling.

Preston was an efficient enough station – but it wasn't pretty. Increasingly grimy layers of coal dust and muck had built up on every exposed surface since the steam and diesel powered giants had been brought out of retirement to serve the needs of a post-Event country with limited energy resources. In its present incarnation Preston Station was like a living museum dedicated to the ponderous glories of the Industrial Revolution.

As Cody, Bella and Josse alighted from their carriage the youngsters stared in wonder at a reconditioned steam locomotive almost shrouded by clouds of steam. It was like a great iron dragon, impressive even when at rest. Another lumbering colossus was pulling away from a distant platform and they watched it gathering speed in the grit thickened air before bursting out into the sunlit world beyond. Josse turned to Cody his face aglow with barely suppressed wonder. They both smiled at each other.

'Come on. Come on. We can't stand here dawdling.'

Bella herded them along to their connecting platform where the train to Carnforth and Windermere was waiting. Once she had them settled in an empty carriage she disappeared saying she had to make some purchases at one of the grimy kiosks and told them not to move from the carriage. Josse watched her go and turned to Cody, his face a mask of impish delight.

'I'm off for a look at that diesel engine over on the other platform. Won't be long. Cover for me if *she* gets back.' And he was gone, darting away out of the carriage and out into the steam and gloom.

'Of all the...!'

Actually, Cody didn't mind having a moment to herself but she was genuinely outraged at Josse for being so irresponsible. Bella was bound to be furious at his behaviour and Cody secretly hoped she wouldn't have to cover for him. Unlike Josse, whose attention flitted easily from one thing to another, she couldn't just throw off the anxieties heaped on her during the last twenty four hours. The hideous things she had witnessed coupled with all that Bella had told her about her 'real' history had effectively removed any impulse to be frivolous. It was like being forced to grow up suddenly and it didn't feel comfortable. Left here, alone in this gloomy old train on this gloomy old station didn't help lift the spirits much either. And it was so cold.

She wondered wistfully what had become of Bron. Bella couldn't be right about her. How could her old friend be imaginary? How? To be honest, right now, she didn't much care what was real and what was not. A dose of Bron's irreverent humour would be most welcome. What on Earth was all that about being a coward and a...what was it, an exile? What did it all mean? Her mind found it hard to hold onto these thoughts. They slipped sideways into odd corners of her mind becoming vaguer with every heartbeat, as unreal as...no!...don't even begin to accept that. Bron was real. She had to be!

She stared listlessly out of the window. A few shadowed passengers drifted through the murk making their way to their various destinations. There was no one near this part of the platform. Everywhere pipes and thick tangles of electrical conduit crisscrossed the exposed brickwork and girders. Nothing had any colour beneath the coatings of filth. What a dismal place. It felt exactly like being underground. A few thin beams of sunlight pierced the overhead gloom from holes in the roof but had no effect on the overall dreariness. It was hard to believe that people were enjoying a sunny day beyond the blackened walls of this dreary place.

Was the cold getting worse? Cody shivered and pulled the collar of her coat up and sank back into the thin cushioning of the dusty seats.

Her chin was sunk onto her chest and she was growing more wretched every moment. Unwanted memories were playing in her mind over and over again. It was impossible to turn off; her father taken from her, mother and Ben struck down by the Shadow Hein; images of Bee, the terrifying exchange with Jesmina and the vile squirming thing that had been in her chest. How on Earth had she known how to deal with that horror?

These moments of recall were interrupted by equally vivid memories of scenes she could not possibly have witnessed herself: someone using two silver rings to destroy a tapestry of writhing, mesmeric shapes; triumphant figures in chains stood before a waterfall; a sunbaked courtyard where some grotesque creature was reduced to scraps of leathery husk by the stare of an unarmed girl; a battle between two flying armies slaughtering each other amongst tumultuous storm clouds…and that face again, always that face, a youth's face merging with the worn features of a mature man, but always the same person – Lucian! Who was…?

She was startled by the loudspeaker announcing a slight delay to the Windermere train. She tried to shrug off her misery and shivered, noticing for the first time how beads of moisture were settling on the windows and the thick varnish of the carriage panelling. Her breath puffed into the still air like smoke. Her coat and hair were covered in dew-like droplets. The air was becoming painfully cold! Where was Bella? Where was Josse?

Annoyed she stepped out of the compartment and into the corridor intending to make her way to the platform and wait there. As she did so a flicker of movement at the corner of her eye made her turn her head. Behind her the floor and walls were covered with a dusting of frost! It was exactly the way the lane outside Bee's cottage had looked during the attack. Her hands went instinctively to the locket chain round her neck and the bag containing the two silver rings and phial. She backed towards the carriage doorway and the platform. Then her eyes slid up to the dark corner of the carriage ceiling and saw it - a quivering jellied 'something' hung suspended in the murk of the roof, a dozen obscene limbs anchoring it to the panelling. The thing was radiating a malevolence so chilling, so intense it was heart stopping. A ring of shadowy dots around its edge could have been eyes or mouths or clusters of stinging cells and wave after slow wave of brain numbing cold radiated from it,

146

congealing the very air itself. She could sense its malice, the pent up hatred pulsing against her mind and body, willing her to submit, to collapse, to die. Her heart began to hammer inside her chest and she felt the now familiar stirring of her phantom hand, but it was sluggish and painful.

She groped her way backwards towards the door, her numbed feet crunching on the coating of crystals. It was as if she was straining against some invisible, chilling wind, pressing backwards away, away from that grotesque *thing*. Somehow she made it to the open carriage doorway, stumbled and fell onto the platform. That too was frosted in ice. What was happening? Where was Bella?

A piece of litter brushed against her legs. The contact made her lurch away from the train but she couldn't get to her feet. She felt she was being exposed to a torrent of freezing water. Shreds of tattered paper were gusting everywhere trailing flimsy gossamer tails. She could feel the threads clinging to her like spiders webs to her hands.

All sense of contact with her surroundings began to fade. She collapsed onto the frosty ground, wiping her palms against the roughness to remove the disgusting shreds from her hands. The razored edges of the crystals made her cry out in pain. Close up she could see that the filmy things were not paper at all but translucent skins of mottled brown leather, like something a snake would shed, only they were supple and clinging. Her legs and body were covered in them and more drifted across her hair and face. She cried out in desperation, her breath white in the air,

'Bella! Josse...oh, Bron! Anyone!'

She could hear a scream, shrill and echoing around the vaulted darkness but surprisingly it hadn't come from her own mouth. It was the shriek of a locomotive entering the station. More of the filthy membranes drifted across her face – she was going to suffocate! The sickening things were coming towards her from every corner and shadow, tumbling and twisting like obscene flaccid spiders. If only she could fight back, but the numbing cold had robbed her of all ability to move. This must have been what had happened to Bee, her poor body frozen near-solid!

The shrill whistling was filling her head with pain as she sank face down onto freezing concrete. Ice crystals sharp as thorns were erupting out of the ground. Her body was being paralysed by frost. She dared not open her mouth for fear of breathing in the disgusting tatters. Her clothing had become cold-welded to the concrete. And no one was coming to help. Where was everyone?

Her vision became cloudy as more of the sickening skin-things shrouded her face. Her mind was shutting down with revulsion at being wrapped in the filthy tangles of wet membranes. She fancied she heard cries and sounds of footsteps. The intense cold was being hammered into her skull by that shrilling high pitched whistle. It didn't matter any more. She was sinking...sinking...

Then Bella was there ripping away at the things on her face and clothing, dragging at the gummy strands and tearing them to tatters. As she did so a high pitched whistle came from her lips. It barely registered on Cody's ears but the things clinging to her were dropping off like dead leaves, curling as they fell. Josse was there too on Cody's other side lifting her, his breath gusting in great clouds with the effort of tearing her loose from the frosted ground. It took several hefty tugs to drag her free of the concrete. A sudden flash of green light threw shadows racing in front of them but there was no time to check what it was. Bella seized Cody round the waist with one arm and ran along the platform carrying her like a sack of vegetables. Clouds of litter swirled and danced out of their way as they jogged past frozen milk churns and trolleys piled with crates. Everything glittered with frost. Bella was shouting at Josse,

'You stupid, stupid youth! You know the dangers Cody faces. When did you have your *brain removed!*' The stress she put on these last words made Cody feel nauseous for some reason. Josse was sobbing, but whether with cold or fear she couldn't tell.

They reached a carriage that was free from frost. Cody tried to protest, tried to warn them about the thing clinging to the ceiling but her voice was trapped in her throat. The door was jerked open and Cody was thrown bodily inside followed quickly by Josse who fell on top of her. Cody could barely crawl so numb were her limbs. Bella jumped onboard and slammed the door behind them before whirling round to charge up the length of the carriage.

'Get her into a compartment Josse,' she yelled over her shoulder. 'And lock the door this time. Do not leave!'

Josse forced a length of steel rod against the inside of the carriage handle effectively jamming it. Then he dragged Cody along the corridor behind him until they came to a compartment.

Somewhere in the distance something began to scream. A high pitched sound, painful to hear, almost on the very edge of audible sound. To Cody it was like being transported back to the village with unseen horrors erupting on all sides. Cody had no sense of time having passed when Bella appeared outside their compartment window and yelled,

'Stay put! You'll be secure if you stay exactly there. Try and get her warm Josse.' Then she raced along the platform towards the head of the train. Nothing seemed to be moving outside their window except drifts of mist against the darkness. There was no sign of any litter. Cody could swear there were figures slumped on the ground glittering with frost.

The train lurched suddenly, crashing its couplings. As the coldness in her skin subsided slightly Cody felt a thin trickle of blood pooling in her right ear and running down her cheek from where it dripped onto her collar. She must have cut herself when she collapsed onto the ice shards. Josse's face had a couple of gashes too but he wasn't saying anything about them. He helped to prop her up on a seat.

When Bella came crashing back along the corridor she gave a quick glance at them both through the carriage window before storming to the rear of the train again.

'Stay put! I will return in a moment.' They could hear doors slamming as she made her way through to the next carriage. They felt the train beginning to inch forward drawing slowly away from the station. The acceleration built up. There was a flash of green light from somewhere on the platform as they pulled away.

It was almost painful when they burst out into the sunlight. Preston station quickly fell behind as the train picked up speed. Cody could feel her face stinging, but oh, the light was so good to see.

Bella returned in a few moments, bristling and oblivious to the reek of smoke and some putrid fishy smell that had entered the carriage with her. With strong quick hands she tended to the cut on Cody's head pulling an array of medical packs and jars from her apparently bottomless shoulder bag. As she did so she explained that the driver had been told to get the train as far away as possible from the station. For some reason Cody had the suspicion they were probably the only passengers on board. No one else would have had time to board amidst all the commotion.

She couldn't stop trembling. Partly it was relief but mostly it was from the terrible terrible cold – that and this latest exposure to yet more

149

things from the realm of tortured dreams. Was this kind of encounter going to pursue her for the rest of her life? The chilling thought only made her tremble all the more.

Sitting on the opposite seat Josse regarded her with a terrible sadness that had reduced his features to a milky mask. This time they were barely able to raise a smile between them.

Profile on Bronco Mason, microlite salvager.

Bronco Mason discovered her passion for flying as one of the tough breed of early Ranger-Salvagers working government contracts in the early Recovery & Resettlement Programme of the 1990's. She became one of the first to successfully operate freelance and was one of only two recorded cases of surviving a crash landing in a Tar Zone. As an adventuress and poet she quickly became a living legend amongst the independently minded microlite culture. Her famous 'visionary experience' whilst riding out a storm above the wilds of Cumbria was used (without her permission) as inspiration for the popular ballad 'A GUARDIAN REFLECTS' (1998). Written from the point of view of a mythical Aelim Warrior who protects humanity it bears startling similarities to a portion of the Peaks Engravings, which, interestingly were only translated after the appearance of the ballad (1999-2000). It also has disquieting resonance with a W B Yeats poem published around 1917.

Article summary by Cullie Brown. Extract from egl.legendofbroncomason.co.uk
For text of ballad see: egl.albionlyrics.co.uk

Nineteen
REVIEW OF PERILS

'Coming events cast their shadows before them.'
Goethe.

BY 12.23 Census Officer Peter Loren and his superior Edwin
Kanulf, head of the Mainland Census Officiate, were one hundred and
twenty feet below ground at Saighton Barracks. The long arched tunnel
had rows of equipment lining the walls on all sides. Myriads of tiny lights
flashed discretely in the shadows. In front of them, parked in the centre of
a floor covered in power cables, was a cylindrical half-track vehicle. The
two men stood on a raised aluminium platform peering through a triple
glass observation window into the vehicle. This highly specialised pod-
craft had been flown to the old British Aerospace airfield at Broughton in
the middle of the night and airlifted by helicopter here to the army base.
The vehicle was a portable S.A.C.V. laboratory or Sealed Atmosphere
Containment Vehicle. Inside the sterile interior, radiant with blue light,
were three figures, two in bulky anti-contamination suits with self
contained air systems and Amuna Shree Jensen who was dressed exactly as
when Loren had first met her except for a pair of gloves and a small face
mask. The bubble suit with a 'Kleiper' name badge on the shoulder was
manipulating controls on a set of remote robot arms inside a further
bubble.

The Tar-body taken from the Old Hall ruins in the village lay on a
ceramic trough-table, dominated at either end by five foot high columns of
water. A mass of stainless steel callipers and probes was being controlled
by the figure in the second suit to prevent tar from flowing back into the
large incision made in the tacky mess. Kleiper was using long grips to
slowly extract a gloopy string of jellied egg shapes from the tar. Strands of
goo trailed between the cluster and the incision.

'What the heaving hell is that?' asked Loren in a level voice, unable to tear his eyes away.

'They are the semi-sentient little buggers that were able to mask the presence of the hostile forces we have just finished eliminating in Clayton Bar,' answered Kanulf without turning around.

'That tells me nothing - sir. What are they?'

'A weapon.' Kanulf flicked a switch on a speaker board ensuring their conversation became private. 'A Slumehig. The Chameleons breed them, as well as a host of other obscenities, in their subterranean breeding chambers. The thing itself is fairly harmless inside that Tar coating but we don't know what else may have been planted in there to stop us tampering. Could be a virus trigger or pretty damn near anything. So we are taking measures.' Kanulf adjusted the eye patch over his left eye.

'Were the ones in the Delamere lorries the same as this one?' Loren was hoping to shame his superior for keeping him in the dark about the results of the earlier find but he was whistling into a well. Apparently Kanulf had no embarrassment gland.

'At one time yes, but yours had already been terminated inside their casings. You remember the ground all around the trucks was reported as scorched? We have an idea how that was done and we have a pretty good idea who by. Five of your Tar bodies from Delamere Forest are now in a containment chamber twenty feet from this one surrounded by 800 gallons of pressurised salt water.'

'Salt water? What good is that?'

'Chameleon breed have an aversion to salt. Also to silver and copper. Salt is cheaper.'

'Is that what's in those columns next to our Tar baby?'

'It is. Quick flush in case of...surprises. The rest of your Delamere Tar-bodies were shipped to our Corsham underground complex outside Bath. We are lucky to have captured this one alive and it's destined to end up at the salt mines at Winsford. We have rather special deep storage and research facilities there, about a hundred and fifty miles of them.'

'Slumehigs are classed as unlifes, Loren,' said Amuna's honey voice from somewhere near Kanulf. Loren glanced at the off switch on the speaker board and Kanulf whispered,

'Separate link.' He tapped a tiny comms unit on his lapel. 'There are no secrets from Amuna.'

'But as anaerobes,' she continued from behind the observation window, 'They are rather special, even amongst Chameleon kind. Not needing oxygen they have very specialised uses. For example, for anything bred in one of their vats to be able to broadcast a Behelian field, or any kind of mind shroud, is an alarming new development. These can do it. Chameleons are adepts in the use of mesmeric control and trance states, but this...'

Kanulf nodded soberly in agreement.

'And you are going to tell me what Chameleons are, aren't you, apart from what I know from kids' tales and legends and such.' Loren was leaning his forehead against the triple glass. His breath misted against the slick surface. A readout within the white S.A.C.V. put the inner temperature at three degrees centigrade.

'Tell him Kanulf. It's time. And in simple terms too. He's been very patient so far - as patient as he is capable of being.'

Kanulf let out a sigh and turned an almost wary eye on the younger man by his side.

'You ready for this Loren? I said I was going to turn your world inside out. You're already over the threshold; now it's time to take a deep breath and dive into the labyrinth.'

Loren looked him squarely in the eye,

'I'm not going to suddenly lose interest at this point am I?' The older man shook his head as if to say, well it's your choice.

'Good god there's a CHILD in here!' came Kleiper's hysterical squawk over the intercom. Loren saw Amuna step close to the bubble suited figure and place a hand on Kleiper's arm. She began to talk to the distraught man in her low soothing tones, Loren couldn't hear the words. In a moment or two the figure went back to work manipulating the remote arms, cutting at the chilled glutinous tar, exposing the muck layered centre. Amuna waved encouragingly at the second suited figure to continue working the callipers. She appeared tiny next to their bulky forms. Her breath did not show in the chill environment.

'That is what we are up against,' said Kanulf, jaw clenched. 'That and a great deal more, Census Officer Loren. That Tar covered thing in there is a Chameleon weapon, a way to generate a Behelian or amnesia field to shield their own breed from detection. Yes, yes, you know this already. What you don't know is that the Slumehig consists of that cluster of jellied eggs sealed inside the Tar coating with the unconscious, though not dead body of a mammal, in this case a human child.'

Loren had steeled himself to take everything thrown his way with no emotional outbursts. Treat all facts, however grisly, as simply data. He intoned to himself – 'I will not unravel. I will not unravel. I have seen worse than this. I am a case hardened anomaly specialist,' – but he couldn't prevent a sense of incandescent outrage building as he listened to the details of this horror. He clenched his fists. A trickle of sweat ran down his spine. Kanulf continued,

'The child was probably snatched from some remote rural community for this very purpose. The Slumehig can keep the mammalian host alive for unconscionable lengths of time until its particular abilities are needed, at which point it is triggered into action. Feeding off the life force and tissue of the dormant human it is able to project the Behelian field and mask the presence of other entities bred in the Chameleon breeding vats. With five or six of these things operating you could mount an undetected attack of almost any size on a selected target.'

Loren opened his mouth to ask a question and Kanulf silenced him with a small gesture of his hand and a shake of the head.

'I'm coming to the Chameleons Loren. OK, so this is it in a nutshell. We are at war. Everyone on Earth is caught up in it but humanity at large has no idea what's going on. We have been at war for centuries, probably more accurately for millennia. There are three main protagonists: Aelim, Chameleon and human. Aelim are a higher order of beings forbidden to act directly in the conflict, except under very clearly defined conditions, of which more later. Chameleons are a devolved sub-set of uniquely gifted humans who have become predatory, one might almost say demonic.'

'Er...just a minute. You're telling me the myths and tales are based on truth? There really are Aelim, and these Chameleon beings?'

'The myths play down certain elements and exaggerate others for dramatic effect, but yes, essentially, the truths correspond. Chameleons prey on humans and wish to subjugate them. There are restraints on the worst of their excesses against humanity...for the most part. The overruling primary deterrent is a rigorously enforced Pact which forbids all overt and direct aggression against humankind. What you see in there,' Kanulf nodded towards the black shape on the table, 'and what you witnessed in Clayton Bar last night was an out and out transgression

154

against the Pact. This action will be severely dealt with. It releases certain restraints on our allies who may now begin moves to intervene directly against this heinous breed who acknowledge nothing except bestial power and have no interest except their own survival and expansion.'

Loren was quick to spot an opening,

'When you talk about allies you mean Aelim don't you?' Kanulf speared him with a look.

'Our allies are the Aelim, yes.'

'Angels?'

'Yes...and no. Very definitely yes and no.'

Loren pulled a face like he'd been given a mouthful of lemon but he pressed on,

'You said three main protagonists Kanulf. Humans are no kind of protagonists in the struggle you describe. They are victims only. So, there are the Aelim, angels-but-not-angels, the Chameleon bad guys...and who else? Who are you Kanulf? Who is this third force and what are you defending? And who is Amuna really? How come she...well, look at her.' He gestured inside the triple glass. 'No protective suit! And this girl you keep referring to. What is she?'

'That's one awfully compacted question,' smiled Kanulf without a hint of humour. 'Her name is Cody Conmar. She appears to be an ordinary twelve year old but she is neither a child, nor in reality, particularly normal.'

'None of this is half the shock you expect it to be Kanulf! I've had years dealing with things that would curdle most minds to porridge. My mind isn't going to suddenly implode at what you're telling me. All that I need are the facts. I can remain functional with facts. All the operatic grandeur of what you are trying to impress on me I will deal with later, when there isn't the pressure to get things done. Right now I have the overpowering impression that there is a great deal to be done – and it doesn't seem to me that we're doing it.'

Amuna's quiet laugh came from within the S.A.C.V.

'Isn't he something Kanulf. You have to admit he really is a turn up.'

Kanulf ignored this interruption. He addressed Loren directly, hissing his words with barely contained intensity,

'You clearly have not grasped the enormous implications of what I am telling you. Hardly surprising I suppose. Nor do we have time for lengthy explanations. You are right, there is a great deal that needs to be done. We need people of action. We need minds which will not curdle or implode. But let me put it in words, plain and direct: this is not just some boy scout adventure for gallivanting heroes Loren. What's at stake here is the fate of humanity itself. Not a thing that keeps everyone awake at night I grant you, because this war is fought in the shadows of this world - but there are those of us who shoulder some of the burden. The only long term hope any of us truly have is tied to the fate of individuals such as the young girl who was kidnapped last night. She is an Eloin, a very unique kind of opportunity for human evolution Loren. And we have misplaced her.'

'My question remains Kanulf. Who are you?'

'We are Sufinam. We are ordinary humans dedicated to protecting those amongst us who are extraordinary. Our sole purpose is to protect young Eloin, like Cody Conmar. '

'Sufinam? What is that? Some kind of secret order?'

'It is exactly that.'

'So you and the Black Set...'

'No! The Black Set are not Sufinam, though we often recruit from their ranks. The Black Set are not equipped to deal with the things we have to face. They are highly valuable foot soldiers but for Sufinam we require a great deal more than courage and the ability to handle high tech weaponry.'

'Like Enwyn Carter you mean.'

'Ah yes, we'd noticed you hanging around our young Amazon.'

'I have not been hanging around...!'

'Pestering her about...'

'Not pestering, dammit! I was interested in that black rod thing she carries everywhere.'

'Her Lodestaff. Specialist issue weapon,' said Kanulf smugly.

Loren refused to ask for an explanation he'd never get from the old bristle-whiskers. He swallowed hard and continued,

'I knew it was a serious piece of kit. She's been giving me some lessons, a demonstration really.' Loren's voice had a sulkiness to it that he wished he'd concealed better. 'I know how to handle myself with staff weapons; I've been taking Kendo classes for years, but...well, those staffs are really something else. I had my work cut out I can tell you. I've got the hang of them now though...I think.'

'If Enwyn's been giving you a workout with the Lodestaff,' contributed Amuna over the mike, 'I hope you wore protection. She's very agitated at present and doesn't hold back.'

'Neither do I!' snapped Loren. He could have sworn he heard Amuna chuckle.

Kanulf straightened his back and stared deep into Loren's eyes. He held the gaze, and held...and held, then,

'I know you don't son. And the damned Chams are going to regret it aren't they, especially if you hit them with as many questions as I'm getting.'

'And Eloin? You said Cody was an Eloin?'

Kanulf took a deep, shuddering breath.

'Short answer – Eloin are our hope. They are everything that is most precious about human beings. They are the potential in us all. They are what we must guard and protect with our lives because the sum of our lives is as nothing if they are wiped out.' Kanulf paused and adjusted his eye patch. 'There's much more to it of course but we don't have that kind of time. It is going to have to be a prolonged process of absorption for you.' Kanulf laid a hand on Loren's arm, an uncharacteristic gesture for the old man. 'Trust me son. You need time on this one.'

Amuna was guiding a reinforced steel container on wheels towards Kleiper. She slammed the seals shut on it the moment he lowered the slimy string of eggs inside. The container trailed a tangle of tubes and wires as she steered it behind a rubber seal door at the far end of the vehicle.

'What about the...the kid. You know, in the tar?' asked Loren, his voice soft.

'Beyond any hope of salvage I'm afraid. Best we can do is ensure no more suffering. That's all we could do for the others. They were too far gone.'

'Others? You mean the ones in the lorries?'

'Yes. Although the Slumehig themselves were terminated and most of the host bodies had died three of the victims were still functioning. They were almost impossible to identify. Their entire neural systems were totally incorporated into the parasite's. All we could do was put them out of their torment. Truth is, we have no idea how conscious they may have been or how long they'd been like that.'

'So you did manage to identify some of them?'

157

'We did with two from the Delamere bodies. One was a girl called Jenny Bartland and the other a lad called Adam Bowman.'

'I know that name. Went missing some while back. Poor kid. My bet is they'll all be registered on some missing file somewhere. Damnation Kanulf, this is…it's…it's beyond words!'

'Keep that fury lidded down Loren. I want you able to direct it at the minds behind this obscenity.'

'That's right,' interrupted Amuna coming back into the main chamber of the S.A.C.V. 'We are looking for a mind at work here. A true mind, not one of these devolved, semi-sentient creatures. They're little more than a collection of instincts bound by hatred.'

Loren was pacing up and down the observation platform scratching at his palms, simmering with a fury he needed to unleash. He spat and unwrapped a piece of the gum he'd bummed off a private at the camp gates.

'Do we have any idea who is behind this insanity or the attacks on the village yet?' he snapped.

Kanulf eyed Loren putting the gum in his mouth but didn't comment.

'Not for certain,' piped up Amuna, 'But we are focusing a lot of attention on a woman who keeps featuring in the emerging pattern. She dresses rather distinctively but still manages to remain somehow unnoticed.'

'I asked for that woman's name to be determined a while back I remember, around the time of Teddy Conmar's death,' said Kanulf crisply.

'She has proven rather elusive Kanulf,' replied Amuna evenly. 'Enwyn and others have been onto it. But the name she uses is Bella Dixon. Almost certainly an assumed name. However, she is a candidate.'

'So who is she?'

'The simple answer is we don't know. She could be a new Chameleon agent on the mainland or she might be someone we have run across before in a new body. Or we may be looking at a rogue agent from within the Sufinam itself. A loose cannon. She may have orchestrated the attacks or be nothing to do with them. At this stage we have no idea. She has kept a very low profile whoever she is. What does seem likely is that she has somehow spirited our charge away. She is the only element we have no proper trail for.'

'No indications that Jerphanion may be involved? This couldn't be Jerphanion could it do you think Amuna?'

'No, at least not yet. Not directly that we can tell. There was a sighting of him in Turkey when this woman was spotted on the Welsh borders so it seems unlikely.'

'I'd dearly love to catch him transgressing against the Pact. I'd lead the punitive raid on him myself if we could establish his involvement,' said Kanulf with passion.

Loren was getting out of his depth again and looked at Kanulf exasperated. The older man threw up his hands in mock horror,

'I know, I know Loren. You want to know who and what and why. Jerphanion is an old enemy. He is one of the most sinister and powerful Chameleons, what is classed as a Lord, which means he is totally predatory and evil. Highly intelligent too unfortunately for us, not like these devolves we've been running into here.'

'And you have rogue elements within the Sufinam?'

'Oh, that. Yes. A few. Very rare but they do exist.' Kanulf obviously didn't want to go into it right now.

'We try to keep track of them but they know all the evasion tactics,' added Amuna. 'They aren't enemies as such, just holders of different opinions about how Eloin need to be protected. If she is the one who snatched Cody there will be no plans to harm her. All we have to do is figure what she intends.'

There was a subdued squawk over the intercom. A man's voice said,

'Excuse me sir, we have an urgent call sign from a field agent. It is coded for *Wren*.'

'That'll be for you Loren. You'd better take it.'

'How...that's through a secure linkup site. How did you know my code name.'

'Secure, ha!' barked Kanulf. ' The definition of secure is that I know it.' He laughed delightedly at the expression on Loren's face. 'Get used to it Loren, we've been monitoring every communication you've made in years, however secure you might think it was. Your little parleys with Census Officer Cas Winters included. Get on it son. See what she has to say. Must be pressing if she's trying to reach you here.' Kanulf indicated a row of consoles half hidden in the shadows amongst a bank of electronic equipment that reached up to the roof.

Loren vaulted down the aluminium steps and ran to a keyboard taking care to avoid the tangle of cables snaking everywhere across the floor. He typed whilst still standing, trying his best not to feel foolish that his secrets were so pathetically transparent. He opened with a code for a secure fastlink to his protected line and took the message signed *Loki*.

'I think you were right,' he called up to Kanulf on the platform. 'This could be something. One of our officers...'

'Cas Winters, son. C'mon, let's just get it running here. We know who Loki is.'

Loren fought hard to keep control of his agitation, but it was difficult whilst feeling like a naughty schoolboy.

'It's a report from Lancaster...from Cas. There was a serious anomaly occurrence at Preston station a short while ago. Some kind of outbreak involving confirmed XK00-9 activity.'

'XK00-9, overt anomaly activity with possible human witnesses,' clarified Kanulf.

'Cas is certain they're both linked and relate to the Clayton Bar attack,' said Loren.

'Great Hades' guns! It's them!' shouted Kanulf raising his arms excitedly. He banged on the triple glass yelling at Amuna inside who had looked up at the mention of XK00-9. 'Shree, Shree, they're heading north. They're heading for Wrayhaven! Get the Black Set fired up. And let's put Enwyn on this. She's desperate for a chance to redeem her self esteem.'

Amuna was already heading for the sealed portal of the S.A.C.V.

'Yes, we should set her on their tail I think. She deserves this chance.'

Kanulf was crashing down the steps and striding across the concrete towards Loren, a look of grim delight on his face.

'Is your gear up to scratch Loren? I hope so because this is where you step off the cliff.'

'Never take my gear off sir,' Loren grinned back patting at the pouches on his utility belt. He felt the almost unbearable pleasurable of anticipation rising from his lower body up through his heart. At last, a chance of some serious action. He'd had enough of talk. It was about time to take a blaze at something.

They left the tunnel and pushed through a pressure door as Amuna joined them hobbling on her stick. A voice came through the tiny comms unit on Kanulf's chest,

'Black Set on alert and ready sir.'

'And about bloody time too,' muttered the old man grimly. 'One can have too much of sitting and cogitating about these things, don't you think Loren?'

Loren's grin said everything that needed to be said.

SIDETIME
THE RUINED ABBEY WALL

THE girl stares down at the translucent sheet she holds in her hands and brings to mind all the previous occasions she has done this in practice; how in the past she has masked small objects such as a silver locket say, or a handful of copper coins or a fine gold chain, and made them invisible with a twist of the light, a strand of cobweb and shadow. But now she must do this in a way that will be unbreachable. The thin page in her hands, little more than a whisp of the light itself, is almost unimaginably precious and must be protected from the pursuers who are tracking her down. She is being stalked for this thing she carries. She knows she must open a liminal gate and hide it here whilst there is still time. Then she must conceal the liminal so totally that no one will ever find it without the exact combination of harmonies and colour to reveal the shell of unbreakable force she will place around it.

And so she stills her breathing, starts the tuneless weaving pattern of little whistles and notes that will focus her concentration. She begins to unravel the tiny forces that bind the space around the key stone in the Abbey wall. Almost immediately there is a shimmer in the air as the forces disengage, fluttering apart like a shoal of fish trailing silvered light that glints and dances without once holding still — a living coruscating window of shimmering fishtails, ceaseless in movement, hypnotically beautiful.

For the unskilled to pass beyond this point would be impossible. They would be trapped, entranced by the mesmeric beauty of this necklace of light, unable to proceed any further. But for a true-mind focused by purpose and honed by practice this is merely the threshold beyond which lies a lagoon of serenity and safety.

As the window strengthens she moves closer, reaching into the non-space within and placing the precious object as far back as she can reach. The beautiful glyphs of the page glow with supernatural radiance. With a sigh of reluctance she withdraws. Her heart aches as she restores the invisible bonds of the liminal and watches it close. The air sparkles as the fishtails disperse and she is...alone. Only now can she give thought to her own safety. It is a long way back to the Haven road by the mountain paths.

Twenty
GHOST MEMORIES

'There are forces controlling so many things that happen around us, and we don't know what the governing rules are.'
Thomas C Morledge

THE eighty five year old steam locomotive trailed a plume of steam as it rattled through sunlit countryside heading towards the Lake District. Onboard Cody was trying to untangle the insane twisting thing that her life had become in the last twenty four hours. She held the cotton wool Bella had applied to her ear to stop the bleeding and she stared out of the window, her mind playing and replaying that old loop of images she could happily have done without; all the horrors of Clayton Bar and now the terror of the attack at Preston Station. What would be waiting for them in the miles ahead?

Bella seemed unaffected by the recent events.

'We'll be safe now until we reach Windermere,' she said leaning out of the window. 'But we may have to get off a little before that.' She didn't elaborate and began to unwrap another dressing from the medical kit in her shoulder bag. She was looking at some blood on Josse's throat. He didn't seem to be aware that he was wounded and looked startled when his collar was turned down to reveal a nasty gash beneath his chin. Bella stared expectantly at Cody for a moment, paused, then busied herself cleaning the wound and wrapping it efficiently in a clean dressing. Josse's face showed several thin cuts which were also attended to. Bella insisted they take a draught of the hot herbal tonic from her stainless steel flask and they settled themselves in for the rest of the journey.

Cody's hands still stung a little from the cold and the roughness of the stone where she had tried to wipe the filthy rag things from her palms. Her temples were throbbing and the coppery metallic tang in her mouth was making her throat constrict. She fought the urge to spit and clear her mouth. At this point in her life she was too disoriented to be scared anymore. All the new ideas Bella had been spouting filled her head. They were only sounds – Eloin, Aelim, Chameleon, Sufinam, and yet…and yet there was a haunting familiarity about everything she had been told. It should seem more outrageous than it did, which in itself was worrying. For the last three years her memory had proved unreliable but she couldn't shake the feeling that a window was about to open in her mind, a doorway onto things she should understand but didn't.

A new series of vivid and unexpected images rose up in her mind; two figures fighting their way through a snowstorm with tiny bundles protected beneath their cloaks; a line of torches planted around a colossal floating boulder of gold; a child with a young-old face, covered in steel plates whispering over an ornately decorated bowl, "*Belerima Lucian nu*"; a burning coffin high on a hilltop; a towering cliff with a jagged cave mouth at its base close by a gigantic Tar circle; Bron dressed in silvery mesh and looking older than Cody had ever seen her before. Somehow the very vividness of these images from somewhere outside of her own life made her think that perhaps they should stay buried. Despite Bella's insistence that she needed to know everything about her past a contrary instinct whispered that perhaps it wasn't the right time for her to look into such dark inner streams of her mind – not yet at least. It all made her long for her mother's face, for her father. She wanted to throw her arms around both of them and be held and protected. And she positively refused to give up the idea that mum and dad were not her true parents. It felt too much like a betrayal of all their years of love.

Preston was miles behind them now. She felt no urge to ask what had happened back there. Her sense of curiosity was exhausted. She knew they'd been attacked, that was enough. The herbal drink sent a heavy warmth trickling though her body soaking into her limbs. Josse appeared unconcerned and was staring out of the window at the passing landscape, though his eyes too were drooping. He alternated between scratching at his chest and hugging himself with his thin, scarred wrists protruding from his sleeves. The gashes on his face looked sore. Her own head wound from Preston no longer throbbed.

She noticed for the first time that her coat had an unpleasant musty odour, probably from where those disgusting skin-things had wrapped themselves around her. She stood up to hang it where fresh air from the window could get at it. To do so she had to lean over where

Bella was sat with arms folded humming almost inaudibly between pursed lips. For a moment Cody wasn't sure where the odour came from, her coat or from Bella. The bulky woman's eyes were hidden behind those opaque green glasses, but Cody felt sure she was being observed. She wasn't sure whether that was comforting or not.

She made sure the carriage window was as wide as it would go and returned to her seat.

No one seemed inclined to chatter and the rest of the journey passed in silence, which was a relief to Cody; she was absolutely exhausted. Frankly she was glad not to be bombarded with any more information. Despite the unpleasant smell from her coat the rocking motion of the train began to lull her. Gradually she felt her eyelids drooping and without offering the slightest resistance she allowed herself to sink into a thick welcoming cloud of comfort.

*   *   *

The next thing she knew Josse was shaking her shoulder gently. She must have slept soundly although her head felt like it was packed with cotton padding.

'Come on Cody. We have to get off soon.' She stretched and looked around surprised.

'Are we at Windermere already?'

'Not quite. We won't be going all the way into the station anyway.'

'Oh?'

'No,' he said excitedly. 'Bella says we're going to jump from the train just before we reach the station. I've never done that before. Have you?' Cody still loved to hear the slight French burr to his accent. It became stronger when he was excited.

'But why? Won't that be dangerous?' she asked.

'Shouldn't think so. The train's already going quite slow. Bella is up front with the driver. She's telling him to slow right down before we sight the station. Then we can hop off.'

Given the events of the last hours it would be foolish to ask why they were taking such extreme measures as jumping from a moving train. They'd been attacked twice already. Anything might be waiting for them at Windermere. Cody merely nodded, though she still did not really understand who was pursuing them or why.

'How's your arm?' she asked.

'Ah, it's OK I guess.'

And so, as the train crested the great range of hills that looked out over the lakeside towns of Bowness and Windermere they could feel the train decelerate, as if recovering from the long uphill haul from the outskirts of Kendal. The sight of the lake itself glinting blue and grey a mile away against a backdrop of towering mountains caused Cody's breath to catch in her chest. It was astonishingly beautiful. The sky seemed so huge. Amazing pillars of light illuminated every imaginable shade of purples, tans and pastel blues on the mountains. She could almost feel the wind on her face.

Apart from the lakes and mountains the landscape in this part of the world was remarkable for the phenomenon known as Bolt Oaks, gigantic trees shooting hundreds of feet into the air and dominating everything around them. They were a post-Event manifestation, common to northern parts of the Mainland with a plentiful supply of open water. Cody had read that some genetic event had been triggered by the extremes temperatures of the Ice Year and any young oak trees lucky enough to have survived Fimbulwinter had bolted into accelerated spurts of growth causing these magnificent giants of the forests to appear. In their present setting they were almost unbearably beautiful. It was all Cody could do to keep from crying out with delight.

But it wasn't just the extraordinary beauty that made her gasp. It was the sudden realisation that she had witnessed this view before. She had definitely been here on some previous occasion, though she had no conscious idea of when. Tears came to her eyes as she drank in the striking panorama. She felt exactly as if she was returning home. How could that be? Again there came that glittering inner stream of fish tails sparkling across her mind's eye. A voice, so quiet it could exist only inside her head, reassured her, '*Cem benith aulem shurimel.*' Was it her mother's voice? Or Bee's? Or some other? This person Lucian? Dad's? Was it Dad's voice? Had she been here before with her dad!

Her mind groped back to the time she had last stood looking out across this view, or one very similar to it with...wait, no, not her dad. The voice was a man's, someone she was very close to, but not dad. Then who? She squeezed her eyes closed forcing the tears to trickle down her cheeks. She was trying to break through to the unclouded memory of who had shared this unique and magnificent vision with her. She was trembling with the unshakable knowledge that here was something of great significance that she must understand. She almost had it too. She…

…Bella swept into the carriage. Cody turned her head away and quietly brushed at her damp cheeks with a sleeve.

'Come. We have only a brief moment before the train picks up speed again. We must dismount.' She ushered them out into the corridor and along to the nearest door which she unlatched letting it crash against the outside of the carriage. Fresh air full of country scents rushed in through the gap taking away the stale stink of the old train. Cody's mugginess cleared instantly. The grass banking outside was moving past at barely more than a trotting pace.

'Watch your footing,' Shouted Bella as she braced herself on the outer step. She dropped from the carriage and landed running besides the track. Without too much effort she kept pace alongside the train and ran holding out her arm inviting them to jump. Josse was positioned behind Cody and had a hand steadying her back. She felt a moment's annoyance that he should think she needed help, an irritation that quickly transferred to Bella trotting alongside the train her arm still outstretched. This was overtaken by a sudden wave of revulsion at what she knew was inside those dark green gloves, the deformed fingers oozing and sore. Without hesitation she leapt into space ahead of the big woman and landed skidding on the heaped gravel banked against the sleepers. The impact on the sloping ground took her slightly by surprise but she regained her balance instantly by windmilling her arms and trotted away from the tracks leaving room for Josse to follow. He too leapt without taking Bella's arm.

'That was great,' he enthused his face alight. 'You know, if this wasn't all so serious I'd say we were having some fun.' He flashed a mischievous grin at Cody behind Bella's back. She smiled in return, glad of his cheery spirit.

'Good, we are clear,' said Bella oblivious to the young couple's amusement. They stood watching the last carriage drawing away from them as the train picked up speed again. Cody noticed it had burn marks all down one side.

Bella led the way into a thick bank of gorse that ran alongside the embankment and they squatted for a moment whilst Bella pointed at the far end of the lake to their left.

'That's where we have to get to, to the south. We are less than a mile from the lakeside here but the ferry we must reach is about two miles walk, at Bowness. We must travel undetected. You understand?' She looked at the two youngsters who both nodded with exaggerated seriousness.

'Is Wrayhaven far?' asked Cody. 'That is where we're heading isn't it?'

'It lies two miles north on the opposite shore,' Bella replied pointing up the lake to their right. 'It would almost be visible from here except for the trees that surround it. On this side of the lake we will have to use alleyways and back roads to keep out of sight. Are you well?' Bella addressed this to Cody seeming to ignore Josse, who had been at least as badly hurt as she was. Cody nodded and looked at Josse.

'Don't worry about me. Tough as old cheese.' He beamed.

'Then let us be off,' said Bella ignoring him.

They clambered over a sagging barbed wire fence choked by creepers and picked their way downhill across steeply sloping fields waist high in waving grasses. Their route took them towards the rear of a row of terraced houses backed by overgrown gardens. Everything had been engulfed by wild vegetation untended for over twelve years. Spread out immediately below them was a panorama of rooftops and chimneys and beyond that the stunning vista of Windermere Lake at its most breath taking. Sun was breaking through a rose hued bank of clouds giving the whole world an almost surreal visionary quality. Everywhere immense isolated trunks of the Bolt Oaks rose above the rich green land like abandoned flagpoles of some giants' game.

This was suddenly shattered by a tremendous explosion from somewhere over the hill behind them. Although softened by distance they felt the force of the concussion hit their bodies like a blow. Cody and Josse stopped in their tracks stunned, their faces frozen by surprise.

'What was that!' gasped Josse.

'Could it have been the train do you think?' asked Cody her mind filled with the most awful image of mangled machinery crushed against collapsing brickwork and screaming broken people. 'Oh, I do hope the train didn't crash.'

'Yes. Let us hope so,' said Bella over her shoulder as she continued downhill. 'Come, there is little we can do about it. We have our own tribulations to face.'

'But the poor driver,' said Cody to the retreating back. 'What about the driver?'

Bella paused and turned to stare at her young charges. For the first time Cody noticed an odd detail on the toes of Bella's boots poking out from under her layers of skirts. They were tipped with sharp edged metal caps. The heads of the nails protruded like spikes. They looked...vicious. Cody felt a sudden alarm regarding this intimidating woman about whom she knew so little.

'Could anyone have survived a crash like that d'you think?' blurted Josse. 'That was a heck of a collision whatever it was.'

'If he did not survive then neither would anything that was waiting for us,' said Bella in a dead tone. Light was flashing on the dark green rectangles over her eyes. 'This is not some childish game! There are forces bent against us that you can only begin to imagine. We cannot spare time for niceties or inappropriate compassions. Now pull yourselves together. We have a long way to go and much is at stake.' She turned and strode downhill without a backward glance.

For a moment the two youngsters stood unsure of what had just happened. They exchanged a horrified glance before racing after the striding figure in black and green. When they drew close they followed in dazed silence. Cody was struggling with more unwanted suspicions about the woman who had rescued her from so many situations in this new unfolding of her life. It was hard to like her despite the natural gratitude Cody felt for the protection she provided. It wasn't just the physical things such as her disfigured hands or the grey marble eyes forever concealed behind those glasses. There was a disturbing dissonance to the woman, some dark hidden currents that were instinctively repellent, rather like the sour odour that came from her clothes. Cody was sure now that it wasn't only her own coat that carried the mustiness she had noticed in the carriage. She could smell it gusting behind Bella as the woman walked ahead.

As a twelve year old Cody's responses were intuitive and simple, but she felt deeply conflicted about her strange saviour. It was important to remember, for example, that Bella had suffered brutal treatment at the hands of her enemies and that could make anyone's behaviour seem cold and abnormal. Cody was a sharp girl, intelligent enough to know such extremes of adult experience were beyond her – although of course Bella had said she was much older than she appeared. That was something else she'd have to ask more about at some point.

Her head was spinning again. To make things worse the coppery metallic taste in her mouth had not gone away. She needed a clean drink to clear the unpleasantness. For now it would be best to concentrate on the simple task of keeping up with her guide and protector. She hurried after the energetic figure striding through the tall grass. The wind dispersed the unpleasant odour clinging to the woman's long coat and skirts.

Overhead birds wheeled in a clear blue sky.

'Unless revived by constant use our personal memories become more difficult to retrieve. And if not accessed regularly they will fade or at least distort. Time is not kind to old experiences and thoughts.'

Article from Function In Memory by Cate Waverly at the University of Bangor.

Twenty One
LAND RUNNING

'Merhaba arr sher beulimas - Well met and good fortune.'
A Sufinam greeting.

THEY found a footpath leading between tangled jungles that had once been gardens and followed it through a passageway separating two houses out onto the paved street beyond. They were in the town at last. The street ran level along the length of the hillside. The next lane downhill in the direction they wanted to go ran steeply at right angles pointing directly at the lake a mile away. Bella whispered that they should move as quietly as possible and keep an eye out for anything unusual that might be watching them. As they walked Cody eyed the derelict houses on all sides warily. They were all solidly built Victorian structures with that massive strength such old properties seemed to radiate. With the rampant vegetation obscuring their lower floors it was like walking amongst ancient jungle temples. Most towns in post-Event Britain were like this, the ones that hadn't been destroyed by Bloom of course. She was familiar with the ghostly quality of the deserted portions of Chester, so this was nothing extraordinary, except that this time they were very probably being hunted.

Thick bushes competed with young trees for space around the base of walls and buildings and everywhere tufts of grass sprouted luxuriantly from roadways and pavements. A good many roofs appeared to be intact and some buildings had glass in their windows so possibly were still habitable. But there was no escaping the creepy feeling that this was definitely a ghost town. Or nearly so...a couple of wild cats stared indignantly at them and then shot away into dark recesses amongst the stone walls. And then they saw a horse and cart pass the end of an overgrown back lane they were using. Bella sent Josse ahead to make sure the way ahead was safe.

'Doesn't anyone live here anymore Bella?' whispered Cody.

'Not in the main town,' Bella replied staring intently at where Josse had ducked around a corner. 'Generally people prefer to live close to good fresh water supplies and open fields or near good roadways.'

'Or railways...?'

'Hm.'

'I guess it's so they can spot outbreaks of Bloom quickly and not be trapped?'

'Yes. Bloom is easier to escape when you're out in the open. You'd only find the odd vagrant camped in these empty areas, those who prefer to be alone for whatever reason.'

Josse appeared ahead and waved them on. He was looking puzzled when they joined him at the corner of the lane.

'Nothing in sight,' he said brightly. 'But there's some weird noises coming from those houses over there.' He pointed off to the right. Bella stepped to the corner and peered cautiously round.

'What kind of noises?'

'Oh not loud. Sounded like a swarm of bees. You know, buzzing.'

Cody could sense Bella go rigid beside her.

'Buzzing? Quick! We have to move! NOW!'

They doubled their speed crouching low and running between any cover they could find. It was tiring running in that position. After a while Cody could hear the noise too. It came from behind them and, more alarmingly, from up ahead too. Stern faced Bella waved them through the sagging door of a large house obscured by creepers and they crouched low by a window peeping out at the street.

'We will wait here awhile,' gasped Bella, 'My guess is that these spore clouds are targeted to find us.'

'So they won't attack anyone else?' asked Cody concerned.

'Not unless someone is foolish enough to wander into them and start flailing their arms about,' snorted Bella dismissively.

'Spore clouds?' asked Josse.

'Swarms, like bee swarms, only more deadly,' answered Cody. 'One attacked us back at the Grove and Bella killed it. That's how I got all these...' she touched her arms and for the first time she realised that all the tiny spots had stopped itching. In fact they had completely gone.

'These what?' prompted Josse.

'Oh nothing. Just some marks. They're gone now.' She could feel Bella's attention on her from the other side of the window.

'Oh, OK.' Josse looked as if he'd have like more explanation but wasn't going to start pestering. Cody thought about telling him of her earlier encounter with the spore swarm that had attacked Doug Feydon and Vas Brown and how she'd saved them back in Bee's kitchen but decided to keep quiet. She had resolved that the more she kept to herself the better, even if not entirely sure why. She would not mention the locket given by her mother or Bee's phial to anyone, Bella included. Bella already knew about the silver rings but Cody was going to trust her more secretive impulses from now on.

Bella kept them in the tumbled down house for a couple of hours during which time they saw several spore swarms flitting along the street boiling like black steam in the air. From time to time she would creep into one of the back rooms, or go upstairs to spy out the land, but mostly they would squat together keeping as still as they could manage. Both the youngsters nodded off glad of a chance to make up for their lack of sleep.

By the time Bella decided it was safe to move the day was getting on. They had eaten sparingly from the meagre supplies remaining and both youngsters were feeling decidedly hungry. Light was beginning to fade above the rooftops as they crept out cautiously. The way ahead still lay steeply downhill. Bella told them they might have to chance using the main road that ran directly between the station and their destination. They were running out of time and she was unsure when the last ferry left.

When they'd covered over a mile they came to a gap in the buildings that gave an uninterrupted view of the houses and streets laid out below them. From this high spot, overshadowed by one of the distant Bolt Oaks towering three, four hundred feet into the air, they stood picking out the best route. A low pitched sound made them look up. A small aircraft was zooming along the length of the lake heading north, in the direction they would eventually have to go. Bella hissed to get down. They watched as the unmarked stealth-grey plane passed the nearest point to their position and droned on into the distance. There had been a touch of the sinister in its lack of identifying features.

'Never seen a craft like that before. Have you?' whispered Josse to Cody. 'What was it? A Forces plane? Some kind of surveillance craft?'

Cody shook her head. Seeing the vehicle disappearing rapidly into the distance made her nostalgic for the freedom of the skies. She thought back to the sheer exhilaration of taking flights with Corbin, the Liter pilot she had done most of her microlite flights with. How she longed to be above the magnificent sweep of the Cheshire planes. How far away that life seemed to her now.

'Oh look,' said Josse.

Some distance below them a couple were pushing a high laden hand cart downhill towards the ferry point. Then a family group on bicycles appeared passing the same way. Such a simple sight was reassuring. However insane her own existence seemed to have become ordinary domestic life continued for most people and Cody took comfort in that. Josse was pointing at some sails far out on the lake when Bella shushed for silence. They stared in the direction she pointed hardly knowing what to expect. Then they saw it.

A black shape was zigzagging back and forth across an open space in a street away to their right. Bella made a side gesture with one hand telling them to sink down. They did so and watched the shape, barely bigger than a dog from what they tell at this distance. Suddenly it stopped. Cody was sure her heartbeat was booming like a drum in the stillness and for a moment she felt the familiar sensation of heat and uncoiling movement in her chest. Then to her horror the distant shape lifted up its face - directly to where they were crouched in shadows! It was hard to tell at this distance but there seemed something wrong with its head.

'A Gaunt!' Bella hissed out of the side of her mouth. 'Do not move if you value life.'

The tableau held for five tense seconds; then the shape bolted forward, its head still raised in their direction. Its speed was astonishing. Already it was out of sight behind the intervening buildings and coming fast.

'Run!' commanded Bella. 'Or we are lost!'

They turned and fled.

Hearts pounding they scurried pell mell, leaping over broken masonry and the thick roots of trees. Bella was leading them the most direct route towards the main road and the lakeshore. Sheer terror pushed them on. There was no time to think, just take the hill in bone jarring leaps and pounding footsteps. They must keep going. They must reach...what? Where were they going? Cody's mind yelled at her in protest...what could they possibly do to outdistance the thing pursuing them! Even without knowing what it was she had seen its deadly speed and knew they would never leave it behind.

So intent were they that they never saw the pony and trap as they burst out of an overgrown thicket and almost ploughed into its side. The sturdy little animal reared kicking out at them, spilling baskets and small barrels from the cart and almost tipping the driver. Goods cascaded across the road as the three fugitives dodged to avoid the pony's metal tipped hooves. They were about to continue their flight when a black shape bulleted out of the thick vegetation behind them and tore towards the group. The Gaunt was upon them. It headed directly for Cody, its open maw a nightmare of fangs and slavering jaws. Fortunately the frenzied pony cut across its path at the last moment and the monstrosity skidded aside before trying to dart beneath the wheels of the cart. The whole group was frantically sidestepping to keep the cart between them and the unnerving creature. The Gaunt was silent apart from a fierce hissing but everyone else was yelling and waving their arms. A few hundred yards up the hill behind them several walkers and another cart stopped and watched in surprise.

The Gaunt made a series of darting swerves from under the wheels and leapt up onto the cart slashing sideways at the driver who fell forward with a choking noise onto the pony's rear and crashed between the harnessing. The poor animal went berserk increasing the fury of its kicks and lurching backwards and sideways dragging the body of the vehicle as if it were weightless. Pausing for balance the Gaunt launched itself across the pony's exposed back and leapt, arrow straight, at Cody. Bella seemed to spin six feet to the side putting herself in its path; her arms blurred, flashing across its body, and the thing wrenched in mid air and fell backwards beneath the pony's hooves. Two, three sickening pairs of blows from the sturdy legs shattered its head and shoulders, the dull snaps distinct even against the confused shouting and whinnying. Even crippled the Gaunt tried to crawl clear but got tangled in the body of the driver and an iron rimmed wheel rolled across its back. Bella shot in and finished it with a cobble stone to the head.

For a moment everyone stood still gasping for breath.

'Calm the animal, quickly,' ordered Bella. She dropped the bloody stone and returned a thin, nine inch stiletto blade to its place in her voluminous sleeves.

They did their best to calm the frantic pony but it took a while to stop its wild bucking. The driver was dead, his throat ragged and open to the sky. Josse stepped guardedly to the corpse of their attacker to have a look.

'Holy Scuz! Look at this,' he gasped in awe. Cody was holding the pony's reins, stroking its flanks and whispering in its ear.

'What is it?' she asked.

'It's got no eyes,' replied the lad, his voice husky. 'There are no eyes…or…anything!'

It was true. The corpse was an ugly sack of filth-matted fur, the musculature of its massive chest giving it the front heavy appearance of some grotesque hyena – except for its head. The head seemed to be all skull and mouth with no other features. No eyes, no nostrils or ears. Just great savage jaws full to the brim with rows of teeth like broken shards of glass. Its limbs ended in claws that could have been rusty iron hooks. A pool of black was seeping onto the roadway around the body and the stench was appalling. Josse staggered slightly as he stepped back.

'Here,' he said shakily. 'I'll help you with the cart.' He started to pick up the straw wrapped bundles and miniature barrels from the road.

'Throw everything out of the cart,' snapped Bella. They both stared at her unable to comprehend.

'But…' began Josse.

'We will use the cart to reach the ferry. It is our only chance. Gaunts do not hunt alone.'

The sudden realisation of their situation stung them into action. They worked in a panic of shaking hands and sweating brows hauling the few remaining crates of bottled fruits and containers onto the ground. It seemed an awful way to treat someone's property. And the poor driver - surely it was wrong to leave him like that. Cody looked uphill to where the small crowd of onlookers had kept their wary distance. There would be no help there.

She put down the box she was carrying and asked Josse to help her drag the unfortunate man away from where the Gaunt lay stinking up the ground.

'What do you think you're doing!' barked Bella, checking the cart's wheels and shafts for damage. 'Leave him, now! I said now! Or we may all end up sharing the same tombstone!'

It was the brutal truth Cody knew, unpalatable but true. Yet it still felt wrong. She took the time to close the wretched man's staring eyes before clambering up on the cart behind Josse. There were narrow wooden seats on each side of the cramped space. Bella stood upright and hauled back on the reins causing the still skittish pony to rear and throw its head angrily. It was not happy to be handled this way.

'Her name's Ringtail,' Cody muttered, her head bowed.

'What? Whose name?' demanded Bella.

'Hers. The pony. It's on her bridle,' replied Cody crossly. Josse shot a sympathetic smile at her as he rubbed his chest. She was too unhappy to smile back.

'Well then! Come away Ringtail my beauty,' called Bella firmly giving the reins a flick. 'Let's be away girl.'

The cart lurched unsteadily for a few yards until Ringtail struck her stride. Then she began to run off some of her anxiety in the good clean exertion of pulling a heavily laden cart. It was all downhill to the ferry, so the weight wasn't a big problem. And they were on the main road now so that even with the frequent potholes it was a clear run and they made good speed. The two bodies lying surrounded by scattered goods were out of sight in seconds. The bystanders up the hill still hadn't made a move to help or interfere. It was hard to blame them.

Both the youngsters kept a wary eye on the buildings either side as they jolted along the uneven roadway. They were highly conscious of how fast the Gaunt had moved. They also knew something else about the repulsive creatures – they didn't hunt alone.

'We have a chance if we can reach the water,' shouted Bella above the sound of hooves on the roadway. 'Gaunts have a terror of water.' Hanging desperately onto the bucking cart this information came as small comfort, though it was all the hope they had. The question was, could the cart make it to the ferry in time?

Twenty Two
DEEP WATERS

'The truly great stories work because they resonate with the readers' experiences and often touch on levels of significance not always understood or intended by the writer.'
Charles Oakham, taken from his Crucible Of The First Thought.
[Commentary article by Cullie Brown on egl.linesofsight.co.uk]

FERRYMAN Tom Kettle and his brother Bill were preparing to make their last trip of the day to the west bank. There were only two passengers on board so far with a string of goats. A few more were straggling down the tree lined avenue that brought traffic to the water's edge. It had been a fairly steady day with all the usual faces going up to the market outside Windermere railway station. Earlier he and his brother had even ferried a couple of cars, not too common a sight in these part, and not locals either. As far as Tom knew there were only a handful of local car owners entitled to petrol rations, not counting the district doctor and constable. So that would be something to tell the kids tonight. So would all the goings on up at the station. Some passengers returning from the market had told them that the terrific crash he and his brother had heard earlier in the day had been the Preston train crashing through the buffers at the end of the line and smashing up most of the platform buildings. He found that hard to believe somehow, though why would his regulars lie to them like that? Unless they were playing one of their jokes on him and Bill. He knew that he and his brother were not the brightest lamps on the street; he knew that people liked to play the odd joke on them. But this was hardly a joke was it. People had been hurt, possibly killed, or so old Mrs Gringot had said. That wasn't funny. The scattered ring of communities around the Lakelands relied on that train for links to the rest of the country. And as for people being killed...well! No doubt they'd get the truth of it by the end of the day. And there was nothing they could do about it right now was there.

He finished bagging the horse and pony droppings for the wife's vegetable garden at home. The brothers would sluice the decks clean after this final trip with buckets of water drawn from the lake. Bill stood at the forward end of the great open platform applying grease to the windlass which would draw the craft across the lake by pulling on a thick cable strung from shore to shore. Tom had already checked the rear windlass and swung his thick tattooed arms around his head jangling the collection of charms that hung from the leather wrist bands. One last crossing and then a pint of local brew at the Claiffe Crier before home time.

'You done Tom?' called his brother.

'Done and ready Bill. Give it ten minutes and we...' A sound made him turn to the shore. Someone was approaching from the north at a gallop. Now that was unusual. No one hurried to catch the ferry even at the end of the day. Late comers always knew that a shout to the brothers would buy them enough time to make the ferry. He could hear the clatter of hooves and wheels magnified by the tunnel of trees that lined the final few hundred yards of the approach road. A couple of foot passengers just visible in the gloom stepped away from the concrete road under the trees as the sounds got nearer.

'Someone in a hurry Tom,' his brother laughed. 'Probably that new postman fella.'

'Oh aye.' Tom added his own dry chuckle but he wasn't so sure. Whoever it was they were coming at an awful lick. This could be an accident in the making. He squinted at the pale shadows masking the far end of the lane.

The pony and trap appeared around the final corner going hell for tomorrow. Even at this distance he could pick out the whites of the pony's eyes, mad and staring, terrified beyond endurance. What was the damn fool driver playing at! Without dropping speed the trap swerved wildly correcting its course in a dead heading straight for the ferry slope. Sparks shot out from the wheels. The pony's hooves skidded. Great Oliver, Tom thought, it's a crash for sure.

'Look out Bill! We got a runaway!' he shouted and threw the bag of manure out of harms way by the railings. As the pony pounded down the uneven concrete it hit several potholes which must have shaken every joint and rivet on the two wheeled buggy. Tom seized the ten foot boat hook, ready in case someone needed hauling from the water in the next few seconds. It was all he could think to do. He could see the figures on the trap clinging on for dear life except for the tall one at the front holding the reins, a woman urging the tough little mare with shouts and lashes of the reins. They were never going to make it!

As the wheels jumped the jagged edge where concrete gave way to loose shale, the driver hauled cruelly on the reins dragging the mount up on its haunches gouging deep furrows in the flinty gravel. The cart skidded violently to one side, rose high up on one wheel, before righting itself with a bone juddering crash. The pony's hooves were inches from the heavy metal edge of the mounting ramp. Tom was horrified and stepped across the upper lip of the ramp to give them a taste of his thoughts – damned idiots!

But the woman, her large frame wrapped in long flapping clothes, had already leapt from the cart and was dragging the poor beast onto the echoing metal. Her eyes were hidden behind dark glasses and her face was like a storm.

'Cast off! Cast off now you fool or we're all dead,' she thundered. 'Cast off! Hell is on our heels!' The two smaller ones were helping urge the shuddering beast onto the ramp.

He was dumbstruck. He was about to shout back that there were other passengers to consider too. Then the fear radiating from all three of the panting fugitives leapt into his heart and took command. He found himself at the windlass turning the great wooden handle with all his strength. The cart bumped over the top lip of the ramp and the two youngsters, who couldn't have been more than twelve or so, led the pony stamping and chaffing to the far end of the flat platform. He saw the other two passengers herding their goats as far away as they could from the new arrivals.

'Haul away Bill. For all you're worth,' Tom yelled over his shoulder as his great arms sent the windlass wheels spinning. The ferry pulled away dragging the metal ramp over the gravel and into the water, spray shooting up on all sides. The woman ran to the stout lever that raised the boarding ramp clear of the water and hauled with both hands leaning back with her whole body. The ramp jerked upwards. Tom was amazed. That was a heavy lever to move. He should know. To his further astonishment she then took a place by his side and seized the second handle. The spinning wheels became a blur. Her strength was incredible.

By now they were several yards from shore. Tom could see the three strange arrivals watching the retreating shore with horror. He followed the direction of their stare. There was nothing. What could have been chasing them to inspire such terror? The other passengers would be furious at him and his brother.

And then he saw it. A bunch of dark shapes skimming along at ground level flowing over obstacles like a tide, silent, threatening and startling.

'For the great love of...!'

'Keep winding!' the woman yelled. 'Wind for your life!'

The ferry was now about twenty feet out and advancing steadily. Tom glanced up again. The speed of the things on shore was greater than anything he had seen, even the swiftest sheep dogs. They didn't run like dogs, the front of their bodies were too heavy, and their legs appeared to have too many joints. Despite their speed his mind registered seven of the shapes, whatever they were, and they were almost at the end of the concrete roadway – and showing no sign of slowing down worth a damn. It was clear what they were intending to do but surely nothing could breach the constantly widening gap?

When the lead shape shot across the unstable shale beach its feet skidded before it launched itself across the watery gap. The thing was moving so powerfully Tom knew it would land on the ferry despite the distance. The other dog things were crowded right behind, launching their muscular frames into the air. Only the last two lost their footing on the shale and twisted awkwardly in mid-air trying to correct what could not be corrected. The lean angular shapes of the pack leaders arced through the air like demons in flight as the rear two hit the water with an impact that sent water pluming as if hit by twin cannonballs. In a second they had vanished from sight.

The lead shape was already soaring over the raised edge of the metal ramp. But the woman had leapt to the bow and struck the creature in mid flight directly across the skull with the metal end of the boat hook. The thing crashed onto the metal deck and skidded along the wet surface like a shattered doll, stone dead. The next three landed short managing to hook their forelegs and heads over the upright edge of the ramp. Their black teeth savaged the air soundlessly and claws raked at the surface trying to get a purchase. Tom somehow registered that there was something wrong with their faces even as their claws gouged at the iron sheeting cutting deep grooves in the metal. In a flash the woman was at them, smashing mercilessly at each of their heads with the pole, stabbing and knocking them backwards into the water where they hit with a frenzy of splashing and sank instantly like stones.

The last monstrosity landed with half of its body across the bow. It seized the shaft of the boat hook in its jaws as the woman struck out, shattering the thick wood like straws. The thing's legs scrabbled at the wet metal hauling it over the obstacle. Oh, for mercy's sake don't let that thing on the ferry, thought Tom. But the astounding woman had already moved with sense-defying speed, snatching the end of the shattered pole from mid-air, spinning the metal spike forward and thrusting it upwards through the thing's throat. The tip shot out a foot through the top of its head. The woman followed through with a hefty blow to the side of the head with the other section of the pole and the thing fell backwards spasming in a frenzy of claws and slashes. There was nothing to grip. It sank into the lake like a lead statue.

All this time Tom had continued cranking at the windlass handle to keep the boat moving. The further they were from the shore and any more of those things the better. He could barely believe what he had witnessed. In his heart he knew the sight of those things spitting and clawing the edge of his boat would haunt him till the day his heart stopped. The terrible memory was made worse by the awful fact that they had had no eyes! Apart from the gaping savage mouths lined to the brim with rows of teeth like a lamprey the entire head had been featureless! No eyes, nothing!

'Tom! You alright our kid?' called his brother from the front.

'Yep, fine. Just get us across eh Bill.' Tom's sinewy arms were shaking as they never had before. The goats were bleating pathetically at the far end of the ferry. He roused himself enough to call back to those still waiting onshore,

'We'll be back in a forty minute. Don't worry. This isn't the last run.' Then he settled to the steady swing and push of the windlass wheel, letting the easy rhythm calm his troubled thoughts. If there were any replies from the shrinking figures on the shore he didn't hear them. He watched the woman use the broken shaft of the boat hook to lever the ugly corpse across the wet metal deck and tip it over the edge. All that remained of the incident was a black oily streak. No matter, he'd have had to wash it down this trip anyway. At least he was alive to do the washing. What a tale this'd be for him and Bill over the evening fires tonight. Better than a sack of manure for the veg garden.

Throughout the brief moments of the ferocious skirmish Cody and Josse had been calming the terrified pony as far from the action as they could on the small craft. Foam flecked the bridle around Ringtail's mouth and its flanks shuddered and twitched from its exertions. Poor thing. Its mind was a torrent of fleeting colours and shadows churned into incoherence by its fear. But she knew it would settle slowly under the effects of continued reassurance and gentle contact. It was a tough little breed similar to those common around Clayton Bar, stolid, dependable and tough, not too dissimilar to the sturdy Belmin imports uncle Ben was always trying to purchase. Her heart sank at the memories that opened up and she focused on the warm sweating flank under her hands.

'Ringtail,' she murmured gently against her ear. 'Good girl Ringtail.'

The two goat minders were trying to calm their panicked charges still bleating and staring wide eyed in every direction. Cody ignored them.

Josse had checked the cart and harnessing for any damage and now made a point of going over to the nearest ferryman and speaking to him in a low voice. Bella was stood apart by the metal rail staring out over the open water where the late evening light rippled across the miles of grey surface.

Cody was surprised at how quickly they were approaching the distant shore. They'd be there in ten minutes at this rate. She glanced over the side at a thick cable that rose dripping from the water. The metal strand wound itself around a large wheel passed along the length of the boat to the rear where it passed over a second wheel and then disappeared again into the grey depths. The technology was simple and effective, like the people of this region. She didn't even want to consider how she knew that. Best to let it drop for now.

Josse made his way back to where Cody was still tending the pony.

'He seems a bit quiet. Shock I guess. Best leave him alone to get on with his work I suppose. Here, do you fancy a sandwich.' He had dug a paper wrapped shape out of a satchel slung beneath one of the seats in the back of the trap. 'I know. It's insensitive stealing someone's packed lunch...especially as...well, you know. But I'm starving. D'you want some?' Cody shook her head. Their mad chase downhill and their run in with the Gaunts had taken away her appetite.

She peered back at the shore. Nothing moved amongst the shadow beneath the trees. Bella had said the Gaunts were terrified of water. If that was true then something other than their ravening ferocity had overcome their instinct for survival. They had been intent on killing Cody and her party ignoring everything else in their paths. That was a frightening thought.

'Did you see how Bella took them all out like that,' mumbled Josse his mouth full. 'How does she move so fast? She may be a grumpy hag but she fights like a Dervish.'

Cody didn't reply. She had witnessed Bella's impressive abilities to deal out violence more than she would have liked. For her it only raised more uncomfortable questions about her protector. Josse was oblivious, happily tucking into the unexpected findings from the carriage. He began feeding an apple core to the pony

It was only when they were half way across the half mile stretch that Cody noticed Bella was still stood by the rail where she'd tipped the carcass into the water. She was staring up the misty length of Lake Windermere as if expecting something to emerge from the grey depths. Cody picked her way carefully around a set of timber and barrels lashed to the ferry's side rail and approached her. The woman's entire body was rigid and her mouth was open in a grimace of...pain...exhaustion? It was hard to tell. For a brief moment her face looked almost inhuman, as if the muscles had slipped. The effect was grotesque, something...chilling to see.

Bella's eyes were fixed on the dark surface of the water as if at a mortal enemy – and she was terrified! Her gloved hands twisted slowly on the metal rail as if trying to wrench it from its mountings. Little gasps were making her chest heave like someone unable to find enough air to breath.

'Are...are you alright?' Cody asked, her own anxiety about their pursuers peaking again and made worse now by the state she saw her protector was in. 'Can I get you anything? Bella?' Bella didn't respond. Her eyes were hidden behind the dark green glasses but from Cody's position it seemed as if they were bulging. Apart from Bella's laboured breathing the only sounds were the slap of waves against the hull and the creak of the ferrymen working the huge windlasses. Thankfully the goats had gone quiet for now. The wind off the water was growing more chilly.

'It's alright. I…the water has always held a great terror for me,' Bella intoned trancelike into the teeth of the wind. 'I nearly drowned once; a long time ago. It has never left me.'

And that was all Cody heard from her for the whole journey.

Twenty Three

NATURE TOOTH AND CLAW

'There will be a taint upon the mighty and a blight upon the
mortal. The hope of mankind will lie in the gifts bequeathed to
us in sleep and stored in flesh by all generations gone before.'
From 'Mortal Fields Of Time.' By TC Morledge. [More details at:
egl.mysteryandevolution.co.uk]

IT was an anxious time, the unknown shore ahead, fear on the
shore behind and uncertainty riding with them on the boat. Cody took
some comfort from the cool freshness of the wind sweeping from across
the massive expanse of grey-blue water all around them. There was a
majesty and calm about the distant mountains that rose in dramatic steps
one mass behind the other like an exaggerated artist's impression of what
mountains should look like. The western shore of Windermere was a
thickly wooded mountain ridge that rose up imposingly against the
darkening sky. They would be heading through there soon. As she scanned
the skyline the wind carried a snatch of what might have been some pitiful
creature's wail from somewhere ahead. Both ferrymen paused in their
work to glance up at the towering heights. One of the goat herders
whispered to her companion,

'It's the Claiffe Heights Crier!'

'Do you think?' asked her friend anxiously. 'I thought that was
just a fireside tale to frighten the kids with.'

'Dear me no. I heard...'

The ferryman harrumphed loudly and indicated the two
youngsters stood only feet away and the women went silent. Cody would
have liked to find out more but they clearly were too terrified to talk to
strangers. Fear was radiating off them like a fever heat. She returned to
Ringtail and took some comfort from stroking her muzzle and neck. The
pony whinnied gently and nuzzled at her hand hoping for another apple

core. The big eyes stared trustingly into hers. Josse made a comment on how good she was with animals.

Bella remained locked in her position at the rail, apparently unaware of anything around her except for the grey undulating mass of water. She only stirred when the ferry nudged the far side of the lake and the forward ferryman lowered the ramp to crash onto the concrete apron that ran into the water. Once the two women had shooed their goats onto the land Cody and Josse led the pony and trap up the ramp before mounting again. Bella's relief was immense. She moved with an urgency that was somehow frightening and Cody noticed how both ferryman averted their heads refusing to look at them as the large woman urged the pony forward faster than seemed safe or wise snapping at its flanks with quick flicks of the reins. When Cody enquired how much the fare was they shook their heads and looked away.

Bella's distress was obviously venting itself in this brusque, almost violent behaviour with Ringtail. Her relief at reaching the solidity of dry land crackled around her like a cloak of energy. Cody could feel Ringtail's pain and confusion return.

'Bella, there's no need to use the reins like that is there? We are safe for now.'

Bella looked at Cody, her face contorted with anger and she seemed about to bark something, but regained control of herself with a huge effort and apologised.

'Forgive me. The terror of being out on open water like that is more than I can bear. It really is, I am sorry. You too little one,' she called to the pony. 'You are a beauty. You really are.' The words sounded forced but Cody understood how terrified Bella had been and made no further comment. Josse stirred uncomfortably before looking away.

'Did either of you hear that cry before,' Cody asked. They both shook their heads.

'What did it sound like,' asked Bella, the mirrors of her glasses flashing with the last dying light of the evening.

'It's hard to tell really,' said Cody weakly. 'It was very faint. Like a cry of pain or something.'

'A lost goat.' Suggested Josse. But Cody just shook her head and decided to let it drop. It hadn't sounded like anything really. Perhaps Josse was right; some farm animal with its head caught in a fence or something.

The path from the ferry point led away from the landing area up a gentle slope before turning a corner to the left and then suddenly swinging right to follow the shoreline north towards the top end of the lake. In the poor light they could see that the gravelled path soon became lost amongst trees covering the steeply sloping ground between shore and the high ground to their left. Soon the lake was only visible in gaps between the trees or when the path veered towards the open water and ran close to the stony beach. Otherwise they were totally surrounded by thick woodland and impenetrable bush at ground level.

They travelled in silence. Cody would have preferred to keep closer to the shore, especially knowing how the Gaunts had an aversion to deep water. She felt constricted. Her emotions were too tightly wound for her to feel safe in such thickly wooded terrain. The view was restricted to only a few yards on either side and it was hard not to feel threatened by every shadow and rustle from the undergrowth.

After about half a mile the shoreline suddenly opened up in a stretch clear of all trees and Bella urged the pony on. The path was pitted with potholes and small banks of shale washed down from the heights so they barely moved any faster but it felt less oppressive out in the open. The light was falling fast now. They were surrounded on all sides by shadow. Far across Windermere tiny lights could be seen twinkling from homesteads dotted along the distant shoreline. They looked comforting in an unavailable kind of way.

'Is Wrayhaven far now Bella?' asked Cody.

'Not far, no. Another half hour is all.'

'Good coz I'm about jiggered,' said Josse. 'Hungry too.'

'There will be food at Wrayhaven,' said Bella. 'And much else besides. Don't give up now, either of you. And no stupidities, such as wandering off.' She glared at Josse as she said this. He was scratching himself and gave no sign of having heard.

Cody was wondering what kind of welcome would be waiting them when they finally got to meet Veriman. What would he be like? Had he known Bee or mum and dad? Like Josse she felt exhausted and was hoping they wouldn't have a lot of uphill walking to do. In the failing light they could see that a drystone wall cut directly across their path. A narrow gate was set into the wall just wide enough for the cart to squeeze through. They all dismounted and Ringtail trotted between the massive slab pillars but suddenly began to whinny almost as soon as the gate swung closed behind them. They walked a few steps without remounting and halted staring at the top of the ridge ahead of them through a gap in the trees. Part of the skyline was aglow with a sickly yellow light. The silhouettes of trees stood framed against the pallid radiance and the steel dark heavens.

'Oh no!' said Josse. 'I bet that's Wrayhaven up there isn't it.'

But no one had a chance to reply because the darkness was suddenly split by the ululating wail that Cody had heard once before on the lawn of Bee's orchard. It came from directly ahead of them. This was immediately answered by a much closer nerve shredding wail from the left. There were Shadow Hein close by! They'd never get the cart turned around and back through that gate in time. They were trapped!

Before they could panic Bella hissed,

'Down, towards the lake. This way quickly.' She went ahead following the line of the stone wall towards the water. Cody tugged on Ringtail's bridle but the terrified animal wouldn't budge. It stood frozen to the spot immobilised by the Shadow Hein's hideous wail.

'Josse, help me,' Cody ordered fiercely. 'Ringtail's terrified. Help me pull her.'

The two of them tugged at the reins desperately urging her to move. Josse shifted his grip to a side harness. The poor creatures flanks quivered as if she were being struck but she refused to shift.

'What are you doing?' came Bella's voice from the darkness ahead. 'Hurry!'

'It's Ringtail,' whispered Cody hoarsely. 'She won't budge.'

'Then leave her,' came the exasperated reply, 'Or the shadows will have us all.'

'We can't. We can't.'

The sound of wailing was very close now. Bella crashed back into sight like an avenging fury and strode up to the couple battling with the terrified pony. At the same moment something huge and dark slid ominously from the edge of the trees. A pillar of slithering black on black pooled at its feet with a great circle of darkness. The Shadow Hein towered over them, its mouth aperture thrown open emitting that paralysing sound.

Cody turned in horror to Bella expecting her to do something but the woman's face was fiercely exultant and she cried above the deafening wail,

'Cody, you must use the rings! The rings! Surely you remember how!'

Cody shook her head desperately,

'I told you, I don't know how. I don't know what to do!'

The column of oily blackness had edged frighteningly close and was only twenty feet away now. Bella didn't make a move.

'You must Cody – *Athaneu Ceuliarim* – you must! The rings. It is the only way!'

Cody's mind had gone blank. She was tugging mindlessly at Ringtail's reins and almost sobbing with dread. Her chest had become a furnace, her phantom hand squirmed and thrashed, but she had no idea how to use the two rings as Bee had to destroy the nightmare at the cottage. Another burst of wailing echoed the first as a second Shadow Hein lurched into the clearing from the direction of the path.

In a blur of speed Bella whipped out the nine inch blade from its sheath on her arm and leapt to Ringtail's flank. For a moment Cody feared the terrifying woman intended to kill the pony but Bella made two quick jabs into the pony's rump. Ringtail screamed and reared in pain. It bolted backwards a few steps dragging it closer to the first Shadow Hein. Cody and Josse hauled frantically on the reins guiding it towards the wall and in the direction of the lake. They were wrenched off their feet as the pain maddened pony lurched backwards and forwards. The cart was being smashed from side to side like a toy. The noise was unbearable. At least they were moving in the right direction but hardly faster than the slithering obscenities. They stumbled on tangled tree roots and soft earth. The cart was being crushed against the wall, wood splintering and shattering with the impacts.

Cody glanced horrified at the black monstrosities. They were close – too close! They weren't going to make it. Faster, they had to move faster! But Ringtail was out of control thrashing and rearing like a demented thing. All three of them were hauling on the reins now but were losing ground.

A quick lash of movement from behind caught Cody's eyes. A black tentacle had shot out from the nearest Shadow Hein's head section and wrapped itself around Ringtail's rear leg. Another black whiplash landed like a gigantic tongue across the pony's haunches. Ringtail redoubled her frenzied bucking causing the cart to twist, shattering a wheel against loose boulders at the wall's base. The cart was wrenched onto its side collapsing in a tangle of snapping wood and reins. Another tentacle lashed out. Bella gripped both of the youngsters roughly by the shoulders and jerked them clear. Cody screamed in protest, her cries echoing those of the tormented animal, but she couldn't break the grip on her shoulder. Her rib cage felt as if it was going to explode with heat. She and Josse were dragged backwards as Ringtail's rear legs gave out and she collapsed to the ground forelegs kicking. The lead Shadow Hein swept forward, seeming to haul itself along by the rope-like tendrils. The edge of its shadow skirt touched the pony and blackness flowed over the struggling form like a suffocating oil slick.

'The rings!' urged Bella in Cody's ear. 'There is still time.'

But Cody's mind was blank. She watched, stunned, as the scene before her merged seamlessly with the stultifying memory of her mother and Ben being engulfed by the same nightmare. Ringtail was trapped against the stone wall and was being absorbed by the monstrous black hulk that towered eight feet above her. The pony's head, eyes wide in terror, was the last to disappear from view. Her whinnying peal of despair was choked into silence.

Bella threw the youngsters ahead of her down the hill, pushing them roughly into the darkness. They were following the stone wall.

'Keep moving,' she rasped. 'The creatures are slow. So long as we do not stand paralysed by their sound they are easy to outdistance. Make for the lake.'

They staggered through the darkness trying to block out the sounds of triumphant hooting from behind. Cody was trying not to think of anything other than putting one step in front of the other. Soon they were at the water's edge. Lights from homesteads on the opposite shore twinkled on the waves. Overhead a clear sky was littered with stars. Behind them the wailing noises suddenly ceased.

'Keep to the shoreline awhile,' said Bella, 'Then we will strike uphill and swing round to approach Wrayhaven from the landward side.'

'What was that yellow light we saw on the skyline before?' asked Josse.

'I fear some kind of attack must be under way,' said Bella adjusting her satchel strap across her shoulders. 'We must be invisible and silent. There could be a great many things seeking us out in these woods. Are you able to continue Cody?'

'Um!' Cody felt speech was beyond her at this point. She had sunk deep into her own dark thoughts and her tongue felt as if it had turned to dust.

'What will we do if we can't get past whatever is attacking the place?' persisted Josse. 'I mean, what if there are more of those things.' He pointed back the way they had just come. 'How are we ever going to reach safety? Will this Veriman even be expecting us?'

Bella stopped walking and turned to stare hard at the lad.

'We will find a way. We must. That is why we have come so far. We have to enter Wrayhaven.'

Cody took this all in in silence. Her mind was a turmoil. The uncomfortable heat in her chest had subsided. The invisible hand was no longer coiling and thrashing like an enraged serpent and merely pulsed ominously in time with each heartbeat. Tears were running freely down her cheeks – tears for the poor terrified Ringtail, for her mother, for Bee and Ben and dad. Tears for herself. She felt lost and desolate, sunk in despair. The thought kept echoing inside her head: if only she had known how to use the rings as Bella had said, she could have saved Ringtail – and her mum and Bee too. And Ben.

They plodded on for twenty minutes then began to take the uphill direction towards the peak they had glimpsed earlier. No starlight penetrated the thick trees here and Bella urged them to proceed with great caution. As they gained height they began to see flashes of the sickly yellow light through the trees. There were sounds too, crackling and the dull crump of explosions. Muffled shouts could be heard, and braying like the sound of animals.

Whatever safety had been promised by the idea of Wrayhaven Cody knew instinctively that it was not going to be anything like she had hoped for. She understood, with a dread certainty, that she had left her own world far far behind - and she passionately wanted it back. Impossible of course. The image of Clayton Bar burned behind her eyes, radiant with longing and lost to another lifetime. More than mere miles now separated her from the life she had left only a day ago.

Twenty Four
DEADLY WELCOME

'Confronting the unknown, our minds reel in fear, but all true life choices test us– and they never leave us alone.'
From Gifts To Come by TC Morledge.

IT was tough work clambering up the steep hill in darkness. Cody was using the demands on her body to push images of poor Ringtail to the back of her mind. There were so many unwanted thoughts packed tight into that crowded part of her unconsciousness now – memories, images, things Bella had said, longings for familiar faces and comforts. When would it become too many, she wondered. When would it all come gushing out, uncontrollable and clamouring for attention!

They were making for where the yellowish glow highlighted the top of the ridge. A thick canopy of trees blotted out the sky overhead and they had to pick their way through dense patches of thorn and bracken undergrowth. In some places it was more like a vertical climb up bare rock slippery with patches of moss. When the ground was level they crawled forward on hands and knees, often scrambling over the fallen trunks of gigantic trees. The area was littered with dozens of flattened pines that lay as if swatted by a giant hand. Everywhere massive root systems poked up into the air, thick with soil and splintered stone gripped by a snarl of knotted growth.

They were much closer to the source of the light flashes now and it was clear that a full scale battle was going on over the brow of the hill. The bitter smell of scorched wood – and other things less definable – drifted on the air. Several times they saw grotesque shapes flitting through the silhouetted trees. The very indistinctness added terrible aspects to their shapes and size. They could have been anything and there must have been hundreds. Dull explosions, snarls and animal screeches were conjuring all kinds of unwanted images in Cody's mind. At one point Bella directed them warily around a part of the ground that, in the occasional flashes, seemed to be writhing in tar-covered worms. From all directions in the darkness came the hoots of Shadow Hein. It felt like a passage through some imagined hell, and that was before they breasted the hill to see what was beyond.

They lay on their bellies beneath a damp smelling thicket of yew and holly looking down at the place they were hoping to enter – the stronghold of Wrayhaven. Through the mass of trees that were still standing Cody could see the outlines of a castle. There were crenulated battlements, high towers and layers of ramparts, but there seemed to be no outer wall, or in fact defences of any kind. A churned up area of open ground went right up to the stonework of the building itself as if no thought had ever been given to the possibility the place might have to defend itself. It was a folly, a decorative Victorian version of a castle, not an authentic fortress at all.

The major visible part of the building seemed in good condition but there were some sections of the stonework that appeared badly corroded, as if something had torn great bites out of it. Between the castle and where they lay Cody could make out groups of scarecrow-like figures stalking backwards and forwards. Some carried gear that clattered or were dragging great barrels on low-slung cart arrangements across the roughly cleared ground. The churned up surface must still have been very uneven because progress was painfully slow.

Other figures were hauling at metal bound wooden crates festooned in chain with crudely hammered plates and animal skins . They were lining the crates up to face the walls of the rambling stone structure of the castle.

'Who are they Bella?' whispered Cody.

'Never mind that,' interrupted Josse's voice from the darkness beside her. 'What are they up to?'

'Sh! Just watch,' cautioned Bella.

A vivid jet of greenish yellow fire had erupted from the front of one of the crates and arced high into the air towards the castle walls. It looked for a moment as if the luminous stream had struck the stonework but Cody spotted a barely discernible halo of blue flickering around the impact point. There was a crackling explosion and a mass of incandescent fragments scattered like a sack of hot coals hitting a cliff. As the lava-like pieces fell to the ground it could be seen that the walls remained untouched. The glowing shower spattered onto the churned up earth sending out clouds of steam.

'What was that?' asked Josse, clearly impressed. Bella pitched her voice low,

'The creature in the cage is a Spitter. Those goading it with spikes are making it eject a dense kernel of corrosive matter at whatever is in front of it – in this case the walls of Wrayhaven.'

'There's a creature in that filthy cage?' asked Cody appalled.

'Of a very low order, yes. It creates compacted pellets of polluted matter within its body which is uses as a form of self defence.'

'By spitting?' said Josse.

'As you say, by spitting. The corrosive kernel adheres and eats its way through anything it touches. Terribly fast acting, totally mindless but effectively deadly.'

'But it didn't reach the walls, did it,' enthused Josse. 'I saw a blue flare just before the thing reached the stone. It just bounced off.'

'You have good eyes. Yes, Wrayhaven has many defences. The light wall is just one. These moronic Chameleon Breed will never breach that, not if they had a thousand Spitters lined up.'

'So why do they continue to attack?' persisted Josse.

'Because Chameleon Breed, these Vil-kind, are mindlessly violent and know no other behaviour. Resistance infuriates them and they are incapable of subtlety. They have been ordered to attack – and they do so. They would probably continue until they were all dead. Only their leaders, true Chameleons, are capable of strategy. Come, let us see if we can get closer without being observed. There may be things we may learn. We still have to get inside.'

'Can we really do it?' asked Cody. 'I mean, look at what we'll have to get past first. Wouldn't we be safer somewhere else?'

'No, we would not.' They had started to crawl forward but Bella stopped them and indicated the castle,

'Watch now. This will be instructive.'

From amongst the outlandish shapes bustling in the shadows below them a couple of figures suddenly darted towards the castle. This coincided with several Spitters shooting arcs of corrosive matter at the ramparts. It was possible to see the figures picked out by the harsh glare. The gangling shapes were patchworks of rag and jagged fragments lashed together with no discernible sense of order. Savage twists of wire and bone protruded from every angle and surface, but, although their movements were scuttling and awkward, they moved with a sinister power similar to that of fast moving crabs. The things were gripped by some kind of frenzy and threw themselves at a low set gate buried snug between two massive buttresses. The moment they got within a few feet of the stone there was a blinding zap of blue and the raging scarecrows were blasted apart as if they'd been struck by lightning. A few oily rags fell smoking to the ground.

'You see,' said Bella grimly, 'Mindless. Completely unable to control their impulses.'

Enraged cawing went up from the darkness in every direction. Shapes darted amongst the trees and even flitted about in the dark sky overhead, but the rest of the hellish gathering kept their distance. The vivid discharge had leapt between two irregular stones, possibly ten foot high, set several yards out from the walls. The slabs resembled uprights at ancient stone circles all over the Mainland. Cody had seen the pictures. Now that her attention had been drawn to them she realised there were many others dotted along the entire perimeter of the building.

'Sentinel stones,' she almost gasped.

'Indeed,' said Bella. 'Only much bigger than those around Clayton Bar. Once we are inside the walls of Wrayhaven we will be safe enough. As you see, the defences are impregnable. And that is only a small part of the vast armaments guarding this place. Come.'

They wriggled their way around the outer fringes of scurrying Vil-kind, hugging every scrap of cover they could find. Fortunately there was a huge amount of noise and the attention of the attacking monstrosities was not on the forested area at their backs. After endless stops to reconnoitre they reached a high point of land some way back from the action. They were about level with what must be the second floor of the gothic pile. This side of the castle featured soaring spires and towers that jutted out from the walls. Several heavily arched doorways and windows lined the ground floor and the vulnerable looking openings must have appeared enticing to the attackers. But the appearance was obviously misleading. Every foot of space around the monolithic stone construction was littered with blackened heaps of rags or steaming pits surrounded by wreckage. As they watched, actinic blue flashes repelled half a dozen fiery missiles. Everything projected from the rows of Spitter crates battered uselessly against the light wall. The steady 'crump' of impacts continued to pound the night air and the unpleasant stench of burning increased.

'Get down quickly,' hissed Bella. 'There, see, loping along that trench by the barrels. There is the mind behind this patchwork haggle of monstrosities. That is Garatunde. It is rare to see a true Chameleon out in the open.'

A row of immense barrels were being rolled to the edge of a furrow cut into the ground and running parallel with the walls. From this deep gash several trenches led towards the castle and as each barrel was tipped over thick glutinous tar slid into the cuttings. Stumping about amidst all this activity was a large figure unlike the skittering stick shapes of the Vil-kind. It was hard to make out at first why this Garatunde, was so unusual. He moved by lurching forward in a series of swings that seemed always about to pitch him onto the ground. But there was an assured balance in the spinning movement that belied the jerkiness of his gait. Then Cody had it...the figure was using two huge poles as crutches. A great barrel chest, criss crossed by straps, kept the tops of the wooden struts attached to his shoulder by metal hoops so that his arms were free to swing about. A sudden flash threw his shadow across the broken ground and Cody saw that the creature had no legs! The man had no lower body at all! That thickly padded trunk was propped atop a single heavy pole like a hideous stick puppet. The impression of some terrifying tripod-thing stomping about barking in a roar like an enraged bull seal was haunting. The Chameleon was laying into everything within reach using an ugly cudgel bristling with hooks and nails.

'He's missing half his body,' gasped Josse in a tiny voice.

'The result of a calamitous conflict some years ago,' said Bella grimly. 'The fury of that is what keeps him upright.'

'And what is he up to with those tar barrels,' asked Cody, fascinated despite her revulsion.

'I could not say,' said Bella. 'But whatever it is we are witnessing a new thing. I do not understand what they intend with that cloying filth.'

Cody noted how the Vil-kind rolling the barrels to the lip of the trench skipped about trying to avoid getting spilled on. This wasn't working because all of them were streaked with muck like black snail trails. It was total chaos. Watching the sludge ooze into the channels it seemed to Cody that glistening, half formed solids slid from the barrels into the trenches as well as the tar. Hard to be sure in this light of course but as she was about to turn away an incident occurred at the junction of two of the channels. One of the huge barrels slipped ponderously out of control sending a scarecrow crashing headlong into the black mess. The figure sank from sight and for a moment the tableau froze. Others nearby stopped and gaped at the reflective surface. Then the tar erupted in a tangle of slow moving limbs grasping blindly for the edge of the trench. The Vil-kind was struggling to escape from the glutinous swamp but getting nowhere. The rest of the Vil-kind gibbered but made no move to help. A chill shot down Cody's spine when other shapes emerged from the cloying surface and began converging on the hapless struggling form of the Vil-kind. Black on black limbs or tentacles wrapped themselves around their prey in slow motion. With barely a ripple the struggling mass sank beneath the surface. The Vil-kind returned to their labour rolling away the empty barrels and being bludgeoned by Garatunde.

Cody felt sick. She had no idea what she had witnessed.

Neither Bella nor Josse had observed this horrible episode. Josse was grilling their protector about how they were going to let Veriman know they wanted safe passage into Wrayhaven. Their furiously whispered debate filled the shadows.

'Any attempt to signal Veriman will attract unwanted attention to us, won't it,' badgered Josse stubbornly. 'So what are we going to do? We can't hang around here for ever. We should leave now.'

Bella's calm tones sounded strained as she explained,

'Our main hope is to convince Veriman to turn off the defences for a moment, however brief, so that we can slip through.'

'No one is going to do that soon are they,' mocked Josse dismissively. 'Not with the mutant circus going on out here.'

'No one inside would notice us anyway, would they,' joined in Cody. 'Not with all this noise.'

'I was rather hoping that by the time we reached this point more of your memories would have returned to you, young Eloin, and you would be able to advise me of our best way to gain ingress. The defences of this Haven would never knowingly be used to harm anyone allied to the light. They are maintained by select members of the Sufinam. Our difficulty is that the defences themselves are blind to whoever or whatever approaches. In this present situation everything is perceived as a threat and simply destroyed.'

This exchange was carried on against the constant background of thunderous crackles as dozens of corrosive pellets spattered against the invisible barrier of the shield wall. By the trench the frenzied tipping of barrels continued without a pause. The three fugitives seemed to have exhausted their ideas for a moment and paused to watch the mayhem below. Another group of berserker scarecrows, driven to a frenzy of madness loped out of the forest carrying a felled tree as a battering ram. An iron head had been hastily attached to the front end. They made directly for a set of mullioned windows on the ground floor scuttling like demented crabs and shrieking meaninglessly. The inevitable blue flash seared them into a million fragments yards from their target. Oily scraps of soot fluttered around the charred remains of the tree trunk.

It occurred to Cody that all this futile activity had the telltale marks of some orchestrated distraction. Clearly nothing was going to penetrate these defences and despite Bella's explanation that the creatures were stupid and battle crazed the question persisted - why did they continue to attack?

She recalled a story called '*Lyuman And The Thorn Seed*' narrated by Old Tom Morledge at one of the Albion Fayre 'tellings'. The tale related the adventures of a group of mismatched heroes outwitting an insane scientist-mage who threatened to release plague on the world from within a heavily defended mountain fortress. The hard pressed team had set up a series of decoy attacks to distract attention from their main force. Cody had loved that story and had always admired Lyuman's use of cunning and strategy to misdirect her adversary. Now, if this assault by Chameleon Breed was a serious attempt to storm Wrayhaven all this pointless mayhem could well be a use of distraction tactics – couldn't it? What were the Vil-kind doing with those tar barrels for example?

Something began to unfold inside her head, like a shimmering doorway, a sense of...of something familiar and frightening.

'We must approach the front entrance,' she blurted suddenly, turning to her companions.

'What?' asked Josse dismayed.

Bella remained very very still, the mirrors of her glasses focused on the young girl's face.

'We must approach in the open, as unthreateningly as possible. It is the only way,' Cody hissed urgently. She got up on all fours. 'And we are running out of time. Something is about to happen.'

199

'Wha...?' began Josse again, but Cody turned to the woman on her other side,

'Bella, where is the main entrance?'

'To our left around the end of those two block towers,' the woman replied.

Immediately Cody began to crawl in that direction.

'Where the raving Nell are you going?' hissed Josse hardly able to believe his eyes. But Cody paid him no attention and scrabbled through the bramble thickets ignoring the thorns tearing at her clothing.

'Cody! Don't,' Josse pleaded from behind.

Bella shoved fiercely at the lad.

'No words now. Stay close. Nail yourself to her heels. This is it! This is what we came for. Events are going to move very quickly from this point.'

Twenty Five
CLOSE RUN

'We carry within us the patterning to become gods or angels. We have certainly been devils; our history condemns us. Our legacy is ashes.'
From 'Origins Of Our Elementary Nature' by Fidious Leath.

JOSSE could hardly keep up as Cody burrowed her way through the undergrowth. The din of the attack covered the sound of their progress and he was too intent on not losing sight of his friend to wonder how this sudden change had come over her.

They came to the edge of a wide open space, a great sweep of gravelled driveway in front of the main entrance to Wrayhaven. Before them double pillars twenty feet to a side spanned high archways covering a set of steps that led up to a narrow set of double doors. It all looked so…harmless, so unprepared. Josse could see tiny gates set into the huge stone masses. Blackened scraps of charred material tumbled with the breeze across the open space. Scorched remains lay scattered everywhere.

They dropped behind a low brick wall, the youngsters panting. Josse expected them to take stock but Cody was on the move again instantly.

'Stay close. No hesitating now.' She rose on her haunches ready to run across the gap. All Josse could think was how horribly exposed they would be out there in the open.

'Wait!' commanded Bella seizing Cody's shoulder.

A group of Vil-kind were scuttling from the cover of trees far to their right. They were dragging one of the iron bound crates on chains. Garatunde stumped behind them, grotesque on his three wooden props. He was lashing out with his spiked cudgel and bellowing guttural phrases. The crate was manhandled to within eighty feet of the two pillared doorway and the underlings began to haul it around to face the building. Garatunde stomped back towards the trees to screech at another team of minions.

Cody turned her head to Bella and whispered fiercely,

'This is our only chance, now, before they get set up. Can you take care of them Bella? We won't need more than seconds. Either we will be inside...or dead.'

At any other time Bella's wolfish grin would have chilled the blood, but Cody felt exhilarated by the power that radiated from the woman. Her nod was a spur to action. Cody was scrabbling in her bag to find the silver and glass phial given her by Bee. She pulled it out by the chain and hung it round her neck. Bella's expression was hard to read but she stared intently at the glittering thing in the dark. Next, Cody dug out the two silver rings and gripped them in her fists. She explained quickly what she intended to do and what was needed from Bella.

To Josse it all sounded insane, but Bella merely indicated her readiness. Cody nodded to her companions, took a deep breath and stood up followed by Bella who grabbed Josse's shoulder and placed him firmly in front of her. They stepped forward and began to walk across the open gravelled surface, Bella and Josse about fifteen paces behind Cody. Cody's arms were raise slightly away from her body, palms facing to the front. Her eyes were half closed in concentration and she moved with an even steady grace as if progressing up the knave of a church. Her path took her in a direct line towards the massive twin pillars of the main archway. It would pass within thirty feet of the snarling Vil-kind by the Spitter's cage.

Cody drew level with the bickering group but didn't increase her pace by a step. Josse was almost out of his mind with terror. He could see details about the Vil-kind he didn't care to know, their shredded faces, their patched together limbs festooned with scars and bound with wire, bone and rags. Everything about them was jagged and brutal. He also became aware of how the tattered scraps of rubbish blowing across the open ground seemed to be flocking around Cody's legs. His knees were almost giving away beneath him but she trod as calmly as if on a summer stroll. Even when strangled screams erupted from within the Spitter's cage the vulnerable girl didn't waver.

Every Vil-kind around the cage screamed too on seeing her. In a heartbeat the nightmare shapes launched themselves in her direction - but her eyes never once wavered from the doorway of Wrayhaven directly ahead. The Vil-kind were so outraged that this tiny fragile figure should ignore them that they were taken completely by surprise by the whirling demon that leapt on them from the rear. Bella was a twin bladed fury of slashing, hacking destruction that tore into them faster than their senses could register. In seconds they lay in ugly tangles on the blackened gravel. Josse closed the distance between himself and Cody kicking at the fluttering shreds that now clung to his trousers. Cody's legs were already wrapped in layers of the filthy stuff.

The outrageous bedlam of the scene increased as more Vil-kind erupted from the tree line and raced across the open space whooping raucously. Bella crashed headlong into the leaders cutting them down with scything sweeps of her matched stilettos. She too was making a battle noise, a shrill whistling note that rose and fell with her exertions. It seemed to paralyse the remaining scarecrow figures long enough for her to leap amongst them and cut them to pieces where they stood. More hideous screams were echoing from beyond the tree line and shapes burst out of the darkness. The sight of three isolated strangers out in the open must have shocked them momentarily because some of them staggered to a halt. Only an outraged screech from the tripod figure of Garatunde triggered the ragged charge that followed. The Vil-kind swept forward like a foaming wave of brutality but even they were overtaken by a dozen fast moving shapes that Josse recognized in the poor light as Gaunts.

Bella hesitated fractionally, still swinging the nine inch blades in graceful arcs around her crouched body. The Pound of feet and claws on the rough ground drummed in their ears. As the line of ravening monstrosities halved the distance to their prey Cody, still facing forward, cried out,

'Bella, Josse! To me!'

Bella raced forward, snatching the lad around the waist and cushioning him between herself and the girl. The lead Gaunts were seconds behind.

'Down!' commanded Cody. They fell to their knees.

A shimmering dome of light blossomed over the three fugitives radiating from Cody's out-held palms and chest. The Gaunts skidded on the broken surface trying to avoid it - and collided with the expanding wave of iridescent blue that suddenly boomed outwards from the walls of Wrayhaven. The ugly bodies exploded in mid air. The dome of light was now inside the expanded defences of Wrayhaven's light-wall. Cody's arms fell to her sides, the dome from her hands collapsed around the trio and Cody yelled into the sudden silence that followed,

'Now! Run! For your lives!'

The three of them bolted across the short distance remaining to the arched pillars and collapsed up the stairway. The doors at the top had been thrown wide open. Quick though they were the Vil-kind and remaining Gaunts were also sprinting pell mell for the opening. With the light-wall seemingly breached the monstrosities suddenly saw their prize undefended and helpless. They howled in glee. A brilliant arc of acid yellow bulleted out from the caged Spitter and shattered against the stairwell scattering fragments of corrosive matter which narrowly missed Cody and her companions. The racing Vil-kind were within yards of the twin pillars when a crackling roar rent the night air and dozens of inhuman shapes burst into flaming tatters, ignited by a pulse of blue radiance. Wrayhaven's defences were complete again. Whirling clouds of sulphurous ash filled the air.

Inside Wrayhaven the gasping fugitives collapsed onto the tiled floor and stared in relief at the carnage beyond the shield wall. Cody was still clutching the two silver rings in her hands and her heart was beating like a trapped animal. The filthy layers of skin-things were curling like dead leaves and dropping to the floor. Josse was batting energetically at the things on his own legs and stomping them to dust.

'Eurgh! Yeuch! Get these things off me!' No one paid any attention.

Through the open doorway Cody saw the figure of Garatunde partly obscured by the whirlwind of sooty flakes. He was gesticulating insanely, though no sound penetrated the castle. Her eyes were still adjusting to the gloom of the entrance hall after the intense flashes outside but she could make out someone slamming the doors shut and then collapsing against them in a heap on the floor. She gathered herself and ran over to help. It was a man, lean faced, stick thin, dressed entirely in black. His left side and arm glowed with a smattering of sullen yellow-green luminosity and he was groaning in agony.

It was Veriman, Veriman Kyle, Sufinam guardian and custodian of Wrayhaven - and he'd been hit by a spatter of corrosive sputum from the Spitter outside.

The man was doomed!

Article by Cate Waverly on Underground Cities and Bases - taken from
egl.subworlds.co.uk

From Napoleonic times, and possibly earlier, sophisticated subterranean fortresses have existed in the British Isles. In times of war underground retreats have obvious advantages. The more far reaching the threat the more sophisticated the bunker mentality response.

Between the World Wars extensive town sized bases were constructed underground and with the threat of nuclear attack from the 60's onwards secret subterranean complexes became high tech, self sufficient and capable of accommodating many hundreds of people. These specially constructed centres and the thousands of miles of natural cave systems throughout Britain became sanctuary for a high proportion of those who survived the fourteen month polar year of 1991-92.

After the Great Thaw (1992) the government Recovery & Resettlement Programme gathered pockets of survivors together, whether individuals, groups or, as in some instances, entire communities. Initial records by early reconnaissance teams listed hundreds of subterranean locations. Not all their findings were made public however, because not everyone with access to heat and food sources made it through the Ice Year. Death had come in many guises during the dark Fimbulwinter. Some findings made by the reconnaissance teams were so disturbing that all traces were covered up, even as far as the locations themselves being sealed off. Many appalling and mysterious events had occurred below ground when ice storms ravaged the surface of the world. A decision was taken at the highest levels that the recovering population didn't need to know all that had taken place in the dark time.

Some indication as to the size of the cover ups may be gleamed from comparing early lists of key locations with more recent official records. Many locations have simply disappeared. Conspiracy theory paranoia...or something genuinely sinister? It is a fair assumption that any top secret bases that did make it into publicly accessible records were the tip of a considerable iceberg. So, how many more must have remained totally secret? And what are they being used for today?

Further related topics on egl.secretundergroundcities.co.uk

Twenty Six

DEPTHS WITHIN DEPTHS

THOSE initial desperate minutes inside their hard won sanctuary were spent trying to help their wounded saviour, though in truth no one knew what to do for him. The material of his black tunic was smoking but he made no attempt to pat out the smouldering patches, as instinct would cry you should. Nor would he allow anyone else to do so. His first coherent words were,

'No, don't touch me. My wounds will kill you.'

Cody had stuffed the silver rings back into her satchel and helped Bella to roll the injured man into a sitting position. The face had a pleasant aspect to it, somewhat lost now amidst lines of suffering. Cody would not have described the features as particularly old, though the character creases showed that the man had seen a lot of life. His black clothing bore no distinguishing features; his only adornments were matched rings, a pair on each hand.

He looked around at them in the half gloom.

'You all made it in safely – good.' Veriman Kyle was low spoken, his words coming through gritted teeth, his lips pulled back like a skull. 'We must get down below. Help me could you?'

Taking great care not to touch the glimmering patches of yellow on his body or arm they carried him up the last steps and through a set of heavy oak doors framed by an arch of stone. Beyond this, a great oak table filled the centre of a wood panelled hall and far above them was a soaring open tower whose highest reaches were hidden in shadows. Veriman directed them towards a set of stairs that swept upwards to the open balconies of an upper floor. When Bella used her whole weight to tilt one of the carved banister posts, as instructed by Veriman, the first nine treads swung upwards revealing a tunnel that plunged steeply downwards into darkness.

Cody barely had time to take in any details of the tapestries or rich engravings on all sides before they were staggering down a spiral staircase built from granite blocks. The stone of the side-walls was worn smooth by generations of hands reaching for balance and the steps continued downwards, downwards until they must have been a hundred feet or more below ground level.

Veriman's breath snapped and puffed with the impact of each step. The severity of his suffering made Cody's chest writhe in sympathy but there was nothing she could do to ease his pain right now. On reaching the bottom step he made a brave effort to move his own legs whilst still leaning heavily on Bella.

'Not too far to go now. Take care, don't touch my arm or chest.'

His undamaged right arm was draped over Bella's solid shoulders, his left hand, also unmarked, rested lightly on Cody's arm. The glowing yellow spatters had sunk beneath his clothes into his flesh. A smell of hot sour vinegar came off his body along with wisps of vapour. Bella and the suffering man murmured phrases to each other in Old Tongue. Cody could almost follow the exchange; it sounded like a ritualised set of greetings interrupted each time Veriman's agony overcame him. His eyes would roll up into his head and sweat poured down his thin face matting the thick tangle of hair to his forehead and temples. A constant groaning sound came from deep within his chest, like a sustained humming.

Josse had been a few steps behind them on the stairway and as they struggled along the wide corridor that now opened in front of them Cody saw him stagger slightly. Had he been hit too? He looked awful, grey faced and strained. His hands were twitching at his sides. She asked him anxiously,

'Josse, are you OK? You weren't hit too were you?'

'No, I'm fine. Just...y'know...tired. I, well I got scared out there being so close to those...you were terrific.' His face was mask of misery. He managed to squeeze out a grim smile, clearly not wanting to say more. Cody returned her attention to supporting the wounded Veriman.

They reached the corridor's end without really seeing it. The light had been poor there but improved as they now passed through a number of low roofed chambers lined with a bewildering array of cabinets and display cases. Some areas were stacked with metal bound chests piled up to the ceiling. Other had rows of mailed gloves mounted on the walls or beautifully wrought silver objects Cody couldn't even guess the purpose of. One corridor wide enough to race two horse drawn carts side by side had a row of alcoves inset into the walls. Each was lined with dark shelves displaying incredibly fine chains arranged in delicate patterns. She even glimpsed what looked like folded lengths of chain mail behind ranks of bluish white crystals in stoppered bottles. There was a richness to the fittings that made her think of treasure trove in an Aladdin's cave. The wall coverings were sumptuous; tapestries hung everywhere, mounted on walls or draped over thick wooden frames. They were in excellent condition and displayed eye pleasing patterns of great complexity in purples and greens and browns. Wherever they went it was hard to detect where the light came from. Either it was subdued or cheerful, without ever being harsh.

The place had the feel of a storehouse filled with treasures no one had yet catalogued from a land no one yet understood.

Cody lost track of the number of doorways they passed; some were barred by thick panelled doors or gratings or simply stood open leading off into the darkness. Each was covered in symbols cut deep into the stone or woodwork. Every symbol was inset with metal. Sunk into many of the thresholds were discs of copper or fine tracings of silver filigree woven into intricate arrangements that Cody knew she had seen in some other context; but it would not come to her. She was beginning to wonder just how extensive this labyrinth could possibly be. Already they must have walked further than the width of the building so far above them.

'The upper part of Wrayhaven is for show only,' said Veriman, startling her by how closely his words followed the path of her own thoughts. 'This is the living part of our sanctuary. Does any of it seem familiar to you?'

Between grimaces of pain he was staring at the girl by his side with an intensity that was not unfriendly but was distinctly unsettling. When Cody shook her head blankly he continued.

'I almost didn't recognise who you were out there. That was a brave step you took approaching so openly in that manner. There was barely time to close down the lightshield before you walked into it.'

Cody was about to ask what he meant by saying he recognised her when a jolt of pain shot through his frame and he had to hunch over to control it. All the muscles of his body were taut as piano wire. He hacked, smothering the cough with his left hand and then stared expressionless at the blood on his palm. 'I only hope we didn't take too many hits from the Spitters whilst we were vulnerable.' He wiped the palm along the sleeve of his right arm.

'Is there anything we can do for you Veriman?' Cody asked, her heart going out to him.

'You are already doing it, young one. Get me to the healing bay. Then perhaps you may help me some more.' Another coughing spasm curled him over. The poor man was plainly struggling, controlling the urge to clutch at where his chest was being eaten away by the corrosive sputum. Bella helped him stagger to a nearby trunk and eased him down onto it until the spasm passed. The large woman took a few steps back giving Cody the room to kneel by his side and place her hands on his shoulders in comfort. Without betraying herself she was feeling tentatively at the edges of his pain with her phantom hand. In her heart she was certain there was something they could do for him if only he would lie down and rest properly. Once again he took her by surprise addressing her unspoken thoughts,

'I will last for a pace. We are close to the healing bay now.' He inhaled slowly. 'Help me to walk a little further. I have things there that will reduce this flesh fire.' Bella came forward and they half carried the dying man through two more passageways and across a large circular dome, covered floor to ceiling in swooping spiral patterns. It was totally empty except for thousands of the symbols they'd seen in every other chamber.

'What's all this?' asked Josse, his eyes drifting along the twists of colour that led the eye in every direction.

Veriman paused for a moment and sank to one knee whilst steadying himself against Cody.

'This is a mesmer chamber. The symbols are mesmer glyphs.' A hacking cough stopped what he was about to say next. The little group waited patiently for him to recover. 'The glyphs and patterns exert an irresistible hypnotic attraction for creatures of simple mentality and hold them here, unable to break away or know why they cannot find a way out of this chamber. It is a trap.'

'Like a moth and lights,' suggested Josse his head moving in slow circles as he followed the fascinating configurations on every surface.

'Ingenious,' said Bella.

'Yes,' continued Veriman. 'Should any mindless intruder burrow its way this far beneath our defences it would be caught, entranced, held by the mesmeric potency of the glyphs, until we could come to deal with it. Simple, and elegantly effective.'

'We?' said Bella, sounding surprised, but Veriman had pushed himself to his feet and was already staggering towards the far side of the chamber. Cody kept level offering her arm. They approached what seemed to her like a blank wall, but as they got closer she could make out an oddly contoured doorway within the swirling motifs. They passed through. Bella followed, pushing the strangely reluctant Josse ahead of her. He stared longingly at the domed chamber over his shoulder until a bend in the next corridor cut off the view.

The healing bay was similar to hospital wards Cody had seen in Chester where she had been taken for check ups after the road accident three years ago. There were glass fronted cabinets and medical apparatus trailing wires and tubes, but there were essential differences too. Rows of narrow shelves were divided into dozens of labelled pigeon holes which filled half of a side wall, like some modernised apothecary's shop. The dominant smell was not the clinical odour of anaesthetics but a pleasing herbal essence that calmed and cleared the head. The lights were a soft blue radiance and the atmosphere resonated with an inaudible note that could be felt in the soles of the feet. Two bodies lay on raised tables in the centre of the room.

'Baria and Farsim, my fellow guardians,' explained Veriman as they eased him onto a sloping couch. 'They were injured in the first attack yesterday, cut down by a Vil-kind stalker pack before we knew what was happening. I was attending reports of an assault on another haven at the time but they took us completely by surprise here.'

'That would have been Clayton Bar,' said Bella sombrely.

'It was. Afterwards it seemed likely the two attacks were coordinated. A few Breed penetrated our defences before the light-wall could be triggered.' He was staring at the nearby forms wired up to life support machines. Their faces and bodies were covered in surgical dressing.

'I have them under sedation because of their injuries. They are…quite severe…but they will survive with proper care.'

'We knew we had to find you somehow,' said Cody, feeling suddenly awkward. 'That's why we came all this way.'

'And well that you did.' Veriman's face twisted in pain. 'We will talk of this soon. For now, will someone fetch me that large open box on the top shelf there? I must act quickly if this venom is to be slowed.'

Bella reached down the box and brought whatever else Veriman asked for whilst Cody helped him arrange the items that emerged from the containers and jars. Josse did not take part but plonked himself down on a stool by the door fidgeting. When Bella finished fetching and carrying she took up a position close by with one wary eye on the corridor outside. Veriman unstoppered an amber flask and swallowed deeply. His hunched shoulders began to drop a little as the painkiller in the draught worked its wonders. He spoke to Bella from the couch as he used scissors to cut away his ruined black top,

'We are quite safe. Our triple shield is operating perfectly. Nothing can breach such defences as we have, from inside or out. So, there is no need for concern.' He had to pause frequently to gather his strength and winced as the disintegrating material came away from his skin revealing his left arm and body grown almost black with bruising and dried blood. Carefully he lifted a small glass and silver phial on a chain out of the way, draping it over his uninjured shoulder. It was a perfect match for Cody's own.

A dozen open sores pocked the mutilated skin containing sullen embers of greenish luminosity within the pitted flesh. The hot vinegary smell was tinged with an undertone of putrefaction now. It appeared unbearably painful. Following patiently delivered instructions Cody assisted him in fashioning a splint of pencil sized glass rods around his upper and lower left arm lashing them into place with a flexible metallic mesh. It never occurred to question why she and not Bella was assisting Veriman. Working this way seemed as natural as tending bees or helping out in her dad's workshop.

Over the layer of metallic mesh went several wrappings of white bandage. Covering Veriman's chest in the same arrangement was more difficult. She had to be scrupulously careful not to touch any of the glowing pits in his skin. Soon the glass rods were in place and the silver mesh wrapped snug. Binding the whole torso with lengths of soft cotton bandage was easier. Veriman explained between small gasps as they worked.

'Careful now. The acidic ichor must be dealt with where it lies. You will have seen what the Spitter's venom can do to our

211

battlements – hm? Nothing can stop it, so beware. Now, these crystal rods will draw much of the active heat component away from the corrosive ichor. The silver mesh disperses it and cools the surrounding flesh. It also acts to sterilise the wound. Unfortunately nothing can remove the ichor itself. Anything touched by even a spot of the poison becomes contaminated and destroyed by corrosive action.' The muscles of his face had become more relaxed as the pain killer dispersed throughout his body.

'The active element of the ichor, or sputum, will be slowed down and I will have time to take care of some matters that need attention. Ironic isn't it. I'm dying because some filthy thing in a cage spat at me. Like a bad day at the zoo! '

No one else in the room laughed and Cody mopped at his brow with handfuls of cotton bandage. For the first time since they had met Veriman's features were unfurrowed. He smiled at her with a radiance that revealed the worry creases in his face as laughter lines. Intelligence sparkled in his eyes as he gazed into Cody's own.

'I know, young Eloin. I know. Questions. Questions and mysteries. But not just now. Trust me.'

He spoke to the room in general,

'Thank you everyone for your help. I am somewhat repaired for the moment. But next,' he said turning exclusively to Cody, 'We must apply one final layer to my walking coffin. Could you reach me the heavy jar from that small refrigeration unit in the corner?'

A ceramic screwtop jar was brought to the couch and Veriman let Cody slather a translucent paste over every inch of his bandaged arm with a glass spatula. When this paste was exposed to the light from an ultraviolet lamp it clouded to a pearlescent hue and went rigid. A similar coating was applied to his chest dressings and that too hardened to a metal-hard casing. They applied several layers of the paste.

'It is a form of lacquer,' Veriman explained. 'Tougher than steel, and lighter. A second skin, better than sheet armour.' He smiled thinly as he tentatively rotated his shoulder. The entire left arm was now one solid mass, bent at the elbow so that he could touch his chest.

'It will darken as it draws the venomous energy,' he added almost to himself. 'Are my companions well Bella?'

Bella was peering at the two unconscious guardians on the raised beds and checking their breathing. She nodded to Veriman,

'Your companions appear stable. But what of you? Will that layer of lacquer halt the progress of the corrosion?'

'No. The various layers slow its progress, each in their own way. It is all that can be done. I have bought myself a little time, nothing more.' Veriman's grin was grim.

'Can anything stop it? I mean completely?' asked Josse, still slumped by the wall and radiating misery.

'Nothing will do that. The venom particles will expand excreting acid into all surrounding matter, penetrating...'

'Alright!' yelled Josse. 'I'm sorry but we get the picture. I don't need details!'

Josse's appearance had not improved since Cody had last looked at him properly. Dark shadows had appeared around his sunken eyes. His skin was sickly white. For the first time since Clayton Bar Cody saw that the tiny network of scars on his hands stood out white, even against his pale skin. He looked worse than Veriman.

'I apologise,' said the custodian, rising gingerly from the couch. 'We must get you all some food and rest. You have had a difficult time.'

Cody's face burned with shame at Josse's inconsiderate outburst. Extremely high levels of tension were radiating invisibly off everyone in the room and she found it hard to separate the turmoil of emotional currents. It was a relief to be able to assist Veriman in donning a clean blue tunic taken from a locker. The garment reached to his mid-thighs and had wide enough sleeves to accommodate the bulk of his lacquered arm.

Veriman hobbled over to his companions on the beds. Tenderly he touched the face of each one mouthing words no one in the room could hear. There was great love in the gesture. With a resigned sigh he turned awkwardly to face Bella by the door.

'We must talk. There are a great many questions to be covered and things to be done. I would know how you came to be knocking on the walls of Wrayhaven unannounced. But first, food. We can walk this way.'

They left the sweet smelling air of the healing bay and accompanied their slowly shuffling guide along yet more corridors. Clearly the man was still in considerable discomfort. Cody shot an angry look at Josse but the poor lad was so sunk into his own misery, twitching and fidgeting like an infected cat, that she hadn't the heart to make her point more forcibly. He would not meet her eyes. She moved closer to

Veriman's left side and let him rest the bulk of his lacquered arm on her shoulder. There was hardly any weight to his body.

Twenty Seven
WONDER BELOW

'Damaged humans, all animals, are dangerous because they have survived great injury and know it is possible to do so again. Also, they will be motivated by notions of revenge.'
Words of a Chameleon Lord taken from 'Legends Of The Six Thorn Seeds' by Suskind Gromsen.

THE room Veriman described as the Parley Room was a large comfortable space with a roaring fire and a long trestle table down the middle. The smell of food, burning pine resin and warmth made it a welcoming place. Books, charts and intricate brass instruments covered the table and many other surfaces around the edges of the room. Here, as in most other places they had seen, unusual items covered the wood panelled walls: small shields, or what might have been shields, it was hard to be certain; arrangements of fine chains; medallions and polished stones on velvet trays; things preserved in blocks of solid glass and racks of what appeared to be short black staffs inset with metal rings at either end. Nothing was familiar, yet to Cody all of it was somehow comforting. The two youngsters slipped their coats onto the backs of a couple of chairs and warmed themselves at the fire.

Veriman indicated a doorway leading to a well stocked kitchen before collapsing exhausted into a chair by the fire. Bella took charge telling the two youngsters to bring food for them all whilst she helped Veriman find a comfortable position with his arm propped out in front of him. The lacquer shell of his arm was turning a deep cobalt blue.

The kitchen area opened further into two large larders filled with open shelves of well wrapped food as well as a walk-in cold room where cheeses and sealed pots stood in chilled preservation. Josse was little help at all.

'Josse, what's wrong. Speak to me.'

'I'm FINE. Just...' He snatched a loaf from Cody's arms and bustled back into the Parley Room. Cody followed him hurt and perplexed but keeping silent. They cleared a space at the table and began to bring plates and stone jars of milk from the kitchen. There was a cauldron of delicious smelling soup on a wide fire range that filled the entire end wall of the kitchen. Cody filled four bowls and carried them out to the table. She caught snatches of Bella's description of their journey from Clayton Bar including their names and smatterings of Old Tongue. Veriman kept shifting and wincing from the pain of his wounds. His face shone with sweat and it was obviously a monumental effort for him to concentrate on what was being said. Bella did not seem to take this into account. She talked with barely a pause. It was Bella's way, Cody knew that by now, but a little less forcefulness would not be amiss with such a sick man.

Both adults refused the offer of food and continued to murmur over by the fire as the youngsters ate at the table. Josse picked distractedly at his plate and continued to sulk. The coppery taste at the back of Cody's throat was fading with the cleansing effect of good wholesome food. As she chewed it struck her as odd that no one addressed the matter of why she had suddenly known what to do with the two rings and the glass and silver phial as they approached the castle walls. She didn't know herself what had happened. Possibly the adults did – but no one discussed it. It was exactly like a thousand other situations in her life where grown ups had treated her this way but this time she knew it was wrong. She was not a child any more, in fact, she may not even be a child at all from what Bella had said on the train. What was it now, about being older than she seemed – or something? Each time she tried to think back the memory of it became shadowy, as if a damp fog had settled itself around those moments. She looked over at Veriman sunk in the slow deluge of Bella's words and felt sorry for him. She knew exactly what it felt like.

Abruptly he rose to his feet and shuffled to the doorway they had entered by,

'Please forgive me,' he said with considerable effort. 'There is a matter I must attend...a personal matter,' he insisted as Bella offered to accompany him. 'Better you wait here till I come back. Please.' And he was gone! Cody hoped desperately that he'd be OK on his own. The three fugitives were alone in the room.

Questions hovered behind Veriman's exit like awkward guests but no one seemed inclined to talk. It was as if their shared adventure had drained them. Bella was suddenly withdrawn, Josse was sullen. He sloped over to the seat Veriman had vacated by the fire and slouched into it. Poor thing, he looked so miserable. Cody concentrated on her food and examined the array of wonders everywhere in the room. What wasn't openly on display was locked inside solid upright cabinets with impressive looking brass locks. The racks of ebony rods drew her eye. What could they be for? Not weapons – they were too short and simple for that. In fact, it seemed to her that the lack of weapons was unusual. You'd expect rows of swords or a couple of crossed axes in a place like this. There was armour alright, and shields (if they were shields) and more gauntlets, oh and the chain mail – if it really was chain mail! It would be wise to make no assumptions about anything from now on, she told herself.

Over by the fire Bella was whispering in fierce tones at Josse who was glaring back at her, wild eyed and defiant. His jaws were working furiously as if trying to spit something out. The emotional waves radiating from him were hot and fiery – anger, frustration, outrage. What was going on between them? The relationship between her companions was a complete paradox to Cody. She'd never been able to read it.

'Josse. What's wrong?' she said without moving from the table. 'What's wrong with him Bella. He's really not well is he. Look at him. I'm worried.'

'I think the demands of the last day have proven too much for our little companion,' Bella replied not taking her eyes off the boy.

Cody could see that Bella had the web of beaded threads woven between her fingers, as she had back at the Grove with Jesmina. Her steel flask was on the floor next to them.

'You don't think he's been infected with something do you Bella?' asked Cody alarmed.

'No!' The large woman was winding the threads around her gloves and stuffing them back into her pouch. 'I think Josse is exhausted. Stress and nervous depletion. Possibly lack of proper nourishment too. But the lad will not take anything. Stubborn.'

'I don't want anything!' yelled the sickly lad jumping up and backing into a corner. 'Leave me alone.'

A voice from the doorway took them all by surprise,

'Perhaps he has something to tell us,' announced Veriman leaning against the doorframe. The lacquered arm had turned completely black by now and matched the sleeveless flack jacket he had donned over the blue shirt.

Cody was almost knocked sideways by a burst of hatred so intense that it swamped the room. Totally disoriented she whirled to see who it was emanating from but the silent roar was shut off instantly as Josse pitched forward onto the floor his limbs thrashing. He seemed to be trying to shout something but was gagging as if gripped by the throat. White foam flecked his mouth. They all moved towards him but Bella motioned the others back saying,

'No, let me tend him. I may have pushed the lad too hard.' She looked at Veriman, 'Can I have the use of your sick room?'

'Back the way we came. You'll recognise the route, three rooms along.'

'Thank you,' said Bella lifting the squirming youth without effort and striding towards the door.

'Perhaps I should come too,' protested Cody, making as if to follow.

'No!' said Veriman quickly. 'Stay here with me. I need you here. She can manage the lad. Is that not so Bella.'

'Indeed,' came the reply as the hurrying woman disappeared along the corridor.

The echoing steps faded away and Veriman whirled on Cody, his face sparking with intensity. His whole demeanour had changed.

'Do not question! Listen only! Josse will be safe for now. You must come with me. Time is not our friend right now.'

'I...'

'*Sercetes Eloin Hauna Ceulimas Bimhir!* Questions in a while, old soul. Help me. There is something we must do together.'

He had used the exact same phrase Bee had spoken when last alive. Cody's mind was made up in an instant.

'Which way?'

'Good girl. This way.' Veriman pointed to a blank section of wall between two panels and took out his silver phial from around his neck. 'Do the same,' he urged.

Cody pulled at the silver chain around her neck and gripped the small crystal and metal object as she saw Veriman doing with the palm facing forward, the phial dead centre of the hand. They walked to the wall. A humming note came from deep within Veriman's chest but Cody's eyes were on the stonework directly in front of her. It shimmered. It gleamed and coruscated and felt apart in an expanding window of glittering fishtails that became a necklace of stars. Her chest had erupted into a furnace of pulsating power rippling outwards with every heartbeat.

'Now, Eloin – push. *Sherimai nu!*' said Veriman's voice within her mind. She did. Her phantom stretched forward through the shoal of stars and beyond – followed quickly by the girl herself.

'All time, past and present
Exist in an eternal future,
With future's roots embodied
In an unborn past.'
From Three Quadrants Of Mind by TK Edwins.

Twenty Eight
SPEECH FROM AFAR

'This is the truth of our lives – that we are none of us alone;
perhaps, in times such as ours, we would be safer if we were.'
From a 1914 lecture pamphlet, 'Deprived Of Form' by Prof David C Beltane.

THE way ahead was blocked by a round bronze door that filled the circular tunnel. In the centre was an ornate copper medallion, wide as a dinner plate and green with age. The carvings on it were very beautiful, some kind of script, possibly. Cody regarded Veriman in silence, waiting to see what they were meant to do next. He stepped close to the door holding his glass phial against the central boss of the design. The whole thing slid open, dividing along interlocking parts of the pattern and swinging back.

Stepping into the large space beyond Cody thought they were entering some sort of library. From where she stood she could see the backs of shelves reaching to the ceiling. The floor sloped steeply downwards so that the centre of the room was at the bottom of a huge inverted dome or bowl shape. The perspective of the place was confusing because as well as the floor sloping away from Cody the shelves got smaller the further she advanced into the room. Veriman led the way still leaning against her for support.

As they neared the lower slope Cody could see more of the room's layout and guessed that the symbol on the doors was probably a plan of the space they had entered with rows of shelves marked out as parts of the radiating, web-like design. And they weren't books stacked on the shelves either. Sweeping around her in rows, like stadium seating, were shelves containing hundreds of bowls. They were every size and colour, every material and pattern, plain, ornate, crude, rounded, tapered, deep and shallow. More bowls than she could imagine a use for.

The end section of each lower shelf was made up of dozens of tiny drawers, like the apothecary shelves they'd seen in the healing room.

The shelves at the lowest part of the chamber were no more than table height with open shelves on all four sides. On one central worktop rested an open tome filled with enigmatic diagrams, a scattering of twenty or so tiny wooden boxes and a large brass bowl.

'Welcome to the chamber of the Chalcis Ymlyr, Eloin Cody Conmar,' said Veriman, in a tone that was hard to interpret. 'Of all the secrets, wonders and mysteries within the walls of Wrayhaven, these are it greatest treasure – or were until you arrived.'

Cody covered her embarrassment by helping him onto a stool set close to the book and bowl. She moved round to the opposite side of the worktop.

'In what way are they so precious,' she asked, noting a wide selection of seeds, crystals and obscure fragments arranged on trays or folds of parchment next to the tiny boxes. A thick amber liquid filled the lower third of the brass vessel.

'What you see in this chamber may very well be why we are under such determined attack. These bowls, the Chalcis Ymlyr, or speaking bowls, are the pinnacle achievements of an obscure science whereby we of the Sufinam may communicate at great distances without being overheard. You see these items here?' he indicated the seeds, shells and so on. Cody nodded. 'When these are placed exactly in each marked section marked out on the bowl's rim we can speak to an exactly paired bowl wherever it is, however distant.'

'It's like the singing Tibetan bowls I read about,' grinned Cody delighted. 'If one bowl plays a certain vibration…'

'…the sound energy of speech will resonate in its twin – exactly. The precise tuning of one to the other is achieved by the correct placing of each element or stone or whatever. If even one element is misplaced, if the depth and nature of the fluid in the body of the bowl is incorrect then its voice will remain mute.

'Every bowl in this room has its counterpart somewhere out in the world and each pair are vital in the ongoing struggle with the eternal enemies beyond our walls. For those devolved entities to gain possession of what we are guarding here would be disastrous. So much could fall into peril. There are six in particular…and the books of lore that go with them…' Veriman was becoming agitated; pain danced across the lines in his face. '...It cannot be allowed to happen! Cody, it will not happen. The defences we have around us...' He coughed wetly and clutched at his lacquered chest, '...but there is another matter we must speak of before time overtakes me.'

Veriman was sweating heavily and rested his lacquered arm on the table top as if it weighed more than himself. Cody waited whilst he wiped blood from his lips and mustered the strength to continue.

'What do you know of the woman who brought you here?' The question was abrupt and clearly intended to be so.

'I...until she rescued me from the attacks on our village I had seen her a few times. No more.'

'What does your heart tell you of her?' Veriman's expression was calm despite his fever bright eyes.

'In all honesty I don't know. She is strong and has saved me so many times these last days...hours, that I...'

'No, that is the response you have been directed into giving. Speak from your heart. What does your heart tell you? What is her nature?'

Cody felt the floor shift beneath her feet and she experienced a sense of plummeting from a great height, her senses swimming, her ears aroar with whistling air. She suddenly had no idea what she was thinking and looked at Veriman blankly.

'Thank you,' he said calmly. 'I have my answer. There are strong barriers within you still, though they are weakening. We must attend to that – if there is time. Come closer. I must explain a thing to you, whilst I still can.' Cody could hardly get any closer but she leaned towards him over the bowl.

'Do you know what an Eloin is, and that you are one yourself?'

'Yes. Bella started to tell me as much on our journey here, but I don't know what it all means.'

'Did she! *Falarime!* Cody, pay attention - Eloin are the next hope of humanity. They carry the potential of all humankind's highest aspirations because of what they can achieve and become. I am telling you this now, and we talk as strangers Cody Conmar, because it seems to you that we have not met before. And yet I tell you we were once old friends. By that I mean that we were both friends, as we were once both old together.'

'Bella kept saying something about me being older than I seemed.'

Veriman could see that Cody was trying to appear helpful but it really wasn't making sense to the girl and he sighed deeply.

'You have been asleep, a kind of waking sleep, for three years. The initial period of true Eloin Awakening is usually in the eighteenth year. For one as young as yourself it will be that much more difficult because your memories have been provoked prematurely. You will find this a challenging phase, old soul. I will try and keep it simple.' Veriman sighed. 'Cody Conmar, I knew you when you were older. We had many adventures together for a forty year or more. Hopefully this and much else will come back to you in its right time and way.'

'Veriman I don't disbelieve what you are saying, truly, but how can it be? How can I be older? Please tell me in a way that helps me to understand because none of it makes any sense.'

The suffering man shifted his shoulders trying to get comfortable. The pain made his face grey and his skin glistened with the dew of illness. He stared at Cody nonplussed, feeling for the words.

'The human race has always been evolving, since before man and woman could stand upright. It is a process that never rests. Some improvements have been achieved in our natures and bodies; some changes have gone tragically wrong. It is the way of things, *Tathata*, suchness: the acceptance of all patterning in life, fortunate and unfortunate alike. But there was one rare occurrence that held great promise – the Eloin!

'Eloin are the hope humankind has been waiting for. Every Eloin that we find we protect and nourish until they reach full maturity. Every mature Eloin is another force for good set loose in the world to work for the betterment of all mankind. All Eloin, yourself included, have the potential to become the greatest healers, innovators, creators, thinkers, musicians, poets, artists, builders and inspirers that the history of the world has ever seen. Unfortunately, not all sentient entities wish the world to become what you and your kind could make of it, as you have already witnessed. They would corrupt you, bend your mind and will, distort what you could achieve. Instead of an Eloin's miraculous abilities benefiting humanity, they would be polluted and used to oppress and enslave. It has all happened before – and will again no doubt.'

223

Veriman was breathing hard, his gasps echoing faintly around the open shelves. Cody was staring numbly at the items on the table top.

'I have no idea what I am supposed to think Veriman. I hear your words but it sounds like some creation of the storytellers. And even if I am one of these Eloin what am I supposed to do? What does it mean that you say I am older than I appear?'

'Alright my dear. I will give it to you bold. You are not twelve years old. You are an Eloin. You are a new emergent. You have grown out of an earlier older life, one in which you reached great wisdom and powers as someone called Ceulwas. Ceulwas was a given name, almost a title; your true name was...something else. You were an accomplished healer and forger of destinies. You and I were friends, great friends. We knew many other...friends...and companions. These too you will come to recall as you your memories are restored.

'At the end of that first life of yours I was one of those who stayed by your side whilst your eighty year old body slept in the safety of a chrysalis shell and reformed into the young one you now inhabit.

'Three years ago you became Cody Conmar with no memory of your earlier existence or those involved in your life. In total you are now almost a century old though your body is that of a twelve year old. All your previous abilities sleep within you, locked into your buried memories. And your conscious memories go back only as far as three years.'

'Three years! That was when the accident happened. It's beginning to make sense! I think. That was why we went to live in Clayton Bar!'

'True, that was when you were taken to the Cheshire haven, but there was no accident. That was merely a story invented to explain your lack of earlier memories.'

'Then how come mum and dad weren't over a hundred years old too if...if...' her words slowed to a halt as her mind unwound. Though both feet were firmly planted on the solid flagstones she was falling through the floor.

'But...but,' she tried to rally her senses.

'Go on Cody,' urged Veriman in a whisper. 'Stay the course. Stay open to what is happening. I sense that your mind shield is about to disperse - *Beleriath shamophane Ceulwas.*'

In Cody's mind the glittering gate of fish tails was arching over her head, through her head, sending shards of light and tiny fireworks of unrecognisable emotions bursting throughout her body and limbs. Her phantom hand pulsed with heat and a parade of images collapsed through her inner mind like a tumble of cards, each a captured moment of some forgotten experience. She saw faces she knew but could not name. She recalled scaling great peaks of rock and rowing subterranean rivers with companions who glowed like deep-sea fish in currents of radiant blue. It was like sinking though the levels of a life familiar but unclaimable as her own. And a face she knew swam up to greet her, holding out a palm wrapped in thin silver chain. Someone else she knew stood behind him – *Lucian?* She grasped the hand and was pulled from some rough edged pit onto fresh grass and sunlight. She looked up to say thank you – and the face was Veriman's, younger and bearing scars but the same. And that other face…?

…Cody opened her eyes. The man holding her hands now, as then, was Veriman. He smiled.

'Are you back Cody-Ceulwas?' He stared, eyes fierce with hope.

'In part, at least, Veriman,' she managed to say. 'Dear Veriman. You helped me clear the vent's mouth at Castle Rigg. It was you. And I see now that your scars have healed.' She did not ask about the name…*Lucian, Lucian, Lucian*…not yet.

Veriman's sharp laughter was like sunlight bursting out from around his head.

'It was some time ago,' he smiled delighted.

'Oh,' she almost cried, her eyes wide in revelation. 'If that's true, then…then my mum and dad…' Veriman stayed very still. 'They were not really my true mother and father. Is that right? It is, isn't it. How…how do I know that? I've been told it before but…now the truth is with me. You are right. We were once great friends. But how long ago was that? What has happened? Where have I been?'

'You have been yourself. And now you begin to come back,' he beamed. 'Do not fret if there is too much at once. It will return in its own way. But this at least is a beginning. The important thing now is not to rush it. No, Mary and Teddy Conmar were not your true flesh parents. They were your guardians. Brave, selfless, dedicated people of extraordinary kindness and courage.'

'And they died for me. As did Bee and uncle Ben.'

'This is true. All such knowledge will be hard to bear at first until your understanding matches pace with your recall. Also, I fear the dangers in your too-early Awakening. Some memories will be hard to bear. We will have to consult on that. But for now, you need to engage in something else, look the other way, as it were; come upon your old self as you would approach a newborn calf. Come, help me.' He made to prop himself up on his lacquered arm. Cody walked round the table top and supported his shoulders, taking care not to pull on his arm.

'Oh don't worry about this old limb,' he smiled. 'It has no feeling left. I dare say I could batter a goodly wall of masonry without undue discomfort.' His grimace of pain told otherwise but Cody did not demur. 'Cody-Ceulwas, I have been instructed to show you something of the skill of bowl lore. Watch what I do. I am about to speak with someone who knows you are here.' She bowed her head indicating readiness and watched what he did.

Whilst consulting an open page of the ledger on the table Veriman arranged a combination of knotted silver wire, glass beads, wood and stone fragments around the rim of the bowl, adding some from the collection of little boxes, shifting others around until he appeared satisfied.

'The exact arrangement changes every time in accord with coded guidelines in the ledger here,' he pointed to the perplexing patterns of lines and symbols on the vellum page. 'The match must be exact for both Chalcis Ymlyr to be attuned, and as you can see there are many bowls to choose from. The speech twins to all of those in this chamber are dispersed throughout the world - a humbling and sober thought.'

He added drops of something to the liquid inside the bowl and slowly poured a measured amount of water from a brass tankard taken from one of the lower shelves. As the level rose up a series of marks scratched onto the inside of the brass vessel a voice emerged from the bowl as if someone was approaching from the far end of a tunnel. The voice grew stronger and Veriman spoke a greeting,

'Merhaba arr sher Beulimas.'

'*Merhaba Beuliman so varrime. Verriman, is that you. Thank goodness. Is the attack continuing?*'

'Yes. Garatunde is very determined for reasons of his own. As yet only the upper structure has taken any damage. Baria and Farsim are still unconscious.'

226

'That is best with the wounds they have. Veriman, you must keep our charge safe until help arrives. Something huge and unsuspected is massing. The dual attacks on Clayton Bar and yourselves were coordinated, and other havens were tested. The Pact is being ignored. We are consulting the 'allies' and preparing our response, which will be severe. The Chameleons will regret this action.'

Cody watched Veriman's eyes rolling up into his head and thought for a moment it might be some necessary state of trance until she saw the grimace for what it was. He was struggling to stay focused against the onslaught of pain! Rivulets of sweat ran down his neck. Cody touched his arm gently as the voice from the bowl continued,

'Veriman, you must be prepared. Sephamon will be arriving at Wrayhaven soon. You must hold her safe until then. Will that be possible...?'

But Veriman was no longer listening. His entire body had spasmed causing his uncontrolled limbs to flail at the air. He crashed to the floor as his lacquered arm smashed into the bowl sending it spinning across the table. Seeds and crystals scattered in every direction as water spilled everywhere and the bronze shell crashed onto the floor. The shattering echo reverberated in the domed silence. Cody leapt to his side, horrified at how the man had become oblivious of everything except his agony. The fire in his flesh was eating him alive. She could well be watching her friend's death throes - if she didn't intervene quickly!

On an instinct she spoke words of invocation, silently in her mind - *Lucian clavimé* - without knowing what they meant - and her inner world slid sideways...

Twenty Nine
WEAPONS FROM THE WALLS

AS Veriman's body thrashed beneath her left hand Cody grasped at the phial and locket hung at her neck with her right. Instantly a curtain of light swept across her mind bringing with it an icy stillness. In her chest there began the creeping heat that made her phantom hand flex and stretch. This time it extended out from her body instantly, as soon as she willed it. There it was in her mind's eye, faint as a mere twist of air in the light, the form of a hand without true substance, little more than a shimmer of radiance but strong, oh so strong. Cody felt as if she could crush steel with the grip that flowed from the furnace of her chest.

Knowing exactly what to do she leant forward and thrust the unthing of the hand below the shiny black carapace of lacquer on Veriman's arm and deep within her friend's limb grasping at the veins of fire that scorched his maimed flesh. Neither the lacquer nor the fine silver mesh was a barrier to her. She began to smother each searing thread of heat with her ghost hand, but it was like trying to pat out fire in a smouldering carpet. When you thought you had put out one part it flared up in another place. She managed to reduce the fire; it slowed, cooled to something little more than a fever heat - but it would not die away completely.

She shifted her hand inside his ravaged rib cage, squeezing and smothering the areas of searing heat there. The hideous corrosion had penetrated past his flesh to the inner bastion of the vital organs. The outer flesh and bones of his ribcage could be sealed with scar tissue but if she was to truly help him she must prevent the progress of the burning ichor and if possible neutralise it. She gripped and smothered with her unhand, doing everything she could think of, but the sullen fire would not be quenched. It was a difficult thing for her to accept. She would not be able to save her crippled friend, only halt the agonising onslaught on his body.

Alright, if that was all she could achieve then so be it! She took a deep calming breath...

The image she summoned was from another time and place, an inner resource of sensations and abilities that had been folded away inside her most shielded memories. She saw a great pool of chill luminous water that splashed into her cupped hands as she first stirred, then swept her arms deep beneath its soothing surface. Lifting her invisible limb she allowed droplets to fall onto the burning flesh. The droplets became a trickle, then a stream and finally a torrent pouring out in a cleansing rush funnelled by her invisible hand over the affected areas of Veriman's body. She sensed the heat drop away to almost nothing, a slumbering pulse of warmth, the heartbeat of an undefeated enemy. Corrosive ichor still slumbered beneath the lacquered shell but for a while Veriman would be free of the maddening pain and perhaps she had bought him enough time to concoct a more permanent measure – she wished she could believe that was possible.

But the opportunity never came. As he lay on the ground groaning the floor shook, followed instantly by a dull explosion. Something pounded the vaulted structure around them and dust fell in streams from the stone roof above. The attack must be making progress to be getting so near! The impact registered on Veriman's senses because he roused himself and gasped.

'Ceulwas? What did you do? The pain is almost gone.' He struggled to sit up and tried swinging his arm experimentally. His grin of delight was almost impish, but brief...

CRUMP! The lights in the chamber flickered, died, flared, then sparked unsteadily before returning to their previous level. Veriman's face became a mask of horror.

'The Luminic power cells are under attack! If they are damaged Garatunde's hordes could break through. We have to get to the core generators!'

*   *   *

They rushed up the sloping floor and out of the chamber, pausing at the end of the circular tunnel whilst Veriman grasped his crystal phial and pushed through the final wall barrier himself. They almost fell into the Parley Room and kept running. Cody had no clue where they were headed and she could barely keep up. Veriman moved like a young man, his body agile, his gait sure, despite a distinct limp. They ran along twisting corridors past storage rooms and vaulted cisterns where water was collected or waste recycled. Cody even glimpsed tanks containing plants lit by rows of lamps – hydroponics! This subterranean complex was obviously intended to be self sustaining, and capable of withstanding a long siege – should it ever occur. It looked like the defensive measures were going to be tested.

Veriman skidded to a halt in front of another set of reinforced doors banded in copper and silver. He grasped a pair of protruding handles the size of rolling pins set wide apart on the wood and metal surface and held fast when blue flashes of energy arced between them. Before the doors had fully opened he was shouldering his way in with Cody close behind.

Inside, another chamber of wonders greeted Cody's astonished sight.

This space was long and narrow sunken in the centre like a chariot racing arena. At intervals around the walls on the upper level were glowing monitor screens and chairs. Freestanding arches hung suspended below the main ceiling dominating the central area like massive stone ribs. Beneath these, set in a line at ground level, were three glowing pyramids of soft light.

Veriman hobble-skipped down the steps to the first six foot high pyramid and began to moving his hands along one of the triangular surfaces. A metal hoop was set into the translucent material and gave off odd wavering tones as Veriman traced shapes in the air around it. The pitch of the sounds varied depending on where and how fast he moved his palms.

Cody drew level and gazed in wonder at the ethereal beauty of three spinning force-fields within each pyramid. They were hypnotically beautiful, and if she did not look directly at the spheres subtle shifting patterns could make out dancing on the surface like shimmering silk. Within the force-fields themselves she could make out faint outlines of constantly revolving rings of colour.

'These are the Luminic core generators that power everything in Wrayhaven,' barked Veriman above the dips and pitches of sound he was evoking from the pyramids. Lines of text and diagrams flowed across the translucent triangular face. Veriman was scanning the readouts at phenomenal speed. When Cody moved her head slightly different levels of script appeared. It was very disorienting. Veriman's arms moved like humming birds.

'I don't understand it. There was an unprecedented drain on the Luminic power with that explosion. There is no damage to the cores but something is wrong. I have no idea what it is.' He looked over at Cody appealing for help but she had nothing to contribute.

'Will your companions be safe?' she asked.

'I don't know. We'd better check on...Oh no! Ceulwas quickly...to the healing room. We may already be too late!'

Again, for all that she was younger, Cody was unable keep level with her injured friend. They left the chamber at a run and he was several yards ahead by the time they approached the facility where Baria and Farsim lay helpless. She called out to Bella but got no reply. Even from yards away a fetid reek of burnt flesh, plastics and scorched metal filled the corridor. They crashed to a standstill in the doorway.

Josse was sat up on one of the raised metal cots in a corner regarding them coldly. The two beds where Veriman's companions had lain were fire blackened ruins. The charred outline of a body lay in the corner opposite from Josse; it was still smouldering. Black spatters of something oily were scattered everywhere on the tiled floor.

'You are too late,' said Josse, with sinister flatness. His eyes were barely visible beneath lowered brows. His face looked terrible, the skin was blotched on one side, blue-black bruises flecked crimson with veins vivid as writhing snakes. His hands were concealed within his sleeves. Cody had no idea which was more appalling, the hollowness of his voice or his appearance. Veriman took half halting steps towards the bodies of his two companions eyes flitting between the beds and the shape on the floor. He was frozen unable to advance or retreat. His whole body trembled.

'Josse! What happened?' gasped Cody. 'Where's Bella?'

'Gone,' was the reply, followed by what could have been a cough of a low chuckle.

'Josse,' she said carefully, as if addressing an injured animal. 'What...?'

'Ceulwas! No more questions!' Veriman's voice was steel. 'Nothing will be gained from the things we see here. Your once-friend is too far gone.' Veriman stalked across the room to stand threateningly over

Josse. He had positioned himself between the lad and the open doorway, clenched fists held palm forwards and away from his body. Fury radiated from his trembling frame. Josse didn't flinch or react in any way.

'I will stay here with...Josse. I want you to retrace our steps to the Parley Room and fetch two of the short black staffs racked to the wall. Whatever you meet return with the staffs.'

'Of course Veriman.' This was not a time for questions.

'And...Ceulwas...'

'Veriman...?'

'Be swift.'

Veriman hadn't taken his eyes off the shrunken figure of the boy. Without a word Cody fled into the twisting corridors outside. The moment the Healing Room was out of sight the devastating kick of an explosion threw her against a wall. The impact sent stars spinning before her eyes but she staggered on shaking her head to clear it. The lights flickered and went out. Then started again, only to die almost immediately. There came cries of pain or possibly exultation from somewhere in the darkness. It was pitch black. A crackling sound made the air ripple and more concussions shook the floor. Then the lights flickered feebly and began alternating on and off, an irregular strobe effect that was most unnerving in the confined space.

Cody half groped her way, half stumbled to the Parley Room which was full of smoke from the smouldering fireplace. Every shadow appeared threatening in the strobing illuminations. The restraining bar across the row of black staffs came away with no resistance. She snatched the two nearest, swinging them through the air to test their weight. They felt good in her hands, beautifully balanced. Then she was running again to rejoin Veriman. There was a stink of burning in the air.

As she passed the luminic generator room she saw that the heavy doors were little more than charred timber and dripping molten slag. The crackling sound from the pyramid cores was louder here and she took a second for a quick glance inside. Her eyes widened in horror.

The shimmering orbs of the middle pyramid were being savaged by forks of jagged black discharge from a point on the pyramid's outer surface! The glowing spheres of energy pulsed and stuttered in time with the strobing lights of the labyrinth tunnels. Ugly cracks flickered across the beautiful spheres like sinister webs. The sound was of an animal in pain.

She couldn't help herself – she ran down the steps moving as quickly as she dared in the alternating blindness and flare of the lights. Such was the force of the electrical discharge thudding around the pyramids that she had to push forward against an invisible wind. Only up close could she make out a detail that had not been there before – a small silver tipped crystal had been hammered into the hard glass shell of the pyramid. It was one of the silver and glass phials! And the poisonous forks of energy rippling from this tiny sliver of matter were shredding the Luminic core that protected all of Wrayhaven!

Without a pause she hooked the end of a staff under the chain of the phial and wrenched it out, flinging it across the room. The Luminic orbs flared into an accelerated riot of blinding light that purged the black tendrils, dissolving them in a series of pulses. The animal whine of distress abated followed by all the lights within the chamber brightening.

Silence!

Cody spun on her heels to race back up the steps. Her mind was in a frenzy to reach Veriman, hoping she hadn't left him too long. 'Be swift,' he'd said. She'd already delayed too long but something else caught her eye on the walls of the chamber. Black trickles were seeping from between the stones and pooling at ground level! Already wide patches were spilling down the first steps towards where the pyramid generators were set. Instinctively she knew it was Tar but had to get closer to confirm her fears. She was right –thick glutinous trickles were pouring into the chamber from a dozen gaps between the stones…no, there were more…even as she watched rows of shiny droplets emerged between the masonry and left gleaming trails as they ran down the stonework. The trickles widened, increasing in size as she watched. The Tar was penetrating from the Chameleon trenches, through more than a hundred feet of earth and solid rock. There was nothing she could do! She must warn Veriman.

She ran past the shattered doors without a glance. Every wall she passed on the way back was bleeding streams of shiny black in the now steady light. There was still a way to go to reach the Healing Room when another explosion pounded the tunnels throwing her to her knees. The crash of collapsing masonry was followed by shouts and screams. The sounds came from a passageway to her left and one of the voices was Veriman's. Without a pause she leapt to her feet and changed direction, swinging the short black staffs at her sides as she ran. They hummed in her hands.

Suddenly the passageway opened up into a large, high domed chamber and Cody emerged to a scene that could have stopped the heart of an ox. A huge section of ceiling had been blasted inwards exposing a tunnel dug from somewhere on the surface far above. A gigantic slope of shattered stone, earth and masonry led up to the opening. On all sides thick streams of tar slicked the remaining walls and had pooled in every hollow and dip of the flagstones. But these were just background details; what held centre stage was a tableau so unexpected that time congealed as Cody's mind struggled to assimilate what she was witnessing.

Halfway up the mound of masonry, facing upslope, stood Veriman, his feet wide apart in a defensive crouch. His ceramic arm was raised in shield position, his right arm swung back low by his side as if about to grip some weapon on his hip. Something metallic gleamed on his hand. Around his feet half a dozen shattered Vil-kind lay twisted like broken dolls. Tentacles of shiny ooze quested from gaps within the rubble like blind worms. Against a far wall lay Josse, limbs at unnatural angles suggesting that he had been thrown there with considerable force. And towering above it all with her back to the shattered tunnel roof stood the terrifying figure of something that had once been Bella. It was the clothing that gave it away since the face bore little relation to the woman Cody had become so familiar with in the last days. It was as if all the facial muscles had slipped revealing a flayed travesty of features that could not stay constant. This grotesque mask was framed by the same flowing mane of hair and the ever present dark glasses. But hell was in that face and although it had been focussed on Veriman, both figures poised as if about to launch themselves in mutual annihilation, the hell visage was now focussed squarely on Cody.

All movement had frozen at Cody's sudden appearance. The air was chill with blood rage and menace. The eternity of confusion in her mind lasted no more than a second but every detail burned into her consciousness. Her chest surged with heat so intense she would have expected to combust on the spot if there had been time to register the thought – but time snapped back into effect with an accelerated blurring of action...

...the Bella-thing hurled itself towards Cody with a predator's shriek, her cloak booming out like great black wings, her arms obscured by the terrible speed of those ghastly nine inch blades cutting patterns through the air. This was how Cody had seen death approach in nightmares.

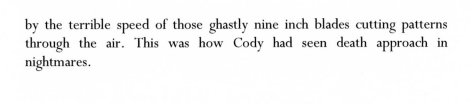

'A good soldier is not violent. A good fighter is not angry. A good winner is not vengeful.' Quote from an article on the writings of Lao Tzu by Beowulf Clark.'
See more on egl.theeffectivehandincombat.co.uk

Thirty
UNFOLDING AND UNLEASHING

'My kind live long, the years refine
Our minds and strength; perfected wine.'
BA Wyeth.

CODY would have gone under Bella's knives had not Veriman
taken the screaming Dervish down in a midair body tackle that smashed
them both into the heaped rubble a dozen yards away. They hit hard,
scrapping like wildcats, limbs locked together in a thrashing tangle until
Bella leapt clear, leaving Veriman struggling to his feet with evidence of
knife slashes across his unprotected right leg. His right hand wore a
silvered gauntlet of plates from which radiated a small wrist shield, the
size of a discus – it glowed the same subdued blue as had the defences of
Wrayhaven.

Bella's attention returned instantly to Cody. The not-quite
vulnerable looking girl stood swinging the black rods in wide circles
weaving a wall of protection in the air around her body. The rods
hummed with electric threat – none of which made Bella hesitate for an
instant. She sprang clear of a wrack of stonework spearing the girl with
her terrible gaze. Her great body was gathered to spring like a lion when
suddenly she screamed an inhumanly high pitched noise that set the nerves
jangling. A needle-thin lance of blue fire had swept across her thigh.
Veriman was on one knee holding two silver rings lined up with the phial
on his chest and aiming the ice-clear beam at the spitting snarling enemy.
The piercing ray lanced at the Bella creature for a second time but her
response was so fast that Cody missed it, although she registered the
swiftness of Veriman's raised arm and the blur of the stiletto that flashed
through the air. The missile ricocheted off Veriman's lacquered shell to
end up imbedded deep in a slab of brickwork.

In the fraction of a breath it took for Veriman to regain his balance two shapes appeared at the gap near the shattered ceiling howling with fury. It was a couple of the grotesque Vil-kind. They slid down the rubble pile in a frenzy of limbs and stabbing spikes only to be cut in half as Veriman swept the blue needle light across their paths. But the man was in trouble from another direction. Thick black tendrils from within the rubble had wrapped themselves around his legs and he began to totter backwards dragged towards the wall. As his attention turned to the new threat another Vil-kind appeared from the breached opening and flapped towards the cornered man like a monstrous predatory bat.

Everything was occurring in accelerated time, and all at once. Some divided part of Cody's mind had registered the fact that Bella had vanished, disappearing up the corridor behind them at a run. Another band of her awareness marked the Vil-kind threat to her friend Veriman with legs clamped by tar black bands. And two more scarecrow horrors had erupted from the shattered ceiling. Her chest became a raging furnace of lava.

And then it happened...

The change...

A wet ripping sensation in her mind!

It was both release and agony together; something at least twice the size of her head erupting inside her skull. The pressure was intense. She went blind. Her bones were exploding. She was flying apart. She was coming together. Her phantom hand rocketed five to six feet from her body then telescoped tight within her chest. Torrential light flooded her torso and limbs. She remembered her life and lives, and the sheer breadth of what crowded into her mind scattered every sense that she had – she was separating, drifting, lost...until...until, at the very centre of her being, in the eye of the storm, she found the balancing point between past present and future. The turmoil settled. Became still.

She was home. Herself. One. Reunited. Integrated. Whole again – and all within the beat of a second.

Slipping a silver ring on each hand she began to spin the twin Lodestaffs like Catherine wheels. They responded as live things about to be set loose. With astonishing strength and accuracy she flung one in a soaring arc that took the lead Vil-kind across the throat dropping it like a stone. Veriman saw this and concentrated on the sludge tentacles clinging to him, burning them away with the light beam perilously close to his own thighs. Cody leapt surefooted up the loose masonry, scooping up the fallen staff as she did so and clashed head on with the Vil-kind before they were half way down the slope. The impetus of the vibrating staffs was unstoppable. Metallic bands were glowing at the ends of the shafts and it was as if the weapons drew energy from the very impacts of the obstacles they shattered.

With wide swings and short powerful thrusts Cody blocked every slow motion move the grotesques attempted with their blackened spikes and blades. Cody's mind hung at the calm centre of a storm that was her own whirlwind body as the twin Lodestaffs battered and smashed her filth encrusted patchwork antagonists to the ground. The last one collapsed headless into a heap as Cody's Dervish pirouettes took her to the open gap of the ceiling and peered in. The opening was at least a hundred feet below the surface from which the Vil-kind burrowers had dug and blasted their way into the depths of Wrayhaven. Faint bellows and roars echoed from the surface but nothing moved in the darkness – for now. The restored light wall was keeping all at bay.

She landed lightly by Veriman's side as the last twitching black tendril slid into the mound of steaming sludge at his feet. The shaking hands that grasped the rings fell to his sides as the blue needle of light died away. His breath came in ragged gulps as he regarded the twelve year old warrior with awe. She had wielded the deadly Sufinam staffs so naturally.

'Ceulwas...are you back now?' he gasped, a trace of desperate longing in his voice. The wounded man was in a state of near collapse.

'Yes...no! I...yes, I am. I am back Veriman, *Arkadash*.' She could tell that the use of the familial term pleased him even as he stepped out of the sludge pool and glanced up at the ceiling.

'Nothing else approaches that way – yet,' she assured him. He looked at her. 'And Bella has fled,' she added.

'Not fled, no. If she can shut down the Luminic cores again her breed will be in here in force, not just these few skirmishers who slipped through whilst our defences were down. She has to be eradicated.'

'You knew it was she who damaged the cores before?'

'I know now that it was. She double bluffed me using Josse as a cover. He has been a pawn in her moves all along, as, I'm afraid, have you. She used you to gain access. Her wiles blinded us all. I wasn't in a state to pay attention properly at first,' Veriman lifted his lacquered arm by way of explanation. 'The pain.'

'No one could blame you for that,' consoled Cody.

'Even so, by the time my wits did return I recognised her as far too dangerous to confront directly. I had to improvise guarded responses as best I could. Garatunde and his hell breed were poised for our light wall to drop before pouring in. The lad was suffering from the parasite he bears in his chest. His will has not been his own and the presence of so much silver and copper was distressing the spore leech and he was paying the price. Poor soul. I had to buy us some time – but she killed Baria and Farsim anyway and infected the Luminic cores. She must have smuggled in a Chameleon viral weapon to infect them. Oh, Ceulwas, the desecration! The loss! I should have known. This is so vile a transgression of the Pact. There will be Hell Geld to pay for this.' Veriman had used the last of whatever reserves of strength he had and his body was going into shock. He sank onto a slab of masonry.

'It was her periapt phial.'

'What?'

'Obviously not a true silver phial as Sufinam have but a disguised Chameleon artefact. It was corrupting the Luminic cores till I removed it.' Cody paused, ambushed by a thought. The expression of dismay in her face alarmed Veriman.

'Ceulwas, what is wrong?'

'I didn't destroy it! I didn't know then. I merely threw it away. Bella could get her hands on it again!'

'It is not done yet,' snapped Veriman. 'We must find her before she spreads her corruption any further.' He started to move forward but his legs gave way and he sank onto the wreckage strewn floor. They both saw how his legs ran crimson from Bella's knives and multiple wounds where the black tendrils had attached themselves. Cody caught his shoulders as he sank backwards and lowered his head to the ground. He indicated one of the pouches on his flak jacket and Cody pulled out a medikit. She bandaged his seeping wounds with expert speed.

'Veriman, you have done enough. Leave it to me.'

Veriman laughed wetly,

'I'm very much afraid I will have to, old soul. I will remain with the lad. I managed to paralyse his parasite so he will have a moment of peace. Protect the light wall Ceulwas – failing that, save the Chalcis Ymlyr, the six I told you of, or we are all lost.'

Cody's decision was instantaneous. It was astonishing to feel her thoughts moving so swift and certain; no time wasting on what-if's and maybe's.

'Veriman, guard Josse. I will attend him as soon as I return.'

'Yes, *verime*.'

'Nothing will get past the light wall and you will be safe - if not exactly comfortable. Can you hold out?'

'I can. Here, take my gauntlet.' Veriman fumbled at the restraints of his metalled glove; the workmanship of the many overlapping plates was exquisite. 'These three studs here activate the wrist shield. This slide broadens its span.'

'No, I have no need.' Cody stilled his shaking fingers picking at the straps. 'I have the Lodestaffs.' She swung them vigorously, exulting in the energy that thrilled along her arms. They hummed ominously.

'And the rings,' added Veriman.

He was right! The nature and use of the ring skills lay open and ready in her mind – at last! She smiled hugely. Oh, what it felt to be whole again, after so long.

'Veriman, I really am back.'

'Though only in a twelve year old body, old soul. Be aware of the limits that will hold you to. Your old life will need time to settle into your new one.'

'Even so...' she grinned at him. 'Hold fast *Arkadash*,' and she was gone racing down the tunnel.

Veriman began to drag himself to where Josse lay against the wall, taking care to skirt the tar pools. The lad lay like a discarded puppet, which was exactly what he had been of course: an Orowghast, a puppet walker, slaved to the spore leech imbedded in his chest and controlled by his Chameleon mistress, that monstrosity of green and black. If only he had not been so blinded by pain as to let that abomination gain access to the stronghold. The creature had played a devious game and it might yet cost them all.

'Don't worry young thing,' he assured the unconscious lad. 'We'll see you right.' In his heart Veriman doubted the truth of this, and the sombre cast of his thoughts was reflected in the fact that at that moment the lights flickered and went out.

*　　　　　　　*　　　　　　　*

As she ran through the sudden darkness Cody knew it was a race against hard odds. The light-wall needed only be down for moments to allow a horde of monstrosities to storm their way into Wrayhaven and the lights had already been out for too long. Somehow her newly awakened sensitivities could cope with the utter blackness of the labyrinth and she picked her way with ease through the twisting passageways and corridors. She slowed at the approach to the Luminic chamber, in case of ambush. The only light was a fitful glow coming from inside the chamber itself. She crept forward.

Bella appeared suddenly at the opening and swept through the wreckage of the doors, her freakish shadow cast before her. Cody ducked behind an angle in the walls and the gruesome shape darted away up a passage at right angles to the main approach. Cody let her go. Her business was with the cores. She moved fast. Priority - restore the cores and the light wall. She slid through the sagging doorways and immediately saw that the central of the three pyramids was dead. The outside two flared under the nightmarish attack of demented spiders, the black flickering spikes of viral energy. Bella's crystal had been rammed back into place in the central pyramid.

By now tar had flowed down the steps to fill the lower level of the chamber with a slick that lapped the tops of each pyramid's plinth. Soon it would begin to encroach on the protective glass of the pyramids themselves. Which meant wading through thigh deep sludge – unless...

Cody spun a Lodestaff around her head till her arm became no more than a blur. When she released it the spinning missile sliced through the air and struck the viral crystal with explosive force. The shard was flung across the chamber to shatter against a pillar high up by the rows of monitors. This time she made sure the thing would be unusable. She ran around the raised upper level of the chamber and pounded it to grit with the tip of her second staff taking care to scatter the fragments with her feet. The first staff had ricocheted into the tar pool and sunk. It was no matter. Cody had other means at her disposal to deal with an aberrant Chameleon on the loose.

A rosy glow filled the chamber from the recovering spheres and energy flowed to the most damaged core kick-starting it until it too began to gain luminescence. Overhead lights flickered back into life. Good! The danger was far from over because of the rising tar levels but no immediate solution occurred to her for that. It was time to leave. There was prey to hunt down, and the cores had been disrupted for too long. Veriman and Josse lay vulnerable and wounded at the mouth of the tunnel which the hell breed had already entered by. The abominations would come again.

Priority – her companions must be got to safety. No more losses of Sufinam or human life would be tolerated. She sped through the subterranean passageways like an avenging spirit. The Chalcis Ymlyr would have to wait.

Thirty One
UNSHACKLED LIGHT

'To route the loathsome foes of shade
Did Waelbeorc's twenty fence the glade.
Great hack-edged shields to guard the mound,
That none may yield or lose the ground.'
From the epic: Waelbeorc's Stand.

VERIMAN was poised unsteadily over Josse's body, the blue
shimmering discus shield of the gauntlet extended to cover the youth's
inert body against the chamber wall. He was holding a ring in each hand,
too weary to raise them to chest level and release the burning blue ice-
fire. A line of twenty or more Vil-kind were scrambling down the rubble
slopes ahead of the tripod figure of Garatunde exultant at the sight of an
enemy at last, especially a cornered one. His brutal features were more
easily discernible in this light including the metal plates set in his skull and
jaw and the filth crusted hooks that jutted from his brow. He roared. The
Vil-kind exploded with guttural cries causing the unstable ceiling to
shower down dust.

When Cody came crashing into the side of the unwary phalanx
they were taken by surprise. Within seconds her whirling Lodestaff was
erupting with the rapid impact of patchwork limbs being shattered. The
construct creatures milled in confusion getting in each other's way.
Veriman took his cue and lanced down the front row of horrors nearest to
him with a needle of searing blue light. The roars in the dust choked space
became unbearable. The bedlam was ear numbing. Garatunde started an
unsteady descent on his wooden supports but a skilfully aimed beam from
Veriman sliced through the central support beneath his body and he
toppled heavily face first down the shifting mound of debris. Cody was

hacking her way to Veriman's side past disoriented scarecrows made clumsy by their blind zeal to destroy.

The instant she reached Veriman's side she threw down the single staff and prepared her circlets of silver to do battle, lining both rings up with the periapt phial at her chest. First she scoured the walls behind them with blue fire sweeping the stonework clear of insidious traces of tar. They needed their backs safe. Veriman's visage was corpse like, more skull than face. He was near spent but grinned gamely at his young ally,

'You came back Ceulwas.'

'Always. We owe each other many lives Arkadash.'

'Are the bowls safe?'

'No time old friend. The priority lay here.'

'So be it. In that case let us make a good accounting.'

They faced outwards lancing the nearest Vil-kind with blue-white beams of pure Luminic energy. The lines of monstrosities burned and fell but there were always more to clamber over their fallen kind. The stench of scorched matter clotted the oily air making it hard to breathe or see.

Thirty feet away Garatunde was incandescent with rage, unable to stand upright and lashing at everything within reach with that terrible barbed club. The brutal face bore deep gashes from his fall; the pain raised the volume of his roars loud enough to drown out the cries of everything in the suffocating field of death crammed between the walls – all except for one sound – a piercing shrill that suddenly brought everything to a halt.

Vil-kind froze with arms raised to stab or hurl or chop. From the entrance sixty feet behind them an imposing figure appeared, a figure in green and black, majestic, terrifying. Bella returned! She advanced with a distinct but haughty limp, the crunch of her feet loud in the uneasy quiet. There was no sign of her remaining stiletto. The gathered Vil-kind twitched and fretted, unable to keep still for an instant but held in check by the woman's whistling note, so high pitched as to be almost inaudible. Bella halted behind her Vil-kind, a good distance from the embattled pair pinned against the wall. She gave no indication of noticing her burned minions and creatures, lying on the tar-puddled ground all around her. The sound stopped. She climbed atop a slab of concrete to better view her enemies.

'You know how this ends,' Bella's voice boomed from the grotesque face. 'Your deaths, and Wrayhaven's secrets plundered or destroyed. It is what I came for.' Her bark of derisive laughter sprayed the air with spittle.

Cody was coolly estimating the chance of a good shot to the Chameleon's head through the swirling murk. At this distance it was a hard shot at best.

'You are thinking that your detestable silver could cut me in half even at this distance, I know,' mocked Bella, 'But the one shot is all you would get – and you know how fast I can move. You will be crushed beneath the sheer mass of bodies.'

Cody knew Bella's astonishing speed, even with a thigh wound. It would be a one chance only. But what was the Chameleon waiting for? Was there to be some bargain? Did she want to gloat? The only sound in the chamber was Garatunde's dismal groans as he struggled to lash the barbed club to the remaining stump of his body pole, trying to improvise a new support for his trunk. In his clumsiness he was tearing gashes in his palms. Bella whirled on him,

'Silence you snivelling slime or I'll have your eyes and innards for my breeding vats! I wanted these maggotry dead and you can't even stand upright in my presence, you stinking mire bred miscast!'

'But Grendelmor...!'

Bella leapt furiously down from her concrete slab as if to charge at her hideous lieutenant.

'NEVER use my name you filth sucking canker blasted gutter spore!'

Cody knew the name Garatunde had let slip. It came with a history, a long ago history involving much pain and destruction. She called across the chamber, wanting to position the Chameleon for a better shot if possible.

'Grendelmor! Do you know who I am?'

'So, half thing,' cawed Bella, her enraged shriek rising a notch, 'Remembrance has come to you at last – *at last,* you maggot food.' She was certainly enraged enough, but did not make the mistake of raising her head above the gaggle of Vil-kind. 'You are sluggish and only yet half formed. I tried everything to trigger your powers but you were too enfeebled to undergo the rigours of recall. You are *rejectus.* You are no further use to me Eloin whelp. Your presence gained me access into Wrayhaven and now I shall take what I want and despoil the rest. Including you. Your death is written on these walls. Time to die!'

The ranks of Vil-kind stirred uncertainly, having no understanding of these exchanges, but they knew the word death and became agitated. They hefted their weapons excitedly without daring to look directly at either of their leaders. Cody continued,

'We have met before Grendelmor. You are better looking now than the way I left you then. The purging at Castle Rigg – you remember? Are your caves still smouldering? Are your scars still hot?'

The jibe struck home. Bella leapt back onto the concrete slab to stare over the massed Vil-kind at her taunter. Good, thought Cody. That's exactly where I want you. The Chameleon appeared oddly conflicted. Then some distant realisation hit her. The hideous flayed features contorted in a snarl of loathing. She tugged off her green gloves exposing the ugly corpse flesh of her fingers and pointed at Cody with the horn claws.

'I know you, bile birth Eloin freak!' she hissed, voice dripping venom. 'None shall tear your life but me. You will end in my breeding vats and be revivified as one of my Vil-kind, my children. Prepare for agony!'

It was at this moment that a new, clear voice interrupted the spew of threats and every head turned to see two figures stood at the top of the debris slope near the ceiling. The stifling murk of the chamber became very still.

'You misjudge badly Grendelmor, as always,' the voice said.

The speaker, an imposing man in dark ankle length coat had a black eye patch and a shock of white hair and beard. The second figure was younger, in close fitting leather jacket bulging with pockets and a pair of crossed belts hung with holsters and a large knife. Both men carried Lodestaffs.

'Sephamon,' screamed Bella-Grendelmor, in a sound more animal than voice. 'You raddle fleshed malloc spawn!'

She flung aside her dark glasses exposing her terrible grey eyes. The air between her and the man rippled with sudden etheric violence as a pulse of blistering hatred tore at the white bearded figure making his long coat crack with tornado force. The man dropped his Lodestaff and ripped off his eyepatch revealing an orb the match of Bella's own. A pulse of raw turbulence shock waved back at his assailant sending her hair and garments flapping like demons. The clash of primal energies tore the air apart before settling into an uneasy maelstrom of near-invisible pyrotechnics part way between the two. Every molecule of air in the dust blown chamber jigged to the awesome destructiveness being unleashed. The younger man had leapt out of the way skidding upright towards the chamber floor like a wave rider.

The stinking ranks of Vil-kind had been let off the leash by the renewal of hostilities and attacked, spurred on by threats of outrageous maiming from Garatunde who had scrabbled out of the way as the two titans slugged it out with their ethereal weaponry. The air around Bella glowed hot green. Around her antagonist a blue shimmering aura flared.

It was clear to Cody that the clashing energies of the two combatants, half hidden by the distorting effects of the power they wielded, was evenly matched. The air boiled between them but none would gain the upper hand unless – unless something intervened to tip the balance. All Cody needed was to get near enough for one clear ring shot.

The athletic young man was carving his way through the diminished ranks of Chameleon breed with an efficiency that Cody found impressive. He wielded the Lodestaff and large combat knife to such effect that within moments he had cleared a way past the milling monstrosities and stood shoulder to shoulder with Cody and Veriman against the wall. The fallen Vil-kind were heaped up in a low wall around the besieged companions impeding further attacks by the scarecrow horrors. On the other side of the chamber the crash of colliding energies continued to rip the air apart.

'Hi. I'm Loren,' yelled the young man as he laid about him with both weapons. The ranks of Vil-kind had thinned but the weight of numbers was still in their favour. 'Looks like you could use some help.'

'Plenty of uglies to go round,' yelled Cody. 'Help yourself.'

It was foolish bravado of course, but the sheer impertinence of the man lifted her heart to something approaching elation. Also, it felt good to stand shoulder to shoulder with a strong companion facing outlandish odds.

Veriman had been using his wrist shield to protect Cody from any spears or other missiles but now sank to the ground with a groan, his blue force field blanketing himself and Josse. Cody and Loren closed the gap and continued repelling the savage onslaught.

'We need a tie breaker here,' yelled Loren. 'These boys and girls don't want to leave empty handed.'

Cody knew time was short and she knew what to do. It was up to her to tip the balance between Bella and Kanulf and she had to get within twenty feet of her deceiver to do it.

'Be my shield wall,' she yelled. He looked uncertain for a moment, then in a flash sheathed his knife, grabbed her discarded Lodestaff from the ground, and nodded seriously.

'Make your move,' he hollered.

Cody leapt up onto the heaped bodies and charged forward burning a swathe through those nearest to her and pushing quickly into the gap between the snarling stabbing horrors. Loren kept pace by her side demolishing whatever came within reach of the whirling staffs. The rapid impacts at every step sounded like gun shots. When they had struggled close enough to see the spittle flecked mouth of the rabid Chameleon leader Cody dropped her hands to her sides and closed her eyes, trusting totally that Loren would give her the time needed for what she had planned.

Mere yards away Garatunde had finally succeeded in lashing the thick barbed cudgel to the remains of his body stump and hauled himself upright. He saw the girl drop her defences and bellowed in mindless savagery throwing himself towards her in a barely controlled stagger. The movement caught Kanulf's eye and he instantly perceived Cody's danger.

'Nooooo...!' He whirled to blast the charging tripod figure.

Garatunde took the full force of Kanulf's energy wave and collapsed in a smoking heap amidst the rubble. The quick shift of focus was all the advantage Bella needed in her foe and she threw everything she had at Kanulf with renewed ferocity. He threw up a defensive shield but was wrenched backwards by the shock wave.

In the midst of all this mayhem Cody had evoked the timeless inner space of stillness in which she could weave or unravel the binding forces of nature itself. It left her physical self terribly vulnerable but she trusted the man at her side as if she had known him for a lifetime. Palms forward, head bowed, she reached out to Bella with her mind pushing the ghostly image of a hand inside the Chameleon's body. Starting with the invisible bondings between molecules she dismantled a rapidly expanding chain of cells. She had done this before and knew how to proceed from step to intricate step – but from somewhere outside herself came a sudden unexpected surge of strength, wave on wave that gathered momentum and turned the ripple of disruption flushing through Bella's inner body into a roaring breaker of unstoppable power! What was happening was the reverse of the healing Cody had applied to Veriman's wounds; instead of repairing and bonding she was loosening and dispersing - but this was so much more powerful! Her efforts were being boosted by an unprecedented Luminic source. She had no idea where it came from, but within seconds Bella-Grendelmor-literally-began-to-come-apart.

A hideous wailing shriek shattered Cody's calm and her eyes flew open to see Bella thrown through the air like a sack of grain, twisting and collapsing inwards as its contents spilled in all directions. Propelled by Kanulf's quivering force wave she hit the wall with a sickening impact causing the bedlam from the Vil-kind to grind to a halt. Even the scarcely functional mentalities of the scarecrow minions registered that something cataclysmic had occurred. They rotated their grisly shredded faces as if searching for something. Where were their leaders? What...?

The few remaining Vil-kind were torn apart by an invisible wind. Kanulf was on his knees but directing the terrible force of his unshielded eye at the remaining breed and within seconds it was over. None escaped the chamber intact. It was done.

Cody regarded her new companions and fallen friends in the sudden silence. The force shield from Veriman's gauntlet had collapsed. This small battle was won. But not the war. A hundred feet above them, beyond the walls of Wrayhaven, hordes of Vil-kind were massed still, ready to attack. And if Kanulf did not know how to stop the rising tar levels the Luminic cores would succumb. The light wall would fall and more Vil-kind would pour in. It was definitely not over yet.

Loren was digging around in a battle stained pocket of his jacket. She watched him unwrap a piece of silver paper and pop something into his mouth. He glanced up and caught her eye,

'Want some gum?' he grinned.

'You are a child of the universe, no less than the trees and the stars, you have a right to be here, and whether or not it is clear to you, no doubt the Universe is unfolding as it should.'
The Desiderata.

Thirty Two
UNTHINGS AND DECISIONS

'To change your life and your way of being and leave it behind is always uncomfortable – and frequently terrifying.'
Bronco Mason.

IN the aftermath of Bella's annihilation everyone still able to walk did so with the slow dazed movements of exhaustion or shock. The air was still slick with vaporized smoke and the stink of carcassed Vil-kind. No one appeared particularly celebratory. Everyone was wounded, even Kanulf. There was numbness and there was exhaustion – and there was definitely no time for sitting around.

The fierce eyed Kanulf had replaced his patch and was staring at the youngster that he had come to rescue. He could scarce believe the Chameleon dismantling he had witnessed. It was unprecedented. And this 'child' had achieved it in the very heat of battle! Now, with the mayhem settled he could observe her up close for the first time in a six month or more.

Kanulf hadn't been in the same room as his goddaughter since his last visit to Clayton Bar during the past winter. He'd wanted to see how she was faring under the Conmar's care. Everything had checked out fine. At that stage her mind had still been safely shielded from all leakages from her earlier life and the slow steady nurturing of her less dramatic abilities was going well...but now...! It was unsettling to realise that someone much older was regarding him from behind those startlingly blue eyes. The dismantling performed on Bella had been evidence enough but those eyes confirmed it. This was no twelve year old regarding him coolly – and yet...was this the fully resurrected Ceulwas?

He felt drained. The exchange with Bella had taxed his strength to the limit and even his relief at the outcome was marred by an exhausting anxiety about what had happened to Cody during her time under Bella's control. He staggered down the last few feet of loose rubble and approached his young, not-so-young charge uncertainly,

'Well met Ceulwas. Times of trial eh!'

'Times of strength,' she replied automatically. It was a traditional Sufinam greeting. 'Hello godfather. Haven't seen you for a long time. We missed you in the village. But your arrival here is welcome. You're both welcome,' she added, graciously including Loren.

'I'm sorry it wasn't sooner,' Loren replied. 'We had a few obstacles to clear at the gates.'

'Yes. We met them too,' Cody regarded her two rescuers. 'We have to move fast Kanulf. The cores are threatened by an influx of tar from above ground. I have no way of knowing how long they will function. You need to take a look at them. They are outside my expertise.' She went on to give them a rapid run down of salient points with Kanulf and Loren nodding in assent at certain junctures. It didn't take long and when it was done it was decided that Kanulf should check on the condition of the Luminic cores whilst Loren and Cody got Veriman and the lad to the relative safety of the Parley Room.

Which was easier said than done. Veriman was completely incapable, having slid into a state of unconsciousness, so that they had two unresponsive bodies to somehow transport to safety. Kanulf walked over to the collapsed form that had been Bella. The large frame was hunched over on itself, the hideous features hidden in the lea of a block of stone. The limbs poking out of layers of torn skirts were covered in swathes of filthy white bandages. One of the vicious blade-tipped boots had come off. Dark fluids leaked onto the dusty ground, evidence of molecular breakdown and the rapid onset of corruption. The effects of a dismantling were startling. The stench was charnel. Kanulf turned away sickened but satisfied there would be no further threat from this quarter.

Loren was for checking that none of the scattered Vil-kind were in any state to give them further trouble but Kanulf told him not to waste time.

'Very little walks after taking the brunt of a psygrypel mind pulse. Best get to our tasks.'

As soon as Kanulf left to check the cores Loren and Cody took poles from several damaged tapestries on the walls and lashed them into a travois or 'A' frame strong enough to take the weight of a man. Veriman was placed carefully on it. Cody would be able to drag the injured man on the frame fairly easily whilst Loren could carry Josse bodily without too much trouble.

'Best not to take them to the Healing room I think,' Cody she said as they left the wreckage strewn chamber. 'It's not in a pretty state. And there are those there that Veriman cared for. I'll fetch whatever medication we need to the Parley Room.'

'As you think best,' replied Loren easily. 'I don't know my way around this maze. You lead.'

As they departed they gave the putrefying form of Bella a wide berth.

*   *   *

Most of the smoke in the Parley Room had cleared and they had the two casualties settled down and comfortable in the warmth by the time Kanulf returned from checking on the cores in the generator room. He trailed smudges of tar on the floor as he entered.

'There is even less time than I'd hoped. I've stabilised what I can and rerouted some circuits but there's no way to stop the tar intruding further. It's part way up the protective shields already and they will fail. I'd say we have half an hour tops before we lose the light-wall. I'd really like to have conferred with Veriman but I fear he's too far gone.'

'Not quite Sephamon,' came a weak drifting voice from the chair by the fire. '*Dum spiro spero.* Where there's breath there's hope.'

'Veriman! You old trooper. How are you?' said Kanulf delighted, rushing over to his side.

'Tough as old iron,' replied the badly fading man, 'But ninety five percent rust I fear. Help me unbuckle this harness would you.' Kanulf bent and undid the straps that held the intricate silver plates of the gauntlet on Veriman's right hand.

Cody came to kneel by his far side taking his other hand which was trembling uncontrollably. There were tears in her eyes. Kanulf was made of sterner stuff; his were only misting. Loren was handed the beautifully linked arrangement of finger guards and wrist clamps and went to place it by a cabinet filled with similar examples of metalwork. He was glad of the opportunity to inspect some of the other wonders in this Aladdin's cave, especially the rack of Lodestaffs. He stayed on the far side

252

of the room giving the little group some small measure of privacy, although he was hanging onto their every word.

'There's something that must be done Kanulf,' said Veriman with an effort. 'The Chalcis Ymlryr. The Six must be taken or hidden. I will sketch you directions for their location in the chamber. Ceulwas and I had no time before we were overwhelmed. She...she came back for me Sephamon. She came back.'

'It was always her way,' replied Kanulf looking at the young girl's head bent over the dying man.

'If it comes to it Wrayhaven can be destroyed rather than its contents falling into the hands of the abominations. You know how Sephamon. But the Six and their tomes can be saved. There is an escape route prepared.' Veriman was scribbling directions with a pencil stub on a page torn from a notebook.

'The lake tunnel!' exclaimed Kanulf quietly.

'Yes. Once you reach the boathouse you will be able to get clear. The building, as you know, is substantial and has its own light-wall protection but once out of its cover you will be vulnerable.'

'Ceulwas,' he struggled to touch the girl's face with the back of a shaking hand. 'Could you please get me a drink. I think my poor body will stand a simple draught of something nourishing.'

'Of course *verime*.' Cody sprinted to the kitchen area and Veriman grabbed at Kanulf's sleeve.

'Don't let her make the decisions for this escape Kanulf!' He leaned his head close to Kanulf's whispering fiercely. 'Her Awakening has started, yes, triggered by events here and before her arrival I am sure, but she will be confused awhile. All her memories will be jostling for dominance. Her abilities will be unpredictable at best and there will be a clash of instincts old and new. She is still incredibly vulnerable. A warrior yes, but one of two minds not yet in harmony. And she must save the Six Chalcis Ymlyr. She can place them in a Liminal.'

'She has the power to do that?' gasped Kanulf aghast. 'Already?'

'Indeed. She opened the door to the Chalcis Ymlyr chamber by instinct. I was intending merely to use the Periapt phials but she responded instinctively. I tell you she can do it!'

'Astonishing. Unheard of.' Kanulf was unconsciously chewing at his lip.

253

'I know,' continued Veriman. 'I think we were right about her all along. There is something extraordinary about this young Eloin. Possibly she is as we suspected, one of the elite Eloin, a *refined*. She is precocious in every sense, and she will not like the idea of us being so protective towards her. Kanulf, you must ensure she reaches the lake safely.'

'We can't escape by water old friend. They will have the lake seething with Fin Swarmers. Any boat out crossing open water will be taking a chance.'

'Worse than that they have at least one Spitter nest trained on the boat house that I know of. But no matter, a small fast force can be clear before the damn Vil-kind get the range.'

'Do you mean the Gnosspelius, old friend?'

'I do indeed. In perfect working order. Checked just before the attacks started yesterday.'

'But that only takes two people...' began Kanulf.

'I will not be going anywhere Sephamon. I am hanging by a thread.'

'Then neither of us will be crossing the lake will we. The important thing is to get Ceulwas clear and to safety. I have planned for two possible rendezvous, Cody by air and us by boat to the south end of Windermere. Loren has the air rendezvous details if anything should happen to me. Once she is clear of Wrayhaven our charge should be as safe as we can divine for now.'

At the opposite end of the room Loren was inspecting an arrangement of fine silver chains on velvet cushions pretending not to hear.

'A remarkable young man. You must be very proud.'

Kanulf flicked a quick glance over his shoulder and fidgeted with his eye patch before dropping his voice even lower,

'I am. He shows great promise. Taken to the Lodestaff like one born to it.'

'Hardly surprising. Good fighter too...Ah, Ceulwas,' Veriman spoke up as Cody returned with a hot beaker.

Kanulf explained to her that they had an escape strategy.

'Ceulwas, there is one way open to us. We must get Veriman and young Josse to a tunnel that leads down to the lake. That is our way out - but we must also attend to the Chalcis Ymlyr first.'

'You're right, I know Kanulf, but I'm more concerned for Veriman's safety. I will stay with him. He's important to me.'

'This is understood. He is important to us all. Never the less, this is what will happen: Loren here will convey him to safety. You and I will attend to the Chalcis Ymlyr and fetch your young friend Josse afterwards. Then we will rendezvous in the tunnel.'

The two of them were staring hard eyed into each other's face over Veriman's head. The air was electric with tension. Then Cody's stubborn expression slipped into the vulnerable features of a child, displaying all the bewilderment of a youngster out of her depth.

'But I don't want to leave Veriman,' she pleaded. 'So much loss. I've lost so many people already.'

Kanulf was unable to speak for a moment, overcome by the desolation he knew she must be experiencing. Her young heart was unable to benefit from the strength of her older self. It tore him apart to witness. When he spoke his voice was deliberately softened,

'Never the less, young one, that is what we must do. Ceulwas, I am addressing you now. It is the best use of our meagre resources. You know this *yulic o traminir*. These things must be done.'

Cody hung her head in resignation and nodded. '*Bashime dor*. I know. Then let's be about it. You said we have very little time.'

'Possibly too little.'

Kanulf put his arm around her shoulders and nodded to Loren to take care of Veriman and Josse by the fire. He walked her to the blank wall at the far end of the room, the concealed entrance to the chamber of the Chalcis Ymlyr.

*   *   *

An Aelim Reflects On The Thanklessness Of Protecting Humanity From Hidden Enemies.

(Supposed translation from the mysterious Peaks Engravings see article by Cate Waverly egl.peaksengravings.co.uk)

My life is trade for mankind's fate
At war among the clouds above.
For those I slay I have no hate
From those I guard I feel no love.

A savage tumult lures my sight,
I weave through fiercely tangled crowds
Where meteor flash of blazing light
Draws me my path against the clouds.

Too late to come to comrades' aid.
Restraining zeal and battle yell,
Must slay this foe of flesh and shade
Must chase unruly forms to hell.

Who'll guard the ones I leave behind?
Or know my fate, my life so brief?
Yet, balanced, all is steadfast mind,
What use are years of wasted grief.

(Also reworked as the ballad — A Guardian Reflects.)

Thirty Three
A GLIMPSE BELOW THE THRESHOLD

KANULF was keen to observe for himself how Cody's nascent powers were emerging and watched carefully as she approached the doorway to the Bowls Chamber – she opened the barrier so casually that she was through the dancing archway of light before he realised what had happened. He followed quickly. Perhaps there would be a better opportunity when it came time for her to conceal the Six Chalcis Ymlyr inside a liminal.

At the centre of the sunken room Cody took Veriman's scribbled note from Kanulf and walked amongst the shelves searching out the first of the Six bowls. Everything was coated in thick dust and stone fragments shaken loose from the ceiling by the explosions and Kanulf had to sweep the top of the central table area clear with his sleeve. There were seeds and various mineral fragments scattered around. A brass bowl lay on the floor, a reminder of how Veriman had been thrown into a spasming fit by his agonies. Kanulf gathered everything carefully into a neat little pile but left them unsorted.

Cody was already carrying the first of the Six to the table. She set down a totally unremarkable object at the far end of the table. It could have been an ordinary household kitchen bowl; made of light brown pottery on the outside its inner surface was white glaze, covered in a network of tiny cracks. It would be easy to imagine someone cracking eggs into a nest of flour and whisking up a simple batter in such a bowl. Next to it she placed a tiny card-backed notebook held shut by a loop of elastic.

'Amazing the power contained in such everyday objects,' Kanulf mused as Cody continued her search amongst the shelves. Her voice echoed around the vaulted chamber from behind the stacks of bowls rising almost to the ceiling.

'Many have no intrinsic value whatsoever,' she said. 'But these Six are unique amongst the unique because of where their speech twins have been conveyed to in the world, often at great cost in skills and life. Replacements sets can be constructed, at least I think they can, but it would be a tremendous task to then transfer them to where they were needed. There was one exactly like that pottery one in Bee's kitchen. I used it myself a few times to mix stewed fruits. Of course I had no idea what it was then. I saw it lying broken the night she died.'

'Your memories appear to be returning well enough now Ceulwas. Do you recall everything?'

'Not everything, no. There are patches that are clear. Most are fragmented. I recall the basic principles of the Chalcis Ymlyr for example. I know that each has a second, or more rarely a third, speech twin elsewhere in the world.'

Kanulf could see her peering at Veriman's scrap of paper as she roamed the labyrinth peering at carved lettering on the edge of each shelf.

'And you recall why the Six are special Ceulwas?'

'Not as such, no.'

'If we were to lose access to the Six major paths of communication we would be blind and deaf in places where we need every sense available to us.'

'Do you know their locations out in the world?' came Cody's voice from behind the shelves.

'Three of them, yes. But the others are deliberately kept unrecorded. Do you know where the Liminal is in this room?'

'Do you Kanulf?'

Kanulf felt he was losing control of this exchange, not an experience he felt comfortable with, especially with someone so young. Cody appeared briefly between the wooden rows and came down to join him at the table. She had located a further two of the bowls,

'No,' Kanulf replied, a little brusquely. 'Liminals are not an area I have any skills in. But my understanding was that it was possible to open one in any location. Is that not so?'

'It is, but a newly created Liminal is never as secure as a long established one. The layers of protection around an established Liminal are so much more ingrained. For our task here the most secure possible resting place is called for.'

'I understand.' Kanulf was clearing space on the table for all six bowls. 'As far as I know there are old established key Liminals all over Wrayhaven but no one knows where. No one has the skills you see. We could be standing on it or it could be in the support stones above our heads.' They both glanced up at the massed stone canopy high above them. 'But there is one here, Ceulwas. Veriman said so. It was prepared decades ago for this very kind of eventuality.'

'Hm. I'm going to need another moment or two then,' said Cody calmly. Her eyes closed. She had slipped into an interior place where she could view the intangible streams of force that flowed alongside the dimensions of the visible world. She drifted back behind the shelves.

Kanulf exhaled slowly and positioned a tall vessel of varnished, mottled iron next to the first bowl; then a vase shaped item of bronze, heavily engraved in interlocking geometric patterns. He was doing his best to remain calm but was acutely aware that their sands were running out.

In a few minutes Cody had the rest of the Six: a flat wide bowl carved of wood pitted with age; an elegant glass shape, straight sided with its entire length marked off in finely etched circles; a squat chubby form of deep blue glazing. Gathered besides each was its accompanying tome of lore, the codes and patterning by which, with prearranged timings, each Chalcis Ymlyr could be attuned to its speech twin. These were as varied as the objects to which they referred: a chart of waxed linen folded four times to wallet size; a loose collection of vellum leaves tied with knotted cords; a scroll wrapped around an ebony rod; a silk bound pouch containing a series of pounded bark cards; a clasped leather volume the size of a paper back novel.

None of them, bowls or tomes, would be too heavy or difficult to transport. In fact that was one of the main requirements of their design. But as a collection it would be impossible to guarantee their safety. Placed in a long established key Liminal they would still be there, safe and unchanged, in months or a hundred years from now.

Without a word Cody darted up the sloping floor and disappeared again amongst the rows.

There was one extra item not on Veriman's list that Cody had brought to the central table; a thick hide-bound volume a hand's span long and half as wide. It was heavy despite the almost gossamer thin pages. On its many hundreds of translucent sheets were finely scripted diagrams and text in many calligraphies and coloured inks, a masterwork of reference duplicating the contents of every other single tome of bowl lore in this great chamber. Unimaginably priceless.

Kanulf opened it briefly and gazed in awe at the glowing radiance of the delicate pages. So fine the penmanship of glyphs and scripting. Breath taking. Mesmerising. He snapped the covers shut and slipped the volume into a deep inside pocket of his voluminous coat and looked up anxiously as the lights of the chamber flickered.

'I have it,' came Cody's voice from behind one of the highest shelves on the outside aisle of the chamber. Kanulf ran to join her.

She was stood looking at a flagstone set in the middle of the floor. It was unremarkable in any way, indistinguishable from any of its companions.

'This is it? Are you sure?'

Cody smiled tolerantly. 'Let's get the bowls up here quickly. I don't want to be opening the Liminal for any longer than need be. It may well contain other secrets that should not be exposed for too long.'

They both ran back and forth between the central table and the flagstone carrying each bowl with its tome of reference resting inside. The sense of urgency increased as the lights dipped again and steadied a couple of times. They knelt just clear of the foot worn edges of the flagstone, the Six bowls close at hand.

'Ready!' said Cody. 'When the Liminal is open hand me each item in turn and I will place it safely within.'

'Be swift,' urged Kanulf. 'Our enemies are pressing close.'

Cody closed her eyes.

Kanulf watched in awe as a wash of iridescent waves danced outwards from the centre of the stone widening until a large rectangular pool of luminous translucence lapped at the surrounding pavings. He had been told, or read, that Liminals manifested differently for everyone. He had no idea what the twelve year old at his side might be seeing but from his point of view she appeared to be placing each bowl he handed her into a radiant shimmering pool of purest blue water. He glimpsed other shapes somewhere in the depths but nothing he could identify.

He handed her the last bowl. She sat back on her haunches, touched her hands to her chest – and the flagstone was solid once more. They both sighed deeply, sounds of regret for some fleetingly glimpsed rapture. It was hard to move from the spot. The chamber seemed suddenly gloomy in contrast to what had opened at their feet.

'We must get back,' said Cody quietly breaking into Kanulf's reverie. 'Veriman and Josse…'

'Of course.' He peered at her sideways. 'What else did you see in there Cody?' She regarded him levelly for a moment, her icy blue eyes radiant in the gloom.

'I too have questions Kanulf; what happened to leave Clayton Bar so vulnerable to attack? Why did you take so long to reach me? Why, for the love of kinship, has any of this been allowed to happen? I mean, what have you and the Sufinam been doing? And what of Lucian? I hope you are not going to keep such matters from me. I may need them to survive.'

'You recall Lucian?' Kanulf became icy still. 'You need to know such things Ceulwas, but this may not be the right time.' A cascade of dust fell between them from the ceiling following the dull shock wave of an explosion somewhere far away. He looked up. 'A reckoning is due for what is happening here.'

'Yes. A reckoning is due.' Cody's voice was scarce more than a whisper.

Kanulf rotated his neck, working the strained muscles.

'And that eye of yours Kanulf…that's new. Why on earth would an Eloin have himself fitted with a psygrypel?'

'These are all good questions Ceulwas. We each have counsel that must be shared it appears, but we need a better place and time than this I think.'

The blue eyes bored into him, as if X-Raying his soul. Seconds ticked by. Then,

'I agree. We should be getting away from here. *Beleriath?*'

'*Beleriath*. Good then.'

It was a truce, of a kind. They scrambled to their feet and crossed the central floor of the chamber making for the doorway opposite that led back to the Parley Room. Part way up the sloping aisle Cody paused and looked round at the massed shelves of precious vessels, rows upon rows of the beautiful and the plain, the elegant and the crude, each a miracle of knowledge and craft, the work of centuries gathered as mute testimony to the creative spirit.

'Will all this be lost Kanulf?' she asked, soberly.

'It is possible. It is always possible. If the Vil-hordes do find a way in, by burrowing or explosives, they will either destroy or steal. It they steal then the bowls will still exist, and it may be possible to reclaim what is ours at some future date. It will be costly but it could be done. In our enemies' hands they could become weapons used against us. But it is likely they will be in the throes of *wael raes*, the rage of battle slaughter, and Chameleon kind can never be relied on to restrain their destructive tendencies.'

'So, we've done all we can here,' said Cody with finality. 'Friends are waiting.' And she spun on her heels and made for the exit. Kanulf trotted at her heels in silence.

'When a sufficiently large number of enlightened minds work together towards a specific goal, a state of critical mass is reached, from which arises a force which nothing can resist.'
Shell Harker (Privacy Booth.)

Thirty Four
DEPRIVED OF FORM

*'The language of friendship is not in words but meanings. It is
an intelligence above language.'*
Thoreau.

IT was a shock to find the warm sanctuary empty when they re-
entered the Parley Room.

'Loren must have decided to take Josse along with Veriman,' said
Cody.

'Perhaps the lad's feeling better,' said Kanulf. 'Veriman too, I
would surmise if he has revived enough to guide the way.'

'That is good news,' said Cody, cheering slightly.

'Come, we can easily catch them up,' added Kanulf briskly. 'Best
to don our warm clothing I think. It will be cold in the tunnel, and outside
too probably.'

Cody slipped her coat on and picked Josse's from the back of a
chair where he had draped it earlier. Kanulf took down two Lodestaffs
from the racks. He led the way, following the route taken by Loren,
shown by the drag marks of the travois poles on the ground.

The parallel lines in the dirt were easy to follow. They led
through a number of echoing vaults, chambers and store rooms piled with
chests and crates of unknowable contents. They also passed some of the
pits and cisterns that honeycombed the rock around Wrayhaven. Even
here the traces of Tar were beginning to show. Thin trickles ran down the
walls or appeared as tiny pools at ground level.

The most arresting space they passed was a mesmer chamber
similar to the one Cody had seen when they first entered Wrayhaven - a
bare open space covered in swooping patterns and mesmer glyphs

263

decorating every square foot of the smoothly plastered surfaces – only this one had a major difference.

Stood in the centre of the space were three Vil-kind, immobile, arms hung by their sides, weapons forgotten, their rag-shred faces twisted up towards the ceiling, heads rotating slowly as their eyes drifted along the flowing hypnotic patterns following the contours of misty pastels. Blushes of colour flitted along the patterns like motes of energy racing along a circuit, incredibly beautiful to watch.

The grotesque figures were making low sounds, soft plaintive moans, as if gripped by some pleasurable pain. They were trapped, held by the mesmer spell. And they would be here still in a month or a year or until their exhausted patchwork bodies fell apart leaving dusty heaps of crumpled rag, leather and bone.

Cody and Kanulf skirted round them, stepping to avoid their eyelines. It seemed wise not to give the monstrosities anything to focus on that might tear their gaze away from their rapture. As the door closed behind them the piteous moaning continued unchanged.

Cody wiped her brow of the cold sweat that had gathered there. Kanulf fidgeted with his eyepatch. But neither commented.

The drag lines eventually disappeared beneath the edge of a massive ornate mirror edged with silver and copper bracing. Kanulf swung it aside and plunged without hesitation into a narrow oval tunnel barely the height of a man. The path sloped steeply downwards with walls gouged into circular ridges giving the appearance of some gigantic throat in the poor light thrown by occasional strip lights. On the left hand side a metal rail ran at waist height, toothed like part of some huge unravelled clock wheel. There were small alcoves scooped into the right wall every fifty yards or so. It was cold and the sound of their footsteps echoed with an unusual percussive reverberation in the confined space.

The walking was difficult on the curved floor but within a minute they had caught up with Loren whose shadow loomed large in the confined space - but apart from the man on the travois frame he was alone.

'Loren! Where's Josse?'

'Don't you have him with you?'

'He wasn't in the Parley Room. We presumed you'd taken him as well.'

'He was still unconscious,' replied Loren as he propped the poles of the 'A' frame carefully against the side wall. His breath was misting in the cold air. 'I didn't want to injure the lad further by rough handling so I thought I'd go back for him afterwards. I'll go get him.'

Loren shot off up the tunnel at breakneck speed darting past before Kanulf could make a grab at him. Cody checked Veriman's shallow breathing with an anguished face. He looked even more cadaverous. He was losing the battle with the embers buried in his flesh. But even so, her heart was torn between staying with her friend and chasing back with Loren to discover where the lad had got to.

'Ceulwas, it's fine. If Josse is findable Loren will find him. He is a good man; capable.'

'If...! Kanulf, if! Where could Josse be? How can he not be findable? Did we miss him? Did he just wander off?'

'He could be anywhere. Doing anything. He is still Orowghast, slaved to his parasite. He could ...'

'Then I need to get to him. I can remove it, the spore. I've done it before.'

'Ceulwas, that was a long time ago.'

'No, it was yesterday! At Clayton Bar. And my name, in this body, is Cody!'

Kanulf was taken aback. He struggled to keep his voice even,

'That was you? You dealt with the Feydon girl? The one we found wandering around the village?'

'She was infected and I took it out with this,' Cody reached into the neck of her coat and lifted out the periapt phial, but she did it with her phantom hand. The phial hung steady in the air between them, apparently unsupported. Kanulf was not looking at the phial but at the quiver of air around it.

'Scaedu folm!' he gasped, 'The shadow hand. There are rumours...only...I have never seen it.'

'It was the only way she could help me,' said Veriman weakly. 'I'd be dead these hours gone if she hadn't taken me in hand.'

'None of this changes a thing,' snapped Kanulf forcefully. 'The one certainty, the one thing that must occur is that we get you away to safety Cody. Nothing else matters.' He was staring hard at her, their faces less than a foot apart.

'Nothing else *matters*?' Cody's voice had a dangerous timbre to it. 'Nothing…was that what happened to Lucian? Was that what happened to my *brother*, Kanulf? Did he not feature in your priorities and got left behind?'

'You do not understand the circumstances of what happened to your twin,' Kanulf snarled, equally dangerously.

'He is right, old soul,' said Veriman. 'There was nothing we could do for Lucian. The shadows took him and we have been pursuing the Chameleon agencies responsible ever since. Believe me *Beuminas*, there were many forces at work. There still are. We have not lost hope.'

Cody was breathing hard, her face set like stone. The air in the claustrophobic space felt as if it was about to take fire, despite the chill. Kanulf looked away and his voice had a catch in it,

'Do not fight us on this, please; or everything will have been pointless.'

Cody stared at him as if about to unleash lightening around his head but reined in her turmoil with enormous effort. She threw Josse's coat across the poles of Veriman's travois and began to haul the frame down the slope being careful not to spill Veriman.

'This is not finished Kanulf. But, as you are fond of saying, this is not the time.' Kanulf nodded in acquiescence and followed on behind.

The sudden sound of footsteps approaching at a run made him spin round. It was Loren, breathing hard.

'Not a sign. None. He's not anywhere. And Bella has gone too!'

The impact of this hit the little group hard.

'What?'

'How…?'

'Then we have even less time than I thought,' snapped Kanulf. 'The hag's recuperative powers are terrifying. She could have reconfigured her body. She could be anywhere!'

'No,' asserted Veriman. 'There hasn't been time for that. At most she may be alive. But she won't be doing any fighting any time soon.'

'You are right,' Kanulf agreed hurriedly, looking somewhat relieved. 'Cody started an unstoppable internal chain disintegration – and I delivered the coup de grace. If she is alive it will not be in a form dangerous to us – not yet anyway. She could possibly jettison parts of her body too far damaged to save but that would all take time. If we can reach the end of this tunnel we will have the means to put an end to her and any hell minions half witted enough to have set foot inside Wrayhaven.'

'So you've decided to destroy Wrayhaven?' asked Cody, marble faced.

'Not quite yet. We are not in the clear yet,' replied Kanulf equally sternly.

'This is not the way it should be,' said Cody angrily. 'No one should get left behind! My friend is back there, somewhere. I can't abandon him. I can save him. I have the power to do it now.'

'Cody, no!' begged Veriman from his position on the floor. 'Believe me, time is against us, in every way possible.'

'Then I'd better be swift,' said Cody and before anyone could stop her she was sprinting back up the tunnel. Kanulf could not get past Loren in the narrow tunnel in time to restrain her.

'Cody, no!' he yelled. 'No, wait. I will come with you.' He turned to Loren. 'Get Veriman as far as you can to the tunnel's end. We will join you as soon as life allows.' And he too began the steep uphill race back to the bowels of Wrayhaven. He was in a frenzy. The little time they had was almost spent!

*   *   *

Josse could hardly place one foot in front of the other so bad was the pain from his damaged body and limbs. The hurt involved in staggering through the abandoned corridors and rock chambers of the labyrinth had been terrible to bear but clambering step by pain raddled step up the sloping mound of rubble had been agony. His feet had slipped back with every suffering advance he'd made up the unstable surface. He'd had to pick his way around fallen Vil-kind avoiding the poisonous looking hooks and black iron weaponry; it was everywhere. Now, in the darkness beyond the gaping hole of the ceiling he trod through tacky patches of tar he could not avoid. The impenetrable blackness stretched ahead further than he could sense though he knew that the surface world was a long way over his head. He found it hard to recall what the outer world was like - but he was not allowed pause to reflect. The voice that compelled him did not rest for a heart beat. It lashed at him mercilessly blinding and stabbing at his benumbed mind, just as the parasite-thing lying coiled within his ribcage tormented his body each time he staggered to an exhausted halt.

The route he had taken was marked in the dust by a trail of black noisesome fluids trickling slowly from the thing that he carried clutched close to his chest. Its voice impelled him without pause, threatening, goading, gibbering with descriptions of torments he would suffer should he pause or let slip his precious burden.

'...drop me you pox maggoted scab curd and I'll lance fire through your veins, your eyes will boil, I'll tear you with rusty iron, open you up...brain to festering crotch you plague damned pus sack...you whelp spawned useless sludge...they unleashed the unbinding on me!...me!...the scurfsome earth crawling secabantes...but they will pay...hell will visit their domain and rip their minds to screaming tatters...their bodies will shrivel and bleed...' and on and on, an unending torrent of abuse and vilification that stung with every mucus splattered consonant, tore with every poisoned sibilant and vowel.

Bella, or what was left of her, rasped into his face with fetid death breath, gusting foulness from lips only inches from his own. Only the head, upper torso and arms travelled in Josse's palsied grip, dripping and putrescent but somehow remaining intact despite the trailing gelid innards that flopped wetly across the boys knees and thighs. The rest of the her lay abandoned in the blast torn chamber below, surrendered to the disruptive forces of unbinding that had almost ended her existence completely.

The fact that Bella lived at all was testimony to the incredible resilience of her Chameleon body's resources. The fact that Bella's mind could focus so ferociously on crimson streaked revenge, despite the awesome brutally of what she had undergone, was testimony to her intractable iron will – and her insanity. It made her heart boil to know how badly she had misjudged the Eloin child, that putrid retch worm of the high breed, who was obviously one of the rare amongst the rare, an Eloin *refined*; not only that but a wittering righteous slug-bred that she had run into before – Ceulwas! The form of the freak brat's new body had deceived her. And the oozing mucus cub had been at the mercy of her claws! Blast and hellfury and six kinds of fetid damnation!

The indignity of being unbound by that whelpic grub of a gore canker was unbearable. What an opportunity lost! But there would be vengeance; scalding, savage, blood soaked vengeance, sweet as razors, sharp as glass. All of the curse- born would perish. They were trapped in the maze of their own making and soon the light cores would fail, suffocated beneath the tar tide, and in would come her ravening hordes of Vil-children to exact their blood levy. Once back amongst her vats and splicing tables she could begin to reform, reshape her body. There might even be a use for this flesh whelp carrying her. He had strong fresh body parts, ripe for harvest – so long as the spore leech hadn't done too much damage, as they often did.

Josse heard the endless awfulness of the spitting, muttering thing that he carried but understood none of it. His poor bruised mind had retreated to levels shut off from his suffering and lay, blind and unknowing, in a remote corner of his inner psyche. This was the only defence he had against the suffocating evil that engulfed him.

Thirty Five
RETURNED TO FORM

'There is an imperative upon us – to excel in at least one area of endeavour and leave a mark upon life.'
Thomas C Morledge. *Taken from Man Completed, Elements Of A Partial Design.*

CODY ran with the winged feet of desperation and resolve to find her friend. The aching layers of loss in her heart drove her on. Too many friends and loved ones had been overtaken by brutality in the whirlwind of hours since the village attack. No more would be lost! And no one would be left behind! This rising tide of malevolence would have to be met with courage and boldness. It was time to draw the line.

She sped through the Parley Room, her senses heightened for any trace of Josse's presence in the endless echoing labyrinth of tunnels. Something was taking her back towards the battle chamber, some faint trace of empathic emotional tones. Someone she knew was this way. She increased her speed.

Sections of the labyrinth had been carved through different strata in the solid rock and sometimes flights of stairs or spiralling staircases linked the various levels. It was at the foot of one of these wide flights leading up to a stone archway, encrusted with copper and silver patterning, that Cody came to a halt. Someone, or something, was stood near the topmost steps regarding her in silence. She slid the silver rings off her fingers and into her palms in readiness.

'Cody. Do you not know me?' The voice was familiar. The figure was not. Some Chameleon shape shifting trick? The shape descending the stairs towards her was tall and had a wide face, framed by loose flowing hair. The body was concealed beneath long robes parted from hip to ankle, arms swaying in wide sleeves. There was a suggestion of metal glinting at wrists, throat and calves below the garments.

The figure paused half way down the stairs and waited in an unthreatening pose.

'I must pass,' grated Cody, rolling the rings in her palms, which were facing forwards but not yet raised to chest level. 'I am missing a friend.'

'Alas,' replied the familiar voice in an easy tone, 'This is a time of many losses, for all of us. Your friend may already be beyond reach I fear.'

'You would prevent me from going to him?'

'I would prevent you from a wasted gesture when higher things are at stake and time is of the essence. You must flee Cody Conmar. You must leave Wrayhaven now. You are needed in other places than this lost domain. Wrayhaven will fall. It cannot be prevented. And your young friend has his own destiny and fate to meet as ever he can. You cannot be here when all this happens.'

Cody was taking slow, cautious steps up the staircase. Her brow was drawn into a puzzled frown. The voice...was familiar. The face...the face was like someone...

'Cody, I know I am changed in this form, but so changed? Do you really not know your old friend?'

'Bron? Bron is it really you?'

'Ah, the changes are not really so extreme after all. Yes, it is me.'

'So Bella was wrong. I knew it! I didn't believe her. How could you be imaginary...I...I knew...I knew...' Cody was stammering, reverting to a confused twelve year old again, struggling to make sense of a relentlessly baffling world. 'You...you disappeared after the train and I had no idea what happened to you. I've missed you Bron, and now you look so... grown up.'

'That is because this is my corporeal battle form Cody. And in a way Bella was right, for all her intention to deceive and misdirect you. It is only your belief in me that has kept me earth bound and able to act. It is only through my links with you that I had any hope of redeeming my former cowardice and dishonour.'

'What do you mean? I thought we were friends.'

'Friends, true, but I was meant to be more. Not a guardian, not a true guardian as such. I was only ever meant to be a witness, a watcher, *bene elim*. I told you before Cody, that I was an exile; the term is *excidiat*. I am working to redeem my past failings. But back in the village I was useless to you because I was craven and afraid. Not all Aelim are heroic Cody.'

'You are an Aelim? Oh, Bron.'

'A poor one, yes. And as an excidiat I existed with very limited powers in the form I took as your friend. I sought to gradually earn my redemption by long service and friendship with you. But the time has gone far beyond the simpler requirements of friendship. The dangers are too great. Too many things are in perilous balance. More decisive action and sacrifice is called for. There has been a call to action – across many levels.'

'Is that why you look so different?'

'Yes. In a short while the defences of this place will fail. Hell breed will pour in and take any treasure and lives remaining.'

'We know. Kanulf is planning to destroy the keep rather than let it fall to the abominations.'

'No! He must not do so. There are measures in hand to halt to the curse-breed. Wrayhaven must not be destroyed in that way. Your sole task is to get yourself clear before the fire of retribution scours these hallways. Even now the time left you before the cleansing is dangerously short.'

'You have begun to remember many things, young Eloin, including the fate of your lost brother. But your recall will be at best a patchwork tapestry. Many parts will be fragmentary, unrelated to the whole. Your past will be confusing to your unharmonised mind as it struggles to integrate your once and present lives. You have awoken too early and many things that you cannot deal with coherently will be distorted or rejected in order to protect you. This puts you in great danger. You will suffer increasing migraines, disorientation and nausea. Despite the knowledge and abilities that are unfolding within you, you will be left incredibly vulnerable until you can be fully restored. This is why you must be taken to a place of safety.'

'But what about Lucian, Bron? I am right aren't I, he is being held captive somewhere.'

'He is, but you have to be strong and in your full power before you go seeking him. You will be no use to Lucian, or anyone, if you get injured or captured yourself.'

Cody bowed her head as if absorbing all this.

'What are you going to do Bron? How is Wrayhaven to be protected?'

'Something decisive – and total is in hand. You must go with Kanulf. You can trust Kanulf and Loren. They know how to convey you to where you must be. You must also trust yourself. You are true. Your are natural. You are hope. But do not act in haste.'

The commanding figure turned as if to leave and Cody's heart leapt in her chest.

'Bron, you're frightening me. What are you going to do?'

'My name in this form is Imbroniel, Cody-Ceulwas. I wanted you to know that. There is a thing I can achieve in this form. Tell Kanulf to prepare the aes triplex. He will know what that means. Now you must go. It has been a great privilege *Ceulwas omnatiir*. Your friendship has meant more than I can express. Now leave!'

And Cody's friend, cheeky, lovable Bron, who could skip stones across a pond better than anyone she knew, turned with grace and dignity and strode swiftly through the archway, passing silently from view. And Cody knew she would not see her friend again. She called out with a forlorn voice,

'Bron! Bron!' Tears burned her eyes. The wrench of another loss was unbearable. When she heard the sound of footsteps behind her she spun round ready to lash out at something - Kanulf was stood there.

'Kanulf!' There were tears pouring unheeded down her cheeks. 'Kanulf, Josse…Bron said…she said…'

'It's OK. I heard. Both your friends are beyond our reach, each in their own way, I'm afraid. Some terrible things must be done in the service of life Cody-Ceulwas. Not everyone has the courage to do them, but our path demands it of us. *Yulic o traminir.* Come, please.'

…and it was then that the lights finally died!

*   *   *

It took them a while but when they finally rejoined Loren and Veriman in the cramped throat of the tunnel everything was in complete darkness. Cody never thought to question how Kanulf kept pace with her. Presumably his eyes too could cope with the velvet blackness. Loren had hauled Veriman's travois several hundred feet further down the slope using a narrow beamed torch from his utility belt to ensure they weren't

273

running into any obstacles. He was panting hard from the effort of keeping a steady footing on the sloping oval floor. He grinned at them,

'No idea how much further, but we must be getting close. The air is fresher down here. Ah'm afraid Veriman is still out of it. Probably best. No sign of Josse then?'

'We need him awake, right now,' ordered Kanulf elbowing past Cody to reach the reclining man. 'Give me your water bottle!'

Loren handed it over. Kanulf tore the top off and splashed the unconscious man's face. 'Quick, get him off that frame and into that next alcove. Help me.'

No one asked questions. Veriman roused himself enough to ask for a drink from the canteen as they crammed themselves tightly into the low scoop in the rock.

'What are we doing sir?' asked Loren. Kanulf ignored him.

'Veriman. Veriman! We must create the aes triplex.'

'What! Are there allies here? Finally?' His voice was faint.

'Just one, old friend. But the light-wall has fallen. Vil-kind will be pouring through Wrayhaven. Our ally is going to perform *immolatus*.'

'Immolatus? Holy Hell, self sacrifice! I see. Quickly Ceulwas, take out your periapt phial. The dome shield you used to protect yourself when entering Wrayhaven's defences...? We must do so again, only this time a threefold shield.'

His words faltered as an unnerving sound came from the gloom of the tunnel behind them. It fell on them softly, as if through miles of rock and across decades of memory, a voiced sound of defiance and exultation, but also of unbearable sadness which tore at the heart. There was a ferocity in it too that set Cody's pulse racing. Close on this came a great rush of air, moaning and buffeting its way down the bottleneck of the tunnel walls, building, building irresistibly to some terrifying yet silent crescendo.

With heads bowed Cody, Kanulf and Veriman held aloft their periapt crystals releasing a scintillating blue canopy over themselves and Loren. It flared against the dreadful carrier wave of soundless light funnelling past them with the fury and brilliance of a comet...

*   *   *

Bella was spitting orders and whistling dementedly at the torch bearing ranks of Vil-kind that surged past her through the breached defences of Wrayhaven. Josse stood blank eyed and desolate, still clutching the twitching half form of his mistress, spattered in filth as the waves of monstrosities parted either side of them. His mind registered none of the shrieking delirium around him. He was gone. Gone from his own body. An empty vessel. A slave shell. An Orowghast.

Suddenly, above the clamour and braying of the bestial minions charging into the darkness came another sound, a voiced ambience, half song, half battle tone. The rabid Chameleon ruin that was Bella stopped shrieking abruptly, her ugly grey orbs frozen open in disbelief at what she heard. There was terror in her voice when she gabbled,

'No! No, it is not allowed!' The frantic horror of her twisted grimacing features strained to hear above the bedlam. In a bellow of curses the hag dame sent Josse crashing against the tide of monstrosities searching, searching, desperate and furious, looking for…looking for…! They came to a side opening, a jagged fissure caused by the explosions used to breach the Wrayhaven foundations.

'There, there!' she screamed, pointing with filthy claws into the gap. 'Run, hide, take cover, conceal. It is coming. It is coming!'

Josse's puppet limbs propelled their ungainly weight into the opening and fell, stumbling as far back as they could into the dank shadow. The rock had collapsed exposing a vertical shaft at the bottom of which glistened the scum crusted surface of a breached sewage channel. The smell was terrible, but there was no time to hesitate. Bella screamed,

'In, down, fly, conceal, protect, juuuump! It is coming! The curse and the fire! Juuuuuuuump!' And he did.

The conjoined bodies fell from sight, ignored by the massed ranks of hell-bred still charging into the heart of the broken citadel. They hit the fetid crust of filth and sank from sight leaving only a cluster of thick scummy bubbles

*   *   *

At some distant but central spot, deep within the labyrinth of Wrayhaven, the haunting non-voice of triumph and loss had ceased. It that moment of silence the air trembled – then took fire…

275

...a soul blistering wave-front of blinding silence surged along every open space and passageway, through every crack and gap, between every column and crevice. Destruction was riding the wings of light!

...the bonding forces of every organic molecule in its path were torn into incendiary atoms by a hurricane force.

...the hordes of rampaging Vil-kind were blasted to incandescence by a force so intense it was beyond sound.

Helmets, clothing, chains, wire and weapons, metal shards, rags, plates of rust, hafts of polished bone, grisly trophies, belts buckles and bolts, charms of stone and links of brass fell from mid air as the organic molecules of the bodies bearing them up were stripped of cohesion and fell apart. Not a shred of living organic matter was left intact, only the inanimate survived. The floors were littered with the detritus of an entire army.

Eight hundred yards from the heart of Wrayhaven, forty feet below the sloping forest of the lake shore, a tiny three layered bubble of protective light shimmered around four forms crouched in the oval tunnel. The inaudible ferocity raged past them with the force of a storm god, a solid yet insubstantial column of disintegrating intensity, a tsunami of condensed lightning, a cleansing brilliance. And within seconds – it was gone!

The haven had been scoured clean of every living thing: tendon, muscle, organ brain and blood were gone. The silence was deafening.

'Fua neé' breathed Cody.

Thirty Six
READY STRATEGIES

'Each path of fate is found within,
In call of blood and bond of kin.
Take courage, summon up the sword,
The bloodline song won't be ignored.
Throw wide the gate, assume the myth,
Seek out your lost and tortured kith.'
From Leoric and Amberym, a New Albion Legend.

IN the desolate silence that followed no one dared move for a moment. Then the triple blue shield fell apart and the four cramped survivors began stretching their limbs, easing muscles that had been clenched tight by fear.

'That was a blast,' commented Loren wryly. No one responded.

They set off following the slope of the tunnel stumbling on the awkward surface. Eighty yards further on the footing levelled off then widened in front of a barrier of blank stone eight feet high and thirty feet from left to right. Loren strode up to the wall and pounded it with the heel of his fist,

'Now tell me someone has a key or something to get us through this because my instincts tell me we're going to have a horde of uglies at our backs some time soon.'

'Not any that were in Wrayhaven though,' said Cody, checking to make sure that Veriman was OK. 'They're all dead.'

'Dead?'

'Dismantled by what roared past us in the tunnel.'

'Dismantled? How?' queried Loren.

'Similar to what happened to Bella, only of a much higher order than most mortals have ever witnessed before.'

Kanulf had taken out his crystal phial and was holding it against the stone wall. 'Everything biological was torn to atoms by an unleashed Luminic force,' he said. 'Only inanimate matter survived – and ourselves of course. But any Vil-kind who were outside the walls of Wrayhaven at the time will have been beyond range. They will be hot on our scent very soon. We aren't in the clear yet.'

'So they weren't all…dismantled?'

'Those in range of the Luminic wave were.'

Kanulf closed his eyes and tapped the wall precisely in three places. Deep rumblings were heard behind the wall.

'But who, or what created the Luminic wave?' persisted Loren, exasperated at having to squeeze for every bit of information.

'A friend,' said Cody. 'Let's leave it at that for now.'

With a puff of dust the middle section of the stone slab grated upwards into the ceiling. Fresh air gusted at them through the opening. There was room for two people side by side.

'In quickly, we have only seconds,' snapped Kanulf hauling Veriman's travois through the gap. The raised section of the barrier wall was three feet thick but a good length of further tunnel lay before them. They stepped smartly forward and the raised slab closed rather sharply on their heels as they staggered into the space beyond. There was a surprisingly rich scent of water in the air – and greenery. And from somewhere at the top of the stone stairway stretching up in front of them daylight bounced off the stones walls.

'Open space at last,' sighed Loren.

'I'd lost track of time,' said Cody amazed. 'It's daylight.'

'Dawn I'd guess,' murmured Veriman.

They all manhandled Veriman's frame up the steps and paused thankfully at the top.

They were stood inside the drystone walls of a massive boathouse wide enough for at least twenty row boats to be tied up side by side. Three craft bobbed gently on the water. Set into the wall opposite them were a pair of fifteen foot wide doors that would let out onto the magnificent expanse of Lake Windermere. The interior was lit by fresh morning light streaming in through an irregular arrangement of slitted or arched windows set high up near the roof. A slate topped jetty ran around three sides of the building with large metal rings set into the floor at regular intervals. Tied to three of these were the three craft: a wooden rowing boat; a twenty foot open decked steam launch, of the sort often seen in museums as examples of turn of the century engineering; and last, was a…well, it was hard to make out quite what it was. Parts of it were tantalisingly familiar, but it was a hybrid thing. The hull rested on twin floats or pontoons. There were struts, rudders and spars with wires crisscrossing everywhere. A three prop propeller sat snug against a compact engine at the rear. Rising vertically from the hull was an oddly angled pair of sails uncannily like the folded wings of some gigantic insect.

'What the Zephyr is that!' gasped Loren, eyes agog.

'An amphibious two man aircraft,' explained Kanulf.

'That is the Gnosspelius,' said Veriman proudly. 'Built for waterborne take off, and as fast as any two-person craft of her size. It's a microlite engine and frame; 32 foot flexiwing span; carbon fibre ribbing with a Dacron skinned aerofoil wingframe, ultra light. The wing fins snap down to standard horizontal position for take off. This is just its storage configuration, more compact you see.' His breath was coming in gasps.

'Veriman!' Cody knelt by her friend and wiped his brow. She could see every vein in his skull and his sunken eyes were like hot coals. 'Take it easy Arkadash,' she soothed. 'No need to exert yourself.'

'Ah Ceulwas, if only there was time. But there is not. We must get you away.'

Kanulf had climbed a set of slate steps to an upper window with a view of the shoreline and the bulk of Wrayhaven just visible uphill through the trees.

'Veriman I can see the Spitter cage you spoke of but no movement,' he called.

'There's a team of handlers dug in behind that low wall to the north,' wheezed Veriman. 'We are going to provide them with a target for the Spitter using the steam launch. This will give the Gnosspelius enough time to get clear. It will be close. But it can be done.'

'Can't you do your eye thing again Sephamon?' asked Cody.

'I'm a little tired for that but perhaps a short unleashing would be possible. I'd need to be in the correct position. And close.'

'That means very close,' added Veriman. 'With me in the steam launch and Kanulf on land you will have seconds to take off and get clear of the Spitter's range.'

'I will not leave you behind!'

'Ceulwas, look at me. No, I mean LOOK at me! Use your sight to go inside my body. Tell me what you find there. Tell me how long you think I have in this broken physical shell. Look!'

'I don't need to Veriman. I know. You will not be with us more than an hour at most. But at least you're alive.'

'No, at most I'm alive! But not for long. Allow me to make a use of my ending Ceulwas. Let me make it count – and it will, if you get clear. Tell me you would not want the same thing in my place. Tell me.'

'Knowing what is true and being prepared to go along with it are two different things. I-will-not-leave-you-behind!'

All three men became completely still, Kanulf perched up by the window and the other two hardly daring to stare too closely at Cody's face. The young Amazon was intractable. No one seemed to know what to do. Veriman spoke to Loren,

'Young man, help me over to the Gnosspelius. I must go over the controls with you.' Cody started to help him but Veriman gently prised her fingers away from his sleeve and nodded towards Kanulf descending from the high window.

'Talk to Sephamon, old one. He will explain to you how we planned our final departure from Wrayhaven. You will be impressed; it has many ingenious aspects to it. You always loved devious strategies,' and leaning heavily onto Loren's arm he shuffled slowly towards the moored microphibious craft. Kanulf approached slowly, almost warily.

'Windermere was the birthplace of the age of amphibious aircraft you know,' he said watching Loren support the struggling Wrayhaven guardian. 'You may recall that, I don't know, I'm unsure how much you really remember. 1911 the first ever amphibious seaplane took flight here. Later in the 1940's we built the great Sunderland flying boats here. Had the greatest unsupported single span building in the world right there over on the east shore. Do you remember that?'

Cody remained resolutely silent.

'Not a single scrap of that building remains today. Nothing. Entire lives were swallowed up and spent there in efforts to develop those aircraft. We were trying to help bring an end to World War II. Do you remember that? Now you'd be pushed to find even a plaque to mark the spot. Things change Cody. Things die, disappear, move on. It's the way of things, *tathata*.'

Cody was glaring at her fingertips.

'What's the plan Kanulf? Veriman said you had a plan.'

'Ah yes, one I suspect that will appeal to you. Involves decoys, split second timing and surprise attack.'

'Go on.'

'We have to distract the Vil-kind so that Loren and yourself can get clear in the Gnosspelius...'

'I don't...'

'Hear me out! I'm making allowances for your disoriented state due to an abrupt premature awakening but you will at least hear me out!'

'I am not disoriented!'

'You are not thinking clearly! Faced with unpalatable certainties you are retreating into stubborn emotionalism. You are not facing facts.'

Cody crossed her arms but wouldn't look at Kanulf. It was like watching a child trying to act like a grown woman – she was struggling to master emotions far more powerful than herself. The gentle sound of waves lapping at the stone walls echoed within the enclosed space. Outside could be heard the morning sounds of bird cries.

'Go on,' she said.

'We fire the rowboat with oil soaked rags and push it out of the right hand gate creating a smoke screen. We shut down the localised light wall from those controls there,' he pointed to a set of dials and two large brass and wood levers set discretely into the wall by the stairway's entrance. 'Veriman takes the steam launch shooting across the lake...'

'I...!'

'Hear me out! Everything must follow on fast and ordered because surprise timing is our greatest asset. I exit through that open window up there on the Vil-kind's blind side.' He indicated an unglassed opening twenty five feet above where they stood.

'I slip out behind the Spitter position using a limited Behelian capability I have. At the same time Loren exits through the left hand gate, opened by you. You jump onboard, Loren snaps the wings into flying mode as soon as you clear the headland – and you take off. You are to rendezvous fifteen miles away up over the Kirkstone pass at Ullswater. You'll be met. You'll be taken to safety.'

'And Veriman may be killed.'

'Veriman is dead already Ceulwas. You know this. He certainly does. And you will deny his dying of any value.'

'I told you my name is Cody!'

'No! You have been Cody for three years only. You were Ceulwas for over eighty years and I have some claim to call you by that name.'

'What about you?'

'Me? I will visit all kinds of hell on this pack of patchwork dogs then slip away to a rendezvous of my own. I have these.' He opened his long coat to display two Lodestaffs stowed into slip-pouches sewn along the lining. 'And this,' he said, tapping at his eyepatch. 'I will be safe. Once the Spitter and its crew have been silenced I will be clear to make my own escape. There are still Vil-kind on the loose but they are easily evaded in the daylight. We will all be where we should be.'

'Except Veriman.'

'Especially Veriman. Our courageous companion, our selfless ally and kin, our friend will be at peace knowing his passing has been well spent.'

'You have ever been prepared to sacrifice others for a cause Kanulf. You would have sacrificed Wrayhaven; you would let Veriman die. I know you do not do these things lightly but how do you bear the cost?'

Kanulf's face was gaunt, his mind filled with the haunting image of a village being engulfed by flames.

'They are lost anyway,' he said quietly turning to watch the edge of a brilliant white cloud through the high windows. 'The centuries teach us that what is lost in honour remains as more than merely dust and ashes. Veriman knows this. You have forgotten it.'

For what seemed an age they both stood unspeaking, listening to the lap of waves, watching the clouds. Over by the microphibian Loren's enthusiastic chatter rose and fell alternating with Veriman's quieter tones.

'Go and be with him...Cody. He does not have much time whichever way he leaves this world. He would value any last moments you can spare to be with him.'

Cody stepped like a sleepwalker along the grey slate pavings towards the spirited discussion the two men were having over by the curious aircraft. Loren was balanced on one of the floats rehearsing the sequence of fast-release levers that would snap the folded aerofoil into a fully deployed wingframe when the time came. His face was alight with appreciation of the little craft's ingenuity. Veriman was propped up on the quay, his back against a large metal tool box surrounded by spanners, wrenches and the well ordered contents of two impressive tool bags. He smiled at Cody's approach.

'Ceulwas, I think your man here has it now. It is not complicated.'

'Not complicated! It's brilliant. It's the most impressive piece of kit I've ever had the chance to fly. She's a total beauty.'

'Tell him why it's named Gnosspelius,' said Cody sinking down besides her friend and dangling her legs over the water. Loren looked up expectantly.

'Ah, Gnosspelius; one of our home grown air pioneers here in the Lake District,' beamed Veriman. 'One of our many great men and women who no one has ever heard of. It is always the way of it, *ne var* Ceulwas. We are ever destined for obscurity and the blank pages of history.'

'*Ita vero,* except amongst our own Veriman. We never forget our own,' said Cody gently.

Kanulf had sauntered up to join them.

'Time presses *Arkadashim*. Are we ready? Are you alright Cody?'

Cody had sat suddenly bolt upright. She was staring at Loren as he tested the tension on one of the wire struts. Without warning she swung out over the water and landed on the craft's nearside float making it buck wildly with the sudden addition of her weight. Loren grabbed at a spar for balance as she seized his wrists and turned his palms face upwards with a strength that took him by surprise. He stared aghast at her intense expression as she examined the tattoos on each hand. On the left palm was what looked like a candle flame rising out of a circle broken by double slashes. In the corresponding position on his right palm was a block of lines and dashes surrounded by short curves.

'Do you know what these are?' she asked in a husky voice.

Loren found the intensity of her voice and face daunting.

'No,' he replied. 'I never have. Had 'em as long as I can recall, well, from four years ago anyway. Never have come up with any explanation. Might have been drunk...or something.'

With one hand Cody tore at the neck of her jacket and withdrew the silver locket and chain given her by her mother. With a battered thumbnail she prised at the edge of the metal oval popping a slim panel aside and revealing a tiny engraving. Loren, one wrist still held in an iron grip, was able to read: *Gill C Beltane 1931,* beneath the black and white photo.

'Is that a relative of yours?' he asked, looking at the bright eyed girl.

'You might say that.' She looked across at Kanulf. 'Alright, we will follow your plan. I'll go with Loren. Your plan has merit.'

'And that's because…?' began Loren.

'It's settled!' snapped Cody, her blue eyes blazing like sunlit glass. 'Settled. You understand. No discussion!'

The men looked at each other and did what all sensible beings do when faced with an overwhelming force, they lowered their gazes and acted as if nothing had happened. Kanulf had seen her opening the silver locket and knew what she had seen there; he also knew that this was not the time to be discussing the meaning of the engraving.

'Let me explain everybody's part in what we must do and the timings if we are to get this right,' said Kanulf cautiously. Cody nodded her agreement.

'It is time to begin taking this war to the shadows.'

Thirty Seven
TIME EXPIRING

'This is the way a tale be made
Each step a cost in blood is paid.'
Taken from: Waelbeorc's Stand. Translation by Brough Savage.

VERIMAN had to be installed into the steam launch and lashed to the pilot seat inside the tiny open cabin. Try as she might Cody could not let go of his hand as they settled him behind the steering wheel. She leant forward and hugged him tenderly. Words were exchanged in Old Tongue; both had tears in their eyes and were unashamed to show it.

'Loren has something in safe keeping for you Ceulwas. I asked him to bring it with him from Wrayhaven and give it to you when you reach safety. It is a gift from an old friend to your old self.'

'Veriman, Kanulf asked me what I saw back there in the Liminal.'

'Did you tell him?'

'No. It was something out of my past. Something pointing me to Lucian's possible whereabouts. I had information once about what happened to him and placed it in there because I did not know who I could trust. Treachery had put my brother in the hands of our Chameleon enemies. That was three years ago. I have to find him.'

'That will not be easy. And you must be sure you are ready. Our enemies do not allow us the luxury of second chances.'

'I know Veriman. Bron told me I would experience crippling disabilities because I have awakened too early.'

'That is putting it mildly Arkadash. I can only say trust your instincts. Act with wisdom, not inflamed passions. As Eloin we must learn to live with constant and terrible losses and judge our time carefully. This is our inheritance and our burden. I must mourn my companions Baria and Farsim. You have suffered the demise of loved ones.'

'Josse…he…'

'Yes. I am sorry. There was nothing anyone could have done. That was the hand that life dealt him.' Veriman paused. 'Ceulwas, my old companion, there are people who will meet you and take you to safety when you reach the rendezvous at Ullswater. Go with them. Heed them. But be always mindful. We are never truly free of the treachery which dogs our footsteps in this shadow war we wage.'

There was a moment of silence. Cody laid her hand on her friend's frail arm.

'Veriman, if there was only some way I…'

'I know *Beuminas*, I know. I feel as you do, but it has to be this way. Go now. Go in love. Go and find your brother.'

The parting was inevitable but did not come easily. Kanulf yelled and threw a lighted match onto the oily rags piled in the row boat about fifteen feet away. They took fire with a whoosh and Cody vaulted from Veriman's launch to haul at the pulley ropes that opened the first set of gates onto the lake. As they creaked open Kanulf dragged the rapidly burning boat along the jetty and guided it out onto the open water with a long boat hook. Thick choking smoke billowed from the tiny craft. Immediately Veriman throttled the steam launch's engine, drowned instantly by Loren firing up the Gnosspelius. Any further communication was impossible with the din magnified inside the confined space. Kanulf ran for the blind side window away from the Spitter position outside, throwing the controlling lever for the protective light-wall as he passed. The boathouse was now unprotected.

With surprising agility the old man scaled the rough stone wall in the same time as it took Cody to race around three sides of the inner perimeter of the building and reach the microphibian on the opposite side. The steam launch with Veriman at the controls surged forward onto the open water as Cody hauled on the pulley for the second set of gates and leapt onto the nearest float of the Gnosspelius. The way was now clear for both escape craft to head out into clear water. Cody scrambled nimbly into her seat behind Loren jamming a leather flying helmet onto her head and pulling down the goggles. There were gloves too. Loren was already kitted up. He grinned insanely at her as she gave him the thumbs up.

Veriman's launch was obscured by the thick smoke spreading across the natural harbour in front of the boathouse but he would be speeding along the narrow spit of land that formed a landing on the right hand side and the enemy would guess that.

Loren gunned the madly revving engine of the Gnosspelius and roared out of the boathouse pushing a bow wave that crashed against the sides of the exit. He yelled something inaudible amidst the deafening noise, his head turning back to check Cody and still grinning. She saw him press a wad of chewing gum to one of the supports. *For good luck*, he mouthed at her. She grinned back.

The odd looking craft crested across open water heading for where the main shoreline on the left extended into a short headland. They would have to clear that before they could lift off properly. Everyone knew that the skulking Vil-kind would have been immediately alerted by the smoke and bedlam of engines starting up. There would be very little time to get away, moments only. Kanulf had disappeared through the top window and would get within deadly range of the encamped grotesques as soon as he could but would he be soon enough to stop them unleashing a broadside of the deadly corrosive pellets? He would be heavily outnumbered. Cody's spine itched with tension.

She caught sight of Veriman's launch as it broke clear of the smoke. It was making good headway and so far there had been no response from the Vil-kind. Seconds later Loren snapped the vertical wings of the Gnosspelius into their horizontal position and almost immediately the tiny craft began to dip and bounce as it tried to unstick from the water. The mad hornet roar of the engine drowned the noise of their crashing impacts but not the pounding the craft was taking. Cody felt as if her teeth were being shaken loose.

And then she saw it – a line of sickly yellow arcing out from the bank and smacking into the waves just ahead of Veriman's boat! A great plume of spray and steam geysered upwards as the corrosive mass exploded. He was in range! Veriman was going to get hit! Kanulf had not taken them out! She could hear nothing above the aircraft's roar, not even her own scream.

With a stomach dropping lurch the Gnosspelius suddenly leapt clear of the water and rose in a steep climb that snatched the breath from her body. It was every kind of churning terror and exhilaration together at once. They were going to get free. Which was when a sizzling bolt of yellow skimmed the right edge of the aircraft and Cody realized with a surge of paralysing fear that they were still in range too. Loren banked steeply to the left but they had too little room to manoeuvre – they were still perilously close to the water. He pulled the nimble craft back into a steep climb followed by a spiralling twist to the left trying to baffle their enemy's aim. But the next moment something hit the left float with a crackling spitting sound and acid yellow fragments were filling the air all around them. Some passed right through the thin fabric of the wing without sticking. In a blur of lightning movement Cody batted away a kernel of hot matter from the back of Loren's head with her phantom hand and then the rest of the fragments were falling back to earth as the craft shot upwards.

The dull crump of an explosion made her spin round. She saw a cloud of smoke billowing from somewhere in the trees near to the boathouse. Kanulf had silenced the Spitter nest! At last.

'Turn, turn,' she screamed next to Loren's ear. 'I want to see Veriman.'

Loren shook his head indicating no. She grabbed him by the scruff of his jacket collar and twisted viciously. He waved frantically, OK, OK! They took a sharp easy curve around to catch sight of the steam launch far below. The water was boiling around the hull as if being thrashed by maddened propellers. She glimpsed a flash of silver amidst the seething mass, squirming fins and fishtails. The launch was being attacked by Fin Swarmers, the vicious piranha-like flying predators! They were gliding onto the deck of the launch and crashing against the tiny pilot cabin.

But then she saw something that would stay with her forever – Veriman was stood, feet apart on the highest part of the decking waving at them, waving at her. Even from this distance she could see that he was smiling, exultant even. And he was holding aloft his periapt phial and two silver rings. That smile bridged the distance between them like an electric spark and held the seconds at bay. He gave one final wave, and then brought the phial and rings clashing together level with his chest. The little launch and everything around it vanished in an expanding orb of brilliant blue fire! When the flash dissipated the steaming water rushed back to fill a bowl shaped cavity in the lake and crashed upwards like the column of a fountain before falling back in on itself. Veriman was gone. Evaporated. A far less devastating self sacrifice than Bron's but not one iota less courageous.

Her head sank onto her chest but there were no more tears to shed.

Without a word Loren banked steeply away and headed north along the length of Windermere. It was a morning of clear skies and a faultless dawn. Ullswater was fifteen miles away over the top of the Kirkstone pass 1,480 feet above them.

*   *   *

Kanulf 's decisive strike had left the Spitter cage and it's attendant Vil-kind a mass of tangled wood, metal and corpses. He replaced his eye patch as he ran trying to ignore the stabbing ache in his eye socket. It was not wise to overuse the arcane psygrypel weapon embedded in his skull. The cost could be debilitating – he felt drained. But he ran, knowing that he had little by way of breathing space to make his own escape. Already other Vil-kind were crashing their way through the smoke shrouded forest alerted by the sounds of destruction.

He had to reach the spot where he and Loren had been dropped from a Black Set stealth helicopter the night before. It was away to the north west and there was a beacon buried there. Once triggered it would have a rescue squad on his mark within fifteen minutes – or thereabouts. In his exhaustion it seemed a long way to go.

From the wooded slopes leading up to the sombre mass of Wrayhaven a mob of monstrosities erupted from cover and swept, howling and slashing at the air with their weapons, towards the boathouse. Straight past the smoking pit of the Spitter nest they crashed against the solidly built stone structure, battering at its gates and swarming up the walls. In no time they were piling in through shattered windows or screaming defiance and rage at the rapidly disappearing microlite, already little more than a dot in the sky.

Kanulf was about to leave when he saw something that changed his mind. He melted into the dense cover of a hawthorn bush and watched.

A wolf-like creature was being urged forward from the forest covering, bowed beneath a massive glass jar. The container was stoppered and carried by a filthy criss-crossing of skin shreds and straps. Amidst shrieks from the mob the jar was removed and set down by a figure masked and hooded in rotting leather. It carried a pair of long handled whip-like rods lashed with beaded strings. Wires led to what was probably a primitive battery pack on its hip. The scarecrow gaggle shrank back as the figure uncapped the jar releasing a dense cloud of whirling dots that danced in the air.

'Spore swarm,' breathed Kanulf, aghast. 'A damned viral swarm!' His heart sank. This was a weapon that was hard to combat, especially when it was closely directed by one such as the leather hooded Chameleon breed. The figure was already weaving the crackling whip-rods and somehow marshalling the mass of mobile spores. When they suddenly shot off in the wake of the distant microlite Kanulf realised he had to act quickly. He wouldn't be able to destroy the swarm, he knew that, but he might be able to prevent it reaching its target. If he could take out the directing mind behind the killer cloud there was a strong chance the swarm might lose cohesion and disperse or even attach itself to another moving object.

Summoning his last reserves of strength he broke cover and crossed the intervening ground at a speed that took the milling monstrosities totally unawares. Their attention had been on the rapidly vanishing swarm and Kanulf was amongst them before they had chance to react. Wielding both Lodestaffs he carved his way past the two nearest abominations and took the leather hooded Vil-kind with a hail of blows. The sounds of the impacts were like gunshots. The controlling rods and their user became instant wreckage.

Without pausing Kanulf reversed his charge and sprang clear of the raging monstrosities, sprinting for the cover of the forest and taking down any of the shrieking scarecrows that got in his way. He had a head start on them, but it might not prove enough. The Chameleon breed could be fast over good ground and if there were Gaunts around he would have his work cut out. He swung the Lodestaffs wide, adding to his forward momentum. The dangerous humming note they gave off was a comfort to his warrior's ear.

Kanulf ran low and fast, setting up a steady pounding lope. The bellows of the pursuing Vil-kind so closed behind chilled his spine. He had to dodge low hanging branches and leap felled trees that had been hacked down by the besieging forces. In his heart he wondered if he had the reserves to keep ahead of the braying malforms as he cut a zig-zag path towards the beacon point.

…the Shadow Hein's shriek almost paralysed him. He staggered and fell, rolling amidst thick bracken and leaf mould. The thing was so close! Recovering fast he was on his feet in an instant, and side stepping clear of the slow wailing column of hideous blackness. The form towered above him. He would have got clear too but for the five other Hein blocking his way in a wide crescent formation. The moment he paused a black barbed tentacle lashed around his lower thighs wrenching him to the ground.

Damnation and stars! he cursed to himself. I was almost clear.

His Lodestaffs slashed across the writhing limb of the Shadow Hein causing it to trumpet in pain and release him. He managed only a few tottering steps before collapsing, unable to move his legs. Rising to his knees he holstered the twin staffs and readied his rings in front of his chest.

Before he could unleash the needle beams of fire a brilliant lance of heat sizzled above his head and cut the nearest Shadow Hein in two. The upright stump and top portion sagged in on themselves like a column of rancid grease. Other beams began carving up the ululating shapes, rendering them into steaming slices. They fell apart like sludge on a hot shovel.

Kanulf's own ring fire took its toll in demolishing the travesties. The things fell apart under the withering rage of the beams. Soon there was silence. A stench laden steam drifted gently on the breeze. Across the clearing Kanulf could make out the diminutive white clad figure of his rescuer forty yards away. It was lowering its arms.

Amuna!

Her goggles glinted in the low light and a huge grin of relief split the pale face. When he tried to stagger to his feet she gestured to a line of black clad figures behind her in the gloom. Heavily armed members of the Black Set swept past her and fanned out either side of Kanulf protecting him from the approaching pursuers. The screams of rage were getting closer. Two of the operatives grasped him under the arms, helping him stand upright. He couldn't have managed it alone. They half carried him to where Amuna stood ringed by more of the imposing black soldiers.

'You are a welcome sight Shree,' gasped Kanulf through gritted teeth. 'There's quite a pack on my heels.'

'They'll be dealt with,' grinned Amuna. 'We need to move fast. Are you alone?'

'Our charge made it clear. She is with Loren heading for Ullswater. Veriman didn't make it.' Kanulf was breathing hard and grimacing.

'We heard the explosions. I'm sorry Kanulf. Dues of war.' Her voice was as melodious as ever, though they were both hobbling and stumbling over the rough ground.

'How are you here so soon Shree? I thought you were hours away.' Their Black Set guards were hacking foliage clear ahead of them to aid their progress.

'The situation changed Sephamon. A massive Luminic discharge was detected coming from within Wrayhaven. I decided I needed to be here.'

'And I'm relieved you did. I'll bring you up to date about the *event* when we have clearance.' Kanulf glanced meaningfully at the operatives around them, anonymous behind their blacked out goggles and night masks. Amuna nodded.

Behind them they could hear the sound of gunfire and what could have been the roar of flame throwers. The shrieks and screams continued without a pause.

'We'll get you lifted out of here soon,' said Amuna glancing back. 'Then get you patched up. Are you in too much pain...?...no? Well, mission a qualified success, do you think? Some losses; we are preparing to take Wrayhaven back soon; our charge is on the way to safety; oh, and you aren't dead.'

Kanulf chuckled grimly.

'No. Not dead yet, though I thought for a minute there...! Ceulwas should be home and free now. She's in good hands. Loren is a good pilot.' He winced sharply. His breath was coming in snatches and gasps. Amuna indicated for the figures supporting Kanulf to stop. She placed her hands over the wounds in his thighs, which were bleeding badly. She held them there. Nothing seemed to happen, except that Kanulf suddenly straightened with a huge sigh and breathed with obvious relief.

'You should have said,' she reprimanded him gently. 'OK, let's keep moving. Not far to go now.' She addressed the two Black Set propping him up. 'Keep a grip on his arms, even if he complains. Ignore him. He's a grumpy old man. Just keep him upright.' They nodded.

It was somewhat easier going now that Kanulf's pain was reduced.

Thirty Eight
PARTHIAN SHOT

*'If hope could put wings on our backs, we would never touch
earth again.'*
The Inherited Landscape by Jean Frecé.

IT was only as the Gnosspelius roared high over the abandoned
town of Ambleside at the northern end of the lake that Cody realised they
were carrying their doom with them. They had begun the long steep
ascent towards the top of the Kirkstone pass when she spotted that part of
the Spitter's corrosive pellet had not just struck but adhered to their left
hand float and was rapidly eating its way into the metal. She felt a lurch as
part of the float dropped away and the microlite bucked with the change
in weight. Loren's head whipped round and they both peered over the
side of the tiny hull to see the sullen line of bile yellow creeping its way
along the body of the float and into the two main struts holding it to the
hull. With a lurch the last of the float dropped away tumbling end over
end until it vanished amongst creeper choked houses on the outskirts of
the town. The creeping horror would reach the hull and engine housing
within a few brief minutes. After that they would come crashing out of the
sky. The plane was being devoured by slow increments the way poor
Veriman had been. And even if by some miracle they managed a forced
landing and survived they would still be miles from their rendezvous!
    'Try to dislodge that forward strut,' yelled Loren. 'Hit it with
something.' Most of his words were stripped away by the wind but Cody
understood. But with what? They were travelling light, there was nothing
she could use to swing at the slow death that was inching its way towards
them. And even if she had, twisting around in the tiny space to reach the
strut was almost impossible. She was crammed up against Loren's back
and every shift of position made the microlite buck and drop. The force of

293

the wind was whipping glowing fragments of corroded matter behind them like a trail of sparks. Unfortunately this in no way diminished the danger; it was furiously decomposing matter that streamed out behind them; the steadily advancing edge of corrosion never diminished, in fact it seemed to be accelerating under the effect of the wind, possibly being force fed oxygen, like the embers of a bonfire being whipped into a furious heat by fanning.

'Hang on. I have an idea. A long shot,' yelled Loren.

They were passing high to the right of one of the gigantic Bolt Oaks that had taken root on the sloping land above Ambleside and Loren put the craft into a sharp turn skimming low towards the top of the magnificent shape. Cody's heart jumped into her throat as she realised what he was going to attempt. She was right. As near as he could judge it Loren took the Gnosspelius to within feet of the topmost foliage and at the last minute dipped the hull as close as he dared to the branches. There was an almighty lurch and explosion of foliage as the forward stump of metallic strut ripped into the Oak. The craft staggered in mid air and nose dived with a sickening twist towards the ground. Cody was sure they would never pull out in time but Loren's piloting skills proved their worth. He was clawing at air, struggling to drag the aerofoil into an alignment that would not smash them head on into the unforgiving ground. With barely spitting distance to go he managed to wrench the shuddering craft around in a turn so tight they both nearly blacked out. With immense relief Cody saw that they were heading in the correct direction upslope again, about fifteen feet clear of the exposed rock and heather that covered the bulk of mountainside. She could see that the forward strut had been successfully wrenched off by the impact leaving a jagged hole in the fibreglass, but they both knew that the lightweight craft wouldn't survive a second impact like that one; and anyway there were now no more trees between them and the summit, only bare rock and dry stone walls. The danger was too great to attempt dislodging the second strut.

Then she had it.

'Head straight for the pass,' she screamed over the wind, pounding him on the shoulder. 'Leave it to me.'

Loren had no idea what she intended but nodded OK and set about gaining altitude. The magnificent land swept majestically towards the peaks above them.

The sparking corrosive patch had eaten most of the remaining rear strut by now and was within a foot of the hull. Cody stretched out with her phantom hand, her Scaedu Folm, as Kanulf had named it. She concentrated on forming the nonlimb emerging from her chest as an ice cold crushing fist of muscle and bone, immensely strong. Without hesitation she grasped the spitting concentration of bile fire and enclosed it in her invisible hand. Her intention was to simply contain the fiery venom, envelope it in an airless impenetrable shroud. She could see it's sputtering reduce drastically, but knew that the thing would not die. It was far too tenacious. She tried wrenching the strut away from the body of the microlite but it was incredibly strong despite its lightness. Fine. At least it had slowed. All she needed to do was keep it inert until they were over Ullswater and they could come up with something, some way to ... but of course they couldn't land, on water or solid ground! Whatever way they came to earth it was not going to be a controllable landing.

Loren twisted round to see how she was doing and nodded encouragingly when he saw no sign of the yellow bile. He had no idea why his passenger was angled half out of her seat in such an incredibly awkward position but didn't try to question her.

'Won't be long,' he yelled almost inaudibly into the face of the wind. 'Minutes to gain height over the pass. Minutes to reach Ullswater. All a downhill glide from top. You OK?'

Cody didn't really catch all he said but gave him a thumbs up to reassure him, never for a moment relaxing her fisted grip on the acidic yellow embers. There was nothing to do but sit it out and improvise some kind of plan when it came time for landing. The ideal solution would be to sink the Gnosspelius in deep water so that the Spitter's venom would be rendered inert and eventually neutralised by the cold, airless darkness of the lake's depths. They'd have to make landfall some other way. There was still time to figure something out.

The Gnosspelius spiralled up and around gaining precious height and in so doing provided a breathtaking view of the mountainous sloping land below them. Back the way they had come the magnificence of Windermere's eleven mile length stretched far into a glorious misty distance. Pale layers of mountains ranged one behind the other to a horizon hazed into an exquisite patchwork of pastels. The contrast between this stunning panorama and the recently suffocating confines of Wrayhaven made her soul soar with delight. She could feel her heart fill with hope and resolve. They would get through this. They were in the clear. Loren had proved his worth handling the craft the way he had and once they reached safety she could plan how she was going to begin tracking down her missing brother. Poor Lucian. It tore at her heart to think what he might have undergone whilst abandoned to the hands of his Chameleon captors - and for three years. Three years! It was almost unbearably painful to even consider.

Her gaze was drifting across the landscape behind them when something caught her attention. Something was following them. Birds? A cloud? She wiped at the goggles and peered more carefully – and her heart nearly stopped.

Spore swarm! And it was gaining on them, fast.

She pounded Loren on the shoulder pointing frantically at the deadly shape to their rear. His face looked grim.

'Are they gaining on us?' he wanted to know.

'Yes. I'm pretty sure.'

Loren began to root around in the tiny cockpit for something. When he found what he was looking for he held it up for Cody to see. A compact metal cylinder the size of an aerosol can with a large plastic cap and some kind of wire pull-cord along one side.

'Phosphor grenade,' roared Loren. 'Veriman provided for everything.'

There was printing along the side. Beneath a danger symbol it said in neat red print: *six second delay*. Well, that was helpful to know.

'Can you drop this in its path?' Loren screamed at her above the wind. 'Can you?'

'Won't it just fall?' she yelled back, puzzled at his request.

'Pull that release wire on the side and throw it high. That's a parachute on the top. If you can time it to drift anywhere near the swarm it should knock the beggars out. Thing is, I can't get a good swing around our canopy and you'll need to chuck it high above us to get the timing right. Can you do it?'

'Yes. I think so. Yes. Yes I can,' she screamed against the wind, suddenly more certain.

'Awkward shot I know. We've got two of these things. Best to wait till it gets closer. You up for it?'

Cody nodded vigorously and took the grenade carefully in her gloved right hand as he passed it back. With her physical hands she knew it was an impossible task. But with her phantom hand...she would have to let go of the smouldering embers to do it but if she was quick the corrosion shouldn't gain much ground. She glanced back at the approaching cloud and tried to estimate how close it was. The shape was shifting and writhing as it sped along. Judging its approach was tricky, especially from her twisted position still gripping the Spitter venom. The next five minutes were extremely uncomfortable. Loren kept glancing back and asking her if she was OK. She nodded that she was.

The Gnosspelius was gaining height steadily and heading for the summit of the pass opposed by a head wind, which not only made communication difficult but, at this altitude, was chilling. All the energy from Cody's chest was directed into her phantom grip keeping the corrosion contained and she was both exhausted and feeling the cold. The strain of everything that had happened in Wrayhaven was taking its toll. Her shoulders and neck ached terribly from holding this awkward position. She desperately needed food and rest and her eyes throbbed with pain. The microphibian bucked and dipped constantly as they arrowed between soaring mountain peaks on either side. Loren was compensating for the ungainly twist caused by the drag of the remaining float on the right hand side. And behind them the poisonous swarm gained ground. There seemed an eternity for Cody's thoughts to roam over the events of the last forty eight hours and there was no lack of unpleasant memories to occupy her. Her temples ached with visions of Bee, Josse, Bron and Veriman. She had many questions about Kanulf, and she was fretting badly about Lucian.

The approach of the swarm came all in a surge of accelerated motion that was as alarming as it was violent. Suddenly, there it was, only a hundred feet or so behind them. Dangerously close! She could almost hear its angry buzz. Cody realised she had lost concentration for a moment but her reactions were quick. Releasing her hold on the Spitter corrosion she grasped the grenade with her phantom limb, tugged the release wire on the side, and hurled it up above the microlite canopy stretching her invisible arm around the taut material in a way she could never have done with her solid limbs. She lost sight of the missile for a moment only to see it almost instantly seventy or eighty feet behind them, a tiny object dangling beneath a tiny orange parachute. It was hard to judge how close it got to the swarm but when it burst apart in a ball of flame the cloud of writhing mites swelled around the explosion, gyrating madly, before instantly reforming and accelerating after them.

'A hit?' yelled Loren, as Cody clamped her phantom hand back around the Spitter venom.

'Give me the next one,' she screamed in his ear. 'I have the distance now.'

'OK. Good luck. This is our last.' He passed the final grenade, taking care not to snag the trigger wire. 'We're coming to the pass soon,' he yelled back at her. 'We'll be able to level off at that point. It'll give you a better shot at it.'

He began to throw the microphibian into a series of swerves and dips as if trying to shake the tenacious cloud of venom off their tail but the thing followed every manoeuvre without any trouble.

'Won't be long now,' yelled Loren. 'Almost at the top. You're going to love Ullswater. It's beautiful.'

*   *   *

In the silent depths of Wrayhaven a blackened shape broke the surface of a tar pool into which it had rolled for protection against the devastation that had scoured the tunnels clean of life. For several desperate moments it choked and spluttered trying to clear its lungs of the cloying intrusive sludge. Then it began a slow crawling attempt to gain some kind of grip on the slippery edge of the pool. Every foot of progress involved repeatedly sliding backwards into the glistening ooze. But painfully, slowly, the shape pulled itself onto firm ground where it collapsed, snatching great gulps of air into its tortured lungs.

Garatunde knew he was lucky to be alive. It was rare to survive a Scouring and there had not been much warning. Fortunately he had recognised the signs in time. Once before he had barely avoided having his atoms blasted to scalding dust by an Aelim unleashing the fires of destruction on him. Only the nearness of the tar pool had saved him on this occasion. His lungs had almost ruptured in the suffocating pitch but he had remained submerged preferring that to having his body scattered in searing agony.

The truncated Chameleon lay oozing glutinous drips and muttering a blethy of oaths and obscenities. He stirred, his eyes glaring a furious red within the dripping black mask, as a questing black tendril slithered around his forearm and tried to tug him back below the glistening surface. The damned things had been nudging at his face and limbs whilst he held his breath in the pool. He bellowed with rage, almost glad of something to vent his fury on. Savage slashes with one of the wire bound blades on his wrist tore the tentacle to messy pulp. He clawed at the muck around his mouth issuing curses that echoed in the dimness of the death chamber before he resumed dragging himself towards the massed heap of rubble that led up to the opening in the ceiling – and eventually to the outside world. Here and there a few flaming torches had fallen into tar patches and flared fitfully giving a hellish light to the litter of weapons and objects scattered everywhere. Garatunde crawled over them all oblivious of everything except the need to reach any Vil-kind who might have been outside the labyrinth when the Scouring took place. His ugly beauties would resume their invasion of the damned stronghold as soon they realised the way was clear, and he would be carried to safety.

By now he'd reached the top of the rubble slope and was dragging himself hand over hand, still half blinded by the tacky coating that he trailed behind him like some obscene slug trail. It was humiliating but he had to reach the place where he had broken into the subterranean levels earlier at the head of a stalker pack. There were weapons and abandoned gear everywhere around him in the darkness. Then he paused...a sound! A sound he knew! From somewhere in the darkness ahead he could hear a voice, a braying shrieking sound that made his heart sink as he recognised it. It was Grendelmor! So, she too had found a way to avoid the Scouring. Damnation and hell fire! The woman was indestructible! He crawled towards the sound like a broken lapdog, dreading yet pulled irresistibly towards the thing he feared and hated most in all the world, his insane tyrannical mistress.

Modern myths of post-Event Britain, The New Albion Sagas.
Article summary by Cullie Brown.

'The popular series of legends and children's tales featuring Leoric and Amberym tell of two heroic individuals, twins, who battled bestial creatures from a mythic world realm. Their foremost enemies were the insane Technosages, lurking in their subterranean caverns, and meddling with the laws of nature. These deviant souls had bred a creeping poison that threatened to devastate the land, one which was only destroyed by the twin heroes unleashing the Fimbulwinter. This devastating Ice Year saved the world, but the cost was great. The Ice Event caused great destruction and untold deaths.

The heroes Leoric and Amberym were aided in their defeat of the Technosages by three Aels or Aelim, beings very like the traditional angel warriors of myth and religion, who sacrificed themselves to precipitate the Fimbulwinter. It is an inspiring tale of epic combat and heroic self sacrifice to save humanity from terrors, subjugation and annihilation. The three Aelim warriors suffered horrendous damage. One was captured by the Technosages and kept immobilised in a shell of debilitating torment. The other two escaped but had to be immersed in a powerful healing soul state or Haelenmir. Whatever recovery might be wrought for them would take years, possibly decades.

The subsequent fate of the two human heroes, Leoric and Amberym, varies depending on which legends are consulted, but they all agree on the fact that Amberym was captured by the inhuman lord of the Technosages and suspended in an unbreachable cage of distraction. Leoric underwent many adventures trying to locate her twin but without success.'

For more information go to: egl.mythsoftheiceyear.co.uk

Thirty Nine
HARD LANDINGS

'The story's final line is crossed
When innocence expires, is lost.'
TK Edwins.

AS the Gnosspelius lurched its way to the top of the valley Cody began to feel nauseous. Spots of light darted behind her eyes making it hard to focus on the pursuing patch of shadow that threatened to kill them in midair.

'Almost there,' roared Loren. 'I'll take it steady and level now. Ready?'

'No problem,' Cody roared back. He gave her a thumbs up without turning round.

The microphibian levelled out, still climbing, but on an arrow straight path. Cody focused on the dark patch of air directly behind them, swirling and weaving like a fish shoal. Her hands were numb with cold and for a moment she feared her fingers would refuse to work properly. She was too exhausted to channel any more heat from her chest. All her energy was going into gripping the glowing Spitter venom.

The timing with the grenade had to be exact. There would be no third chance at this. She had six seconds after pulling the trigger wire to place the explosion directly ahead of the swarm for maximum effect. Could she do it? There was only one way to find out.

She had considered using her ring skills – they were always a last resort of course – but that would involve removing her gloves, twisting around to face the rear and targeting every single mote in a shifting, nebulous target. She would also lose focus on her Scaedu Folm for as long as it took to burn the swarm out of the sky. How long would that take? There was no way of knowing. No, this was their best bet.

She had one advantage. She needn't do this alone. Locked away in her mind was over eighty years of learning, skills and experience of warfare. She could tap into that, use her inner resources. Closing her eyes she sank into that place of glittering fishtails, the inner icy stillness behind a curtain of light. It was there that she found the peace she needed. This was her centre, her place of knowing. Her still focus of action.

Snapping open her eyes she gauged the distance to the swarm. They were closer. Time to act. Now, simple steps. Pull the trigger wire on the grenade. Count – 6 – 5 – snatch the grenade with her invisible fingers – 4 – lean backwards, twist and hurl – 3 – 2 – 1! The tiny orange parachute drifted down in perfect alignment with the darting mass of motes – and blossomed into an expanding ball of fire directly in its path. For a second she lost sight of the swarm. Minute blazing sparks radiated outwards on all side of the fireball, dispersing like a firework. The burning motes dropped downwards, already falling far behind as the Gnosspelius sped away from the explosion. A shockwave buffeted the craft briefly making it lurch and drop. But Loren had it under control and they roared on. Loren looked back. She gave him a thumbs up and he let rip with a rebel yell.

'My girl!' he whooped. 'What a champ. Yeeee bloody haaaar!'

Behind them a diminishing cluster of sooty grains drifted to earth beneath a dispersing mushroom of smoke. Threat vanquished. With a start Cody remembered to slap her phantom hand back around the deadly corrosion still eating into their craft. It had flared up alarmingly from the sudden supply of oxygen. It died to a sullen glow as her unhand enclosed it.

She felt a tremendous elation. Success. Satisfaction glowed along her body momentarily banishing the dreadful cold that had seeped into her bones. They might make this after all.

By now the Gnosspelius was passing over the roof of an inn on their right hand side, at the very point where the land levelled off before beginning its six mile downhill slope to the waters of Ullswater. Cody could see that the building had been demolished by a patch of Bloom at some time, half of it having been absorbed by the edge of an expanding circle of creeping blue fungus. Now, of course, all that remained of the Bloom was a fifty foot wide circular patch of black tar. The inside of the inn was exposed to the elements, half of its walls lying in tar coated rubble inside the perimeter of the tar spot. There were three other circles dotted around the plateau, one cutting directly across the narrow road linking the Ullswater valley to the lowlands of Windermere. Even from this height Cody could see how tyre marks and cattle prints skirted the ominous black expanse before meeting up again with the old roadway.

'Are you OK?' yelled Loren.

'Yes. Cold though.'

'Don't worry. There she is. Not far now,' he assured her.

Water glinted between two steep sided angles of the great valley far ahead of them. Ullswater Lake. It was time to start seriously planning their moves. Their swift powered ascent changed into an effortless glide taking them through a landscape that seemed to the exhausted Cody to be rushing around them like the walls of a tunnel. There was so little protection between her and the vast spaces that yawned beneath the flimsy structure of the microlite. It seemed to her that she was flying with no discernible means of support, weightless, soaring on wings of air. She tried to blink away the dots dancing behind her eyes.

'When we get to the water watch the right bank. Should be someone waiting for us there,' yelled Loren.

'Who?'

'Friends. Four of them. We'll get as close as we can and ditch parallel to the shore.'

'We can't,' yelled back Cody.

'What?'

'We can't. Have to ditch in deep water.'

Loren's head twisted round, this time assessing more fully what it was his passenger was doing leaning over the side so awkwardly. It was impossible to see the phantom hand in the bright sunlight, but he spied the blackened stump of the strut and the tiny glowing embers. His intelligent face flickered between Cody's eyes behind her goggles and the stump, then turned back to his controls.

'OK,' he called after a pause. 'Deep water. Damn, that's gonna be cold.'

Cody's already high opinion of this capable young man rose another notch. No unnecessary questions or quibbling, no asking for details or needing reassurances. He accepted her assessment of the situation and was prepared to act on it. She liked him. Actually he reminded her of someone – but she didn't want to spend time chasing down that particular thread of connections at this moment. Her mind wandered instead, back to her last exchange with Bron and her friend's comment about a call to action...it wasn't all clear in her mind yet, not by a long count, but she knew there were things that needed attending to – some of them urgently.

With a start she realised that they were rapidly approaching to within a few hundred feet of the glittering expanse of Ullswater. The Gnosspelius levelled off and swung closer to the right hand shore line. Loren took them to about fifty feet above the shimmering surface.

The magnificent body of the lake curved like a great crescent to the right so that the next stretch of water was continually obscured behind steep slopes and cliffs of beautifully coloured rock dotted with bushes and pine trees that sprouted at picturesque angles against the skyline. They passed a few boats, rowing boats mostly, though there was one small steam launch with a red funnel and a couple waving at them from the open cabin. For a moment Cody thought that this might be their intended rendezvous but Loren roared past them, with a cheery wave. Just ahead was one particularly spectacular mountain buttress jutting out of the water like the monolithic walls of some primeval fortress. The view suddenly widened. Ullswater broadened out here and it was possible to see the top most shore where a passenger steamer, tiny in the distance, was pulling away from a landing beneath a cloud of white steam. The air was crystal clear.

'Should be a jetty somewhere on the right,' came Loren's voice above the roar of the engine. 'Rendezvous close by. Howton pier. May not still be there of course.'

They kept about a hundred feet clear of the shoreline which had lush overgrown meadows and trees coming right down to the water's edge. Beyond that the land rose gently before shooting steeply up to the line of mountain peaks that bordered this portion of Lakeland beauty.

'There they are!'

It was impossible for Cody to see much to the right of the craft twisted as she was to the left side of the hull, but when Loren circled the Gnosspelius in a tight turn she got a good view of what he had spotted onshore. Four figures stood in a line on the stony water's edge signalling with coloured scarves and waving. Loren turned the microphibian in a wide circle so that they would pass left handed along the shore and Cody could get a better view. Loren and one of the figures exchanged rapid hand signals and the Gnosspelius circled for another pass. The second time they paralleled the shore Cody was taken aback to see one of the figures in the water swimming strongly away from the shore. A second figure was discarding a jacket and taking a running dive to do the same. By the third pass Loren had the plane barely skimming the water and aimed approximately ahead of where the two swimmers were racing with powerful strokes. He looked back at Cody,

'Ready?'

She nodded vigorously.

'Countdown 3-2-1.'

The impact with the water started as a gradual skimming action, the lower hull and remaining float kissing the tips of a few waves, but from that point on there was nothing gradual or gentle about their descent. The craft lost momentum rapidly and dug into the water smacking ferociously with a judder that skewed the whole frame forwards onto its nose. The remaining float was torn away. The delicate aerofoil wing tilted and chopped into the waves like a knife before collapsing like a swatted butterfly. Spray obscured everything and Cody was instantly and totally submerged beneath a rush of chilling waters. Cold pressure crashed against her chest and head so suddenly that she was immediately overwhelmed. The aircraft had no buoyancy at all. The Gnosspelius was sinking like a shattered stone pot. Cody released her grip on the corrosion infected strut and kicked herself away from the sinking trap of wires and clinging fabric and metal. The engine had died within seconds releasing an explosive wave front of steam. The dying craft was in danger of dragging her with it into the chilly dark depths. She hadn't taken in enough air and what was in her lungs was being squeezed out by the shocking pressure. She had to fight against the drag of her coat and satchel that had filled with water. Her goggles and helmet had been torn off by the initial collision. She tugged her gloves free. Streams of bubbles erupted from her mouth. Her heart was hammering like a tortured animal...and the glittering surface and safety was far above her head, out of reach and getting further away with every second. Her strength had abandoned her. She went limp, her cold eyes watching the tangled carcass of the Gnosspelius preceding her into the depths, its torn wings flapping languidly and getting dimmer as it sank further...and further. At least, she thought, at least nothing will be infected by the Spitter venom now.

Something wrenched at her collar jerking her up towards the surface. Something, someone was dragging her upwards with powerful kicks and arm movements striving for the blessed light. Were they going to make it...was she going to breathe again? She'd like to.

The pain of breaking through the shimmering surface and gulping in tortured lungfuls of air was more shocking than the pressure of not being able to breathe at all - at first – but at least it was a living pain, not a dying one. She thrashed about blind, deaf and inarticulate but overwhelmingly grateful for the strong arms that hooked about her waist and chin supporting her. Voices were calling urgently to one another; someone was splashing nearby. Nothing made sense. She felt herself being towed through waves that slopped into her mouth and nostrils. Something bumped against her head, something solid, plastic, hollow. Her arms were raised and thrown over the hard shape that bobbed beneath her weight. A voice said,

'Hang on Cody. Hang on. We can push you to shore. Are you OK?'

She nodded, unable to form words. Water still streamed into her mouth and nose. Hands hitched her up higher onto the bobbing shape. It was the second float from the Gnosspelius. As she numbly did as she was told and clung on, a face came into focus on the opposite side – Loren. He too was gripping the slim serrations of the float's plastic skin and hanging on grimly. A livid bruise coloured the entire left side of his face and his chin was gashed. Her grinned at her.

'Hope you're not going to sue me for that landing,' he laughed. 'Best I could do.'

Her returning smile was suffused with relief and gratitude. She coughed.

'Thanks Loren. Best landing ever.'

She focused at last on the other two figures in the water besides them. On Loren's side was a strikingly beautiful face she had never seen before. Radiant green eyes glowed against smooth coffee skin.

'This is Cas. Cas Winters,' spluttered Loren. 'Old friend.'

Cody nodded then turned to the figure with a protective arm still around her back. She started to say thank you but choked to a halt,

'Enwyn!' Her already befuddled mind reeled. 'What are...where...?'

'Just hang on the pair of you,' said Enwyn, not unkindly but very business like. 'We'll push you to shore. Kick your legs if you can but we'll do most of the work. Steady now. Nice and easy.'

'Enwyn, thank you. I...thank you.'

'I know Cody. It's fine. Save your breath. Soon have you to safety.'

They kicked the rest of the way to shore in silence.

*   *   *

There were two other figures waiting for them on the sunlit pebbles and shale. One at least was familiar. Cody hadn't seen Corbin Sleath since she and Bron had run into him and Enwyn at Martin's Gate market by the Telford junction in Chester. She knew him well enough, of course, having taken many Albion Fayre rides in his grey and black liveried microlite *Skyhound*. The other was a stocky Liter still wearing his leather flying helmet. Both of the men rushed into the water to offer support as she staggered out of the shallows on Enwyn's arm.

'Corbin! What are you doing here?' Cody's teeth were beginning to chatter.

'Oh, hanging around, you know. Can't swim,' he added nodding at the lake behind her. 'Never learned.' He looked sheepish.

'No, I mean here, waiting like this. Are you part of all...this...' she gestured vaguely as if trying to include everything inexplicable and mysterious that could have brought them together on this stony beach so far from the simplicities of Cheshire.

'Well, Enwyn here needed the loan of a microlite, and I could get her the use of one...I kind of owed her a big favour.' He and Enwyn exchanged significant looks for a moment.

'On condition he could come along naturally,' added Enwyn fussing Cody out of her coat and sodden top layers.

'This is Wrace, by the way. Wrace Jackson.' She indicated their companion who smiled warmly at them both and busied himself digging out packs of survival foil from his backpack. He had removed his helmet showing a typical Liter haircut called a bunce crop. Like so many flyers he wore a leather jacket, neckerchief, dozens of pockets everywhere and lightweight ankle boots, probably intended originally for skydiving.

Corbin immediately started to stash their dripping clothes into plastic bags and then into his own shoulder bag. Enwyn had started wrapping layers of the insulating plastic around Cody's limbs and torso tying them off with lengths of cord. Cas was doing the same to Loren. He didn't seem to mind at all. Both the women wore only close fitting black all-in-ones that ended at elbows and mid thighs, garments Cody had only seen before in pictures of athletes and extreme sports enthusiasts. All four of them from the water were shivering in the chill air.

'Like the togs,' said Loren with a mock leer. Cas pounded him on the shoulder and told him to turn around whilst she secured his crackling foil layers. He obeyed meekly but protested when she tried to remove his utility belt of pouches and holsters.

'Cas, please! I mean...!'

'Alright, keep your toys. But they go on outside the foil. No arguing now.'

'We don't have a lot of time,' interrupted Enwyn, her manner brisk. 'We have to get airborne and on our way.'

Cody tried to ignore the feeling that she must resemble a Mardi Gras mummy in her layers of gold and silver wrap.

'Airborne? Where are we going?'

'Blea Moor,' said Cas over her shoulder. 'You'll be safe there.'

'Another haven? Bawnhaven perhaps?' said Cody quietly.

Everyone stopped. Enwyn stared at her.

'Cody, how much do you remember?'

'A great deal. Enough anyway. You're Sufinam aren't you. You too I guess Cas. How about you Corbin, Wrace?'

The silence hovered like an unexpected guest. Waves slapped at the pebble beach. Swallows dipped and dived above their heads.

'Did Kanulf plan all this?' continued Cody, now trembling continuously. 'He did didn't he. And he intended for himself, and probably Veriman to be here too. That's why the four microlites. But things went wrong. We're the only ones who made it out of Wrayhaven safely.'

'Didn't Kanulf make it?' asked Enwyn, sounding alarmed.

'Possibly,' answered Loren. 'He and Veriman were covering our take off. He...'

'He may have done,' said Cody. 'Veriman didn't.' The faces of the rescuers looked stricken.

'How did you know we've got four microlites,' asked Wrace quietly.

'Saw them camouflaged in that field over there – from the air,' answered Cody.

Wrace burst into laughter. 'Cool.' He seemed delighted.

'Alright, explanations later I think,' said Enwyn glancing at the other rescuers. They nodded. 'Our task is to get you to safety. We can do that at least. This way, through the meadow. Don't worry about your wet things. Corbin and Wrace'll bring them along. They'll dry just fine when we get to Bawnhaven.'

Both women retrieved their own discarded clothing and added padded leggings and jackets plus leather helmets over the top of their wet layers.

'You'll soon warm up,' explained Corbin as he helped Cody into a spare quilted jacket taken from another backpack lying on the ground. 'Works like a wet suit. The inner layers of air and water heat up. You'll feel like toast in no time.'

It was true. In a matter of moments, with the zipper pulled tight under her chin and the hood covering her wet hair Cody could feel the beginnings of warmth moving along her limbs. She added a discrete release of heat from the slumbering furnace in her chest to speed things along and was soon feeling distinctly better, if rather sleepy. They waded through the waist high grass towards where the microlites were parked alongside an overgrown tarmac road. Cas applied a plaster dressing to Loren's cut chin, brushing aside his feeble protests. He was obviously loving the attention.

After being handed a slab of granola emergency rations by Wrace Cody was bundled into a grey and blue winged craft with the name *Chohim* stencilled on the side. Enwyn sat in the pilot seat. Loren climbed in behind Cas in the second machine, *Cloud Glyphs*. Corbin stashed their sodden clothes into lightweight saddle bags strapped to the sides of the tiny hull of *Skyhound* and fired up the engine. Within minutes the powerful little craft were taking off from the bumpy surface and arcing out over the lake. Wrace's yellow and black bird, *Zu Zu's Petals*, protected their rear as they made a wide turn to gain height and clear the ring of peaks around Ullswater. Once clear of the ground Cody opened the granola bar and devoured it hungrily as they rose above the sunlit panorama and left the lakes behind. She could begin to relax a little. Despite everything set against her, she had made it. And now she had the time to pay due respect to those that hadn't. She would do that in her own way.

*   *   *

The landscape so far below was lush with sweeping forests and the glory of radiant mountains that stretched to the horizon. Recovering Britain was a rich and verdant country now, punctuated only by Bolt Oaks or the blight of Tar circles. From the air it resembled pictures Cody had seen of the Amazon rain forest as it had been twenty or thirty years ago. The treetops seemed to go on for ever. Very rarely, thin tails of smoke showed where some isolated communities carved out a living in the new wilderness. What a beautiful land. What a lesson it all was, recovering and gathering its strength, as was humanity itself. There was hope abroad in the world – which would be needed because there was also a terrible darkness.

Calmly Cody trawled through the interior world of her eighty year old memories, cataloguing what she knew of the place they were going to - Bawnhaven. 'Bawn' was an ancient word meaning fortified dwelling. She had spent time there before, a lifetime ago, and knew they'd be safe once they reached it - not that she would be staying for long! She had plans to make for what lay ahead and she intended to be well prepared. There would be those who would oppose her going in search of her missing twin, she knew this. But they could be dealt with. Some terrible and brutish events lay in her past but they would not claim her or deter her. Nothing would.

Her only priority lay in tracking down where Lucian had been incarcerated and getting him out. Her being alive meant that Lucian had a chance. In all likelihood he would be a shadow child now – but he could be redeemed, reclaimed. She knew things that no one else did. There were also the links of blood that connected them in ways invisible to other beings, Eloin, human, Sufinam or Aelim.

Such terrible things had been done to her and her kin. The Pact had been broken. The Chameleons had transgressed by taking the Shadow War into the open. For this there would be a reckoning. True, Bella-Grendelmor was dead and her revolting henchman wiped out; a great many Vil-kind had been eliminated, but right now, none of that seemed enough. It did not feel as if anything would be sufficient to still the rage she felt at the atrocities that had been committed. The attacks on Clayton Bar and Wrayhaven had not been opportunistic raids but parts of a planned campaign. She could perceive the pattern behind it all now. Bella-Grendelmor was not the only Chameleon agency who had been involved in planning and executing those assaults. It was time to take the Shadow War into the nest of the enemy. It was time for the light to reach into the darkness and burn it clean.

For this she knew she must learn quickly how to control the abilities and knowledge she had at her disposal. Such evolved combat skills as she had displayed in Wrayhaven astonished her. It seemed that a whole world was at her beck and call and for one of her age that was a daunting prospect, especially in so young a body. It was all happening too soon! But she would cope. If necessary she would die trying. It was vital that she stay focused and think of what lay ahead – plan. Plan and anticipate. As Ceulwas in her previous body she had known how to do that.

All that mattered at this present moment was that she was alive, and so was Lucian. She *knew* it. She sensed it as she sensed the living insidious evil of those who guarded him. The phantom hand flexed in her chest, strong and reassuring, a thing to be reckoned with. Despite being so exhausted she could feel its power. And she was now able to deploy it at will.

So, let them beware. She was coming. Let them *beware*!

Across fifty yards of crystal clear air Loren waved at her from behind Cas Winters in the *Cloud Glyphs*. She smiled and waved back. Seeing her staunch new companion was a reminder that there would be allies as well as enemies in what lay ahead. With good companions she would endure.

'Be at peace Lucian,' she whispered to the air and sky. 'I am coming.'

SIDETIME
APPROPRIATE PAGES.

A single stream of light cuts through the gloom of a stone walled chamber protected and remote from the conflicts that rage across wild regions of the Isles. Though distant and hidden this place is yet woven into the fabric of the Shadow War that is erupting into the everyday world. Many secret things have been discussed and decided here over the decades. Many more will be spoken in the decades to come.

A thin figure sits stooped over a spread of varied objects scattered across a broad oak table. The man is selecting and positioning them with great care around the rims of three bowls arranged on the table. A whispering voice can be heard coming from the smallest of them. The man leans forward listening intently.

'The halls are taken,' the voice says. 'The enemy rampages within.'

'And our young Eloin? Has she too been taken?'

'No. The Eloin old soul is free and running. It is time Aemenir. She is coming. She is awakened before time and is in peril for that, but she is alive and well.'

The man leans back wearily. His hands are shaking.

'We can thank the dreaming heavens for that at least. We should prepare. She will be seeking her brother and no doubt be prepared to use violent means to do so. I fear her wrath may turn against her own youthfulness.'

'Indeed. Great caution would be advised. She will need to be handled carefully. We are all heading for territory that none of us have trod before Aemenir, not in a mortal span. Her powers may be beyond anything we yet know but the dangers to her are great.'

'Falarimé. These times will test us all Arkadash. I will break now. There are things I must put in place.'

'Var macuni Arkadash — times of trial.'

'Var ko — times of strength my friend.'

The man removes the nine objects from around the smallest bowl and places them in their respective boxes and containers. He glances a last time at the page in the leather backed tome he has been consulting. Aloud, he translates a small passage scribbled in the margin:

'Each ending urges us
To another purpose,
Another road, pale with distance,
A goal beyond the one we figured.'

He smiles sadly before gently closing the page with hands that still tremble. Finally he stands and moves to a high window where he draws back the heavy drapes and flings open a window. Golden-green light and clean air stream into the chamber dispelling the stale atmosphere. He takes his time gazing at the view beyond.

'So, she is coming. Coming at last. But will she be ready? Will she? We can only hope; and the shadow of that hope will be a price for her deliverance. The war is out. May the dreaming pathways aid us all.'

'The meaning of our journey
On arrival, is revealed as hollow,
With purpose lost or broken on the path behind,
In that very moment of completion.'
TK Edwins.

The Severed Twin - Volume Two Of The Shadow Histories!

Allies And Horrors — A Lost Identity — Omens And Marvels In The Next Stage Of Cody Conmar's Journey Through The Shattered Landscape Of A Recovering Homeland.

Revelations, nightmares and Vil-breed await Cody Conmar as she searches the remote regions of post-Event Britain to locate her lost twin Lucian. It is a race against time but in her prematurely awakened state she is still vulnerable. The inner turmoil of her mysterious past creates conflicts within her own mind. And yet, armed with newly awakened instincts and barely controllable abilities she must defeat every form of Shadow-breed and treachery that her Chameleon enemies can throw at her.

So far her phantom limb, her Scaedu Folm, has saved her life, but what if it should prove to be something beyond her control, with a life of its own?

As the nature of her new role in the Shadow Wars begins to become clear she realises she must enter the subterranean Breeding Vaults of the Technosages. This realm of malice lies at the heart of a festering labyrinth of nightmares. Somewhere in those hellish depths Lucian is being subjected to unimaginable suffering and torment. He may even have become Orowghast, a shadow slave.

He is still redeemable but time is running out. It is a path through madness and brutality. Only the certainty of death lies ahead.

Cody must just certain the death is not her own.

For more details on the unfolding Shadow Histories universe go to:

www.shadowhistories.com

Printed in the United Kingdom
by Lightning Source UK Ltd.
116748UKS00001B/126